BESTSELLING AUTHOR COLLECTION

In our Bestselling Author Collection, Harlequin Books is proud to offer classic novels from today's superstars of women's fiction. These authors have captured the hearts of millions of readers around the world, and earned their place on the *New York Times, USA TODAY* and other bestseller lists with every release.

As a bonus, each volume also includes a full-length novel from a rising star of series romance. Bestselling authors in their own right, these talented writers have captured the qualities Harlequin is famous for—heart-racing passion, edge-of-your-seat entertainment and a satisfying happily-ever-after.

Don't miss any of the books in the collection!

BESTSELLING AUTHOR COLLECTION

New York Times and *USA TODAY* Bestselling Author

MAGGIE SHAYNE

KISS of the SHADOW MAN

TORONTO NEW YORK LONDON
AMSTERDAM PARIS SYDNEY HAMBURG
STOCKHOLM ATHENS TOKYO MILAN MADRID
PRAGUE WARSAW BUDAPEST AUCKLAND

Recycling programs
for this product may
not exist in your area.

ISBN-13: 978-0-373-68876-0

KISS OF THE SHADOW MAN

Copyright © 2010 by Harlequin Books S.A.

The publisher acknowledges the copyright holders
of the individual works as follows:

KISS OF THE SHADOW MAN
Copyright © 1994 by Margaret Benson
REGARDING REMY
Copyright © 1994 by Marilyn Pappano

CONTENTS

For my own Katie, a heroine as feisty
and tough as any I've ever written.
And as smart and beautiful, too. I love you.

KISS OF THE
SHADOW MAN

New York Times and *USA TODAY* Bestselling Author

Maggie Shayne

MAGGIE SHAYNE

"Tasty," "tension packed," "haunting,"
"bewitching" and "better than chocolate" are
just a few of the ways *New York Times* bestselling
author Maggie Shayne and her award-winning
novels have been described by critics and
colleagues alike. Maggie is equally at home
penning romantic-suspense novels that will stop
your heart and paranormal romances that will
haunt your nights.

Chapter 1

Some there be that shadows kiss; Such have but a shadow's bliss.

—William Shakespeare

The pain lanced her head like a dull blade, sawing, cutting, ripping its way through. It was all-encompassing. At first, that was all she felt. Then, slowly, as if the lights were coming up in a darkened theater, she became aware of other sensations. The hard, irregular shape of her pillow. Her fists clenched around it, and the words "steering wheel" surfaced in her brain. She wasn't even certain what that meant. Then it came to her.

Next, the warm, steady trickle along her neck. She lifted her hand to touch the skin above the pulse point, only to find it soaked and sticky. Her fingers moved upward to trace the source, and located the gash at her temple. She pressed against it and a sharp pain made her wince. Still, she held the pressure there. It would stop the bleeding. She didn't know how she knew that, but she did.

Sounds filtered through the dense fog surrounding her mind. Sizzling…like bacon in a frying pan. No. Rain. It was rain. She lifted her head slowly, fighting the rush of dizziness the action brought, and peered through the darkness. Rainwater cascaded in sheets over the shattered windshield. She could see nothing beyond the spiderweb pattern of the broken glass, and the rain. Only darkness, filled with the howl of a vicious wind.

At first, she thought the wound to her head was what made her feel off center, out of balance. But when she tried to sit straight, she realized the car was at a strange angle, tilted with the driver's door pointing downward.

"I've been in an accident." She said it aloud, trying to take stock and finding it difficult. But the sound of her own voice made her gasp and jerk herself rigid. It wasn't her voice. It couldn't have been. It was the voice of a stranger, a voice she'd never heard before in her life. She blinked rapidly, looking around the car's interior, though she could see little detail in the darkness.

Then there was a flicker of light, a snapping sound, an acrid aroma.

Fire!

Her hand closed on the door handle, and she shoved desperately, again and again. It wouldn't budge. Panic giving her strength, she clambered up the sloping seat toward the opposite door. Her knee banged against something, a stick shift on the floor. Her skirt caught on it when she tried to move. She tore it free, and the sound of ripping fabric somehow added to the fear exploding inside her.

Her body shaking, she groped for the door. The latch gave when she wrenched at it. But the door wouldn't open. No. It would, it was just gravity making it difficult. The car was tipped on its side. The door, nearly horizontal above her. She pushed with all her might, bracing her feet against the hump in the center of the floor. The door lifted, and she growled deep in her throat and pushed harder. It wouldn't swing far enough to remain open on its own. She could only hold it up, her arms straining above her head, as she inched her way up and out. She braced one foot on the dashboard, the other on the seat's headrest and shoved herself upward, still holding the door. Another step. She pushed and shoved and hauled herself inch by inch through the opening, then out into the punishing rain and brutal wind.

Her legs gave way as soon as she hit the slick, muddy ground. She fell, curling into a small ball in the mud. Pain screamed through her brain. She could barely tell up from down, she was so dizzy. Her entire body throbbed with pains she couldn't isolate. She was cold, and afraid. So very afraid.

She only struggled to her feet again when the flames began to spread. Brilliant tongues of fire licked a path from the front of the vehicle toward the rear. The sharp scent of gasoline burned her nostrils. She pulled her mesmerized gaze from the hungry flames and bolted, only to skid to a halt in the mud. To her right, a sheer drop stretched endlessly into blackness and pouring rain. To her left, a steep, muddy embankment angled sharply upward.

Cold rain beating against her face, pummeling her body, frigid wind buffeting her every step of the way, she started up the bank. She clawed with her fingers and dug with her toes. She wore no shoes. She had no idea what had happened to them.

Countless times she slipped, losing more distance than she'd gained as the cold, wet soil scoured her palms, her knees, her chin. Each time, she grated her teeth and began once more. She'd be damned if she'd die here in this mud and misery. She gripped every protruding twig or outcropping of rock that she was fortunate enough to encounter. Slowly, agonizingly, with blood spilling over her neck and dampening her shoulder, she made her way to the top…to the twisting, narrow and utterly empty road.

An explosion rocked the ground beneath her, and she nearly fell from the force of its percussion. Bits of metal and glass rained around her and she shielded her face with her arms, frightened beyond rational thought. The car from which she'd escaped became a blinding ball of flame, and she had to turn her eyes away. The pounding in her head and the pressure against her temples grew stronger with every ragged breath she drew.

She heard the sirens then. In the road ahead of her, vehicles with flashing lights and flapping wipers screeched to a halt. Men emerged, and several hurried toward her, shouting.

Again she felt an inexplicable fear. She whirled from them and ran headlong in the other direction, bare feet slapping on cold wet pavement, raindrops ricocheting in front of her, lashing her face and legs. Headlights rounded a curve. The car swerved to miss her, skidding to a stop on the shoulder. She went rigid as the door opened.

She could only see his outline. He stepped around the car, the headlights at his back, rain pounding his body, and came toward her. He was no more than a powerful, menacing, black silhouette. A shadow.

Her heart hammered and she couldn't draw a breath. It was more than fear she felt. It was stark terror. He would hurt her, she was sure of it. He would kill her. He kept coming, closer, closer.

She screamed. It was a shriek of unbridled horror, and it froze the big, dark shadow man in his tracks. Again, she turned to run blindly. The paramedics were in her path, hands held out as if to gentle a frightened pony, voices soft. "Easy now, just calm down. We're here to help you. Easy."

She shook her head, pressing her hands to the sides of it. One came away dripping crimson and her throat closed off. She backed away from them, turning again only to find the shadow man there, so close she could smell the rain on his skin.

She screamed again when his arms closed around her like a steel trap. She fought, thrashing in his grip, kicking, pounding him with her fists.

"Dammit, Caitlin, that's enough!"

His voice was deep, loud, frightening. But it wasn't his voice that made her stop her struggling. She blinked, and shook her head, looking up into a face that was no more than a grouping of angles and planes in various shades of gray. A square, wide jaw. High, defined cheeks. Full lips. Prominent eyebrows.

Her voice a croak, she whispered, "What did you call me?"

His grip on her eased. She felt, rather than saw, the shock that rippled through him. "Caitlin." His arms freed her, but his large, hard hands gripped her shoulders. "Caitlin," he said again.

She was aware of the others closing in behind her. She shook her head, and dizziness swamped her like a small boat in a hurricane. "No...that's not my name." Her legs seemed to dissolve and her upper body sagged. She fought the sensation, leaned into the hands that supported her and managed to remain standing.

"Then what is?" It was nearly whispered, but there was a coarseness to the words that rubbed at all her nerve endings.

She closed her eyes, searched her mind. It was a simple enough question. What was her name? She squeezed her eyes tighter, trying to extract the information from her mind like juice from an orange. Nothing came. Her answer was an empty hole. A dark, empty hole in her mind where her identity should have been.

"I...I don't know."

"You don't know?" He seemed to be searching her face but she could barely see his. All crags and harsh lines, and beaded droplets of rain. Deep-set eyes. Wet hair that looked like a windstorm. No colors. Only shades of gray.

She felt the fear well up in her throat. She didn't know who she was. She didn't know where she was. But she did know that she was afraid, terribly, paralyzingly afraid. Of what, or whom, she had no clue. Right now, it was of everyone, everything. Most of all, this broad, hard-faced shadow man. She tried to pull free of him, but he wouldn't release her.

"Let me go!" She twisted her shoulders back and forth, heedless now of the icy rain pelting her, the streams of it running between her shoulder blades and soaking her clothes. "Let me go!" Again and again she screamed the words until the dizziness returned. The varying grays around her lost their form and blended into one cold, dark color. And then, even the pain in her head drowned in the gray sea.

Dylan Rossi stared through the double-paneled glass with the wire mesh between the panes into the room where they'd just wheeled his wife. He couldn't see her now. He only saw the backs of doctors and nurses in their pale green scrubs, with the white strings tied in neat little bows up their backs. He saw the dome of chromium steel above her, the blinding light it gave. And he saw the monitors. Their waving white lines coming erratically, the beeps without rhythm. The white sheets on the table that held her were spattered with crimson.

He couldn't see her. Not now. But he'd seen her less than an hour ago, when she'd struggled against his brutal grip in the pouring rain. In the glow of his headlights, he'd been able to see just fine. The gaping wound in her head, the blood pulsing from it, soaking her hair, her face, mingling with the rain on her neck.

And he remembered her eyes, the fear in them. It had been real. She'd been afraid…of him. And he couldn't say he blamed her. She had every reason in the world to be afraid of him.

Dylan paced away from the double doors marked Sterile Area, No Admittance. His wet shoes creaked over the polished tiles. The scent of the place turned his stomach.

No, no, it wasn't the damned scent that was making him sick. It was *him.* It was what he was thinking, what he was feeling right now that made him want to puke his insides out. But that didn't stop him from feeling it, and nothing could stop him from admitting it, at least to himself.

And he shouldn't hate himself for acknowledging what the rest of Eden, Connecticut, already knew. It would be best for everyone concerned if his coldhearted bitch of a wife never came out of that room.

Thirsty.

There had never been a desert dryer than her throat was right now. She forced her eyes open, but the room was blurry, dim. She licked her lips and tried to sit up. Her body responded with little more than a twitch of several muscle groups. And even that small effort left her limp with exhaustion. God, what was the matter with her?

"Caitlin?"

That voice sent a shiver up her spine. She tried to turn her head toward it, even as she felt herself instinctively cringe farther into the stiff sheets.

The form, dark as before, and blurred by her errant vision, rose from a chair to lean over the bed. "You're awake." His finger jammed repeatedly at a button on the side of her bed. "How do you feel?"

She twisted away from his touch, frightened to have him so near. Her back pressed the rail at the far side of the bed. She turned fast, startled. Her head throbbed with pain.

"Take it easy. Caitlin, you're in a hospital. You're going to be fine."

She swung her head around to face him again, though the movement increased the pain abominably. "Who are you?"

He frowned. Her vision was steadily clearing, and while the room was only dimly lit, she could now see his features. His eyebrows were dense and dark. His hair a jumble of deep brown satin waves, mussed as though he'd run his hands through it.

In a flash, she saw him doing just that. Not here and now, but somewhere else…before. He was tall, solidly built and he looked as if he were trying to see through her eyes, into her mind as he stared at her.

The door was very wide and made of wood. She noticed that as it swung open and a miniature nurse came through, took one look at her and whirled to run out again.

The man never moved. He only continued staring at her, eyes like melted chocolate, glistening, probing. "You don't know who I am?"

She shook her head, then closed her eyes because the action hurt her.

"Do you know who you are?"

Tears stung her eyes, so she squeezed them tighter. She felt droplets work their way through to moisten her lashes and roll over her cheeks. He swore, low harsh words that made her spine stiffen.

She heard the door again, the shuffling of feet and a feminine voice, very low. "You'll have to wait outside, Mr. Rossi."

Rossi. The name meant something. Bells sounded in her mind, but there was no more. Nothing but the vague feeling that she ought to know the name.

"You told me there was no sign of brain damage." The deep, rumbling tenor voice, Rossi's voice, came to her as he was urged toward the door.

"I told you we couldn't be sure until she regained consciousness."

"She says she doesn't know who she is," he growled. He sounded as if he doubted it to be true. "So run your damned tests and tell me if this is legitimate, pronto."

"Please, try to be patient. I know you want your questions answered, but right now we need to examine your wife."

An electric shock zapped through her body at that word. "No!" The denial flew from her lips, riding her coarse voice to fill the sterile-smelling room. "No! I'm not his wife. I'm not. I don't know that man. I don't know him, I swear it! I—"

"Calm down, Mrs. Rossi." Cool hands on her shoulders, then her forehead.

"Don't call me that!" she shrieked. She sat up, flinging the covers from her. She had to get out of here. Everyone here was crazy. She swung her legs to the floor, only to feel her arm grabbed firmly and jabbed with something sharp. She caught her breath. By the time she drew another, her head was swimming, and someone was pushing her back onto the bed.

She looked toward the door. He still stood there, staring at her. She met his gaze and moved her lips, forcing words with an effort. "Keep him…away from me."

He shook his head, yanked the door open and left as quickly as possible.

Night again.

God, why was it dark whenever she opened her eyes? Was she to live in darkness from now on?

"You're sure she's not faking this?"

It was his voice. The man they'd said was her husband. And it was filled with contempt.

"Mr. Rossi, why on earth would she want to?" The feminine voice paused, awaiting an answer. There was none. "Amnesia is rare," she said at last. "But it does happen, and I'm convinced it has happened to her. She needs patience and understanding right now. Not suspicion and mistrust."

The shadow man's head turned toward her in the darkened room. Caitlin closed her eyes again, and lay utterly still, waiting.

"She's been through a terrible trauma, Mr. Rossi."

"All the more reason not to tell her. Not anything. If she's faking, I'll know soon enough. If not…" He let the sentence hang for a moment. "If not, then telling her would only do more harm." It wasn't, Caitlin thought, the ending he'd intended to tack on to the sentence.

"Quite frankly, I'm inclined to agree with you. She's better off not knowing too much. Yet. She'll have to be told, though."

"Yeah, well, I'm her husband, so I'm calling the shots. I decide when and how much."

"*I* am her doctor, Mr. Rossi. And as soon as she shows me that she is on stable mental ground, you'll no longer be in a position to decide anything about her care. If you haven't told her by that time, then I will. Make no mistake about that."

"Fine."

The door opened, closed again.

A sense of solitude slowly invaded the room. She was alone again. With no more answers than she'd had before. God, could she really have lost her memory so completely? Could that big, frightening shadow man really be her husband? And what was it they intended to keep from her?

Caitlin rolled over, very slowly so as not to aggravate the dull throbbing in her head. There was something else, something that was missing, something precious. She couldn't put her finger on what, exactly. She only knew a ball of loneliness rested in the pit of her stomach. She felt empty inside, aching for something she couldn't identify. Not her memory. Not the man who claimed to be her husband. Something else, something she missed so terribly that it was a gnawing pain in her heart.

A teardrop worked its way from between her lashes, and she closed her eyes tight before a flood of them could follow. She wrapped her arms around her pillow, hugged it tight to her chest. When the floodgates finally broke, the sounds of her sobs were muffled in the fabric.

"I've dimmed the lights, Caitlin. The brightness will aggravate the headache, and hurt your eyes. It's better this way."

She turned toward the woman's voice. The tall, blond doctor sat in a chair beside the bed. She wore a white coat, and the tag pinned to it read Dr. Judith Stone, M.D., Ph.D.

She had a pretty face, but hid it behind black-rimmed glasses. Her hair was pinned to the back of her head.

"My name is Judith. Yours is Caitlin. Do you mind if I call you that?"

"How do you know?"

"Your name? Well, your husband told us, for one thing."

"He's not my husband. I don't know him."

Dr. Stone tilted her head to one side. "Caitlin, we're not just taking his word. He had photos of you. We checked your fingerprints, too. We'll bring your brother in to confirm it, if you like."

"I don't have a brother."

"Well, there is a man running around claiming to be your brother, with a birth certificate that has your parents' names on it. It's all a matter of public record." Dr. Stone paused for a moment, to let that sink in, she thought. Then she added, "Come to think of it, there is a marriage license that says you're married to Dylan Rossi. Also a matter of record."

Why did the name feel so…important? Unless it was true. He was her husband.

"If I have a brother, why hasn't he been in to see me by now?" No one had come to see her, she added in silence. Not her professed husband, or her parents, if she had any. No friends, no one at all.

"I thought it would be best not to allow visitors, Caitlin. Seeing a lot of strangers who claim they know you would only add to the stress."

She probably had a point. "Why can't I remember anything?"

Judith leaned forward in the chair, her eyes attentive. "How much *do* you remember, Caitlin?"

She shook her head slowly. The name still felt odd, like a pair of shoes broken in by someone else. It must be hers, though. The doctors were certain, had been insisting on it for days now. You couldn't argue with a birth certificate.

"Nothing. I woke up in a car, in the rain. Before that,

there's just…nothing." She opened her eyes and faced Dr. Stone. "I've answered these questions before. Every doctor that comes in here asks me the same things. I'd like some of my questions answered now."

Dr. Stone blinked, but smiled gently and nodded. "All right."

All right. Just like that. She didn't know where to begin, there were so many things she wanted to know. Where she'd lived, what she'd done for a living, who her friends had been.

"Am I ever going to get better?"

Narrow fingers closed on the black-framed glasses and removed them. "Caitlin, you were in a serious accident. You saw firsthand the distance your car fell, and how much farther it could have gone. If you'd been unconscious another few minutes, you'd have died. If the car had landed differently, you could have been paralyzed, or worse. I want you to keep all of that in mind."

Caitlin—she was finally trying to think of herself by that name—braced herself. "As things stand," Judith Stone continued, "you escaped almost unscathed. The head injury was serious. You already know you spent a week in a state of coma before you woke up three days ago. Many times, patients who experience that never regain consciousness, or when they do, they're—"

"Please, stop preparing me and just say it. I'm not going to get my memory back, am I?"

She sighed. "I'm afraid I can't answer that. Not yet."

Caitlin sunk back against the pillows as tears threatened. She blinked against them.

"Only time will tell, Caitlin. There's just no medical way to predict whether you'll regain some or all of your memory. But in the meantime, you have to begin again. You have to start right now, today."

"Start what?"

Hands gripped hers and squeezed. "Learning who you are."

"I don't remember who I am." She wanted to wail the words, but she only whispered them.

"Not who you were, Caitlin. Who you are. Who you will be from this day on. That's the most important thing for you to accept. You aren't that woman anymore, and if you spend too much time trying to find her, to become her again, you'll drive yourself crazy. I want you to remember that." She tilted her head again, as if trying to read Caitlin's reactions on her face. "Any more questions?"

She licked her lips. "My full name?"

"Caitlin Amanda O'Brien Rossi."

She turned that over in her mind. "So I'm Irish?"

"Sure sounds Irish to me."

Caitlin nodded. "It does, doesn't it. What about my family?"

"Parents are deceased. You have…no children. There's your brother, Thomas, and your husband, Dylan."

She nodded, glancing down at the rings on the third finger of her left hand. "How long have I been…married?" The word didn't come easily.

"Five years. You're thirty-three. Your brother is twenty-nine."

She met Judith's brilliant green gaze. "And Dylan?"

Pale brows rose. "I never asked him. Why don't you?"

"He hasn't been here since I woke up."

"No, that's not quite true. He's been a fixture around here. He only doesn't come into the room because you made it clear you didn't want to see him, and because I thought it would only upset you if he did."

"Oh."

"Do you want to see him now?"

She bit her lip. "I don't know."

"Caitlin, there's something else I need to let you know. Your stay in the hospital is no longer necessary. Physically, you're fine now. You need to start thinking about where you'll go when you leave here. Surrounding yourself with familiar things can often be helpful in regaining memory."

A cold finger of panic traced a path around her heart. Where could she go? "My b-brother?"

"He and his wife live with you and your husband."

The fear she'd felt right after the accident resurfaced, and she searched in vain for its source. "Doctor—"

"Judith," she gently insisted.

"Judith," Caitlin said. "What do you know about the accident? Where was I going? How did I end up going off the road?"

Judith licked her lips, and for the first time, she didn't meet Caitlin's eyes as she answered. "The police department would know more about that than I."

Caitlin sighed. The answer was no answer at all. She had a feeling the accident was important, somehow. Almost as important as that wellspring of sorrow she felt inside her. More pressing, though, was her situation now. It looked as if she would have no choice but to return to her former home, if Dylan Rossi would even have her.

And there was another thing bothering her. "Why are there no mirrors in here?"

Judith rose slowly. "I asked that they be removed. I wanted to be sure you were ready to see your reflection. It'll be kind of shocking at first. Like looking at someone else's face."

Caitlin drew a deep breath. She knew her hair was a deep, dark shade of auburn. She'd pulled a lock of it around her face to stare at it. It was very long, and she felt curly bangs on her forehead. "I'd like to have a mirror. I think I'm ready now."

"There's one in the room next door. Feel up to a walk?"

Caitlin nodded. Judith opened a closet and pulled a pretty, red satin dressing gown from it. "Here, put this on."

She got to her feet and let Judith help her slip the robe up over her arms. "Whose—"

"Yours. Your husband brought some things when you were still in the coma."

At the mention of her husband, Caitlin stiffened, and her nerves jumped. "When do I have to leave?"

Judith walked with her to the door, and held it open. "Tomorrow."

Chapter 2

Dylan went rigid when she scuffed out of her hospital room, Dr. Stone at her side. He'd been at the desk only ten minutes, just getting the full report of how she'd passed the day and what progress had been made. He hadn't set foot in her room since she'd screamed that he be kept away from her. Seeing her now brought a sickening twist to his stomach and a jolt of memory to his mind. Again, he saw her caught in the beam of his headlights, frightened as a startled doe, as he moved toward her. Again, he saw her fear of him when he called her name, heard her scream, watched her turn and run away as if he were Satan himself.

Later, he'd wondered if she'd really had sense enough to think she might finally have pushed him too far, or if her fear had all been an act. One more scene in the never-ending play where she was always at center stage. One more bid to tear him apart a little more. He couldn't imagine what more damage she could hope to exact. But if there was anything, if she even imagined there was anything left that could hurt him, she would do her damnedest to use it. Cold, spoiled Caitlin. She would never change.

But she hadn't faked the injury, or the coma. And now this amnesia. Real, or a ploy? She had the doctors fooled, there was no doubt about that.

Dr. Stone opened the door to the room beside Caitlin's. "Do you want me to come with you?"

"No." Caitlin seemed to hesitate before answering, but when she did, her voice was firm. "No, I want to do this by myself."

"Okay. I'll be just down the hall if you need me. And I'll come back for you in five minutes."

Caitlin nodded and Judith Stone walked away. Dylan watched as Caitlin seemed to brace her shoulders, and stepped into the room, shoving the wide, brown door farther, and allowing it to swing slowly shut behind her. He was curious, and no one seemed to be paying much attention at the moment. He walked with deliberate casualness across the pale gray tiles of the hall, toward the door she'd entered. He pressed it open, just a little, and he peered inside.

She stood as if transfixed, staring into a full-length mirror on the inside of an open closet door. Dylan looked at her reflection, seeing everything she saw. The soft, ivory-toned skin, the high sculpted cheekbones that gave her a regal look. Her long, wavy hair, the color of an old penny. Her eyes, huge and round, wide-set and penetrating. They were wider right now than he thought he'd ever seen them, and greener. Like emeralds. Shocking, glittering green. Too green to belong to her.

Her hand rose slowly, and her fingers touched her cheek, then slipped slowly downward, over its hollow, tracing her jawline to her small, proud chin.

Her fingers were trembling.

Her gaze moved downward, over her slender frame, her endlessly long legs. When her eyes met those of her reflection again, there were tears brimming in both.

Dylan retreated in silence.

If she was acting, she was doing a hell of a job.

She was silent in the car, head turned away, eyes pretending to scan the roadside as they passed. Dylan kept a steady pressure on the accelerator as he negotiated the narrow, twisting strip of pavement that passed for a road.

She'd fastened her seat belt the second she'd slammed her door. It surprised him. Caitlin never used a seat belt. Oh, but he was forgetting Dr. Stone's lecture, wasn't he? This was not the same woman he remembered, not the woman he'd married, not the woman he'd known. This Caitlin was a new woman, a perfect stranger.

But that was the punch line, wasn't it? He and his wife had been strangers for a very long time now.

She certainly didn't look any different. At least, not now that she was dressed up in one of her chic, designer label skirts, with its brilliant yellow color. The matching jacket was cropped at the waist to show off its minuscule size, and flared at the hips to accentuate the way they would sway when she walked. The pumps were the precise shade of the suit. She did tug at the hem of the jacket once or twice, though. And she shifted in the seat as though uncomfortable with the amount of slender, long thigh exposed by the skirt. And she hadn't put her hair up. She hadn't gone out in public in more than a year without a classy French braid or a twisting chignon. Today, she just sat there with her coppery curls spilling all over the place.

So she'd forgotten how to braid her hair. So what? She hadn't changed in any way that mattered. It was still painfully obvious that she wished she were somewhere else, anywhere but with him. Not that the feeling wasn't one hundred percent mutual. So where was this big change he'd been told to expect?

He sighed and returned his attention to the pale gray ribbon that stretched ahead of him. In a way, it was good she'd continue being distant and cold. It would be easier to keep his secrets that way. There were some things she was far better off not remembering. He'd had a hell of a time convincing Dr. Stone of that, but in the end she'd agreed. If the amnesia was real—he glanced toward Caitlin, and felt a resurgence of doubt—she was better off.

She ran one hand over the supple leather seat. She knew, somewhere in the tangled jungle of her memory banks, that it was a luxury car. It seemed to have all the extras. The air conditioner silently cooled the interior, while the sun outside made heat waves dance above the pavement ahead. It smelled new, good. She tried to remember what the other car had looked like, the one she'd seen go up in a ball of white hot flame. She frowned, searching her mind, but nothing came.

"What is it?"

She jumped, startled by the suddenness and resonance of his deep voice. She was still afraid of him. Just being in the same car with him had her nerves standing on end, and seemed somehow to intensify that emptiness inside her. "I was trying to remember the car. The one that burned."

He slanted her a skeptical glance. "You don't remember your car?"

"Only that it was small, and there was a stick shift. I remember banging my knee on it when I was trying to climb out."

He shook his head. "It was a red Porsche." He released a low chuckle. "Figures that would be your first question. You thought more of that car than..." He shook his head, leaving the sentence unfinished. His face darkened, and his lips tightened.

His answer made her hesitate to ask any further questions. She sensed his disapproval. Still, there were things she needed to know. "What...what do I do?"

"What do you mean, what do you do?"

"For a living."

His eyebrows shot up and he stared at her for so long, he

had to jerk the wheel when he finally glanced back at the road. He gave his head a quick shake. "For a living? You? Give me a break."

Caitlin felt a prickle of knowledge make its way into her brain. Dylan Rossi didn't like her. Not at all. In fact, she was feeling the touch of his intense dislike right across the space between them. She tried to find some patience for him. After all, he had lost a wife and gotten back a perfect stranger. He had reason to be short-tempered. "Look, it would help if you could put a damper on the sarcasm and simply answer me. Do I have a job or not?"

He glanced at her from the corners of his eyes. "Not."

She nodded. "Can you tell me why not?"

He shrugged noncommittally, flipped down the visor, and pulled a pair of black sunglasses from it. When he slipped them on, his eyes were completely hidden.

She shook her head, exasperation growing with every minute. "I need to know. You were her husband—" She bit her lip. "I mean, my husband. If you don't know, then who does?"

"You don't work because you were born rich. You don't need to exert yourself any more than it takes to sign a check and you have all the money you could want. Happy?"

His words stung her. "No, I'm not."

"No," he repeated. "You never were."

He turned the car onto a long, winding driveway. She felt the crunch of the tires over gravel, but didn't hear it in the silent interior, as the car moved beneath a tunnel of overhanging trees. It was shadowy, and darker. He could easily have removed the sunglasses, she thought. He didn't.

They rounded a bend, and the house towered before her. Old red brick, everywhere, most of it covered with clinging, creeping vines that seemed to Caitlin as if they were trying to smother the place. The windows, narrow and arched at the tops, were surrounded with bricks in fan patterns. The entire place was a harsh combination of severe corners and dull colors. It frightened her, this house.

In an upper window, a curtain parted, and the shadow of a face peered out. Caitlin caught her breath, but before she could say anything, the curtain fell once more.

Dylan was already getting out of the car. He glanced in at her, as he replaced his sunglasses on the visor. He frowned when he saw she wasn't moving. "Something wrong?"

Yes. God, everything was wrong. Why would she feel such terror at the prospect of entering her own home? Why was there a gnawing sadness digging a pit into her soul? Why was she so uncomfortable with the man she'd married...perhaps even loved...once? She shook her head, and instead of asking any of the questions that truly troubled her, she asked a safe one. "Who else lives here, besides us?"

"Your brother and his wife, and..." He stopped, cleared his throat. His gaze moved away from hers for just a moment. A quick flicker of those dark eyes, and then he faced her again. "And my great-aunt, Ellen Rossi. Other than that, there are only Genevieve and Henri Dupres." He pronounced both names with a perfect French accent.

"Who are they?"

He sighed as if running low on patience. "The French siblings you insisted on hiring last year. Genevieve worked for your family once, but your old man let her go right after your parents' divorce. You always liked her."

As he spoke, he moved around the car to her side. His hand gripped her arm to urge her to her feet and draw her along beside him, an automatic gesture, she was sure. But the warmth of his touch, the pressure of each finger on her skin disturbed her. It sent her nerves skittering in a hundred directions, and a shiver over her nape.

"So when she showed up with her brother to answer your ad for hired help, you gave them the jobs. She's our maid and he's our cook."

Caitlin stopped walking, vaguely aware she'd missed most of what he'd said. Something tickled her consciousness, teased her senses, tugged at her. A scent. *His* scent, clean and pleasantly spicy…and familiar.

She frowned as an image flickered in her mind. His face, very close to hers. His eyes filled with dark fire, staring intensely into hers, as his strong hands held her to him. She felt his skin, hot and damp against hers, felt his warm breath on her face as his lips came nearer.

"Are you coming in or not?"

She gasped and blinked up at him. His brows drew close, and he reached out a hand. She instinctively took a step backward. Strong hands caught her shoulders, preventing her from going any farther.

"Caitlin, what in hell's the matter?"

She closed her eyes slowly, willing herself not to pull away from his touch. The image had shaken her, but she didn't want him to know. A heat spread up through her cheeks. Her skin seemed to burn where his hands rested, though that was all in her mind, of course.

"Nothing. I'm fine." She drew a steadying breath, and began walking at his side again, trying to act as if nothing had happened. Her feet sunk into the hot gravel. The humid, stifling air bathed her. Perspiration broke out on her forehead in the seconds it took to reach the steps. She felt her skin growing damp and her clothes sticking to her. And she smelled the Atlantic.

She frowned, tilting her head to listen to the sounds she hadn't noticed before. Waves crashing against rock in the distance, and the discordant harmony of seagulls.

There seemed little lawn. Mostly the place was surrounded by shrubs and trees and plants of every size and variety. It was like a miniature jungle here, with the humid, heavy air to match. Not a single breeze stirred a single leaf. But she imagined that on the back side of the house, closer to the shore, there would always be a breeze. The idea was appealing at that moment.

"Caitlin?"

"Hmm?" She tore her mind away from the ocean and the gulls and the imaginary breeze, and glanced at him.

"Coming?"

She'd stopped again, at the base of the steps this time. She nodded, and made herself move. Already, the gravel she stood in was heating her feet right through the soles of her stylish, torturous pumps. Dylan walked beside her up the wide, stone stairs to the front door with the oval window of frosted glass through which one couldn't see. He opened it, held it and waited. Knees trembling for no reason she could name, Caitlin stepped inside.

The house had the chill of a meat cooler.

Her footsteps echoed over the deep blue, marble floor, floating up to the high, vaulted ceiling and vanishing there. A twisting stairway of darkly polished hardwood began at one end and writhed upward, out of sight. A tooled, gleaming banister supported by elegant spindles wound its way alongside the stairs. The place smelled of oil soap and old wood.

She absorbed it all, shuddering at the darkness of the decor, and at the cold. A woman descended the stairs, very slowly, one gnarled hand gripping the banister for support. Snow-white hair was twisted into a smooth bun at the top of her head. She wore silver-rimmed glasses, Coke-bottle thick. And as she reached the bottom of the stairs and came nearer, Caitlin saw that her eyes were as brown as Dylan's.

Dylan rushed forward, extending a hand to help her. She waved him away. "Leave me be, boy. I'm not crippled."

Dylan's lips curved into a crooked smile, and he stepped back. Caitlin caught her breath. He was looking at the old woman with tenderness and a sort of indulgent smile. Real affection lit his eyes, and for some reason, it made her feel more alone than she could remember feeling.

"I've brought Caitlin home, Aunt Ellen." He walked beside his aunt, watchful, ready to reach out if she stumbled.

The old woman moved slowly, her feet scuffing the floor. "I can see that. I'm not blind, either." When she was standing six inches from Caitlin, she peered into her face. "So, you're back, are you?"

Caitlin smiled at the woman. "Yes. It feels good to be out of that hospital."

The woman sniffed. "Been better if you'd stayed there. For all of us."

"Ellen." Dylan's voice held a warning.

"What? She might as well know my feelings on the subject, or is that supposed to be a secret, too?" Caitlin shot Dylan a questioning glance. He averted his eyes. "You never liked me, girl. No more than I liked you. They tell me you've forgot all that, but I imagine it'll come back to you soon enough. Old habits die hard, you know."

Caitlin opened her mouth to deny it, then closed it again. How could she? She remembered nothing.

"Ellen, where is everyone?"

She faced her nephew, squinting. "How would I know? No one around here ever tells me anything." She shuffled into the adjoining room—the living room—and Dylan and Caitlin followed suit.

Caitlin almost smiled at Ellen's remarks. Despite Ellen's frosty attitude toward her, she was like a petulant child. And at least she was up-front with her feelings, not brooding and sending her veiled glances, the way Dylan had been doing.

Another woman entered the room then, coming through the arched doorway. She was tiny, with her jet hair cut in a pixie style, and huge, dark, Liza Minnelli eyes. She wore the regulation uniform of a maid, black dress with white collar and cuffs. Stiff white apron.

She came forward, smiling nervously when Caitlin's eyes met hers. "Madame Rossi, I am so glad to see you home. You look well." Her speech was laced with a silky French accent. She stretched both hands to clasp Caitlin's, and squeezed softly. A gesture that suggested familiarity, yet Caitlin felt none.

"I'm sorry. I don't—"

"I know," she said softly. "It is all right, you will be well soon, *non?* I am Genevieve—"

"Our maid," Caitlin filled in, more to solidify the information in her own mind than anything else.

Genevieve's hands fell away, and Caitlin noticed her nails. They were immaculate, not excessively long, but far from cropped. They were hot-pink at their bases, with a black diagonal line bisecting them. The top portions were white, with tiny black dots.

"More than your maid," Genevieve was saying. Her voice had dropped an octave, and was softer than before. "We are friends, as well."

Caitlin looked up, saw the expectancy in the woman's eyes, and offered her a smile that was far from genuine. "That's good to know, Genevieve. I could use a friend, right now."

Dylan cleared his throat, drawing both gazes toward him. Ellen had settled herself in a broad rocking chair that looked ancient, and was rocking back and forth rapidly.

"Monsieur?" Genevieve inquired. "Is there something I can get for you?"

"A cold drink would be terrific." Dylan all but ignored Caitlin, though the old woman's eyes never left her as she rocked.

"Ice tea?" the maid asked.

"Fine. It's pushing ninety again today. Air's so heavy you can barely breathe outside." He slanted a glance toward Caitlin. She felt his eyes on her face and knew it was beaded with perspiration, though not from the stifling heat he'd mentioned. The house was as cold as a tomb. "One for Mrs. Rossi, too. Ellen?"

"I'll get it myself. Haven't had any servants waiting on me in ninety-two years and damned if I need 'em now."

Dylan's mouth pulled upward at one corner, but he quickly remedied that twitch, and nodded toward Genevieve. She left, and Ellen stopped rocking all at once. "That gal's bucking for a raise, mark my words. Friends. Bah! I never did like her."

"You don't like anyone, Ellen," Dylan gently reminded her.

Caitlin shook her head, confused. "I don't understand. Am I friends with Genevieve, or not?"

Dylan shrugged. "Like I said before, you always liked her."

Ellen sniffed, pulled herself from the rocker and scuffed out through the arched doorway, taking the same path the maid had. Dylan was watchful of her every step until she moved through the doorway and out of sight.

"I guess your aunt and I didn't get along."

He faced her again, his eyes skeptical. He sighed, shook his head and walked to an elegant eggshell sofa, with scrolled wooden arms and clawed feet. He sat down, reaching for a newspaper on the matching end table. "She's my great aunt. And no, you never got along."

Caitlin remained standing, watching him as he shook the paper twice, then began scanning the headlines. "Why not?"

He lifted his head, his gaze meeting hers, still packing thinly veiled distrust. He opened his mouth, but snapped it shut again when Genevieve reappeared carrying a tray and two tall, dewy glasses. Caitlin moved forward and took one. "Thank you." Her throat was suddenly parched. She sipped the beverage gratefully.

Genevieve handed Dylan's glass to him, sent Caitlin an encouraging smile and vanished again. Dylan took a long drink. Caitlin's gaze affixed itself to him, the way his lips parted around the glass's rim, the rippling motions of his throat as he swallowed repeatedly.

A sound floated to her ears then, breaking the tense silence between her and her husband. A soft, demanding cry. It pierced Caitlin's nerves like a blade. She stiffened, and a second later heard the glass shattering at her feet. She didn't look down, only stepped past it, vaguely aware of the crunching beneath her shoes, and moved out of the room toward the staircase. Dylan jumped to his feet, then stood motionless, poised.

Again and again the tiny wail came. Caitlin felt her eyes moisten, and her heart twist. She turned to face Dylan. "My God, no wonder I've felt so empty.... Why didn't you tell me?"

"Caitlin, wait—"

She ignored him, whirling once more and racing up the stairs. She had a child. A baby! No wonder she'd felt so utterly bereft since she awoke in that hospital. It made perfect sense now. She'd been aching for her child.

She ran as fast as she could along the maze of corridors, following the sound of the baby's cries, paying no attention to the countless rooms she passed on the way. She didn't even pause when she came to the closed door of what had to be the nursery. She flung it open and hurried inside.

The infant lay on its back, eyes pinched tight, mouth round. Tiny arms and legs stretched out and trembled with every wail, then relaxed in between. Dark, thick hair swirled over a small head, and chubby fists clenched with frustration.

Without hesitation, Caitlin bent over the crib and scooped the small, wriggling bundle up into her arms. The child wore only a diaper and a tiny white T-shirt. Caitlin rescued the receiving blanket that had been kicked into a wad at one corner of the crib, and wrapped it around the baby, holding the child close to her chest, resting her cheek against the silken hair.

The crying stopped at once, and Caitlin looked down into huge eyes that were so blue the whites of them seemed tinted blue, and thick, long lashes and chubby cheeks. So soft, the skin on the pudgy arms and legs. And the baby smell that filled her senses was like pure heaven. Caitlin ran her hand over the baby's fuzzy dark hair, and bent to press her lips to a soft cheek. She closed her eyes as they filled with tears, and held the baby against her once more, rocking it slowly in her arms.

"God, I don't even know if you're a boy or a girl. But you're beautiful. You're beautiful, and Mommy is home now."

She heard his steps stop in the doorway, but she didn't turn. She just held that child to her breast and let the tears of joy and relief fall unchecked over her face. "Everything is all right now, little one." She felt as if her heart would explode, it was so full. That emptiness inside her was filled. She had the part of her that had been lacking. Everything *would* be all right.

"Caitlin." His voice was hoarse.

She turned slowly, smiling though her lips trembled. "You should have told me, Dylan. If I'd known we had a—"

"She's not ours."

Those three words spread a blanket of ice over her heart. She shook her head in denial and held the baby closer.

"Caitlin, that is not our child." He took a step closer, and she backed away.

"No."

His face was tight, his eyes glittering with something. Anger? "She's your brother's little girl, Caitlin. She's Thomas and Sandra's baby."

Again, she shook her head. "But…but—"

A young woman with a towel wrapped like a turban around her head joined them in the room then. She stopped when she saw them there, her wide blue eyes on the baby in Caitlin's arms. She wore a jade dressing gown, tied with a sash, but it gaped at the neck, giving a more than ample view of her swollen breasts.

"Cait." She shook her head, in self-deprecation, perhaps. "First day home an' here I've got you babysittin' already. Sorry," she said with a sexy Southern drawl. She tipped her head back, fixing Dylan with a potent stare, her eyes huge and jewel-like. "I thought for sure she'd sleep long enough for me to take a shower." She came forward, and took the baby from Caitlin's suddenly numb arms. "Come on, Lizzie, come to Mama."

Caitlin felt colder than ever all at once. She shivered, and tried to blink back a new rush of tears. This couldn't be true. Holding the baby had felt so right, so natural. How could she not be her child?

"Caitlin, this is Sandra—" He broke off, his gaze leaving Caitlin's face when the narrow-faced woman sat down in a rocker near the crib, baring one plump breast as if she did so with an audience every day. Lizzie nuzzled, found her target and latched on with vigor.

Caitlin turned away, and pushed past Dylan into the hall.

Dylan braced one hand against the door frame, and watched her run away. She disappeared into one of the guest rooms, and he heard her lock the door after she'd slammed it.

"Gee, what's wrong with her?"

Dylan didn't answer. He couldn't, just then.

"What's wrong, little one? Not hungry?" She sighed. "I swear, she must have a tiny tummy. Eats just a little, and twenty times a day."

He heard the brush of fabric against skin as Sandra righted her robe, and then rose. "I'm taking Lizzie back to my room with me while I change. Then we're going out for a walk, aren't we, Lizzie?"

He ignored her artificially pitched voice as she murmured to her daughter all the way down the hall and out of sight. Dylan stepped back into the nursery and closed the door. He stared for a long time at the crib, and the litter of stuffed animals inside it. Mindlessly, he reached down, and stroked the silky fur of a teddy bear with a big red bow at its throat. When he'd walked in here, when he'd seen the way Caitlin held Lizzie in her arms, the ecstasy on her face, the relief, the tears of sheer joy…

It was like getting hit between the eyes with a two-by-four.

His hands clutched the brown fur until the bear was twisted into a grotesque blob, his chin fell to his chest and Dylan Rossi cried.

Chapter 3

She had no idea how long she huddled on the bed in the obviously unused room. She cried, but she didn't know why. It was ridiculous to feel such devastation over a simple misunderstanding.

Then why was she devastated? Why did it hurt so much to have believed she was a mother for a few precious seconds, and then to learn that she wasn't? Why?

When the knock came, she sat up, and swiped at her tear-stained face with the backs of her hands. It would be Dylan, she had no doubt of that. She got to her feet, and pushed a nervous hand through her hair. She wanted it to be Dylan, she realized slowly. She wanted him to explain what she was feeling, and she wanted him to comfort her, perhaps even hold her, the way a husband would hold a wife. His arms were big, strong, his chest wide and firm. It would feel good to be cradled there, even if it was only a gesture. Even if it meant nothing at all.

She opened the door and frowned at Genevieve's curious, dark gaze.

"You are ill?" she inquired, scanning Caitlin's tear-stained face.

"No. I'm fine."

Genevieve shook her head slowly. "You do not look at all fine. Something troubles you, *non?*"

Caitlin only shook her head. "Really, it's just a headache. I'll be all right." Friend or not in the past, Genevieve was no more than a polite stranger in the present.

The maid looked Caitlin over with a narrow eye, and finally nodded sharply, just once. "Fine, then. Your husband asked me to show you to your rooms. You'll want to change for dinner." She shook her head in that way she had, that made it seem as if she were scolding herself. "I don't know why I did not think that you might not remember the way. My head is not, as you say, screwed straight, I think."

Caitlin smiled a little, looking down at the rumpled yellow suit she wore and nodding. Yes, she would like to change, into something that didn't look like an ad from some fashion magazine. But when the maid led her to her rooms, she began to wish she'd stayed where she was. She stood in the doorway for a moment, blinking. Crimson chintz draperies with blousoned valances adorned the tall windows like debs at a Southern ball. The bedspread was satin, as vividly red as the drapes. The wallpaper's soft ivory tone was splotched with scarlet roses.

For an instant, she saw that shattered windshield, splashed with blood. Her blood. She shivered.

"Is something wrong?" Genevieve's hand touched Caitlin's shoulder from behind. "It is beautiful, *non?*"

She turned slowly, tearing her eyes from the decor to stare at Genevieve. She blinked twice at the woman, who was glancing admiringly into the bedroom, then turned to look at it once more herself.

Beautiful? Maybe, to anyone but her. Maybe the colors seemed vibrant, and alive to the casual viewer. But all Caitlin could see was the red, and she could almost smell the blood, and beyond it, the sharp odor of gasoline, and the pungent smell of fire. The room might have seemed beautiful to her once, but, God, not anymore.

"I'll send Monsieur Rossi for you when dinner is served. If you have no memory, you won't find your way." She stepped back, and closed the door.

Caitlin drew a bracing breath and made herself walk through the bedroom. She peered into the adjoining bathroom and found it just as troublesome. Red curtains, even the shower curtain, with a frilly ruffle bordering it. The carpet was the same plush ivory tone as that in the bedroom, and that was a welcome relief. There were even red towels, huge and plush, hanging from the racks. She shook her head in disappointment. She hadn't needed one more bothersome thing to add to her list. She'd hoped for a haven, something familiar in her rooms, something that might jar her memory. The only memory this room jarred was that of the accident.

She returned to the bedroom and tugged open a closet. At least she could get rid of this expensive outfit now. But as she sorted through the items hung in neat rows, she found the clothes were all the same. Cropped and tight, in vibrant shades and prints. All expensive, chic and sporting designer labels.

She sighed her disappointment—she'd been longing for something casual and comfortable—and turned to the bureau, already half-sure of what she'd find inside. One drawer spilled over with silken lingerie. Another was filled with workout wear that looked as if it'd never been worn. Finally, buried in the bottom drawer, she uncovered a pair of designer jeans. She was so relieved, she could have cried as she pulled them on.

They were too tight to be comfortable, even though she'd lost weight. They must be old, she thought. Everything else was conspicuously loose on her, though obviously designed to fit like a second skin. She took a green silk, sleeveless blouse from one of the suits in the closet and buttoned it. She added a belt, from the fifty or so she found hanging on a special rack all their own, and knelt to search for footwear. The pumps that lined the closet floor were all alike, except in color. There seemed to be a pair to match every suit that hung above them. At last, she located a pair of running shoes, no doubt top of the line. It seemed the old Caitlin had never settled for anything less. They were as white as if they'd just come off the shelf, and she saw not a crumb of dirt in their tread.

She pulled them on, wondering if Caitlin had been the type who wanted to look great when she exercised, but rarely did so.

She was on the edge of the burgundy-cushioned Queen Anne chair, bending to tie the shoes, when she heard the door open. Dinner was served, then. And her hostile husband was here to fetch her. She felt again that emptiness inside her, and didn't turn to face him. She told herself not to be disappointed that her homecoming wasn't what she'd hoped for. What had she expected? For that hard-faced shadow man to take her in his strong arms and shower her with kisses? That he'd be so glad his wife was alive, he'd overlook the rest? Had she really expected this family to welcome a stranger into its midst?

Strong hands came to rest on her shoulders. She stilled utterly, shocked at the tenderness of that touch after his earlier coldness.

A second later, his head came downward, and lips nuzzled the crook of her neck. She closed her eyes.

They sprung open again when she felt the tickle of a mustache against her skin. She flew to her feet, whirling to face him at the same time. The man who stood there smiling at her was not Dylan. She'd never seen him before. He was shorter than Dylan, but just as powerfully built. His swarthy complexion and blue eyes were unfamiliar, as was the thick black mustache.

"Who are you!" She was breathing hard and fast in her anger.

The man looked stricken. "Surely, you have not forgotten me, *ma chérie?*" He studied her face for a long moment, then shook his head sadly. "Ah, but you have. It is I, Henri. Do you not remember the man who has begged at your feet for so long?"

Henri. Their cook, she recalled. My God, what on earth was going on in this house? She shook her head quickly and fought to find strength to put him straight. She stiffened her spine, and made herself meet his suggestive gaze head-on. "If you ever touch me again, Henri, I'll…I'll tell my husband, and he'll probably fire you on the spot. Is that understood?"

He smiled, one side of the mustache tilting upward. "Do you really believe he would care so much, *ma petite?*" He shook his head. "*Oui,* I dare much in saying so, but it is so clear to me, he does not know how to love a woman like you, he does not know what a treasure he holds. He is a fool—"

"That's enough!"

He stopped speaking, eyes downcast, lips tight. "My apologies. I forget myself in my joy to see you safe and sound once more. It is only that, I assure you, nothing more." His head came up, and his eyes, black and full of mystery, met hers. "Know that *someone,* at least, is happy to see you home again, and *alive* as well, *chérie.*"

His eyes were filled with meaning, and Caitlin felt a chill snake over her spine. "Maybe you'd better go, now." The words were spoken firmly, despite the tremor that shuddered through her body.

He nodded once. "Forgive me if I have upset you. It was not my intent." He turned and left the room.

Caitlin found herself slamming the door behind him, and throwing the lock. Stupid, senseless behavior, she told herself. He hadn't harmed her, or threatened to. And his affection would probably have been flattering, under any other circumstances. But, God, there was enough of a rift between her and Dylan without this added burden. Was Henri in the habit of flirting with Caitlin? Had she allowed such behavior in the past? Or was he truly only reacting to her close brush with death, as he'd implied?

She leaned her forehead against the cool, dark wood and closed her eyes. He'd implied that not everyone was glad to have her back, and the emphasis he'd placed on the word "alive" still rung in her ears. What had he meant by that? Was he giving her some cryptic warning? She'd felt sheer terror at her first sight of this house. Might there be a reason for that reaction?

She straightened and paced away from the door. They were keeping things from her. She already knew that. Part of her had agreed to come back here just to unravel the questions of her past, to learn what secrets Dylan was keeping from her and why. But another part, the part that had trembled at first sight of this house, and still trembled, in something other than fear, whenever she was close to her husband, wanted to leave. To go someplace where no one knew her and start fresh, and forget she'd ever had a past that had been erased from her mind.

She shook her head slowly, knowing even as the thought occurred to her that she wouldn't run away. She had to learn about her life before. Something inside was insisting on it. She might never be whole again, until she did.

Dinner was like a wake. A wake in a cold mausoleum filled with false smiles and stilted conversation. It was difficult for all of them, she realized dully. Sitting with a woman they'd once known well, a woman who was now a stranger. Knowing she didn't remember a thing about any of them.

The glasses were crystal, and the table shone with polished silver and the muted glow of the candelabra on the sideboard.

Caitlin wished she'd never come out of her room when the timid maid had found her there. But she had. She'd dried her eyes and tried to squelch the devastation she felt tearing her in two, and followed Genevieve to the formal dining room, achingly aware that Dylan hadn't wanted to come for her himself.

She picked at her food, eating little. She had no appetite tonight. The entire room was filled to the breaking point with tension, and she knew too well that she was the cause.

Dylan sat at the head of the glossy, dark wood table, eyes sharp and always moving. He paid close attention to every move she made, every bite she took. His features were tight, drawn as if he was in pain. He wasn't, though. She imagined he was just disgusted at having her in his house, in his elegant dining room with its dark-stained woodwork and its immaculate high ceilings. She certainly didn't feel she belonged here, beneath the muted glow of an antique brass chandelier.

"It would be a welcome relief if this weather would break," Dylan observed, spearing a bit of the succulent roast beef with his fork. "It isn't usually this bad here, Caitlin."

"I hardly notice the heat," she said. No, what she noticed was the lighted candles spilling their warm glow on his face, softening it in a way that was utterly false. "The house is so cool, and I haven't been outside at all."

"You used to…" Thomas stopped before he finished the sentence. He was just as tall and solidly built as Dylan, but his hair was brilliantly carrot-colored and wildly curly. Freckles spattered his face, and his eyes were troubled. "Sorry. You don't want to hear about what you used to do."

"Yes, I do," Caitlin told him. "What were you going to say?"

He met her gaze, a look of uncertainty in his. "You used to love to walk along the cliffs at night. Said you could hear the wind singing with the sea."

Caitlin closed her eyes, wishing she could recall that feeling.

"That was before. It wouldn't be a good idea to indulge in that habit now, Caitlin. You're not familiar with the cliffs, and there are some dangerous spots out there."

She frowned at Dylan, at the tone of command she heard in his forbidding voice. And then she stilled utterly, just staring into his dark eyes, glittering in the candlelight. She'd seen them glitter before…but in moonlight…and the strong emotion in their dark brown depths had been passion, not anger.

From somewhere far away, she heard an echoing whisper, a masculine voice, his voice. *Always, Caity. No matter what.*

"He's right, Cait." Thomas's voice intruded on her dream-state. "Better stay clear of the cliffs until…unless—until you're better." Her brother's lips thinned, and he broke eye contact with her to stare without much interest at his food.

Caitlin's stare was drawn back to Dylan. To the muscled column of his neck, the taut forearms revealed by his rolled-back sleeves. Her stomach twisted into a knot.

Across from Thomas, Sandra lifted her pale golden eyebrows. "It's not like she's crippled, you guys." She shook her head, and sent Caitlin a glance. "Don't let them start bossin' you around, or you'll never leave the house again. Believe me, I know 'em. Not just Tommy, but Dylan, too," she drawled sweetly. "Matter of fact, now that you lost your memory, I prob'ly know him better than anybody."

She glanced up at Dylan as she said it. He sat at her elbow, and returned her quick glance. His might have been slightly amused, but it was too short for Caitlin to be sure. She felt a sudden, swift jab of jealousy. It was ridiculous. After all, Thomas was only twenty-nine, and if Caitlin was any judge of ages, Sandra couldn't be more than twenty-two. She was practically a child, for God's sake.

Still, she was beautiful, her long, silvery blond hair hanging over one shoulder, her rounded breasts straining against the clingy fabric of her skintight black dress. It was short, exposing most of her shapely thighs to anyone who cared to look. Her voice, laced with that delicate Southern accent, made every sentence she spoke like a caress. Besides all that, she was the mother of the child Caitlin had thought was her own.

"We're in for a storm," Ellen remarked. "Been building up to it all week. I feel it in my joints."

"And your joints are usually right," Dylan returned, his gaze softening when it lit on Ellen's.

Caitlin picked at her food, and told herself not to feel animosity toward her sister-in-law. Sandra had done nothing to deserve it. She turned her attention to Thomas, who sat beside her. Her brother. How could her own brother seem like a perfect stranger to her? There was a strong resemblance between them, she noticed. His green eyes looked a lot like her own.

"Something wrong, Caitlin?"

He'd caught her staring at him. She shook her head. "No, I...I was just trying to remember."

"To remember what?"

She shrugged. "Anything. What it was like growing up together. Whether you were a jock in high school, whether I..." She sighed and shook her head.

Thomas set his fork down with exaggerated care. "Our parents divorced while we were in high school. You stayed with Dad, I went with Mom."

She licked her lips. He seemed uncomfortable with the subject, but her curiosity was pestering her. "Why did they break up?"

"Because he was a bastard."

The sentence was clipped, and Thomas's eyes became hooded. "You never believed that, though."

"Is that why I stayed with him?"

He shook his head. "You were his princess, Caitlin. You blamed Mom for the breakup. No one really expected you to leave the lap of luxury and live the way we did."

Her eyes widened as he spoke, and she searched his reddening face, then glanced toward Dylan.

"That's enough, Thomas. What happened wasn't her fault."

"It's all right," Caitlin said quickly. "I want to know—"

"No, Cait." Thomas lowered his head, pushed one large hand through his curls and sighed hard. "Dylan's right. I'm sorry. It gets to me sometimes, that's all." He met her puzzled stare. "It was a mess. A big, ugly mess." He shoved his plate away from him, pushed his chair back and stalked out of the opulent dining room.

"Why'd you have to bring all that up? Dammit, Caitlin, he'll be ornery for the rest of the night, now."

Caitlin blinked rapidly at the woman who was her sister-in-law. "I'm sorry. I didn't mean—"

"Don't apologize, Caitlin." Dylan's gaze met hers for the first time that evening. "Your brother is still angry—"

"With good reason," Sandra cut in.

"Sandra O'Brien, it's time someone taught you some manners!" The declaration came loudly from Ellen, who sat across from Caitlin, and was accompanied by a wrinkled fist banging the table.

"Oh, hell, you're all treatin' her like she'll break in a strong wind!" She glanced at Caitlin. "If Thomas is still mad at you, it's no wonder, and I don't blame him!"

Dylan stood slowly, purposefully. "Go and see to your family, Sandra." His words were not shouted, but their tone carried the same impact as if they had been. And suddenly, the tall, powerful form of Caitlin's husband seemed terrifying. "Now."

Sandra rose, glaring at all of them in turn. Dylan sat down slowly, saying nothing.

"Fine. That's just fine." She threw her linen napkin down on her plate, and hurried from the room.

Caitlin sighed, and leaned her head into her hands, elbows propped on the table. "I'm sorry. I didn't mean to spoil everyone's dinner."

A low, rasping chuckle brought her head up, and she met Ellen's glazed brown eyes, which were crinkled at the outer corners. "Didn't spoil mine, girl. I'd much rather eat without that kind of comp'ny."

Caitlin shook her head. She looked across the table to Dylan. "Why is my brother so angry with me?"

"He's not angry with you. Only at what happened. Your parents' divorce is ancient history now, Caitlin. He got over it a long time ago."

"But he was so—"

"It bothers him to talk about it, that's all. He was a kid, his family split up. It's understandable, isn't it?"

She bit her inner cheek, and finally nodded. "I suppose so."

"He doesn't resent you, Caitlin. When Sandra got pregnant, he didn't have two dimes to rub together. You're the one who offered to let them move in here—"

"And nagged Dylan until he gave the worthless bum a job," Ellen cut in.

"I did?" Caitlin shook her head. It was difficult to picture herself nagging Dylan. His very presence shook her to the marrow.

She looked up then, curious, scanning his handsome face with sudden interest. "What kind of job? God, do you realize, I don't even know what you do?"

He licked his lips, his eyes narrowing as if he wasn't sure she spoke the truth. "I'm an architect."

"Best architect in the state," Ellen added. "Owns his own firm, a whole office building's worth."

Caitlin nodded, looking around the richly furnished room. "That explains this place. You must make a lot of money."

His head came up, eyes alert. "You want to talk money now, Caitlin?"

She frowned, not understanding the sudden bitterness in his tone. Had she said something wrong?

"It's your house, not mine. I never wanted it. I still don't."

Caitlin was stunned. She sent a glance toward Ellen, who only nodded her affirmation. She shook her head. "I don't understand." She felt sick to her stomach. The more she learned about the past, the more confused she became. But she had to know, didn't she?

"Water under the bridge," Ellen declared all at once.

"And here's dessert. You both better dig in, 'cause I hate to eat alone."

Genevieve crossed the room with a tray of dessert plates, laden with chocolate cake and whipped cream. She set one in front of Caitlin. Caitlin closed her eyes. "I don't think I can—"

"Sure you can. Barely touched your dinner, girl. You're already thin as a rake. Eat up."

Ellen lifted a forkful to her lips, and sighed as though she'd found ecstasy. Caitlin couldn't help but smile at the older woman. Ellen might dislike her, but Caitlin was beginning to wonder if she might have good reason. There had obviously been a lot of animosity in this marriage. Ellen pretty clearly adored her nephew.

"You really must try to eat," Genevieve put in. "I can see how much weight you have lost since the accident. You'll get well sooner if you eat."

She felt Dylan's eyes on her, and knew Genevieve was right. She had lost weight. The designer clothes hung looser than they should. Her curves didn't strain the seams the way Sandra's did. She dipped her fork, and lifted it. She'd force herself.

The fork was slapped out of her hand with stunning force just before it reached her lips. It clattered to the floor, smearing cake and cream all over the marbled black tiles.

"Ellen, what the hell—"

"It's carob!" was her shouted answer to her nephew's unfinished question. "Did you eat any, girl?"

Ellen was shoving her own water glass into Caitlin's hands as she spoke. Dylan was on his feet, shouting at Genevieve. "What in God's name were you thinking?"

"I didn't know! I swear, Monsieur Rossi, I had no idea."

He brushed past the trembling maid and stood beside Caitlin. "Are you all right?"

She set the water glass down and stared up at him in

shock. Was that concern or fury she heard in his tight voice? She nodded. "Yes, fine, but I don't understand. What in the world is carob?"

Dylan sighed hard and pushed a hand through his hair. "A bean from some Mediterranean evergreen. It's used as a chocolate substitute, among other things. You have violent reactions to carob, Caitlin. Rare, but potentially lethal. This damned dessert could have killed you."

His gaze met Ellen's, and there was some hidden knowledge that passed between them. "How did you know?"

Ellen shook her head. "I know real chocolate, boy. This stuff has a bitter aftertaste to it." She made a face.

Dylan glared at the maid, who was crying loudly. "Get Henri in here. I want to get to the bottom of this."

She nodded jerkily and hurried out of the room.

"You're sure you're all right?" Ellen asked. "You didn't eat any of it?"

"No, not a crumb." Caitlin felt the trembling in her hands, and she tried to force it to stop. First the accident, and then this, an inner voice whispered. Almost as if someone were deliberately out to get her. She gripped herself mentally, and shook. It was ridiculous. She was only being paranoid.

The dark look that passed between Ellen and Dylan just then made Caitlin's heart skip a beat.

She turned toward Dylan, certain there was something he wasn't telling her. She opened her mouth to demand an explanation, then closed it again. She was tired, upset. It was her first day home after a serious accident, a week in a coma and a total loss of her own identity. Her judgment was far from what it should be. She was overreacting to what surely must have been an accident. Dylan disliked her enough without her shouting accusations of conspiracy at him over dinner. Her head throbbed. She rose slowly, closed her eyes at the increased pain in her skull.

"Caitlin?"

She opened her eyes and faced him. "I'm just going upstairs to lie down. It's…been a long day."

Genevieve reentered the dining room, with Henri at her side. His eyes met Caitlin's with a silent reminder of his earlier, veiled warning glowing from their onyx-black depths. Dylan moved toward Caitlin, one hand on her arm telling her to stay where she was.

"Henri, I want an explanation for this dessert. And it had better be a good one." Dylan's voice was dangerous, and its depth made her tremble. He shot her a brief, sidelong glance. He must have felt the vibrations shuddering through her arm, where his hand still rested. He took it away.

"Monsieur Rossi, I promise you, I had no idea the cake was made with carob. It was delivered this afternoon."

"*Oui*," Genevieve added quickly. "I answered the door."

"Delivered from where?" Dylan demanded.

"The box said Alyce's Bakery. There…there was a card." Genevieve's voice trembled.

"Get it."

As she scurried out of the room once more, Caitlin looked up at the towering, angry form of her husband. "Dylan, I'm sure it was an honest mistake. Please don't—" She broke off at his quelling glance.

"The *madame* is right," Henri put in. "She must know *I* would never do anything to hurt her. This was simply a tragic error."

"I'll be the judge of that." Dylan snatched the small envelope from Genevieve's hand when she returned. He pulled out the card and read, "Wishing you a speedy recovery. It's signed, the Andersons."

"Who are they?"

He frowned down at the card, answering Caitlin's question without looking at her. "Our nearest neighbors. They live a mile farther down the road." He shook his head. "I'd better call them, just to be sure—"

"No chance of that, boy. They left for Europe yesterday.

An extended vacation. Mahalia Anderson called to say goodbye just before they left." As she spoke, Ellen got up from the table.

Dylan sighed hard. "From now on, Henri, no food comes to this table unless it's prepared by you. This might have been a fluke, but it could happen again."

"Of course." Henri turned those knowing eyes on Caitlin. "I am terribly sorry, *madame*. I hope you believe that."

Caitlin only nodded. "Of course. It wasn't your fault." She glanced up at Dylan. "I really would like to go up and lie down now."

"Fine."

She licked her lips. "I'm not sure I remember the way. Genevieve brought me down and I wasn't paying much attention. This place is so big…"

His gaze slid past her to Genevieve and for an instant she thought he would abandon her to the maid's care. The Frenchwoman's eyes were wide, nervous, before she averted them. Poor thing. Caitlin knew *she'd* hate to be on the receiving end of Dylan's anger.

After a moment's hesitation, Dylan sighed, took her arm and turned her toward the doorway.

She felt three pairs of eyes on her all the way out, and she suppressed a shudder. Dylan led her up the stairs, through a number of tall, narrow corridors, all lined in that same gleaming, dark wood. The grim paintings all looked alike, abstract displays of dull colors that meant nothing. She was sure she'd never learn how to find her way around this mausoleum that was supposedly *her* house.

Finally, he paused and opened a door. Caitlin stepped inside and stopped, glancing around. The deep red decor stared back at her. Her feet sunk, but refused to move, in the plush carpet.

She shook her head and took a step backward into the hall. All that red. God, why couldn't she shut out the image of the blood-spattered windshield? She felt the sticky, warm flow on her neck again, and she closed her eyes tightly to block out the vision.

"You don't like it? Caitlin, you decorated it yourself."

She turned away from him, and drew several deep breaths. "It'll be fine."

He caught her shoulders and turned her to face him. "Look, Caitlin, if you don't want this room, say so. There are plenty of others." His hands stilled on her outer arms. He'd only need to bend his elbows to pull her against him. She almost wished he would. She almost longed for his hard chest as a pillow, his muscled arms as blankets, closing out the confusion, the pain.

She shook her head. And then she felt the phantom sensations like whispers on her body. Friction. Skin against skin. Hot, wet, frantic. Something skittered through her midsection. A tensing, a longing. Why didn't he pull her into his arms?

"I—um—" She fought to pull her thoughts into order. "I don't want to be difficult—"

"Since when?"

Her chin rose at the cynicism in his voice. It had hit her like a bucket of ice water, shocking her back to reality. She met his gaze and saw the censure in his eyes. Had she thought he might harbor a single spark of feeling for her? Was she insane?

"The room is fine. Thank you for bringing me up." She forced herself to step back inside, refusing to look at the stifling, dramatic red that surrounded her. She closed the door behind her.

Chapter 4

The disappointment was like some living force, draining the energy from her body. But then, what kind of homecoming had she expected? One where her loving family members would hug her hard, one by one, their eyes filled with genuine joy that she was alive and back with them, instead of suspicions and secrets?

And it wasn't only the anticlimactic first day home that was getting to her. It was compounded by the still unidentifiable sense of loss, the gnawing ache for something she couldn't identify, the feeling that she was on the brink of tears all the time. Not being able to remember the reason did nothing to dull the pain.

Then there was this other feeling, the invisible threat, the menace of this cold, echoing house. The way the circular knots in the wood's dark grain seemed like evil eyes, always watching, waiting.

God, waiting for what?

It was ridiculous to feel so vulnerable, so much at risk, and she knew it was more a result of the trauma she'd been through than any real danger. She was in *her* house, with *her* family. There was no reason for this insane feeling that she was being stalked, or that the carob-laced dessert had been a deliberate attempt to hurt her.

It had been a gift.

But Caitlin couldn't help but wonder if it was more than just a coincidence, as she recalled again the speaking glances Dylan had exchanged with his aunt, and Henri's earlier words, laden with meaning.

She hadn't lied when she'd said she was tired, but instead of resting, she paced like a condemned prisoner. Again and again she moved past the foot of the tall, four-poster bed, its wood nearly charcoal, gleaming, its posts rising as high as gallows.

Gallows? What made me think that?

Finally, when she knew she wouldn't close her eyes until she did so, she picked up the phone on her bedside stand, dialed information and got the number for Alyce's Bakery, in Eden. She dialed that number, and waited.

"'lyce's. What can I do for you?" The feminine voice was one that sounded as though it answered the phone in the same way many times each day, even dropping the "A" in "Alyce's."

Caitlin licked her lips. "My name is Caitlin Rossi. A cake was delivered to me today, but, uh, the card was missing. I wanted to thank whoever sent it to me, if I could."

"Just a minute." The answer was quick and brief. Not even a pause, as if Caitlin's story sounded fishy. "You said Rossi?"

"Yes."

"That cake was sent by Mr. and Mrs. Jacob Anderson."

"Oh."

"You have a nice—"

"Wait!" Caitlin drew a steadying breath. "Can I ask…how it was paid for? I mean, credit card, cash or—"

"Sure, just a sec." Pages riffled in the background. "Cash,

Mrs. Rossi. Was there a problem with the cake? Is someone looking for a refund, or—"

"No, nothing like that. There was just a question as to who sent it. The Andersons are in Europe, you see, so…"

"Hmm. Well, maybe they asked someone to take care of this for them. The order was waiting when we opened up this morning."

"Waiting?"

"Yup. Cash and instructions in an envelope, slipped through the mail slot in the door. We get those all the time, 'course they're not usually cash, but once in a while…"

"I see. And the instructions, did they specify carob instead of chocolate cake?"

"That's right."

No one actually saw the person who placed the order.

A tree branch scraped across the window glass, like fingernails on a chalkboard.

"Thank you for your help."

"Anytime, Mrs. Rossi."

And they paid in cash, so there's no way to trace the source.

Caitlin hung up the phone, an antique replica, gleaming black with brass trim and a bell-shaped mouthpiece. It was just coincidence. There was no reason to see diabolical plots around every corner. She could well imagine Mr. and Mrs. Anderson, whoever they were, hurrying to the airport to catch their flight early this morning before the shops opened, and remembering at the last minute that today was the day their critically injured neighbor was to come home from the hospital. So they'd improvised, stuffed some cash and some instructions in an envelope, and dropped it off at the bakery, barely breaking stride in their rush to catch their flight.

It was possible.

But not very likely.

She shook herself, vowing to put the entire incident out of

her mind, and went into the adjoining bathroom. A long, hot soak might help her rest.

She'd only peeked in here briefly before. She was unprepared for a spigot in the shape of a lion's head. She shuddered, and adjusted the knobs until steamy water spewed from the gaping maw. The tub had clawed feet. She'd missed that before, too. She'd been too busy noticing the blood-red decor. She looked around a bit more now, while the tub filled. A spider wriggled its legs, in a high corner, while a fly struggled to free itself from the web. She bit her lip, trying not to liken herself to the fly. She was being ridiculous, melodramatic, overly afraid.

She forced grim thoughts aside and left the tub to fill while she searched for a comfortable nightgown. She had in mind an oversize football jersey or a dorm shirt. What she found, instead, were long and flowing, softly feminine nightgowns. Every fabric from cotton and soft white linen, to silk, and sheer gauze. Every color from one end of the spectrum to the other.

Apparently, the old Caitlin had a touch of a romantic inside her. Had she bought so many attractive nightgowns with her husband in mind? Or was it just that she'd been fond of pretty things?

Caitlin stilled, holding a white muslin gown held up by its spaghetti straps. One thing about this room was obvious. It was hers, and hers alone. There wasn't a single thing in it that suggested the presence of a man. Not a bit of masculine clothing anywhere. No men's colognes or shaving implements in the bathroom. Only one toothbrush, standing alone in a cup on the edge of the basin.

How long had they used separate bedrooms? she wondered. Had Dylan moved his things out since the accident, in an effort to make things easier on her? Or had it been this way far longer?

Another unanswered question to add to her growing list.

Sighing, she took the nightgown with her into the bathroom, and twisted the knobs to stop the flow of steaming water. It brimmed near the overflow drain, and already the mirror and small window were coated in mist. Clouds of it rolled off the surface of the water, invitingly. Caitlin stripped off the designer jeans and silk blouse. She wasn't overly fond of either of them. They looked like the clothes of a rich, well-placed, confident woman.

Maybe that was why she felt so uncomfortable in them now. She didn't feel rich or well-placed, and she was anything but confident. She felt alone and afraid, unsure of herself and everyone around her. Putting on the expensive clothes was like putting on a disguise. They belonged to another woman. A woman she no longer knew.

The long, steaming bath she indulged in did little to settle her nerves, though she did her best not to look at the spigot, or the spider.

Her skin damp, she pulled on the nightgown, and slid beneath her satin sheets, but was unable to sleep for hours. Countless questions and myriad possible answers flooded her brain each time she closed her eyes. Finally, though, exhaustion took over, and she did sleep, only to be tormented by vivid, disturbing dreams.

She was standing in warm, wet sand. There was rain pelting her skin. Her wet hair clung to her neck and shoulders, until large, strong hands pushed it away, and moist lips moved over her skin where it had been.

There was a chilly wind. Goose bumps rose on her arms and naked thighs. Those hands moved down over the curve of her spine, long, graceful fingers kneaded her buttocks, pulled her close to hardness and heat, held her there.

She couldn't see, in the dream. Her head was tipped back and her eyes were closed. She could only *feel,* and what she felt made her breath come in short little gasps, and her heart beat faster.

A mouth covered hers, and she parted her lips in silent welcome. A tongue probed, thrust, suggesting things that heated her blood to boiling. She reveled in the feel of it and curled her arms around his neck, threaded her fingers in his hair, pressed her hips harder against his.

Then the mouth lifted just slightly, lips still brushing hers as they moved to form words. "I love you, Caity. I always will. No matter what."

"Dylan…"

She'd spoken his name aloud in her sleep, and the sound of her own voice roused her, broke the seductive spell the dream had wrapped around her, brought her back to cold, harsh, lonely reality.

She sat up in the bed, blinking in the darkness. Her fingers rose of their own volition to touch her lips, which seemed to burn with the memory of those phantom kisses, then brushed over her breasts to find their nipples taut and yearning. She shuddered. Had it been a dream, or a buried memory? Had Dylan ever held her, touched her like that? Had he ever whispered those words against her lips with such passion? Or had it all been a figment of her imagination?

She pressed a hot palm to her sweat-slick forehead and lay back down. Would she ever know? God, had she really had something that intense once, only to let it slip away?

It was 5:00 a.m. when the baby began crying. Caitlin was wide-awake, curled into a ball on her own bed, still shaken from her dream of making love with Dylan, still dreading its return…and longing for it. She lifted her head, listening, waiting for Lizzie's cries to be answered. But they went on and on. No one seemed to be in any hurry to check on the poor little thing.

Caitlin flung back her covers and got out of bed. She chewed her thumbnail and began to pace the room. Surely, someone would pick Lizzie up soon. They had to. She felt it wasn't her place to step in and care for the child herself. Sandra might resent the intrusion, and so might Thomas. She didn't want to do anything else to alienate her family.

"I'm being utterly ridiculous," she said firmly. "I'm her aunt, and no one else is bothering to take care of her."

Caitlin pulled her door open and strode out into the hall. Darkness greeted her. No light spilled through the drawn draperies, which stood between the night beyond the towering windows and the darker halls within. No lamp had been left aglow to show her the way. She glanced up and down, all the same, as a chill assaulted her body, and the hairs on her nape prickled with electricity. She narrowed her eyes, gazing into utter blackness as if by doing so she'd somehow sense if anyone was there, watching. There was only the scent of rich wood and oil polish, and the sound of Lizzie's cries. She told herself there was no reason to think anyone would be, but the shiver up her spine argued that point, so she looked, anyway. She felt nothing but emptiness. Utter isolation. She was alone, right to the soul of her.

The baby still cried and Caitlin turned in that direction, stepping softly, her bare feet making no sound on the plush carpet. She strained her ears to hear if anyone else was up, moving around, maybe answering the baby's demands already. She heard nothing. Or did she?

She halted, glancing over her shoulder, puckering her face in concentration as her heart was slowly filled with ice water. There was a sound. Not footsteps. No, something much more menacing than that.

Breathing, all but silent; slow inhales, deliberately quiet exhales came to her in steady rhythm. It seemed to grow louder as she listened. Or was it in her mind? Was the stalker coming nearer? Was that his heart she heard pounding, or her own?

She whirled and ran the rest of the way. The baby's cries still guided her, drawing her in as surely as a lighthouse guides a ship among the rocks and reefs, to shore.

She didn't slow down at the nursery door, only gripped it and flung it open, ducking inside and closing it behind her; turning the lock by sheer instinct.

She leaned back against the cool wood, fighting to catch her breath, and calm her rapid pulse as the baby kept crying in an odd sort of cadence that worked to ease her panic. She got her breathing under control. As jumpy as she was, it might well have been her own slow breaths she'd heard out there just now. Or even the rhythmic respirations of someone sleeping with the door open, in one of the bedrooms she'd passed.

It was neither of those and you know it.

She ignored the voice of her fears and moved toward the crib. There was a fluttering, then a clenching of Caitlin's abdominal muscles, a heavy sort of ache in her breasts.

She leaned over and scooped Lizzie up. "Hush, little one," she murmured, cuddling her close. "Ooh, you're wet, aren't you? No wonder you're so grouchy."

Her attention was only half-focused on Lizzie as she laid the child on the changing table, stripped her down and washed her pink bottom. The other half was busy glancing every few seconds at the locked door. Despite her silent rationalization, she almost expected to see the handle move as someone tried to get in. It didn't, and in a few more moments, Caitlin shook her head slowly, wondering if she were losing her mind.

Naked, Lizzie kicked her feet and waved her hands, cooing and chirping like a little bird on the first day of spring. As Caitlin taped a fresh diaper in place, Lizzie grinned broadly, dimples in her cheeks and her chin, toothless gums fully exposed.

Caitlin found herself smiling back. "Your auntie is a little bit paranoid, Lizzie. Must have been that bump on the head." She struggled to capture Lizzie's flying feet, one at a time, and fit them into the legs of a soft sleeper. Then her arms. "Anyone could have been out there in the hallway tonight. Right? You were crying loudly enough to wake the dead. Just because no one around here is overly fond of me, doesn't mean they spend their nights following me around this gloomy old place. Does it, Lizzie?" She fastened the snaps, and scooped the baby up once more, heading for the rocking chair near the window.

Her explanation wasn't very convincing. Sure, someone might have been on their way to see to the baby, but if so, why hadn't they spoken? Why try so hard to keep their presence behind her a secret? And even if she could make herself believe it was just a coincidence, it didn't erase the earlier incident. Somehow or other, a cake that was poison to her had wound up on her dessert plate tonight. She'd tried to explain it away as she lay in bed, but combined with the presence in the pitch-dark hallway just now, she wondered. The "accidents" and "coincidences" were beginning to pile high.

"I cannot find her, Monsieur Rossi."

Dylan frowned over the morning paper and his coffee cup at the maid. "What do you mean, you can't find her?"

"She is not in her room."

Dylan glanced at his watch, and shook his head. He had to be in the office today. He didn't have time to play Caitlin's games.

"Not thinkin' of going off to work without even seeing her, are you, boy?"

He tossed the newspaper down none too gently. "As a matter of fact, Ellen—"

A crooked finger was waggled near his nose. "Head injury like that, no tellin' what's become of her. Might have gone for a walk and taken a fall. Might be lost, maybe passed out somewhere. Can't just leave, Dylan Rossi, no matter how you feel about her. That explosive temper of yours makes you forget things. She's still your wife, your responsibility. I taught you better than that."

Dylan drew a deep breath, to keep his "explosive temper"

from raining down on Ellen. "I'm not going anywhere until I know what she's up to."

"You're not worried?" Ellen demanded. "After the accident, and that close call last night?"

"Ellen, there was no proof that accident was anything but accidental."

"The brake line—"

"Was torn, not cut." He spoke slowly, carefully.

"You might try saying so without sounding so defensive, boy. And what about that cake last night?" Ellen squinted at him through her thick-lensed glasses.

"Are you sure she didn't send it herself, Ellen? Just another ploy, though God knows what she could hope to get out of it. Attention? Or maybe she's trying to set me up for attempted murder, so she can take the whole shebang."

Ellen looked stunned. She stopped eating and blinked down at the plate in front of her. "Well, I never heard of such a thing," she muttered.

"I'm not saying it's a fact, just that it's something to keep in mind. Don't get taken in by her acts. I don't intend to."

"Dylan!"

He looked up at Sandra's shout and saw her coming toward the table, wringing her hands. "What is it now, Sandra?"

"I can't get in the nursery. Door's locked from the inside, and I—" She broke off, glancing around the table. "Where is she?"

Dylan felt a small fist poke him in the gut. "Where is who?"

"Oh, Lord, she's in there with Lizzie, isn't she? That knock on the head was more serious than anyone thought. She's gone off the deep end and now she's holed up with my baby. Dylan, do somethin'!"

Dylan was on his feet before she finished her tirade, gripping Sandra's shoulders to calm her down. "Did you try knocking?"

"N-no. I didn't want to wake the baby. We can't just go up

there and knock, Dylan, it might set 'er off." The more agitated Sandra became, the thicker her twang grew. "Git the key. Please, for God's sake, git the key."

"All right. All right, just calm down." She pressed herself to his chest, clinging to his shoulders as if she would fall down without his support. Dylan rolled his eyes. Sandra was nothing if not overly dramatic. "Caitlin would never do anything to hurt a baby, for God's sake."

"How do you know," she moaned. "She's different now. Like a stranger."

Dylan shook his head.

Ellen stood, slapping a hand to Sandra's shoulder from behind. "You want to blubber, girl, go find your own husband to hang all over and let Dylan get that door opened up."

She gave a rather ungentle tug and tore Sandra from Dylan's chest. Leave it to Aunt Ellen not to pull punches. Dylan knew damned well Thomas was still in bed, sleeping. Thomas had been up pacing the halls half the night. Dylan knew, because he'd been restless last night, too. After he'd called the bakery the cake had come from, only to be told his wife had already called, after he'd demanded they tell him, word for word, what they'd told her, he'd been too keyed up to sleep.

He turned toward the kitchen, and located the right key on the rack. Then he went back through the dining room, and on to the foyer and the stairway, with Sandra right on his heels. Thomas's young wife had one valid point. Caitlin was acting differently, strangely. Quiet, almost timid. Her usual assertiveness seemed to have disappeared along with her memory.

As he stopped outside the nursery door, a little ripple of apprehension went through him. Suppose Sandra wasn't overreacting? Suppose there *was* some lingering aftereffect of the accident that had left Caitlin less than sane, and suppose that baby in there was just the shove it took to push her over the edge? Maybe his problems would be solved in a way he hadn't even considered. If she were dangerous, maybe Caitlin would have to be institutionalized. Hadn't he wondered about her mental state all along? It was why he hadn't told her the secret he was keeping. She might know, though. She might have remembered. She might have some kernel of subconscious awareness buried in her mind, and it might be just a little more than her injured brain could take.

He turned the key in the lock, twisted the doorknob, and pushed it silently open.

Caitlin sat in the rocker, with her head leaning to one side, eyes closed, her long lashes just touching her sculpted cheekbones. Her hair was a wild tangle of auburn curls and there wasn't a trace of makeup anywhere to be seen. She wore a thin white nightgown, and her arms, thinner than he remembered, and bare to the shoulders, pale from being hidden from the sun for too long, were wrapped protectively around Lizzie. The baby was cradled to her chest, sleeping just as soundly as Caitlin. The relaxed little cherub-face was nestled in the crook of Caitlin's neck.

A searing hot blade sliced cleanly through Dylan's heart, and he grated his teeth against the flood of pain that would have liked to cripple him. He blinked twice, cleared his throat and made himself move forward as Sandra stood in the doorway, sighing in relief.

He leaned over, lifted a hand toward his wife's face, then lowered it. "Caitlin," he said.

Her eyes flew wide, and she stiffened.

"It's all right, it's only me." He searched her emerald eyes for any sign of insanity and found none. She calmed at once, drawing a breath, shaking her head self-deprecatingly. She lowered her gaze to the baby in her arms, and the most tender smile he'd ever seen whispered across her lips. She slowly got up, walked to the crib and lowered the baby into it, careful not to wake her, then tucked a tiny blanket over Lizzie and turned.

A finger to her lips for silence, she tiptoed into the hallway, past Sandra. Dylan followed, and pulled the door closed behind him.

Sandra turned on Caitlin the second the door was closed. "Do you mind tellin' me just what the hell you think you're doin'?"

"Shh, you'll wake her." Caitlin frowned at the door, then at Sandra.

"She's my baby, Caitlin. I'll wake her if I want to."

Caitlin shook her head. "I know whose baby she is." She frowned until her auburn brows touched. "What I don't know is why you're so upset. Last night she cried for a half hour before I got up and went to her. She was soaking wet and probably hoarse from all that yelling. You didn't get up so I did. What's the problem?"

Sandra closed her eyes slowly. "Oh, God, it must have been the antihistamine I took last night. I never heard her." She opened her eyes again, and in an instant the anger and worry that had clouded them was replaced by regret. A second after that, her blue eyes narrowed again, searching Caitlin's face. "But that doesn't explain why you locked yourself in the nursery with Lizzie. I was scared half to death when I couldn't git that door open."

Dylan put a hand on Caitlin's shoulder, firm, not comforting. "Caitlin, why did you lock the door?"

She whirled to face him, blinking twice before she seemed to understand. "Oh...so that's what..." She lowered her head and pressed one palm to it. When she looked up again, it was to face Sandra. "God, no wonder you're ready to strangle me. I'm sorry I worried you, Sandra, really, I didn't mean to." She lifted her hands, palms up, and shook her head. "I did it without thinking. I was scared half to death, and I—"

"Scared of what?" Dylan caught her arm and turned her to face him again.

She licked her lips, and met his gaze only briefly, before looking away. "I don't know. It was probably nothing but a case of nerves."

Dylan frowned. "Tell me what happened." His hand still clasped her upper arm.

"Really, Caitlin. If somethin' scared you that bad—"

Caitlin shook her head slowly. "I didn't sleep well."

He nodded. He'd already noted the puffy eyes, the beginnings of dark circles forming beneath them. She was pale, too, and on edge. "Bad dreams?" he asked.

Her green eyes pierced his like arrows, and for just a second, he glimpsed a raw longing in their depths; a longing that shook him right to his frozen core. "Dreams. Not bad ones, though." Her cheeks flushed with color, and she turned away, facing Sandra instead of him. "I woke when I heard Lizzie, about 5:00 a.m. The halls were pitch-black, and I don't really know this place well enough to find light switches in the dark. I just followed the cries."

Her lips thinned, and Dylan saw her throat move as she swallowed. He jerked his gaze upward again. "Go on, Caitlin."

She shook her head. "I thought I heard something…behind me. Someone…breathing. It seemed to get louder, as if they were coming closer, and when I moved, it kept pace." She sighed. "I panicked, and ran the rest of the way. When I got to the nursery, it was a reflex to slam the door and throw the lock. I didn't even think about it, just did it." She lifted her gaze to Sandra's. "I'm really sorry I scared you, Sandra."

Sandra drew a deep breath, then let it out as she nodded. "It's okay." She shifted from one foot to the other. "Look, next time, why don't you just wake me up, all right? I'd really rather see to her myself."

Caitlin nodded. "If that's what you want." She couldn't keep the hurt from her voice, or hide it from her eyes.

Sandra nodded and turned to leave them. Dylan took Caitlin's arm and began walking. She tugged it free.

"We need to talk, Caitlin, and we can't do it here. Come on." He resumed walking, not touching her this time, and she followed. He stopped at her bedroom, opened the door and held it as she preceded him in.

She moved slowly toward the bed, then turned to face him. "What is it we need to talk about?"

"What happened last night? Did you see anyone?"

She looked down at the floor, closed her eyes slowly, shook her head from one side to the other. "This is like walking blind through a maze."

"What?"

She bit her lip, met his gaze again. "What kind of a marriage did we have, anyway?"

He opened his mouth to answer, but she hurried on. "I feel like I've just stepped into another woman's life, without a clue how she lived it. I've been handed this part to play, but the roles aren't what they're supposed to be, and the lines keep changing, and…" She turned, strode to the walk-in closet and whipped open the door. "Look at these things."

Dylan frowned. "Your clothes? What's wrong with your clothes?"

"Not *my* clothes, not anymore. There's nothing wrong with them, they're just wrong for me. Wrong for the *me* I am now, not the *her* that I was then." She reached in and began yanking tailored suits, narrow skirts, cropped jackets off hangers, and tossing them onto the bed. "They're bright, and expensive, and chic, and they're just not me."

He caught her shoulders, stopping her from emptying the closet entirely. He stood behind her, and her shoulders slumped forward, her chin touched her chest. "Didn't she even own a pair of jeans without a designer label? A sweatshirt?"

Dylan couldn't allow himself to fall for the act. This vulnerability, this confusion, was just a mask she'd put on. "Not in a long time," he said softly.

She turned toward him, searching his face. "You hated her and now you hate me."

"I never said I hated you, Caitlin—"

"Were the separate bedrooms your idea?"

He shook his head.

"No, I didn't think so." She closed her eyes, and the tensing of her throat muscles made him think she was fighting tears. Or at least, that was what she *wanted* it to make him think. "How long…how long since we made love?"

He licked his lips. "Eight months. Except…"

"Except?"

"There was one time."

Her face pinched tighter as he spoke the words. "One time. Why in God's name did you stay with her?"

He shook his head, fighting the image she was trying to project, angry that her apparent pain was so convincing. "You, Caitlin. Not *her*. You. Why did I stay with *you*." He said it as much to remind him as her.

Her brows lifted, green eyes meeting his, clear and direct. "Well?"

"I didn't have a choice."

She shook her head. "I don't know what that means."

He shrugged. "Doesn't matter. We've veered way off the subject here. You said someone was in the hall last night, following you."

She waited a long moment, and he thought she might insist on an explanation from him. It wouldn't matter if she did. He damned well wasn't going to say any more. He wasn't even sure who she was anymore.

She stared at him for a long moment, searching his soul, it seemed. Finally, she sighed, long and low. "I've told you everything I can. I didn't hear anything except breathing. I saw nothing. No one touched me or said a word. I have no idea who it was, or even if I imagined the whole thing, and I wouldn't even have mentioned it, except to explain why I locked the nursery door. Okay?"

He examined her face with skepticism he didn't bother disguising. "Okay."

"I didn't mean to send Sandra into hysterics." She looked at the floor for a long moment, then shook her head slowly. "Maybe I just ought to leave."

Dylan was stunned. "Leave?"

She nodded and glanced again toward the closet. "I don't even need to pack. There's not a damned thing here I want."

"Caity, you love this place. You'd never leave—"

"What did you call me?" Her head had come up all at once, those sharp eyes probing again.

He shook his head, still confused by his own reaction to her suggestion. He'd known the end was at hand. He'd been eager to get it the hell over with. "Sorry. I know you hate it. It just slipped out."

"Caity," she said once, then again. A rush of air came through her lips even as they pulled upward at the corners. "God, all this time everyone's been calling me Caitlin, and I've felt like it was someone else's name. Not mine. But Caity…" She smiled fully. "That's who I am." She hugged herself and laughed softly as her eyes fell closed. "Oh, God, that's who I am."

Dylan saw a single tear work its way from beneath her lashes, and travel a slow path down her face. His gut twisted into a hard knot, and he had to clench his hands into fists to keep from reaching out. Whether to wring her slender neck for blatant deception, or to brush that tear away, he couldn't have said.

Chapter 5

Caitlin dashed the tear from her face with the back of her hand, nearly limp with relief at having found a shred of her identity to cling to.

Dylan shifted his stance. "Why don't you get dressed, come downstairs and get something to eat. You'll feel better."

She shook her head. She didn't want to put on the other woman's clothes, or eat at her table. She wasn't even sure she liked her. "No. I really think I need to get out of here."

"And go where?"

"I don't know. Anywhere. A hotel, a—"

His loud sigh stopped her from completing the sentence. "You're *not going* to any hotel. I've told you, this is your house."

"*Her* house. *I* don't want it."

Dylan turned from her, pushing one hand through his hair and pacing slowly away. "Look, you're two days out of the hospital. This is no time for you to be on your own."

"I don't care."

"Well, I do." He blinked fast after he said it.

"The hell you do," she said very softly.

He lurched forward, gripping her upper arms hard. "You're still my wife."

"Your wife is dead."

He stared hard into her eyes, and she felt his searching, probing, and doubting. She kept her gaze level with his, staring right back. She noticed for the first time how dark his eyes were, like melted chocolate. She felt the contained strength in the hands that held her, and glanced downward, at the corded muscles of his forearms extending from rolled-up sleeves. Again, she felt herself wishing he'd fold her into those strong arms. That instead of digging his fingers into her flesh and despising her, he'd rock her against him and tell her that everything would be all right. She closed her eyes at the image, and battled back new tears.

His hands fell away, but when he spoke, his voice had not gentled. "Get dressed. You want out, I'll take you out. You can buy some clothes that meet your latest set of standards."

"I—I don't have any money."

His eyebrows rose slightly. "Caitlin, you're *rich*. When your daddy died, he left you every dime he had."

She shook her head. "Don't you understand? That isn't my money. It was hers. I'm not her, Dylan." She stepped nearer to him, and in her desperation to make someone understand, she caught his face between her palms and tipped it downward. "Look at me. She is gone. I'm not her. I'm not sure I even want to be."

For a long moment, he said nothing. Then slowly, one hand came up to stroke a slow, crooked path over her hair. For a fleeting moment, she saw his eyes lose their glittering harshness. "God, I wish I could believe that." Then his face hardened into the stone sculpture that was becoming familiar. "You'd like me to believe that, wouldn't you?"

Her hands fell to her sides, and she bit her lip. "But you don't, do you?"

"I can't."

"Why?"

He took a step away from her and shook his head slowly as she lifted her gaze to his face once more. "Sheer self-preservation, Caitlin. Go on and get dressed. If you feel you can't spend your own money, then consider it a loan."

She swallowed the lump that tried to choke her. She frowned, then, recalling what he'd just told her. "You said I inherited everything from my father. What about Thomas?"

Dylan's face went still. "Thomas was excluded from the will. He and your father never got along, and when he took your mother's side in the divorce, the old man disinherited him."

Caitlin blinked rapidly. "No wonder Thomas resents me."

"He doesn't resent you. Let's not rehash all this now. I haven't got the time or the inclination. I'll meet you out front in an hour."

She looked up briefly. "I'll only need twenty minutes."

Aside from a brief frown, he said nothing. Then he was gone.

She saw that frown again and again that morning. Dylan drove in silence to the bank and helped her through the process of claiming the replacement bank credit cards they'd been holding for her. Hers had all burned with her car. He was quick, efficient and seemingly emotionless. She felt oddly guilty accepting a new card from the teller, but she took it, silently vowing she'd find a way to replace every dime she had to spend. She'd repay the woman she considered dead, the woman Dylan Rossi distrusted so openly.

Back in the front seat of his plush car, he turned to her. "I'll drop you at Eden Mists."

"What's that?"

"Your favorite boutique. Very chic."

She grimaced and shook her head quickly. Then her stomach rumbled loudly enough to be heard.

"Maybe we ought to start with breakfast. I forgot you hadn't eaten this morning. We'll swing by Milford's?"

"Another chic spot?"

"Four-star cuisine." His tone was deep, level, unfriendly.

"Don't we get enough of that at home? What about that?" She pointed to the golden arches in the distance.

"You're kidding, right?"

She shook her head and opened the car door, leaping to her feet. The gloom of the drafty house and its hostile atmosphere were wearing off fast. Even Dylan's grim face couldn't keep her mood from soaring, with the brilliant sun spilling all over the neat little city. There was so much to do, so much she must have done once, but couldn't remember. The small city of Eden was bustling, even this early in the morning. Cars buzzed up and down the broad lanes, people walked in groups of two and three, in and out of shops and businesses.

Dylan caught up with her, and they walked side by side to the fast-food restaurant, and through the double doors. Caitlin inhaled the delicious aromas, but hesitated at the crowd standing in front of the counter. She was suddenly uncertain of what to do. She didn't like the large number of strangers around her. She pressed closer to Dylan, not even fully aware she was doing it until he frowned down at her, and his arm came around her shoulders. It was like an automatic act. His face said he regretted it, but when she felt his arm begin to move away, she scrunched closer, and he let it remain.

"You want to leave?"

She gazed up at him, feeling the warmth of that arm around her, seeing the real concern in his black-fringed eyes. His strength seemed to flow into her. She wanted to turn into his embrace, feel his arms surround her…the way they had in her dream.

"No. I'll be fine." *As long as you hold me.*

Dylan's hand rested nervously on her shoulder, and he propelled her along beside him. "What'll you have," he asked, leaning closer as he spoke above the noise. His warm breath fanned her ear.

She shrugged, glancing at the menu high on the facing wall, then at the pastries under a clear cover on the counter. "Those look good."

"Cheese Danish?" He stared down at her for a moment, an odd look in his eyes, then he blinked it away and strode to the vacant spot near a cash register. "Two cheese Danish and two coffees."

A moment later, his arm was no longer around her, because he was carrying their meal on a cardboard tray as he made his way to an empty table. Caitlin sat across from him, unwrapped her pastry and took a bite, then closed her eyes in ecstasy. "Oh, this is terrific."

He only watched her and shook his head.

"What is it? Have I done something wrong, or—"

"We used to come here a lot," he said slowly, carefully, as if he was afraid something would slip through his lips against his will if he didn't watch every word. "You always ordered those."

She set the Danish down and studied his face. It seemed taut, as if he were in physical pain. "When?"

He averted his eyes. "A long time ago, Caitlin."

"Caity," she said quickly. "Can you please call me Caity?"

He lifted his Danish and met her gaze briefly over it. "I don't think so."

She was doing a hell of a number on him, and the worst part was, he felt himself starting to fall for it. First the fast food, then choosing Kmart over all the stylish dress shops in the city, and now—

Dylan had to blink down his gut-wrenching memories when she came out of the fitting room in a pair of five-pocket Levi's jeans and a T-shirt. She had the T-shirt tucked in, and the jeans hugged her slender hips and buttocks just the way they had all those years ago, when she'd blown him away every time he looked at her. So long ago, before her mother's suicide, before she'd inherited all that money from her old man. Before she'd started to change, to close herself off from him, to change into the unfeeling woman she'd become.

They'd been something then. Like a live flame and gasoline. When they were together... He closed his eyes, remembering the way Caitlin used to make love to him. She'd put everything into it, heart, soul and body. But he'd soon begun to sense her slipping farther and farther from him, disappearing inside herself, drawing away. He'd responded by drawing back a little, himself. He'd poured even more time and attention into the business, stung by her coolness. And that had only seemed to make her build more walls. And eventually, what they'd had had died. He'd lost her. He'd finally accepted the facts, and resigned himself to ending his farce of a marriage.

And now, she was coming off like the girl she'd been before all that. She acted innocent, trusting and naive, and so damned vulnerable. Afraid, nervous. Pretending to enjoy his company. It was all an act. It was impossible for her to have changed so completely, virtually overnight. Impossible.

She picked out three more pairs of jeans, a half-dozen tops and a couple of simple sundresses, then added a pair of flat summer shoes to her collection. When they left the store, she balled up the bag that held the designer suit she'd arrived in, and stuffed it into a trash can.

She faced him smiling, her eyes glittering with pleasure, the wind whipping her long auburn tresses into mass chaos. "What next?"

Ah, damn, she looked like a teenager.

"We'd better call it a day. I need to go into the office so—"

"I'd love to see where you work!" She slung the shopping bag over her shoulder and started for the car.

He stood where he was, stunned into motionlessness. When she glanced back over her shoulder and saw him there, she stopped beside the car and turned. "What did I do now?"

Dylan shook his head. "You've never given a damn about the business." He made his legs carry him to the car, and slid in behind the wheel. "You sure you want to do this?"

She got in beside him, carelessly tossing her purchases onto the backseat, before studiously fastening her safety belt. "Of course I am." She looked up at him and her smile died. "Unless…you'd rather I didn't. I really didn't mean to monopolize your entire morning like this. I wasn't thinking—"

"It's all right, Caitlin."

She sighed and sat back in her seat. "You can take me back to the house if you want to."

He started the car, and backed out of the parking space. What the hell was she up to? She wasn't genuinely interested in the business all of a sudden. She couldn't be. She'd always seen it as a bother, a drain on his time and attention. She'd had enough money for them both, so why waste time on such a difficult project? She was just pretending, because she was up to something. He hadn't figured out what yet, but she was definitely up to something.

Or was she?

Doubts about his sanity pestered him, but he drove toward the office just the same. He'd give her enough rope to hang herself, and then he'd know for sure.

Caitlin stood just outside the glass-paneled office building, blinking. In gold letters across the front door were the words, Rossi Architectural Firm. Then his hand was on her arm again, and he marched her through the doors, into an elevator that whisked them up to the fifth floor.

The place even smelled successful, like new carpet and leather. He led her down a corridor, nodding to people who passed. They all greeted him with deference, "Hello, Mr. Rossi." "Good afternoon, Mr. Rossi." "Good to see you, Mr. Rossi." None smiled, though. They all looked rather pious when they looked at Dylan.

He took her through a door marked Dylan Rossi, CEO, into an office that would have suited the president of IBM. His desk was huge, his carpet, plush silvery gray. A drafting table stood near the windows with a stool in front of it. A computer monitor held court on the desk, with notepads and pencils and books piled around it.

"This is incredible."

He glanced at her once, and once only. He took the thronelike chair behind the desk, and began rummaging through file folders.

It didn't bother Caitlin. She moved around the office, impressed beyond comment at the place. And it was his. She wandered to the drafting table, and looked at the drawing there. The lines and angles, numbers and codes jotted all over the thing meant little to her.

She paid scant attention to Dylan as he spoke on the phone, and made notes in several files. When he finally took her on the promised tour, she felt a little guilty. He obviously had a lot more pressing things to do. Still, it was pleasant, and he seemed to swell a bit with pride as he showed her the various offices and storage rooms in the building, and introduced her to several young architects who worked with him. All the while, he was watching her, studying her reactions. What was he waiting for?

He showed her the small office her brother occupied, but Thomas seemed elbow-deep in something pressing, and only muttered a greeting.

Hours later, as Dylan led her back through the lobby and to the car, she looked back once more and shook her head.

"What?"

She glanced at him, seeing more of him than she had before.

He was talented, successful, determined, capable. The people who worked for him respected him, and when he spoke to them, it wasn't with the same coolness in his eyes that always seemed directed at her. "Caitlin must have been proud to be your wife," she said, and her voice was strangely hoarse and soft.

He shook his head. "Not exactly."

Caitlin frowned hard. She couldn't believe the woman she'd once been had been indifferent to her husband's abilities. "She must have been. Maybe she just…never said so."

He looked at her for a long moment. "No, she never did."

"Then she was a fool." She swallowed hard, cleared her throat and made herself continue. She had to begin somewhere. She had to try to right some of the wrongs her old self had wrought. But first she had to find out what they were. She'd alienated her husband, somehow. She touched his arm as he leaned over to open the car door for her. He straightened. "She must have been a fool, Dylan, but for what it's worth, I'm not."

He searched her eyes so deeply, she felt his burn into her soul. Then he broke eye contact, leaving her feeling cold and alone. He jerked the car door open. "Get in, Caitlin. It's going to pour any minute."

Caitlin glanced up at the darkening sky. The sun was rapidly setting, and ominous black clouds roiled in masses overhead. She got in without another word, and they drove in silence.

By the time they approached the looming house, rain poured over the windshield in sheets. The headlights did little to pierce the wall of water, and Dylan drove slowly, braking with care as the drive came into view.

Caitlin sighed, drawing his attention.

"Something wrong?"

She shook her head. "I was just thinking…wishing…" She bit her lip and looked at him. "Wouldn't it be wonderful to just keep on going?"

He frowned, pulling to a stop at the end of the drive. "What?"

"Just keep driving," she rushed on. "Right past this house

and on to…I don't know, someplace cozy and warm, and… and kind."

He looked at her strangely, then pulled the car into the long, curving drive and up to the house. A chill raced up the back of her neck when the house came into view. So grim, towering there with its dark red bricks and masses of clinging vines. It seemed even more spectral in the middle of the night, with the rain pouring down. She fought to suppress it, but felt herself shiver, all the same.

"Running away wouldn't solve anything, Caitlin."

"Wouldn't it?" She faced him in the darkness of the car.

"You can't just walk away from your life, you know. It's not that simple."

She shook her head. "I know I can't. Not yet, anyway." She hurried on before he could ask what she meant by that. "I don't want to go inside yet. You know, all I've seen of this place is the front…all I can remember, anyway."

"Cait, it's raining."

She sighed long and low. "Feels good, doesn't it? It's been so hot." She opened the car door and got out. For a moment, she just stood still and let the rain pour over her. She tipped her face up and let the downpour bathe it.

She didn't hear him come toward her, only the sounds of the wind and the rain battering the ground, pinging and ricocheting on the car roof. His arm came around her shoulders and he urged her toward the house.

She pulled free. "No. I want to walk out back, by the ocean."

"The cliffs are dangerous at night, Caitlin, especially when it's raining. You could slip—"

"I'll be careful." They stood facing each other. His hair was already drenched, plastered to his head. His jaw was set and rigid.

"Cait, this is crazy." He pitched his voice loudly to fight the storm, and again it carried that tone of command that made her tremble.

"I'll be fine. Go on to the house, Dylan."

"That's exactly what I'm doing." In a second, he'd scooped her up into his arms and was striding toward the front door. He flung it wide, carried her through and kicked it closed behind him. The light in the foyer was too bright after the murky darkness outside. A shiver moved through her and his arms seemed to tighten just a little. He looked down, into her eyes. She stared back into his. Her arms had linked themselves around his neck, and their faces were close. She could feel the heat of his body through her wet clothes. And all at once, she wanted to kiss him. She wanted to know if it could be the way she imagined it…or had she remembered it?

Her fingers slid upward, into the dripping sable waves, and she brought her face closer to his. Her heart pounded harder. She closed her eyes, and eliminated the last inch of space between their mouths. She pressed her parted lips to his, felt them move in response, felt her mouth captured by his gentle suction. Then everything changed. His arms clutched her tighter, so tight she could barely breathe. His mouth took hers in a frantic, desperate assault. His tongue plunged and dove, as if he couldn't taste enough of her. She kissed him back just as eagerly. Her body strained against his, her tongue twined with his in a sensual dance…

…that stopped all too soon.

He pulled away and abruptly set her on her feet. He looked at her once, his gaze narrow, almost wary. Then he shook his head and strode away.

Chapter 6

She got turned around in the labyrinth of corridors on her way down to dinner. She knew she was on the ground floor, but she'd somehow taken a wrong turn from the foyer, and wound up in a part of the house she hadn't seen. The towering ceilings and darkly stained wood, the hardwood floors and tall, arched windows, were the same as the rest of the place. The house was gloomy, unwelcoming, even with all the lights blazing. The rain slashing against the windows and the wind howling through the trees outside, only made it seem worse.

She walked over the cold, hard ceramic tiles of the strange hallway, peering through one darkly stained door after another to try to get her bearings. She found a cluttered office, with wall-to-wall file cabinets, a desk full of computer equipment, and a printer. Maybe Dylan worked at home sometimes, she mused. She drew back, closed the door and moved along the hall to the next. She was just reaching for it when she heard soft voices farther down. She hurried toward them. Then stopped at the low, throaty laughter.

"Of course, I love you, *mon cher,* but I cannot wait forever." The voice was Genevieve's.

The one she heard whisper a reply startled her. It belonged to her brother. "It'll all be yours, baby. You just have to be patient."

"I run out of patience, playing servant to these people. And your wife, she treats me like a dog. How much longer, Thomas?"

"I need a little more time. I promise you, we'll be on top…and Dylan Rossi will be sorry he ever underestimated me. I'll show him. It'll be a lesson he won't forget."

Caitlin drew a sudden gasp and her brother's words stopped. A second later, he appeared in front of her, stepping out of the room—a cozy, private parlor, from what she could glimpse—where he'd been having his little chat with her maid.

"What are you doing here?" The words had the ring of an accusation, but the expression on his face was one of pure guilt—and something tugged at her mind.

"I, uh, got lost on my way to dinner." She fought to keep what she'd heard, and what she was feeling, from showing on her face. "I'm glad I ran into you. I was afraid I'd never get back on track."

Thomas's hooded green eyes tried to hide his offense, but at the same time he stole quick glances at her face to see if she knew. He took her arm and started off in the direction from which she'd come.

The image came to her then. The pudgy red-haired boy, in a grimy Little League uniform, looking up at her just the way he was right now, as he tried to wipe the white foam from his shirt.

She squinted, trying to fine-tune the memory, then clapped a hand to her mouth to stifle the burst of laughter when it all came clear. "Tommy, *you* were the one who shaved Mrs. Petrie's poodle!"

He stopped walking, faced her, blinking. "Mrs. Pe—" He grabbed her shoulders, smiling broadly. "You *remember* that?"

She grinned back, nodding hard, mentally hugging the memory to her, wanting never to let it go. "I covered for you. Helped you ditch the razor and cleaned the foam off you before anyone saw."

"Damned dog had it coming." He shook his head, and laughed. "Stole my lunch at practice. I thought I'd starve before I got home."

"I think you went overboard in your retaliation," she teased.

"I only shaved the puff from the top of the mutt's head." He turned, and began walking again. After a few moments, he said, "So, um, how long were you standing out there?"

She frowned up at him. She wanted very much to get close to her brother again, especially now, having regained such a cherished memory of him as a child. But she'd just heard him threaten her husband, unless she'd completely misunderstood. She couldn't trust him. Not yet. "Not standing, walking. I was just wandering aimlessly and you stepped right into my path."

"Oh." He looked relieved.

He guided her through the maze of corridors until things began to seem familiar to her. It seemed to take a long time, though. She realized why when she finally entered the dining room to find Genevieve had managed to get there before them. She was already setting covered platters on the formally set table. Dylan rose when Caitlin came in.

"There you are. I was getting ready to send out a search party." His voice was level, controlled, but there was tension in his eyes.

Caitlin sat down just as Ellen entered the room behind her, and did likewise. "Enjoy your day out, Caitlin?"

Caitlin glanced up at the older woman and nodded. "Very much."

"I see you got some new clothes." Ellen looked down at Caitlin's jeans and shook her head. "Not your usual style."

"It is now."

Platters were passed, and Caitlin frowned across the long table at her husband. "Shouldn't we wait for Sandra?"

Dylan shrugged. "You've always insisted on promptness at dinner. She knows that it's one of your favorite rules."

"It's a stupid rule."

Genevieve stopped halfway across the room with a bowl in her hand. Dylan paused in filling his plate. Thomas stared at her.

Ellen chuckled. "I always said so. Still, I think we may as well get on with it. Baby was fussing. Sandra probably won't be down for a while."

"Is Lizzie sick?" She directed the question toward her brother.

"I don't know. Just cranky, I think."

"Don't worry about it, Caitlin," Ellen said. "Tell me about your trip. What did you do?"

Caitlin was worried, and vowed to check on the baby after dinner. In the meantime, though, Ellen seemed genuinely interested, and Caitlin wanted to build some bridges with the woman.

"Dylan took me on a tour of his offices."

Ellen frowned, her silvery brows bunching behind those thick glasses.

"I had no idea how successful he was until I saw for myself. I was very impressed."

"Did he tell you he started in one room, and not a big room, either. Built everything from the ground up. Designed that building himself."

"No, he didn't."

Ellen nodded. "That's his, girl. I won't stand still to watch anybody try to take it from him, and that includes you." Her bony finger poked into Caitlin's shoulder as she spoke.

Caitlin only shook her head. "Why would you think I—"

"I know what you're up to. You just remember that."

"That's enough, Ellen."

Ellen shot her nephew an impatient glare, and returned her attention to her plate. Caitlin let her chin fall to her chest. She'd honestly believed she might be making some progress with the woman.

Sandra's hasty entrance brought her head back up, and then she shot to her feet. Sandra held little Lizzie in her arms. The child's eyes were heavy-lidded and dull. She lay limply, as if exhausted, her head resting against her mother's shoulder.

"She's burnin' up!" Sandra drawled thickly. "I cain't get the fever down."

Caitlin raced forward, instinctively placing her palm across Lizzie's forehead, feeling the unnatural heat and the clamminess of the baby's skin. Sandra's eyes were pleading as they met hers.

Thomas stood, but didn't make a move to approach his daughter. Ellen rose with effort, moving slowly forward.

"Landsakes, you're shaking like a leaf, girl. Give her here, before you drop her."

Sandra surrendered the child to Ellen, who, in turn, placed Lizzie in Dylan's arms, obviously unaware, or unconcerned that Dylan would prefer the child were anywhere other than in his grasp. He held her stiffly. The veins in his neck bulged.

"Take her upstairs," Ellen ordered. "Sandra, call the doctor if you think you can talk straight. I imagine by the time you get done on the phone, the fever will be down, but call anyway."

Dylan left the room with the baby clutched awkwardly to his chest. Ellen hobbled behind him. Sandra went to the living room and picked up the phone. Thomas, to Caitlin's amazement, sat back down to his dinner, but he didn't really eat any of it.

"Aren't you going to go up there?"

He shook his head. "It's not that I'm not worried. I am, I just…she's so tiny. I feel like a giant when I hold her. I'm…not comfortable, you know?"

Caitlin frowned at him and shook her head. "No, I really don't." She followed Ellen up the stairs, knowing she wasn't wanted or needed, but too afraid for Lizzie to stay behind. In the nursery, Ellen gave calm instructions.

"Dylan, just sit and hold her. Caitlin, make yourself useful and run some water in here." She handed Caitlin a small plastic tub. "Make it cool. Not cold, but cool to the touch. Go on, hurry it up."

Caitlin nodded and took the tub into the adjoining bathroom to fill it. She carried it back into the nursery, and placed it atop the changing table.

Dylan had the baby in his lap. He was peeling the little sleeper off the child, then removing the diaper. His lips were drawn into a thin line, brows furrowed.

As she watched, Caitlin felt her eyes fill. Ellen dipped a gnarled hand into the tub. "Just right. Set her in here, Dylan, but keep hold of her." Dylan rose. "Better get those sleeves rolled up first."

He looked down at his white shirt, then glanced at Caitlin. She hurried to him without a minute's hesitation, unbuttoned his sleeves and rolled them to his elbows. Her fingers moved over the curling hairs on his forearms and she felt a pain twist inside her.

Dylan stepped away from her, and haltingly lowered Lizzie into the tiny tub. The water just covered her chubby legs. "There now, Lizzie," he said softly, falteringly, clutching the infant under the arms as if afraid she'd dissolve in the water. "You like baths, don't you? Sure you do. There we go."

"Now cup your hand, Dylan, and just pour the water over her chest. That's it."

Dylan followed Ellen's instructions, bathing the hot little body in cool water as Lizzie stared trustingly up at him, looking sleepy. After a few minutes, Dylan leaned Lizzie forward, over his arm, and bathed her back in the same manner. He even managed to wet her head and neck, all without upsetting the baby at all, though his hands shook visibly.

Sandra burst into the room then. "What's happenin'? Is she all right?"

"What did the doctor say?" Caitlin asked.

Sandra glanced at Caitlin, then frowned. "You shouldn't be here, Caitlin. You can go now. *I'm* her mama."

God, was Sandra threatened by Caitlin's presence, her fondness for Lizzie? Was she jealous?

"Answer the question, Sandra, 'fore I cuff you upside the head for ignorance," Ellen scolded.

Sandra shot Ellen a nearly blank glance, before she answered. "He said to put her in a cool bath and keep her there until the Children's Tylenol has a chance to work."

"When did you give her the medicine?" Ellen asked.

"I—I couldn't get it down her. She was fussin' so much, and then she got so hot, I just—"

"Well, she isn't fussing now. Get that medicine in here."

Sandra went into the bathroom and returned with the little bottle, and a baby-size medicine spoon. She poured the dose and handed the spoon to Dylan.

"Uh…hey, Lizzie, look what Uncle Dylan has for you." He spoke as if he were talking to an adult. He slipped the spoon between Lizzie's lips and she took the medicine without a fight. Then he returned to his messy, nervous bathing of her heated body. His shirt was soaked, as were the fronts of his trousers and a good deal of the floor.

Sandra paced, Ellen sat in the rocker and Caitlin just stood and watched Dylan with the baby, a lump in her throat making it difficult to breathe. After twenty minutes, Ellen ordered the baby removed from the bath. Dylan scooped her out and wrapped her in a towel. As he patted her dry, she fell asleep in his arms. Dylan stared down at her, some secret turmoil in his eyes. He blinked it away at once.

"She feels cooler now." He placed her in the crib.

Ellen got up and touched the sleeping child's forehead. "Put a diaper on her, Sandra. Nothing else. Get that medicine down her every four hours. If you can't, or if that fever shoots up again, you come and get me."

"Yeah, okay. And I'll take her to the doctor in the mornin'. He said he'd see her first thing."

Ellen nodded and left the room. Caitlin turned to go, as well, but stopped cold when Sandra slipped her arms around Dylan's neck and pressed herself close to him. "I was so scared," she whispered. "Thank God you were here."

Caitlin saw Dylan's arms creep around Sandra's waist. Dylan's back was to Caitlin. But not Sandra's, and that blond head lifted from Dylan's shoulder just long enough to send Caitlin a look of unmistakable meaning.

Biting her lower lip to fight the tide of burning jealousy, pure and bitter, that rinsed through her heart, she turned and fled the room. It was obvious that Thomas's young wife had designs on Caitlin's husband. And from the looks of things, Dylan wasn't putting up too much of a fight. Not that Caitlin could blame him. After all, he hadn't slept in her bed in months and months. What had the old Caitlin expected him to do?

She raced past her bedroom, tears threatening. She felt more an outsider than she thought possible. Seeing Sandra in Dylan's arms, seeing the truth at last, in the other woman's eyes. God, she needed to get out of here!

She took the stairs at top speed, and went right out the front door into the rain-filled night. And then she stopped, and stood, tilting her head up into the black rain, razor winds and the night's bracing, icy hands.

It was almost as if the rain could wash away the person she'd been before, leaving her clean and free to begin again. She closed her eyes and let the drops roll over her heated lids, drenching her lashes, rinsing the hot tears from them, cooling the burn.

Almost without thinking, she began placing one foot ahead

of the other, as her clothes slowly soaked through and began clinging to her skin. She followed a worn path in the grass that took her around to the rear of the house, down a mild slope, and through a small wood.

The sounds of waves hurling themselves against jagged rock were like a siren's call, luring her onward, until she stood at the very lip of a cliff. The wind blew in off the sea, razing her face with the stinging, chilled droplets it carried. It smelled of the ocean, and of the rain. Freshness and freedom. It sent her wet hair snapping behind her, and she closed her eyes and just felt its touch. She forced everything else from her mind, and lived only for the moment, for this experience.

God, it felt good.

She opened her eyes, but ahead there was only darkness, roiling clouds and curtains of rain. She edged closer to the granite lip, and let her gaze fall downward. White foam seethed from the surface around glittering fingers of rock, far below. More white exploded from each black wave that battered the shore.

She was as wet as if she'd been swimming, fully clothed, but she didn't care. She needed to think, and here was the best place to do it. She couldn't keep a clear head in that house.

The woman she'd been had left behind as much devastation as a hurricane. All of it, it seemed, was now hers to clean up. She had to begin somewhere.

But how?

She obviously couldn't mend any fences with Sandra. The woman was after her husband, there was no way around that. Sandra had declared her intentions in no uncertain terms.

The question was, what did Caitlin intend to do about it?

Would she surrender? Give up without a fight? Stand quietly by while the sleek little blonde seduced Dylan?

That the first option rubbed her wrong told her something about her personality. Whether it was the old Caitlin or the new one, she wasn't sure. But she knew that having something that belonged to her stolen while she watched was not a plausible answer. She couldn't do it.

And the only other option was to keep him for herself. And of course, she had no idea if she wanted that, either...or even if he'd have her.

She turned and walked along the edge for a time, letting the wind buffet her right side. When she came to an oblong boulder, she sat down upon its slick surface, and turned to face the sea again, her feet dangling over the rain-filled space between her and the shore.

"You should have died in the accident, Caitlin."

The voice rasped near her ear, just as she felt the gloved hands settle around her throat. She tried to turn around, but one fist closed in her hair, and she couldn't move her head. The voice went on, throaty and gruff, neither masculine nor feminine, unidentifiable.

"But you're about to have another one."

Even as the hands at her neck loosened, she felt the impact of a foot at the small of her back. Her body arched forward, pain slicing her spine. Her hands grappled for something, but only slid from the wet rock.

She was going over the edge. There was nothing to stop her. The cry she released was one of pure fear, and it split the night, pierced the walls of rain and drowned out the wind as she tumbled and twisted and grabbed for salvation.

Somehow, her fist closed on a jagged outcropping. Razor-edged stone cut into her palm, but she clung tighter, even as her body twisted and slammed into the sheer stone face. Frantically, she moved her toes and her other hand, in search of more support. One foot found a niche in the rock, and dug into it.

She was panting, breathless with fear. The rain battered her back and the sounds of the waves crashing to shore below were louder, echoing through her consciousness. She lifted her head, to look above at her assailant, but saw nothing.

Only the jagged edge from which she'd fallen, and the inky sky above. She hadn't fallen far. Surely she could climb back up.

But what if he's still there, waiting? What if he pushes me again? She closed her eyes and prayed for courage, and strength to hold on. She dared not try to scale the wet, sheer wall. If she let go, she would fall, there was no question in her mind, but she couldn't remain where she was, either.

"Caitlin…"

The howling wind seemed to cry her name, then again, louder this time. It wasn't the wind. Someone was there, looking for her. The call came again, and she recognized Dylan's voice. She parted her lips to answer, then bit the cry off before it left her throat. What if Dylan was the one who had pushed her? What if he were only calling out now to ascertain whether his mission had been a success?

Seconds ticked by. Then other voices joined the first, calling her name. Thomas's, Henri's, even Sandra's.

"This way," Dylan's voice shouted into the wind. "I heard a scream."

"*Mon Dieu,* do you think she has fallen—" Henri began.

"Here," Caitlin cried out with every ounce of strength left in her. Whoever had pushed her, they wouldn't try again, not with all of them there to bear witness. "Down here. Help me!"

There were footsteps, then lights above her, glaring down into her eyes. She averted her face. "Hold on, Cait. Don't move, just hold on!" The light moved away, and she heard Dylan's voice once again, gruff and unsteady. "I can reach her, hold my legs, Thomas." There was shuffling, movements of bodies on the wet stone. She looked up again to see Dylan's dark shape. He lay facedown above her, and bent at the waist until his upper body hung over the edge. His arms stretched down for her, his strong hands closed like vises around her wrists.

"Let go of the rock, Cait. Hold onto my arms."

She didn't. She couldn't. What if he just let her go?

"Let go," he said again. She tilted her head up, and looked at him. "Trust me for once, dammit! I won't let you fall."

She had no choice. She couldn't hang on much longer, anyway. Trusting Dylan with her life right now was her only option. She released her precarious hold on the stone, and gripped his wrists just as he was gripping hers.

"I have her," he shouted. "Pull me up."

Slowly, she was dragged up the wet, cold, washboard face of stone, and onto the blessedly level ground again. She lay facedown on the uneven stone, head buried in her arms. Dylan's hands on her shoulders urged her to her feet. His eyes scanned her face, her body, as the fear enveloped her all over again. With a strangled cry, she threw herself against him, and his arms closed around her. He held her against him with all the strength she'd known his arms would possess, and as she shook violently, she noticed that he was trembling, too.

His hands stroked her wet hair, her back and shoulders. "It's all right, Cait. It's over. You're safe now. It's all right."

She couldn't make the tears stop flowing. She couldn't let go of him. So she was glad when he scooped her up into his arms as if she weighed nothing at all, and turned to begin back toward the house. She kept her arms tight around his neck, her face pressed to the warm, wet skin of it. She knew the others walked with them. She felt their curious eyes on her, but she didn't care. She'd experienced raw terror in the last few minutes. She was clinging to her sanity by clinging to her husband. It didn't matter what they thought.

She knew he'd mounted the front steps. She heard the door open and felt the rain stop lashing her as he carried her inside. Then he was lowering her onto the sofa, leaning her head back against the armrest, sitting right beside her.

Caitlin couldn't take her eyes from his face, as he looked her up and down. His hands moved anxiously over her arms, then her legs. "Are you all right? Were you hurt?"

She shook her head as someone handed him a blanket, and he tucked it around her. Then he stared at her face, and shook his head, and the hardness crept over his features, little by little, until the ice sculpture was complete. "Dammit, Caitlin, I told you not to go out there tonight. I told you how dangerous it was, that you could fall—"

"I didn't fall." She blurted the words quickly, and everyone in the room stilled, looking toward her.

Dylan's face contorted then. He shook his head slowly as if in disbelief. "You didn't…my God, are you saying you…"

"Can't say it, Dylan?" Thomas's voice was laced with bitterness. "She jumped. Tried to take the same cowardly way out our mother did." Caitlin caught her breath, but Thomas went right on. "We all could've been killed trying to pull you up, big sister. Next time, try something a little smarter."

Dylan whirled on Thomas, fists clenched. Caitlin threw back the blanket and leapt to her feet, only to sway on weak knees. She gripped Dylan's arm, both to keep from falling at his feet, and to keep him from hitting her brother. "Stop it! For God's sake—"

"Caitlin, don't do this." Thomas's voice cracked and changed pitch. The next sentence was an octave higher, a plea. "I'll never forgive you if you do what she did—"

Caitlin released Dylan's arm, only to grip both of Thomas's. "My mother…are you saying…suicide?"

"It was cruel, Caitlin, and I hate her for it! Damn you, for trying—"

"I didn't!" she shrieked. Thomas went silent, and she saw actual tears swimming in his eyes as he searched her face. More calmly, she went on. "I didn't jump off that cliff. I was pushed."

"Pushed?" Dylan gripped her shoulders from behind, turned her to face him. He'd paled, and his eyes were wider than she'd seen them yet. "Who—"

"Did you say 'pushed'?" Caitlin turned her head to see Ellen, scuffing into the room, followed by Genevieve.

"Oh, *mon Dieu!* Are you all right?"

Caitlin's eyes met Dylan's, and she nodded. "For now I am." Silently, she heard her heart begging him, *Please don't be the one.*

Chapter 7

The room went utterly silent. Dylan only stared at Caitlin, and said nothing.

"*I* think Caitlin ought to pay another visit to that shrink of hers."

She glanced toward Sandra's doubting eyes and shivered. Was the woman that desperate to latch on to Caitlin's husband? Desperate enough to kill?

Caitlin shivered again. Dylan's gaze narrowed on her. "You need to get into some dry clothes before you get sick."

She turned toward him. "Is that all you have to say? Dylan, someone tried to kill me tonight!"

He searched her face, and she saw the skepticism in his eyes. "You don't believe me."

"I didn't say that."

"You didn't have to." She pulled free of the tempting warmth she could feel emanating from his body, turned and walked calmly toward the staircase and up it. She focused on the cool, smooth feel of the banister as her hand glided over it, on the number of steps her feet climbed, on the pattern of the wood grain on them. Anything but the feeling of their eyes on her back, and the fear that still made her heart thunder.

No one followed, only the grim specter of fear that seemed to grow larger with every minute she spent here. She closed the bedroom door, and flicked on the lights. Her nerves tingling, she moved slowly through the room. The closet loomed ahead of her like a dare, and she answered, stepping forward, flinging it wide and scanning the dim interior.

Nothing inside except the mounds of clothing she detested, and the few things she'd chosen for herself. But a chill raced up her spine, and she whirled. The bathroom door was closed. Hadn't she left it ajar?

She stood for an eternity, barely breathing as she listened. She heard only the howl of the wind and the hands of the rain slapping her windows. She moved forward, slowly, mindlessly closing her fingers around something cold and hard and heavy as she passed the nightstand. She gripped the doorknob, turned it and holding her breath, flung it wide.

When she saw only the dark shapes of the fixtures, she stiffened her spine, reached in for the light switch and snapped it on. Oh, God, the shower curtain was pulled tight.

She swallowed hard, snagged the curtain in one hand and lifted her makeshift weapon in the other. She tore it open. The porcelain tub stood gleaming, empty.

"Caitlin."

She spun at the sound of his voice, again lifting the weapon instinctively. Dylan stood near the bedroom door. It was closed behind him, and Caitlin's darting gaze quickly noted that it was locked, as well.

"What do you want?"

He frowned, his eyes focused on the object in her hand. "You won't need that, Cait. Put it down." As he spoke, he moved forward.

Caitlin blinked as her hand lowered. She studied her weapon, a shiny onyx-colored vase with a scarlet rose painted on the front. A thin rim of gold encircled the lip. It would be about as useful against a would-be killer as the pillow on her bed. She closed her eyes and stepped into the bedroom, replacing the vase on the stand.

She heard his sigh as he stepped closer. "You're still shaking."

She rubbed her arms and shrugged.

"Tell me you didn't try to jump, Cait."

She lifted her head, met his eyes. He stood very close to her now. "I didn't jump. I told you, I was pushed."

"By whom?"

She tipped her head up and studied the planes and angles of his face. It was a strong face, with deep brown eyes filled with emotions she couldn't begin to fathom. "I didn't see. He came up behind me."

"He? It was a man, then?"

She shrugged. "It could've been. I'm not sure, the voice was deliberately disguised."

"He spoke to you?"

She nodded. Dylan's hands came to her shoulders and her heart beat a little faster. It was a stupid reaction. For all she knew, it could've been him.

"Cait, what did he say to you?"

She swallowed hard. "That I should've died in the accident. That I'd die tonight, instead."

"And you still didn't get a look—"

"His hands were on my throat. I couldn't turn my head."

Brows bunching together, Dylan's glance dipped to her neck. His warm hands touched her skin there, and tilted her chin upward. His head lowered. An onlooker would have thought he was about to kiss her, she thought, and a shudder rippled through her at the vision. His long fingers touched her throat and she wished they'd explore lower. She knew those fingers had teased her breasts, had taunted her center to throbbing readiness.

How can I want a man who may have just tried to kill me?

"He left marks. There'll be bruises tomorrow."

"So now you have to believe me."

Dylan's hands fell away. "I believed you in the first place."

"Then why—"

"I thought it would be best if we discussed this alone."

Her eyes darted once again toward the locked door. She shivered.

"You're still soaking wet." He reached to the bedpost, where her red satin robe hung, and picked it up. "Here, get into this."

Cait took it from him and stepped into the bathroom, closing the door. She quickly shimmied out of her clothes, and wiped her skin dry with a towel. She scanned the room for something besides the robe to put on, but saw nothing. Not even underwear. Sighing in resignation, she pulled the robe on, and tied the sash tight.

When she stepped back into the bedroom, Dylan was pacing. He faced her and stopped, his eyes narrowing as his gaze moved briefly down her body. He snapped it upward again.

Caitlin felt the touch of his eyes as if they were hands, and she fought the wave of heat that rose to engulf her, even as goose bumps dotted her arms.

"So, what do you want me to do?"

She saw his eyes widen slightly. "What?"

"About tonight," she clarified. "Shouldn't I call the police?"

"I'll talk to them in the morning," he said.

Caitlin's heart skipped once, just once. "Why?"

"Because I'd like to keep this quiet if I can." He took a step toward her. "Cait, we have to handle this carefully." At his second step in her direction, she took one backward.

He froze where he was, his eyes narrowing. "What is it?"

She shook her head. "Nothing. Nothing, this is all just a lot to deal with. I just want to go to bed, and—"

"You're afraid of me, aren't you." It was a simple statement of fact. "You think it was me."

She licked her lips and forced herself to meet his gaze. "I don't know what to think."

He shook his head in disbelief. "You put down the vase."

"Maybe I ought to pick it back up."

"You think it would do any good?" He took another step forward, his hands closing on the outsides of her arms.

"I think you're trying to scare me."

"Am I succeeding?"

She felt her lips begin to tremble. "Yes," she whispered.

His eyes moved over her face in rapid, searching patterns. "Good. I hope you're scared enough to use some sense from here on in. Walking into that storm, going out to the cliffs on a night like this was insane, Caitlin. What on earth were you thinking?"

He still held her arms, and the angry sparks in his eyes were real. "I was upset. I just had to get out of this house."

"Why?"

She closed her eyes, shook her head quickly. "You don't know when to quit, do you?"

"I don't know the word 'quit,' lady. Tell me why you took off like that."

"Because I saw the way you were holding Sandra, all right?"

"The way I—"

"She was pressed so close, I couldn't have fit a matchstick between you."

Understanding seemed to dawn on his face. "In the nursery—"

"And you didn't seem to mind it at all, Dylan. And forgive me for being human, but seeing that hurt."

He shook his head slowly. "Hurt?" He repeated her own word as if trying to remember its meaning.

"She wants you, you know." She turned and paced away

from him, relieved that she'd released the tension burning inside her. "And she intends to have you."

"How do you know?"

"She told me. No, not in words. Women can communicate without parting their lips sometimes, and she made her intentions perfectly clear to me. She wants you." Her back was still to him.

He came to stand close behind her. "And what do *you* want?"

A sob tried to escape, and she choked on it. "I don't know. I only know I want to believe you aren't trying to kill me. I want to believe it very much."

His hands crept up to her shoulders. "But you don't, do you?" She sniffed, and shook her head. "No."

"What's my motive, Cait? You think I want your money? I've never given a damn about money. I could've let you fall out there if I'd wanted to get rid of you so badly. Have you thought of that?"

She laughed, though it came out as a short release of air. "What do you think?"

He turned her to face him, brows furrowed. "My God, you were thinking it at the cliff, weren't you? You were hanging over the side, clinging to nothing but my hands, half convinced I was going to let you go."

She nodded. There was no sense in being dishonest about it, no sense lying.

He shook his head hard and blew an angry sigh. "Believe what you want, Caitlin. Go to the police yourself if you don't trust me. Do whatever you have to do."

He turned toward the door, but her next words stopped him. "Have you slept with her, Dylan?"

He shook his head without turning to face her. He stood poised, his hand on the doorknob. "Do me a favor and stop worrying about my relationship with Sandra. It's none of your business...unless you'd care to make me a better offer."

He stormed out and slammed the door behind him.

* * *

She took a long, hot bath to soak the chill from her bones, but it did little to soothe her frayed nerves. There was just too much she didn't know. Had her car accident been another attempt on her life? It seemed more than likely, given the assailant's words at the cliff. And the carob-laced dessert now looked like yet another. Someone wanted her dead, and badly.

But who? She knew so little about her life, it was difficult to judge who had a motive to want it to end. Did she have enough money to give Dylan a motive? Why wouldn't he simply divorce her if he wanted out of the marriage? And what about Thomas? She already knew he'd been disinherited. And she'd gotten everything. He'd sided with their mother in the divorce, and she'd apparently taken her father's side. What she hadn't known before tonight, was the manner in which her mother had died.

Suicide.

Had Caitlin been to blame for that? Had her decision to remain with her father added to her mother's depression in any way? And how could it not have? Maybe Thomas was resentful of the part she'd played in their mother's death, and maybe he was striking out against her, as a result.

Could she make amends with him now? And should she? She could offer him half of what she'd inherited from their father. It was only fair. He should have gotten it to begin with.

Snippets of the conversation she'd overheard between Thomas and Genevieve floated through her memory and she bit her lip. Thomas had said he would teach Dylan a lesson he'd never forget. Whatever he was planning, she couldn't very well help him along by giving him what he needed to carry it out. No, nor could she tell Dylan about what she'd overheard. She felt an instinctive urge to protect her brother, and sensed it was just the way she'd felt when they were growing up together. If she'd misunderstood, she might cost

Thomas his job, and his wife and child their home, all without cause. That would only make him hate her.

God, she had so little to go on! If she had any sense at all, she'd probably pack her things and get out of here while there was still time. But something kept her from making that decision right now. Tomorrow, she decided. Tomorrow she would do some digging into her past, and decide how best to proceed. Tomorrow.

She dried her hair, and tried to get some sleep, but every time she began to drift off, she would hear footsteps outside her bedroom door, or the wind moaning at the window, and her eyes would fly wide once more.

She drifted off to sleep eventually, but the entire time, she tossed and turned in the throes of a nightmare she couldn't later recall.

A soft wail stroked at the edges of her consciousness, tugging her out of the dream. In the nick of time, it seemed, she emerged into the soft folds of her covers. The baby was crying.

Caitlin wiped the sweat from her forehead, and tried to settle her breathing into a normal pattern. It was just a dream. Nothing more. She was safe.

It was then she felt the presence in her room. She froze and held her breath, listening. There was no sound or movement. Just a feeling that she wasn't alone.

She tried to shake it. It was silly, she told herself. Of course no one was in her room. She was shaken, from the dream and from her close call on the cliffs, tonight.

The baby cried again, and Caitlin felt answering tears well up in her own eyes. She wished, with everything in her, that Lizzie was her own. During those few, brief times when she'd held the baby, she'd felt as if everything would be fine. It had seemed so perfect. She'd had an identity. She'd found something to cling to in this sea of unanswered questions. It hurt too much to hear that child cry, and then stop as someone, probably Sandra, picked her up. Why the hell did it hurt so much?

She rolled to her stomach and buried her face in the pillow, clutching it tightly. It absorbed her stinging tears, but gave no comfort.

Then she heard the audible click of the door closing, and sat bolt upright in the bed. Someone had just exited the room, she was sure of it. She shot to her feet, switching on the lamp. Its glaring light made her blink, and showed her nothing. The room was exactly as it had been before.

Caitlin went to the door and yanked it open, her eyes scanning the dim length of the hallway in both directions. There was no one in sight, but she heard, just for an instant, the soft padding of feet on the carpet.

Terror gripped her, and she backed into her room, closed the door and turned the lock. Someone had been in here, standing over her while she tossed in the throes of her nightmare. Someone had stood, silently, just watching her.

Why?

What would have happened if she hadn't awoke?

She sat on the bed, with her back to the headboard, and her knees drawn up to her chest. She didn't close her eyes again.

In fear and desperation, she finally got up, determined to find the guest room where she'd taken refuge that first day back. She would sleep there tonight. Not only would she feel better, but it would make finding her more difficult for the killer, if he decided to try again.

Dylan poured another shot and tossed it back in a single swallow. It did nothing to erase from his memory the feel of his wife in his arms. When he'd pulled her up from the cliff face and she'd thrown herself against him, he'd experienced a longing that was like an addict's craving for his drug of choice. He'd wanted her.

Wet. She'd been soaking wet, and shivering with cold, and her nipples had pressed against his chest so hard, he could feel them right through his shirt. And her face was damp, and her throat, and he'd wanted to lick the rainwater from her skin. God, how could he want any woman as badly as he wanted her, let alone one who'd caused him so much pain?

But she was different now. No longer the haughty princess of the manor, but unsure of herself, and softer-spoken, and—

Damn straight she's soft-spoken. She's scared to death I'm going to kill her and if I had half a brain I'd probably oblige her. Hell, I should have dropped her out there at the cliff.

His hand closed around the neck of the bottle and he splashed more scotch into the shot glass. Damn her for coming back when he'd thought he'd finally been rid of her for good. Damn her for changing everything just when he'd finally broken the grip she'd had for so long. Damn her for pretending she'd changed when he knew it was impossible. He'd waited five years for Caitlin to change. It hadn't happened. Why would a bump on the head do what all his arguing and pleading with her hadn't?

He poured the searing liquor down his throat and closed his eyes as it hit his stomach. He couldn't let her go now. He needed to watch her night and day until he settled this thing. And knowing that made him angry. And the anger made him reach for the bottle again. It was a night for anesthesia. Because as much as he'd vowed to set himself free of her, Caitlin was slowly drawing him in again.

And she wanted him to call her Caity.

For just a second, he let the image of her when she'd been Caity to him, rinse through his mind like a spring breeze. Then, she'd been as happy in tattered cutoffs as she was in a designer dress. She'd turned her nose up at her father's fancy meals to sneak out for pizza with him. God, if he could have that girl back again…

Ah, but that was idiocy! She didn't even remember those times. That Caity was dead and buried. So, she'd like him to believe, was the cold and distant woman she'd become.

But he wasn't so sure.

He drank and he paced, until his pacing became an unsteady weave and his head floated far above his shoulders. And then he mounted the stairs, thinking he ought to be drunk enough to sleep. As he climbed, clutching the banister for guidance, he recalled the conversation they'd had in her bedroom. She'd admitted that seeing him holding Sandra had hurt her. The old Cait never would have done that. And she'd looked at him like…like she wanted him. But he might have been seeing things that weren't there. And then he'd challenged her to make him a better offer. Like she would. And pigs would fly, too.

He forced himself farther along the hall, groped for the door handle and leaned heavily on it as it swung open. He stepped through, swaying slightly, but catching himself. He closed the door behind him and stood in complete darkness. He knew he was drunk. He didn't mind admitting it. The way he saw it, he had reason to get good and drunk tonight. Besides, he doubted he'd have been able to close his eyes sober. There was too much going on in his mind. Too many painful memories churning to life from the enforced death he'd imposed on them. Not memories of Caitlin. Memories of Caity.

He fumbled with his buttons, his fingers feeling too big. He dropped the shirt to the floor.

Hot, eager Caity. Her skin warm and coated in sweat, her body shuddering at his every touch, her soft whimpers as he played her. He knew how. He knew her every secret, knew her scent and her taste…

He groaned, and lurched forward, dragging the belt out of his pants and clumsily peeling them off. He kicked free of the rest of his clothes, amazed he managed to do so without falling on his butt.

Naked, he stood still a minute. The nearly frigid chill from the blasting central air unit felt good on his tormented flesh.

It shot a little sanity back into his fevered mind. He pulled back the covers and crawled beneath them.

Warm, soft flesh was there to greet him. Long, silken tresses brushed against his unclothed chest. A curvy, bare backside rubbed over his groin, and he knew it was his wife. Naked, warm and waiting for him.

He released an anguished sigh and let his eyes fall closed. Finally, he thought in relief so great it was painful. Finally, the estrangement was at an end. She wanted him again.

His throat oddly tight, he rolled her onto her back, slipped his arms around her slender waist, and pressed his chest to hers as his mouth sought her lips. He found them and kissed her, and as long-denied passion hit him full force, his body grew fervent with need. He felt her slack, willing mouth tighten as she came fully awake, but he chose to ignore it. He forced his tongue inside, and he jammed his knee between her thighs to press them open. Already, he was hard and ready. He nudged against her opening, and felt it moisten in readiness. Oh, God, it had been so damned long.

He felt her hands pushing at his chest, and he was afraid she was changing her mind. Aided in his decision by the scotch, he gripped them both in one of his and pinned them above her head to the mattress. Her frantic twisting beneath him only served to heighten his lust. He kissed a hot trail from her lips to her jaw, and she immediately let out the beginning of a piercing shriek. His free hand clamped over her mouth.

"Baby, don't tell me to stop now," he said, panting with longing. "Please, don't tell me to stop. You don't know what I've gone through, night after night, always knowing you were just down the hall, always wanting you. God, how much I've wanted you."

He moved his mouth lower, captured one impudent breast between his teeth and worried it roughly, biting and tugging the hard little nipple until he felt it pulsate against his tongue. Muffled whimpering sounds escaped from beneath his palm, inflaming him beyond rational thought. Her nipple stood stiffer, hardened to a throbbing nub and he licked and sucked it before turning to the other one, and giving it equal attention.

Her opening wept for him, her juices coating his head where he pressed it against her. She was ready. So was he. He pulled back slightly. This first sheathing of him inside her would be to the hilt. It would be sheer ecstasy.

Her teeth closed on his hand so hard, he was certain she drew blood, and when he relaxed his hold on her in response to the pain, she yanked one hand free, and slammed it across his face.

"Get off me, you drunken lunatic! Get off me now or I swear I will scream until the windows rattle. I'll call a cop. Get off, get the hell off!"

He rolled to one side, swearing a blue streak and trying to figure out what the hell had happened. His arousal throbbed with need. His brain, with frustration. He felt her leave the bed on one side. He quickly left on the other, and unerringly found the light switch. As soon as the room was flooded with brilliance, he saw her. She'd been looking for something to put on, and apparently hadn't found it. She stood there, facing him, not a stitch covering her. Her lower lip was bleeding slightly. There were teeth marks on her dampened breasts, tiny little ridges around the nipples. Angry, red rings encircled her wrists.

But her nipples still stood in quivering hardness, gleaming with the moisture put there by his mouth, and he knew she'd been as aroused as he had been.

"Stop looking at me," she cried, snatching the comforter from the bed and tugging it up to her chin.

"If you didn't want me looking at you, why the hell were you naked, and waiting in my bed?"

"You're drunk," she cried. "This isn't your bed!" She gulped, blinked at tears that might have been manufactured, and shook her head.

Dylan frowned, and glanced around the room, now flooded

with light. It was a guest room, the one right next door to his own. The furniture was situated in an almost identical pattern, and he had come in during utter darkness, not to mention falling-down drunk.

"You...said I could find another room if I didn't like the one I had. I—this was the only one I felt comfortable in."

He moved toward her, around the foot of the bed. She backed away until she was touching the wall. "And you didn't notice that it was right next door to my room? That didn't have anything to do with your choice?"

"As a matter of fact, it did. Someone was in my room tonight, watching me. I was terrified, and for some idiotic reason, I wanted to be closer to you." Her face fell, contorted with pain. "God, I'm a fool!"

Her words made their way through the scotch-induced haze of his brain, and he felt like groaning aloud. He looked at her again, at her dilated pupils, her tear-stained cheeks, her goose bump-dotted flesh. Then he glimpsed the corner of a dressing gown sticking out from under the bed. He reached for it and she jumped. Very slowly, he pulled it out and held it up to her.

She snatched it from his hands, held the blanket in her teeth and slipped the robe on. When she dropped the comforter at last, she lunged past him for the door.

He caught her arm. "This wasn't my fault, Caitlin. Not entirely. I stumbled into the wrong room by accident. What the hell was I supposed to think when I found you in what I mistook for my own bed, like this?"

She faced him, hair tousled, eyes blazing. "You damned near raped me, Dylan."

"If I were the kind of man to take a woman by force, you'd still be on your back under me, lady."

"If that—" she pointed an accusing finger at the rumpled sheets "—was an example of your technique, I'm not surprised your wife requested separate bedrooms."

His gaze lowered, and he ran the backs of his fingers over her still-distended nipple, where it poked through the material of the robe. "Oh, yeah. I can see how turned off *my wife* is."

"You're right," she shouted. "That's the worst part, Dylan. I thought I wanted you. I've stayed awake nights, wishing… Oh, God, I'm going to be sick!" Her face crumpled. She pushed her way blindly past him, and stumbled down the hall toward her own bedroom.

Chapter 8

It was morning, but not yet dawn. And despite her nightlong expenditure of energy, she was still thinking about him. Dylan.

Tears blurred her vision, and she sank onto the bed's edge, amid the piles of clothes, drained of all ambition. She'd wanted so badly to trust him, to believe he was the one person in this house she could turn to in the midst of this chaos. He was her husband. She should be able to trust him.

Then why didn't she?

Though she'd been determined not to, she recalled the events of last night with brutal clarity. His hands, holding her wrists to the bed. His mouth claiming hers with punishing force, his hardened groin digging into her. She'd felt the anger inside him, all of it, seemingly focused on her. She'd felt his contempt in his touch.

And his desire.

His throaty declaration haunted her, even now, ringing in

her ears until she pressed her hands to them to stop it. But still she heard his gruff voice, the pain and frustration palpable in its timbre. "...night after night, always knowing you were just down the hall, always wanting you. God, how much I've wanted you..."

She closed her eyes as the tears spilled over her face. So many emotions assailed her, it was difficult to know what she was feeling.

So she told herself to stop analyzing and reliving it, and she stood up, and got back to work. She tightened the sash of her red satin robe, recalling as she did the coldness in Dylan's eyes as he'd held it toward her in one outstretched hand. She shuddered. She'd have to add it to the pile of clothes to be discarded, just as soon as she returned to her room with some boxes.

Sleep, of course, had not been an option last night. She'd left the guest room devastated, and angry, and confused, and too full of emotions to rest. She tried to count the nights since she'd actually slept decently, and realized there'd been none. Not since she'd come back here.

She picked her way through the mounds of clothes, all separated into piles on the floor, and on the bed, and left the bedroom, stepping silently into the hall, flicking on every light switch she came to along the way. She'd memorized their locations since her last scare out here.

The house was cold, as always, and quiet as a tomb, which was fitting, she thought bitterly, since someone was trying so hard to make it hers. She wouldn't run into Dylan. No chance of that. As drunk as he'd been, he'd probably passed out right after she'd left him. He might not even remember... She almost hoped he didn't.

She padded softly down the stairs, barefoot, and made her way to the kitchen without interruption. She hoped to find Genevieve and ask for a box to pack the clothes in, or maybe just find the boxes herself.

But the kitchen was empty, spotless and dark. She didn't

know where the light switch was in here. She stood for a moment, in the doorway, her eyes moving slowly over the shapes of gleaming pots and pans hanging from racks, the cabinets, the range. With a sigh of resignation, she slipped farther inside. She pressed her palm to the wall and walked sideways, feeling for the light switch. As soon as she let it go, the door swung closed, and Caitlin found herself surrounded by utter blackness.

Panic welled up in her throat until she almost choked on it. She walked faster, both hands racing over the wall now, in search of the switch. She'd been stupid to come down here. What was she thinking of, groping her way through a darkened room where a killer might very well be waiting?

Her fingers touched a switch. Limp with relief, her pulse thundering in her temples, she moved it, and the room filled with brilliant light.

A hand dropped to her shoulder. Caitlin whirled, a scream of terror catching in her throat.

"Do not be afraid, *chérie*."

She took a step away from Henri, but her back touched the wall. "I…I was looking for Genevieve." Caitlin tried not to squirm at the notion of being alone with him, and standing so close. He hadn't lifted a finger to so much as touch her. And just because his eyes were so intense, it didn't really mean anything. So, he found her attractive. So what?

With her back to the wall, and him standing so close, she couldn't really move without shoving him aside, and looking like a total idiot. "Tell me what it is you need, what it is you want. I will take care of it."

Was it only admiration she was seeing in those dark eyes? Or was there more? A suggestion…a meaning she didn't get because she didn't remember. My God, had there ever been something going on between her and Henri? The thought shocked and shook her. Had the old Caitlin cheated on her husband? Was that why Dylan was so hostile toward her now?

She looked up, into the now-smiling face, and shook her head. No. If Dylan thought that, Henri certainly wouldn't still be employed here. Dylan wasn't the kind of man who'd take something like that lightly.

"Chérie?"

He was awaiting an answer. "Boxes. I, um, I need to pack some clothes I don't want, and I need boxes."

"Ah." He stepped back just slightly, pinching his chin. Then he snapped his fingers. *"Oui,* I have it. There are some in the storage room. Wait here."

And just like that, he was briskly walking across the kitchen, and out another door, beyond it. Caitlin slowly released all the air from her lungs. She knew she was simply overreacting to everything everyone said or did, because she knew that someone in this house hated her enough to kill her. She forced herself to calm down, and recalled that Henri tended to call every woman in the house *chérie,* even Ellen, on occasion. She shouldn't start reading a history of illicit liaisons into his friendliness.

He was back in seconds, with three boxes, each one fitted neatly inside another. She took them. "Thank you, Henri."

"It is nothing."

The sun never really rose. It was there, but you couldn't see it beyond the black clouds and pouring rain. Caitlin showered, hanging a washcloth over the ugly, lion-faced spigot, then slipped into jeans and a sweatshirt. She dried her hair and pulled it into a ponytail to keep it out of her face. When she stepped out of her bathroom, she folded the red robe over her forearm and dropped it into one of the boxes she'd filled with clothes.

And then she reached for the delicate antique-looking phone. She'd come to only one conclusion all night long—that she needed to talk with Dr. Judith Stone. And then the police. She'd be damned if she'd sit here and wait for the next attempt on her life without taking some kind of action. The thought of just walking away from all of this pirouetted through her mind, but vanished just as quickly. She couldn't leave until she'd made some kind of sense of her life, found some shred of her identity. It wasn't even an option. This was her home; these people, her family. She'd never know peace until she solved this thing.

She brought the receiver from its elevated cradle to her ear. She was surprised to hear voices on the line.

"Just do it. Withdraw the bid."

The voice was low, resolute, and Dylan's. Caitlin was about to replace the receiver, but the answer came, and it caught her attention.

"Dylan, we need this contract. We're going to be in the red if we don't land it. Dammit, there are only two competitors, and one of the company's CEO is involved in that child molestation case. The state won't award a guy with so much scandal attached to him any kind of contract, so we—"

"We withdraw the bid."

Caitlin frowned, recognizing the young male voice on the other end as one of the architects she'd met at the office yesterday.

"We're about to have some scandals of our own come to light, Patrick. I'm on my way to the police right now, and you know how things leak from one government agency to another. Just pull out and maybe we can salvage our reputation."

"What scandal?"

"Not on the phone."

"It's a private line, Dylan. What scandal?"

Dylan sighed loudly into the mouthpiece. "Within the next hour, I will probably become the chief suspect in the attempted murder of my wife. Scandalous enough for you?"

There was a moment of stunned silence, then, "I don't need to ask if you did it."

"No?"

"No." There was a long sigh. "I'll pull the bid, Dylan. Call if you need anything."

"Right."

Two clicks sounded in Caitlin's ear, and she blinked down her shock. A second later, she placed her own call.

His idiotic boozing last night and the hangover it left him with had not in any way dulled his memory. Dylan almost wished it had. For the briefest of moments, he'd thought… hell, it didn't matter what he'd thought. He lifted his fist and pounded on her bedroom door harder than he needed to.

"Who's there?"

He closed his eyes and willed the throbbing that encompassed his skull to lessen. It didn't. She sounded scared and he imagined she was. Her fear wouldn't lessen when she knew he stood on this side of the door, either. Perhaps it would increase. He was madder than hell right now and rationalization didn't help. He hadn't hurt her last night. If anything, she'd been just as aroused as he was, but she'd never admit it. She'd hold his cavemanlike behavior over his head and make him squirm with guilt. Hell, she already had. The hurt in her eyes last night haunted him, even now. He felt like a bastard, and he was good and angry at her for that, even though it was his own fault. Not only that, but she was afraid of him. And that angered him still further.

"It's me," he said belatedly, in answer to her question.

He expected her to stand on her side of the door and speak through it. He was surprised when the handle turned and the door opened widely. Even more surprised at her murmured, "Come in."

He entered, and she closed the door behind him. She didn't meet his gaze as he looked her over. There were dark circles under her eyes that told of the sleepless night she'd spent. He might have been prone to insomnia last night, as well, if he hadn't been too drunk to stay conscious. Not too drunk to dream, though. And looking at her now, in the snug-fitting jeans, her face free of makeup, her eyes wide and wary, brought those dreams back to him full force. Dreams in which she hadn't stopped him, where he'd finished what he'd so clumsily begun last night.

He was aware of the stirring in his groin, and it only added to the discomfort he already felt. And that added to his irrational anger at her.

"You look like hell," she said, when she finally made her eyes move over his face.

"Good. I'd hate to feel this bad and not have it show."

"Hangover?"

"Mother of them all," he answered.

She nodded.

"You don't look too good yourself." He noticed the boxes of clothes stacked around the room, and the open, nearly empty closet.

She shrugged. "Couldn't sleep."

Here it came, he thought. The guilt trip. "Stay awake all night waiting for an apology?"

Her head came up and her gaze narrowed. "I was afraid if I closed my eyes, someone might sneak in and slit my throat."

"Me?"

"Maybe."

He sighed, and broke eye contact, turning to pace away from her. "I'm not going to apologize, Cait."

"I didn't ask you to."

"There's only so much deprivation a man can take."

"Then you *haven't* been sleeping with my brother's wife?"

He spun around to face her. "Show up naked in my bed again, Cait, and you're liable to get the same reaction."

"It wasn't your bed," she reminded him. "Or do you intend to get so falling-down drunk you can't tell the difference often?"

She was so damned calm, so detached. He wanted to wring her neck. God, he couldn't get the image of her unclothed body out of his mind, or the feel of her moistened opening against his throbbing need, or the taste of her mouth, her skin, her tongue, her nipples.

"It won't matter if I'm drunk or sober."

Her fine auburn brows arched. "Thanks for the warning. I can't say much for your brand of lovemaking, so I'll avoid it from now on."

"That wasn't lovemaking. Just plain lust. And you can argue all you want, but it was mutual."

Finally, a hint of something flickered beneath the cool green waters of her eyes. She lowered them, and cleared her throat. "Was there some point to this visit, or did you just come here to harass me?"

"There's a point. I'm on my way to the police station, to report the unfortunate attempt on your life last night."

She released a short burst of air that might have been intended as a laugh. "What do you consider unfortunate, Dylan? That someone tried to kill me, or that he failed?"

He glared at her. "I came to ask if you want to come along. You're so convinced I might be the guilty party, I know you'll want to share that suspicion with the police."

She turned her back on him, walked toward the bed and sunk onto it as if too exhausted to stand up any longer. She closed her eyes.

Dylan carefully kept any hint of concern out of his voice. "Are you sick?"

She shook her head slowly. "Just tired. Mostly of you and your hostility. You're a real bastard, you know that?"

"And you're Sweet Mary Sunlight, babe. Are you coming with me, or not?"

"Yeah."

She didn't move, or look at him. She was pale this morning, he noted. Her cheeks hollow. She'd lost weight while she was in the coma, not that she'd had any to spare. And she didn't look as if she were putting any of it back on since coming home.

"Get something to eat. I'll wait in the foyer."

She shook her head, and rose slowly, like an old woman with aching joints. "No, let's just go."

She ought to eat. He ought to insist on it. Then again, she was a grown woman with a mind of her own. She didn't need a keeper.

"There's no hurry. We have time—"

"If I eat this morning, I'll probably puke in your fancy car. Let's just go, okay? And will you send Genevieve up for these clothes? I don't want them."

"What do you want her to do with them?"

"I don't care. Wear them, give them away, burn them, for all I care."

He was glumly silent on the short ride into Eden, and Caitlin felt nauseated, even though she hadn't eaten. It was fear gnawing at her gut, fear and confusion. As angry and afraid of him as she'd been last night, she now harbored a slight doubt he'd tried to hurt her. The phone call she'd overheard was strong evidence of that. He wouldn't risk his business by reporting this to the police unless he was innocent. He'd have tried to talk her out of going to the authorities.

Or was this his way of covering his tracks? Did he simply know she would report the incident either way, and want to be there when she did? She almost asked him to forget about it, or delay the visit, but she was too afraid he'd agree readily. She was also afraid the killer would try again, and the police were the only people she was sure would try to help her stay alive.

And there was something else…something she'd not been fully aware of in her fury over his rough treatment of her last night. Something that had only begun to dawn on her in the cold light of day, with his childish refusal to apologize, and his obvious guilt about his actions.

When she'd left him last night, there had been pain in his eyes. Stark, black agony. Loneliness as acute as her own. He had wanted her, had thought she was there waiting. And the truth had been like salt in an old wound. She'd hurt him. Again. She'd obviously done the same in the past. Enough to make him hate her? she wondered. Enough to make him want her dead? He wanted her. She could feel it. Passion ricocheted between them in waves so thick, they were all but visible. But murder was a crime of passion. Wasn't it?

Police Detective Jack Barnes was a big man, with a voice to match. He sat behind his cluttered desk in a brilliant, touristy button-down shirt, leaned back in his chair and removed his rectangular bifocals, staring at Caitlin in the same distracted manner he'd had when she'd first walked into the beehive of activity.

"I'll have to come to the house, interview everyone who was there last night." His voice was deep, booming, as if it echoed back and forth in some cavern behind his barrel chest before floating out to her ears. "We'll send a forensics team to the scene, but with all this rain, I doubt there's any evidence left. Probably not even a footprint." He eyed Dylan for a long moment. "Might have been last night, if we'd been called right away."

"I don't think so, Detective. The cliffs are solid rock, not a very good receptacle for footprints."

Barnes nodded slowly. "So, you went to your wife's room, to check on her, found she wasn't there and got worried?"

Dylan nodded.

"Any particular reason you would worry so quick, Rossi?"

"Hell, Barnes, you're the detective. You figure it out. I've already told you about her condition. It was late at night, not to mention pouring rain."

Barnes's gaze narrowed, then softened just as quickly

when he looked at Caitlin. "Why'd you go outside, Mrs. Ros—"

"Caity, please." She instinctively liked Detective Barnes, except for his gruff, suspicious manner with Dylan. Then again, she couldn't blame him for that. She was suspicious of Dylan, herself. "I was told I used to love to walk along the cliffs at night. I wanted to try it…see if I could remember." There was no sense telling him about how upset she'd been, or about the way Sandra had thrown herself into Dylan's arms. It was irrelevant.

"And who told you that?"

She frowned. "My…brother. Thomas." *Who happens to resent me for inheriting when he didn't, and who's having an affair with my maid, and who I overheard plotting against my husband.*

Thomas? Is he the one?

Barnes made a note. "Okay." He looked at Dylan again. "So, you found she wasn't in her room. Then what?"

Dylan glanced at her, and she thought he was uncomfortable having her hear him retell the story. "I searched the house, and then I realized she must have gone out to the cliffs. She'd mentioned earlier that she wanted to—"

"And Dylan warned me not to go out there alone," she put in quickly, then wondered why she'd defended him.

Dylan sent her a strange look, before returning his attention to Barnes. "Then I went out to look for her."

"Alone?"

Dylan shook his head. "I took Thomas, his wife, Sandra, and our chef, Henri, out with me. Genevieve and Ellen stayed in the house to look after the baby."

Barnes pulled a tissue from a box on his desk, and casually wiped the lenses of his glasses. He looked as if his full attention was focused on the rectangular specs. "You all left the house together?"

"Yes. We walked out to the cliffs, and then we split up."

"Who was closest to her when you heard her scream, Rossi?"

Dylan shook his head. "It's impossible to say. We all sort of ran in that direction from where we were."

Barnes replaced his glasses on his nose. "You have a will, Caity?"

She blinked. "I, um, I don't know." She looked at Dylan.

"Yes, she has a will. Last I knew, I was in it. So was her brother."

Barnes licked his lips. "Who's your lawyer, hon?"

She shook her head, not a bit put out by the endearment. He was at least fifteen years older than she, and he seemed to have some genuine concern for her. "I don't know."

Barnes shook his head, and glared at Dylan. "Done a good job of keeping her in the dark, haven't you, Rossi?"

"She's barely been home three days, Barnes. It hasn't come up in casual conversation." Dylan took his wallet from his pocket, pawed through it for a minute and extracted a business card. He snapped it down on the desk, and pushed it toward Detective Barnes. "Here's his card."

Barnes examined it, and nodded, slipping it into his shirt pocket. "You have any plans to leave Eden in the next few days, Rossi?"

Dylan opened his mouth, but Caitlin cut him off. "My husband makes a poor suspect, Detective Barnes."

The man's smile was obviously forced. "It's Jack, and I wish you'd let me decide who the suspects are."

She licked her lips and swallowed, refusing to glance Dylan's way as she spoke. "When this comes out, his business is going to suffer. He's already had to withdraw a bid on a government contract because of it. This whole thing is costing him money." She bit her lip, only now realizing how vehement she'd sounded. But she'd only spoken the truth, and Jack Barnes ought to have all the facts before he came to any conclusions.

Barnes pursed his lips and rose from his seat. He moved to the file cabinet across the room with measured strides, while Caitlin remained in her hard little chair beside Dylan. She felt her husband's eyes on her. She didn't look back.

Barnes returned, and slapped a file folder onto his desk. "This is the report on the accident you had, Mrs. Rossi. We were suspicious then, but there wasn't enough evidence to warrant an investigation. The brake line was torn, not cut. But I can tell you, it wouldn't be too difficult for someone to have done it deliberately. I suspected it then." He tapped the folder with his glasses for emphasis. "Now I'm certain of it." He slanted a glance at Dylan as he spoke. "You and your husband had a loud argument just before that accident, Caity. You left the house, driving like a bat out of hell, from what witnesses say. He went after you a few minutes later."

Caitlin wasn't aware of slowly shaking her head from side to side, or of rising to her feet. Her gaze turned inward, and when she spoke, she was addressing herself more than she was Jack Barnes. "But he pulled me up the side of that cliff last night. I wasn't holding on to anything but him, and if he'd wanted to drop me, he could have done it right then. No one would have believed it wasn't an accident. Not when he was hanging half over the side himself just to reach me."

Barnes sighed and got to his feet. "That doesn't prove anything," he said gently. "Caity, you're a nice girl. I don't want to see your name cross this desk in a homicide report. Take my advice. Move out for a while. Go stay with a relative—"

"I don't have any, except the ones who live with us."

"Then a hotel. You're somebody's target. You ought to get out of the line of fire."

She sighed hard, shaking her head. "I'll give it some thought." She already had given it thought, though. She just couldn't bring herself to leave. Not yet.

"I think there's another side to that argument, Barnes," Dylan said. She looked at him as he spoke, tried to read his motives in his fathomless, dark eyes. "In the house, there's one person who wants her dead—maybe—and four who don't. In a hotel, she'd be alone, and the killer wouldn't have much trouble tracking her down."

Did Dylan want her to stay, then? Why? To keep her from being killed…or to keep her within his reach?

The detective shook his head, ignoring Dylan. He addressed Caitlin. "Don't trust any of them. I'll be checking up on you."

She nodded. "Thank you."

"Stay in touch. Let me know if you decide to leave." His gaze sharpened when he turned it on Dylan. "Don't let anything happen to her, Rossi." His tone held a warning that couldn't be missed.

Dylan took her arm and walked her out to the car. Once he'd pulled out of the lot, he spoke without looking at her. "Since when are you my staunch defender?"

She shook her head at the sarcasm in his voice. "I was going to make a call this morning. I heard your conversation with Patrick Callen."

"So?"

"So it doesn't make sense that you would risk the business just to get rid of me. It would be simpler just to file for divorce."

"Oh, yeah. That would be a real simple solution, wouldn't it?"

She slammed her fists on the dashboard, and his head swung toward her. "Damn you!" She grated her teeth, squeezed her eyes tight, but the tears came, anyway. "You won't even deny it was you, will you? You can't even give me that much! Did it ever occur to you that I *need* to trust someone? That I need someone on my side right now? I can't…" She bit her lips to stop the endless flow of words that wanted to tumble through them.

"And you want that someone to be me, is that it? You want me to come to you on my knees and swear I'm innocent, beg you to believe me, vow to protect my loving little wife, no matter what?"

"Go to hell, Dylan."

"I'm already there. Don't expect me to come to you, swearing my innocence. If you can't trust me now, you have no one to blame but yourself."

"I don't even have that, Dylan. Because I wasn't around when some woman I don't remember was making you hate her. I was dropped into the middle of her life, not even knowing her name."

"Maybe *you* don't remember her, Caitlin. But *I do*." He braked to a stop at an intersection and waited for the light to change. "So are you going home, or to a hotel?"

She shook her head. "I don't have a home."

"How about a straight answer for once?"

She nodded, and swallowed the lump in her throat. "Take me to Dr. Stone's office. I have an appointment."

The light changed and he pressed the accelerator. "And then?"

"And then leave. When I decide where I'm going, I'll call a cab."

Chapter 9

"I have to agree with Detective Barnes, Caity. It seems to me, you'd be safer somewhere else."

Caitlin continued pacing the length of Judith Stone's office. The knotty-pine walls and gas jet fireplace were supposed to be cozy, comforting, she supposed. But there was nothing comfortable about the way she felt.

"You're probably right."

"But?"

"I'm not sure I can leave yet. There are still too many things I don't understand about…about her."

"Caitlin Rossi?"

Caitlin nodded.

"You told me you considered her a stranger, one who's dead and buried. Someone you didn't know."

"I *don't* know her. But I feel I *have* to. I feel as if I'll never understand myself unless I come to grips with who I was."

Judith shifted in her chair, reaching for the cup of tea on

her desk. "Is there one specific thing you want to know about, or just her life in general?"

Caitlin stopped, and faced the psychiatrist. "I need to know how she could have been so cold to her husband. How she managed to alienate him so completely, and why."

Judith calmly sipped her tea. She held up the mug. "Are you sure you won't have some? It's chamomile."

Caitlin only shook her head.

"Caity, are you developing feelings for Dylan?"

"I don't know. He acts like he can't stand to be near me most of the time."

"And the rest of the time?"

Caitlin walked to the huge window and looked down at the street. "When he took me shopping, there were moments when he let me glimpse the man behind the mask. But every time I started to feel some sort of closeness starting to develop between us, he pulled back."

"And you didn't want him to."

"No. I guess I didn't."

Judith lifted the tea bag from the mug with the spoon, wrapped the string around the spoon three times and gave the bag a dainty squeeze. "What do you want from him?"

Caitlin drew a slow breath and held it. She closed her eyes. "When he pulled me up from the cliff…"

Judith leaned forward in her chair. "Go on."

Caitlin swallowed hard. "He held me so tightly I could barely breathe." She closed her eyes and replayed the incident in her mind. Not the terror, but the crushing strength of his arms around her. The way his heart had thundered beneath her head, and the way his body had been shaking almost as much as hers. "For those few minutes, I didn't feel so alone. He told me everything was all right, and I believed him. He held me like he'd never let me go."

"You felt close to him then?"

Caitlin sighed. "Yes, I guess that's what I want. I want to

be able to turn to him when I'm afraid, when I feel so alone I want to die. I want all that strength to be with me, not against me. I want to have someone I can depend on, trust in, and I want so much for it to be him."

"But it isn't?"

Caitlin faced Judith levelly. "How can it be? He won't even deny that he's the one who wants me dead."

"If he *were* the one, he'd probably deny it loudly. Sounds to me like his pride's been wounded."

"If it has, then it's because of the woman I was. I just don't know how to fix the damage she did." Caitlin began her pacing again. "He wants me."

"Physically?"

Caitlin nodded. "I went looking for another room last night, and chose the one nearest his. He came in later, drunk, and—"

"And what?" Judith rose from her seat.

"Things got a bit rough. He thought I was there waiting for him."

"Caity, are you telling me this man raped you?"

"No. It didn't go that far. But it was close."

Judith shook her head. "And how did you feel about that?"

"I don't know. I was afraid. There was so much anger in him, and it scared me. But I can't deny that there was a part of me that responded to him."

"You wanted to make love with him?"

"I did. I do." She turned in a small circle, pushing one hand through her hair. "I keep getting these flashes of us together, and it's...it's incredible."

"The sex?"

Caitlin nodded. "It's so frustrating. I don't know if they're memories or fantasies. I only know I want him. Madly. But not like that. God, how can I be attracted to a man who seems to despise me? Am I that sick?" She walked to a chair and slammed herself into it. "I disgust myself."

She closed her eyes, bit her lip. "But then, I look him in the eye, and I think he isn't being honest. I think he might not hate me as much as he pretends to. Dammit, if I could just go back and find out what went wrong, I might stand a chance of making amends." She lowered her head, then lifted it again as an idea occurred to her. "What about hypnosis? Could you put me under and make me remember my past?"

Judith crossed the room and knelt in front of Caitlin's chair. "It could work, Caitlin. But there is a very high risk factor involved in your case. The trauma of remembering might be more than your mind could take. You could end up worse off than you are now."

"It might be worth the risk."

Judith straightened, looked down at Caitlin and sighed. "That will be your decision. But I want you to give it careful thought. And I want you to try to work things out in the present, before you go delving into the past. If these flashes you've described *are* memories, hypnosis might not be necessary at all. Let's save it for a last resort, all right?"

Caitlin nodded.

"In the meantime, Caity, why don't you try to get him into an honest, open conversation. He might be as confused about your feelings as you are about his."

"How's Lizzie?"

Sandra looked up from the book she was engrossed in, when Dylan crossed the room toward her. "She's gonna be just fine. The doctor put her on antibiotics. She's got a slight chest cold, is all." Her gaze swept the room behind him. "So where's the lady Caitlin?"

Dylan shrugged and said nothing. He had no idea where Cait was right now, and he told himself he didn't give a damn. The police had been roaming the place all afternoon. Detective Barnes in his loud shirt and khaki trousers, with his suspicion in his eyes every time he glanced Dylan's way had been almost too much. They'd questioned everyone, even Ellen. And their forensics crew had only just packed up and driven off, having found nothing on the cliffs.

Sandra rose and stood near him. Her hands rested lightly on his shoulders. "I don't know what I'd have done without you last night."

"I care about Lizzie." The glint in her eyes made him uncomfortable.

"More than her own daddy does."

"That's not true, Sandra. Thomas just—"

"Just what?" She shook her head. "He don't want her. Or me, either. You treat us better than he ever has."

"He needs time to adjust to the idea of being a father." Dylan went to step backward, but her hands slid around to the base of his neck.

"Lizzie's three months old. How much time you s'pose it's gonna take?" She sighed and a slight smile touched her full lips. "It doesn't matter. I don't want him, either." Her grip tightened, pulling her body closer, until it pressed tight to his. "You know who I want."

"Sandra, for—"

Footsteps behind him made his spine stiffen. He knew without turning that Caitlin had come in. He caught the smug glance Sandra threw over his shoulder, before she lowered her head to it.

Dylan caught her hands, unwound them from his neck, pressing them to her sides, and stepped away from her. He turned, but only in time to see Caitlin's rigid back as she marched up the stairs. He swung his gaze back to Sandra. She was smiling.

"Dammit, Sandra! Do you know what she's probably thinking?"

She shrugged. "I really don't care *what* she thinks."

"It was deliberate, wasn't it?" Dylan's voice was far louder than necessary, but he did nothing about it. He had enough trouble right now, without Sandra adding to it with her theatrics.

"She might as well know where things stand," Sandra yelled back. "You don't want her. I'd be so much better for you than she's ever been, can't you see that?" She lunged toward him again, throwing her arms around him.

Dylan shoved her roughly away. She staggered backward, tripped on the book she'd dropped and fell to the floor.

"What the hell is going on in here?" Thomas strode into the room, with Genevieve at his side. When Dylan glanced up, he saw Caitlin standing halfway up the stairs, staring downward. All of them had seen him shove Sandra. Cait must have heard the entire exchange.

Thomas crossed the room and reached down to take his wife's hand and pull her to her feet. "What are you two arguing about? We could hear you yelling all the way in the kitchen."

Sandra glared at Dylan. He pushed a hand through his hair and moved past them all, not saying a word. Let Sandra explain the fight. He had no doubt she could come up with a lie right on cue.

Dylan went to the library and reached for the bottle of scotch in the cabinet. Then he stopped himself. It had been stupid getting drunk last night. He needed a clear head, not anesthetic.

Caitlin's voice coming from behind him brought him around, still holding the bottle by its neck.

"I wish you wouldn't."

He glanced at the bottle, then at her. "Why not?"

"I want to talk to you. I'd prefer you sober."

He shrugged, and replaced the bottle. "So talk."

She came the rest of the way into the room, and turned to close the double doors behind her. Then she crossed the carpet to the sofa, and sat down. She pinned him to the spot with her eyes glittering like polished emeralds. "How do you feel about me, Dylan?"

He said nothing, but moved to the sofa, and sat on its opposite end.

"Do you hate me as much as you seem to?"

He shook his head. "I don't hate you."

"Dislike, then?"

He closed his eyes. "Why don't you just ask the question you came to ask? You want to know if I'm planning your murder, don't you?"

She shook her head. "No." She sighed, and averted her eyes. "You turned Sandra down. Thank you for that."

"I didn't do it for you. Contrary to what you might think, I'm not the kind of man who gets his kicks by sleeping with his sister-in-law."

"I know. More and more I'm seeing just what kind of man you are." She cleared her throat, licked her lips. She was nervous. "I want you to tell me…tell me about us. Our past. I want to know what went wrong. I need you to give me this one chance…"

"Chance to do what?"

She brought one knee up onto the sofa and leaned toward him. "To show you who I am. I'm not the woman who hurt you, Dylan. You can't keep hating me for the things *she* did. You don't even know me. I'm a stranger that looks like your wife, that's all."

"No, that's not true. You're a lot like her. The way she was when…" He stopped, blinking fast, averting his eyes. God, she was getting to him. He hated his weakness.

Caitlin frowned. "When what?" She slid nearer, placed her hands on his shoulders. "Please, tell me. Turn on a light so I can find my way through this maze. Give me a candle."

Dylan felt the heat of her hands through his shirt. He fought with the ridiculous arousal her touch brought, and he fought with the equally ludicrous hope that kept leaping up when she was like this. But he lost the battle. Her voice was almost a plea, and in her eyes he saw nothing but confusion.

"Fine. Fine, you want to hear a bedtime story, I'll give you one. But I warn you, the ending isn't happily-ever-after."

She sighed and gave him a soft smile that he couldn't keep looking at. He glanced away, toward the massive bookcase opposite the sofa. "We met in college. You were nineteen. We started dating the day we met, and stayed together right through your graduation. By then, I'd already started the business."

"What was I like then?"

He looked at her. He couldn't help himself. She was the image of the girl he'd known then, right now, and the pain of seeing her and knowing she wasn't *his* Caity was almost paralyzing.

"You were different." He fought to keep the emotions from his voice, his face, as he spoke. "You lived in a mansion, had more money than you could count, but never wore anything but jeans. And your hair was consistently in one of two styles. Either long and loose, or up in a ponytail. You hated what you called snobs. You treated your father's household staff like guests instead of employees. Genevieve was one of your favorites. And you never gave a damn if I couldn't afford to take you to the best restaurants or the hot concerts in town. You were just as happy to go for a walk, or a fast-food joint."

She turned to lean back on the cushions, and the act brought her side right up to his. She tipped her head backward and closed her eyes. "And what about you?"

Dylan wanted to recite the facts without getting caught up in the memories, but it was difficult. Her pale arching neck was right under his nose, and he had the ridiculous urge to run his lips and tongue over that satin skin.

He cleared his throat, and his mind. "I was struggling to get a new business going. I spent most of my time working. All I wanted was to be a success, so I could give you what your father could. You said it didn't matter. Maybe I knew, even then, that it really did."

"What kind of grades did I get?"

"Strictly Bs. You could have done better. You had this philosophy that spending too much time studying was unhealthy and a waste of your youth. You liked cutting classes now and then, dragging me away from my shabby little office to the beach." He licked his lips, remembering. "We used to strip down to our skin and swim. Then we'd get out of the water and make love in the sand." Even now, after all this time, Dylan could recall the feel of her warm, wet skin beneath his hands, the grate of the sand coating her damp body, taste her hungry mouth beneath his.

Her head tilted sideways until it rested on his shoulder. Part of him wanted to pull away, but most of him didn't. Against his better judgment, he kept on talking. "I remember once, a couple of the guys who worked for me followed us and stole our clothes. We drove back to my little apartment in nothing but our towels." He caught himself smiling at the memory. "I ran a red light and got pulled over. I'll never forget the expression on that cop's face."

She laughed aloud and the sound was like a knife in his heart, like a ghost from the past sneaking up on him to implant the blade. His smile died.

"When did we get married?"

The blade twisted.

"After you graduated. Your father insisted on throwing us a huge wedding, and you insisted we let him. I didn't like that he was footing the bill, but I wanted to make you happy, so I went along. By then, your parents had been divorced for years."

She turned her head, and when she spoke her breath fanned his neck. "What happened to them?"

"I don't know. It was one of those things you refused to talk about. Your mother and brother moved away, and you stayed with your father. I think that was when you started to change."

"In what way?"

Dylan shook his head. How many times had he cursed

himself for missing the warning signs? "You kept things from me. You used to go and visit your mother, but you would never let me come along, even after we were married. You'd come home depressed and short-tempered, but you wouldn't tell me why. I do know that your mother took nothing when she left your dad. So I imagine she had it pretty rough."

She frowned, but in a moment went on with her questions. "Where did we live?"

"With Aunt Ellen. She had a big old house that was practically falling down around her. She wouldn't let us pay rent, but I chipped in what I could toward repairs. It wasn't much. Those first years were lean. And then your mother died."

She nodded, her hair brushing his neck with the action. "She killed herself."

Dylan nodded. "I was working that night, so I wasn't there when you got the news. You wouldn't talk about it at all, just said you wanted to forget. And the next thing I knew, you'd decided to buy a house. I wanted to wait until I could afford to do it, but you were adamant, almost obsessed with the idea. You picked this place, and just dipped into your trust fund to pay for it. It's all in your name. One big investment. You hired decorators and went crazy with remodeling it, and then we moved in. The one concession you made was to let Aunt Ellen move in, as well. I refused to leave her alone."

She gasped, and straightened to stare into his eyes. "I didn't want her?"

"She raised me. My parents were killed in a car crash when I was ten, and she was there for me. I wanted to return the favor. You didn't argue about it. You never really voiced an opinion at all. I have no idea how you felt."

She closed her eyes and gave her head a quick shake. "I don't know why I would have disagreed with you."

"It nearly killed her to leave her old house, but she couldn't afford to keep it up on her own. And I knew she shouldn't be by herself at her age."

"You were right."

He shrugged. "I couldn't seem to talk to you about anything then, Cait. You were so closed off from me. After a while, I stopped trying. I just poured everything I had into the business, while you worried about investments and stock options and whether our property value was increasing. You became so involved in making sure your money was gaining top interest, there was no room for me anymore. Things just went downhill from there."

"And then Thomas and Sandra moved in."

"Yeah. Your brother thought he'd be all set when your father died, but he was cut completely out of the will. I was surprised when you didn't offer to split your inheritance with him. But I guess I shouldn't have been. That money meant everything to you. By then, the business was on solid ground, so you pressured me into hiring him. About the same time, you hired Henri and Genevieve. We ended up with the life you'd always scoffed at. Our house was as big as your father's."

She shook her head slowly. "Dylan, why did you stay with me?"

He searched her face. It was as innocent and vulnerable as he'd ever seen it. Her sparkling green eyes wide and trusting. He couldn't tell her the rest. He couldn't cause her that kind of pain, not again, no matter what had happened between them. He wasn't looking at the woman he'd known a few months ago. He was looking at the image of the girl he'd fallen in love with. Even if she was no longer that girl on the inside.

"I can't answer that."

"Can you at least tell me why…why we slept apart?"

"You were afraid you'd get pregnant." That, at least, was true.

"But there are so many—"

"You didn't trust birth control, Cait. There's always a slight chance of failure and you just couldn't stand the idea of it.

That's why you were so upset the night of the accident. We'd both had a few drinks that night. And we wound up in your bed, together." He shook his head, remembering how he'd thought then that maybe things were going to turn around. "When you woke later, found yourself naked, in my arms, you freaked. Accused me of taking advantage of you when you were drunk, said you'd never have allowed it sober. We had a hell of a row, and you threw on some clothes and stormed out, terrified I'd gotten you pregnant."

"And you came after me."

"I knew you shouldn't be driving."

She licked her lips. "I wish we did have a baby."

The blade ran right through him, and turned hot. Searing. Dylan had to close his eyes to hide the pain those words brought. "So do I." Suddenly, he felt her fingertips brush gently over his damp eyes, and he opened them. Hers were wet, too.

"Last night, in your room, I—"

He shook his head, and silenced her with a finger to her lips. "That's not the way it was with us, Caitlin. I was drunk and I was frustrated—"

"I know." She smiled, but it was shaky, watery. "How was it, before things went wrong? What was it like when we made love?"

He shook his head. He wouldn't feel anything. He *wouldn't.* "Explosive. Mindless." He closed his eyes, and thought of the nights they'd had together, despite his vow that he wouldn't. She knew him so well, knew how to touch him and make him tremble. And he was keenly aware of every sensitive spot on her body. He could reduce her to a trembling, whimpering mass of longing in minutes. Seconds.

She touched his face, her palm drifting over his cheek, until her fingertips traced his jaw, and his chin. He looked at her. "I want to start new, Dylan. I want to get to know you, to find out if it can be like that for us again."

He shook his head. She wanted him to trust her again, to

let himself care again. And just when he was out of his mind in love with her, she'd get her memory back. She'd become the old Caitlin. She'd shut him out. "Not on your life, lady. I wouldn't go through that hell again for anything." It would kill him this time.

"It won't happen, I swear it." She looked at him intently as she spoke. "Dylan, I need you so much. I can't face all of this alone, please…"

"Ah, Caity…" He couldn't resist the plea in her eyes, the little cry in her voice. He wrapped his arms around her, cradling her head in one hand, and pulling her face close. He caught her mouth with his and her lips parted instantly. He licked her mouth inside and out, and her tongue responded. Her fingers curled in his hair and he kissed her, tasted her, held her close and wished she were closer.

He was in danger. He knew it, and only a supreme act of will made him draw away. Panting with need, he searched her face. Her breathing was just as ragged, her eyes glazed and damp.

"I want you, Cait. I want you so much it hurts, but that's all. I'll try to be your friend. I'll even be your lover, but I'm not going to love you again. Don't hope for that. Don't even consider it a possibility. It isn't going to happen."

She stiffened her spine and met his gaze. The light in her eyes faded slowly and her breaths, by sheer force, it seemed, grew more regular.

"My friend?"

He nodded. "I'll try not to hold the past against you, at least until it starts repeating itself."

"It will never repeat itself."

"I can't be sure of that. It's all I have to offer, Cait. Take it or leave it."

She nodded, but didn't look him in the eye. "Friends, then. I suppose it's better than enemies." She stood and turned toward the doors. "Thank you, Dylan." She moved forward, opened the doors and walked out, leaving him alone and painfully aroused. Apparently, friends was okay.

Lovers was not.

Chapter 10

She couldn't sleep. She wasn't surprised. She'd probably never have a good night's sleep in this house. But tonight, her reasons were different.

It was Dylan's kiss that kept her awake. The way he'd plundered her mouth, and the way she'd responded to the invasion. It hadn't been anger she'd felt emanating from him in waves this time. It had been desire. A desperate, long-denied desire that wouldn't be put off much longer. An answering need had flooded her body from the first touch of his lips on hers.

She wanted him. God, how she wanted him. And she still wasn't completely sure that was wise. She wanted to believe he could never hurt her. But the sight of him shoving Sandra to the floor haunted her. He was like two men in one body. He had a streak of brutality in him. She'd seen it when he'd pushed Sandra, felt it when he'd assaulted her in his bedroom so recently.

His passion was fierce, frightening. Especially where she was concerned. She'd felt its intensity when he'd pulled her from that cliff, been alternately touched by its warmth and burned by its heat. Then, last night, in the library, she'd seen the injured side of him as he'd told her things that obviously hurt him to talk about.

He'd said he could never love her again. Why, then, was there some fool inside her saying that he could? That he might?

She wondered which was the real Dylan Rossi. Which one would make love to her if she were to go to him, right now? Would she feel the violent side of his passion? Or the side that wanted her as badly as she wanted him? Or would she encounter the wounded, wary man who was afraid she'd hurt him again?

"Hell, it doesn't matter, because I'm not going to him." She kicked her covers aside and rose, marching across the room and back again in her silky-soft green nightgown, her arms and shoulders bare. "He made it clear he doesn't want to try again to make our marriage work. Why on earth would I even consider sleeping with him under those conditions? Am I insane?"

He said he'd be my lover. All I have to do is go to his room.

She could have kicked herself for thinking about it. Even up and out of the bed, she kept envisioning erotic images of her and Dylan, their bodies wet and coated in warm sand, making frantic love on a deserted beach. She closed her eyes and willed the image away, but instead, it only intensified. She could feel his hot lips on her throat. She could feel the heat of the sun on his back as her hands moved urgently over it, and the cool spray of the surf as it showered them. She could taste the drying salt the sea had left on his skin.

Her eyes flew wide, and she gasped. She remembered! The images were too vivid, too real to have been imagined. Her breathing quickened and she fought for more. She scanned her mind in search of some other tidbit, something of her past to cling to. She saw the beach for just an instant, in her mind's eye. A horseshoe-shaped patch of sand, surrounded by craggy boulders. He was there, on her, inside her, thrusting, possessing. His lips whispered across hers, the words as soft as his breath. "I love you, Caity. I always will. No matter what."

And on one of the ragged stone faces that stood like protectors around them, someone had scratched a heart, with their initials inside. D.D.R. loves C.A.O.

She bit her lip as tears blurred her vision. In another brief flash, she saw Dylan, wearing cutoff denim shorts, barefoot, his hair longer, damp and tangled, painstakingly chiseling the stone with a pocketknife.

She searched for more, but there was nothing.

Oh, but it wasn't nothing, was it? She remembered. And in that one precious moment of remembering, she'd felt more than the physical sensations his touch evoked. She'd felt the warmth of his love surrounding her like invisible armor, and the strength of her own love pounding back to him.

How could she have had something so sweet, and let it slip away? Why? God, if she could only go back to that place, have that kind of love again, she'd cling to it with everything in her. She'd never let it die.

She brushed the tears away with a swipe of her hand. It was too late to try to change the past. The most she could hope for was to alter the present. Dylan had told her he'd never love her again. But that might change. Maybe with time, he'd see that she wasn't going to revert to the woman who'd hurt him so much. Maybe he'd believe in her, someday.

Exhaustion swamped her as she paced the room, wishing for memories, finding none. God, fate was cruel, giving her just that snippet and nothing more. Just enough to realize what she'd lost. Just enough to make her want it back.

Maybe she should go to Dylan right now, and tell him. She gripped the bedroom door, pulled it open and stepped into the hall before she stopped herself.

Tell him what? That she had a tidbit of their past and that it was killing her? That she wanted a time machine so she could go back there? That she wanted—now, more than ever—to believe he hadn't tried to kill her?

She shook her head sadly. Wanting things didn't make them true. Painful as it was to admit that, she had to force herself to accept it. She turned and stepped back into her room. Just before she closed the door, a strange sound caught her attention. A sort of rattling wheeze. Almost a choke. And it came from the foyer, or the stairway. She paused, one hand on the door, listening.

There was only silence, and the dull moan of the dying wind as the storm blew out to sea.

"Is someone there?"

No voice replied. The dark hallway loomed off in both directions, daring her to brave its blackness. She didn't want to take it up on that dare. But something was wrong. She felt it as surely as she felt the shiver of apprehension dance over her spine. She stepped into the hall, and turned toward the stairway.

The wall switch was at the top of the stairs. Just as soon as she reached it and filled the darkness with light, her fear, this *feeling,* would vanish right along with the shadows.

The house was utterly silent. The wind and rain of the past few days had finally died, the clouds were dispersing, and as she approached the stairway, she saw the full moon's glow filtering through its coat of clouds to streak the floor below.

She reached for the light switch, but her hand missed its mark, and fear tiptoed over her soul. A thrill of dread raced up her spine, and yet she felt some sense of urgency drawing her toward the stairs. She fought it, but took one step down, then another. A tingling sensation raced over her spine, and she stiffened. God, here she was wandering the darkened house alone, at night, knowing full well someone under this very roof wanted her dead. Should she go down, and try to locate the other light switch, or go back to her room?

She took a step backward, but couldn't seem to turn around. There was something tugging her gaze downward. Something down there wasn't right.

She took another step back, bringing her to the top of the stairs. The clouds shifted slowly. Moonlight streamed through the tall, tapering windows that lined the foyer below, and moved across the floor. Its soft glow spilled over the hardwood, spreading like melted butter that coated everything in its path. Finally, it slowed to a crawl, having found its target. Like a spotlight, moonglow illuminated a mound of scarlet satin at the foot of the stairs.

Caitlin frowned. That looked like…

"My robe," she whispered. The light spread slower, as if it were congealing and could barely move, until it touched the pale skin of a still hand. And there it remained, motionless. Caitlin screamed at the top of her lungs.

She raced down the stairs, propelled by panic, her palm burning with friction as she clutched the banister too tightly. She fell to her knees at the bottom of the stairs, her hands gripping satin-clad shoulders, turning the woman onto her back.

The moon's light bathed the still face, and glinted on the crimson strand that trickled down one side from her ear, across her cheek. "Sandra!" Caitlin touched her face, and her voice was a shriek. "Sandra, wake up! For God's sake, wake up!"

There was no response and Caitlin's heart, once thudding wildly, seemed to skid to a painful stop in her breast. She was frantic, pressing her fingers into the warm skin of Sandra's throat in search of a pulse, when light flooded the room. She heard Henri's curse and Genevieve's sob, as both rushed in from the archway on the other side of the foyer. Caitlin felt no pulse beneath her fingers, and she rose slowly, moving toward them, dazed. "I think…I think she's dead."

Henri lurched forward, rushing to the body. Genevieve turned to lean against the wall, folding her arms to cradle her head. Caitlin kept walking, to the telephone on the other end of the room. She picked it up and dialed 911.

Vaguely, she heard steps in the hallway above, then

Dylan's voice, hoarse and too loud. "Caity!" His steps pounded down the stairs, and she turned in time to see him stop short of the body on the floor, blink down at it and draw three openmouthed breaths that were ragged and deep. His gaze rose, and when he saw her, he closed his eyes. He looked down at Henri where the man knelt beside Sandra. Henri only shook his head.

"I need an ambulance, and the police." Caitlin's voice sounded dead as she spoke into the mouthpiece. "A woman's been killed." She muttered the address as Dylan crossed the floor toward her. He was barefoot, like her, and wore only a pair of briefs beneath a knee-length, terry robe that gaped open. His hair was wild, his eyes wide, and moving over her rapidly as she put the phone down.

For a long moment, he said nothing. Not a word. Then, very slowly, he lifted his arms, and she fell into them, clinging to his shoulders, shaking violently. He held her hard, his hands threading through her hair.

"Caity...I thought it was you."

She stiffened in his arms. *"What?"*

"The robe. It's yours. When I saw it from the top of the stairs, I thought..." He drew a deep breath and crushed her closer. "Doesn't matter. You're all right."

But the trembling that had begun in her from the moment she'd seen Sandra's body assaulted her anew, and fear made her dizzy. His words brought the truth to her with sickening clarity. "Someone else thought it was me, too," she whispered. "The person who killed her."

She heard an oath and looked up to see her brother on the floor beside his wife. His chalky face contorted, he pulled her upper body to his chest, and murmured her name. From above, she heard the baby crying, and tears filled her eyes. "Oh, God, Lizzie. Poor Lizzie."

Ellen appeared at the top of the stairs then and made her way slowly downward, stopping short of the bottom, clutching the banister until her knuckles whitened, sending a fear-filled glance toward Dylan and Caitlin on the other side of the foyer.

Dylan only held Caitlin tighter. She felt his heart hammering beneath her head, heard his ragged breaths. If he didn't care at all about her, he was certainly doing a good impression of someone who did. She closed her eyes, twined her arms around his neck and clung to him, her one anchor in a world gone crazy.

Dylan paced the library floor, feeling like a caged animal. He'd be arrested this time. There was no doubt in his mind of that as Thomas sat still as a stone, and told Detective Barnes about the argument he'd witnessed between Dylan and Sandra the day before.

"He was yelling at her. Loud enough to be heard in the kitchen."

"What was he saying?" Barnes wasn't bothering with his notepad this time. He had a tape recorder running. Henri was being questioned in another room. Genevieve had already given her statement, and was in the dining room, watching over Ellen, who was badly shaken. And Cait...Cait was upstairs with Lizzie. Thank God. Thank God it hadn't been her at the foot of those damned stairs.

But if he let himself get arrested, it might well be her next time. Damn, he felt helpless.

"I couldn't hear clearly," Thomas was saying. "I went to see what was going on, just as he pushed her."

"Pushed her," Barnes repeated. "Pushed her, how?" He walked right up to the overstuffed chair Thomas occupied. "Get up and show me."

Thomas rose as if his legs were too weak to hold him. He brought his hands upward to Barnes's shoulders and gave him a shove. "It was harder than that, though. She fell to the floor."

"It *wasn't* harder than that, and she only fell because she tripped over something."

Dylan stopped pacing to whirl around. Caitlin stood in the doorway. She hadn't bothered to change. She still wore the floor-length, emerald green nightgown that shimmered like silk. Her auburn hair was as tousled as a lion's mane, and hanging down to the middle of her back. Her eyes were no longer frightened, or confused, though. They were glittering and angry.

Dylan crossed the room to stand beside her, ignoring the others. "How's the baby?"

"I managed to get her back to sleep. I didn't want to bring her down here with…" She didn't finish, only glanced in the general direction of the living room, where Dylan knew Sandra's body still rested. Barnes's faithful forensics team were as busy as ants in autumn. He could still hear the whir of the camera as the police photographer snapped pictures at the medical examiner's direction. He thought they'd have at least covered Sandra's face by now.

"Caity, if you don't mind…you witnessed this argument, too?"

"Yes."

"Then maybe you can tell me what it was about."

Her gaze shifted to Dylan. "Sandra had been doing her best to alienate me since I came back. I guess she didn't like me very much. I assumed Dylan was angry about that, but I'm not sure, since I came in at the tail end of the discussion. You ought to ask my husband if you want more details. Not that I think it's relevant. The killer obviously mistook Sandra for me in the dark."

Barnes looked skeptical, but turned to Dylan. "I suppose you're going to tell me you were alone in your room all night, and didn't hear a thing, right?"

"I—"

"Not quite alone, Detective," Caitlin said.

Dylan frowned at her.

"Before you go on, Caity, I ought to tell you I've already

interviewed your employees. They said you and your husband haven't shared a bedroom in months."

"That was true, until last night."

"You telling me you two slept together last night?"

Her chin tilted upward. "I was afraid and alone. I needed someone with me last night, so I went to my husband. That isn't so farfetched, is it?"

"What time?"

"Early. Around nine, I guess."

Barnes cleared his throat, and he kept glancing at Dylan. Dylan fought to keep his surprise from showing on his face. He couldn't believe Caitlin was lying to a cop just to cover for him.

"But you slept sometime. He could have gotten up, and—"

"I didn't *sleep* at all." She sidled nearer Dylan and slipped her arm around his waist. "Dylan dozed off around midnight. I was still restless, so I got up to get a book from the library. That's when I found Sandra."

"Uh-huh." Barnes's gaze narrowed, and Dylan stiffened. If he caught on to Caitlin's lie, he'd be more suspicious than ever. "So what you're telling me is, that you and your husband have reconciled."

"Reconciled?"

"The divorce is off, right?"

Dylan felt the shock that jolted through Caitlin's body. He closed his eyes, and put his arm around her shoulders, squeezing her to his side. If she faltered now, he'd be behind bars before dawn. "Nothing's been decided, Barnes."

Caitlin pulled free of him, turned her back on Barnes and walked, on shaking legs, across the library. She reached into the liquor cabinet and pulled out a shot glass, and the same whiskey bottle Dylan had been holding earlier. Her back still to them, she unscrewed the cap, set it aside and poured a healthy splash into the glass.

"If that divorce is still on, Caity, your husband has a huge motive to try to kill you. I'm sure you're already aware of that, but I just want to remind you. The settlement you and your lawyers hammered out have you keeping everything you own, the house, too."

She downed the shot, and sucked air through her teeth. She cleared her throat, but didn't turn. "Of course I'm aware of it."

"Then you also know that your husband fought this settlement tooth and nail for months. Then, suddenly, agreed to everything without a hitch. Right before your accident."

She said nothing. Instead, she only tipped the bottle again, then calmly replaced the cap and put it away.

"It wasn't the settlement I was fighting, Barnes. It was the divorce. I didn't want it." Dylan felt like wringing the bastard's neck for spilling everything that way. And he seemed to be enjoying it, too. He had to know Caitlin hadn't been aware of their pending divorce, just from her reactions. "I'd have nothing to gain by her death."

"What you'd gain, Rossi, is half of everything she was planning to take in the settlement. What's hers is willed to her brother, and to you, in equal portions, more or less. Your share alone is a small fortune."

Caitlin turned to face them, her face expressionless. She glanced toward Thomas, and downed half of the whiskey. "I'm being rude. Would anyone else like a drink? I could make coffee."

"No, thanks anyway." Barnes frowned at her. "Will you reconsider what I said about getting out of here for a while?"

Dylan stiffened, waiting for her to say yes, and leave with the detective. If she walked out now, knowing what she knew, knowing he'd deliberately kept the truth about the divorce from her, she'd never come back. He was as sure of that as he was of his own name. He was equally sure he didn't want that to happen. Not like this. He hadn't realized it until he'd looked down those stairs at her satin robe, surrounding a dead woman's body, and thought for one heart-stopping second that it was her. But since then, he'd come to some damned painful conclusions.

She simply shook her head. "My niece needs me now, Detective Barnes. I can't leave her." She finished the drink and set the glass down. Her hands were shaking, but her face betrayed nothing.

"I'll need statements from each of you." He looked at Caitlin. "Caity, can you tell me why the victim was wearing your robe?"

She nodded. "I packed up some old clothes and asked Genevieve to get rid of them for me."

Thomas nodded. "Yeah, Genevieve brought them to our room, told Sandra to pick out anything she wanted, before the stuff went to charity."

"Did the maid go through the clothes herself?"

Caitlin shook her head. "I doubt she bothered. I'm so much taller than her, nothing would have fit."

Barnes nodded. "All right. You can go see to the kid, if you want. I'll get your statement later." She nodded, and started toward the door.

"You watch your back, Cait Rossi. This isn't over yet," Barnes added in a low voice.

She only nodded, and before she left the room, her gaze met Dylan's. There was a wounded look in her emerald eyes, a look of betrayal, and a shimmer of tears she refused to shed. She walked out with her back rigid, her shoulders so stiff, they shook with it. And all Dylan wanted to do was run after her.

Chapter 11

She felt his presence even before the bedroom door opened. It was like an energy, an awareness of him that preceded him into the room. She stayed where she was, lying on her side on the bed. She'd been wishing for sleep, even while knowing she'd find none.

Dylan stood in the doorway. She felt him there, and without looking up, she felt his gaze on her.

"I'm glad Lizzie's too young to know what's happening." Caitlin kept her voice very low. The entire house had the air of a funeral home, even though Sandra's body had finally been removed. "If I'd died in that accident, she might still have a mother."

"Caity—"

"When were you going to tell me about the divorce?" She blinked, and finally turned to face him.

His face was tight, and his eyes revealed nothing. "When I thought you could handle it."

Or maybe not at all. Maybe you weren't going to say anything, Dylan. Maybe you figured I'd be dead long before you had to.

"You think I did it, don't you?"

She stiffened a bit. Was her face so transparent? Or was he reading her mind? "I don't know what I think." She rolled over and sat up, with her legs dangling over the side of the bed.

"Last night, you believed I was innocent."

"Last night, I thought you didn't have a motive. But you did. And you kept it from me."

He stepped farther into the room and closed the door. He leaned back against the wall, his arms crossing over his chest. Her gaze followed his movements. He wore a snug-fitting black T-shirt that strained to contain his muscular shoulders. His forearms were hard, tight. His biceps, in this position, bulged. A soft stirring in her stomach troubled her. Was it because he was so attractive, because she still wanted him so badly? Or because she knew he could break her neck without working up a sweat?

"Why'd you lie to Barnes?"

His liquid brown eyes searched her face, but they were cold, without feeling. Or maybe he was deliberately hiding what he felt.

She got to her feet, walked to the window and gazed out. The sky was as brilliant as the meat of an orange. The sun's huge upper curve was just visible in the distance; neon fire. On impulse, she released the latch and pushed the windows open. Warm, sea-moistened wind bathed her face, blew through her hair. She tipped her head back and inhaled.

"It was like this that time on the beach," she said. "Early morning. Everything so fresh and new...like we were." She leaned out a little, wishing she could see the shore from here. She could hear it. Waves pounding stone. Foaming surf. Crying gulls. And she could smell the tang of saltwater in the air. She could even feel the sea. The breeze that caressed her face was wet with it. "That was the time you carved our initials into the rock."

She turned to gauge his reaction to that. He'd moved. He was standing nearer the bed now, stopped in the act of coming toward her. His gaze locked with hers over the bed.

"You remember."

She only nodded.

"When—"

"Last night. We were so happy together. What we had…it was so real, I wanted to believe it could be that way again, wanted to believe in us…in you." She sighed, and turned to the window once more. "That's why I lied to Barnes. I didn't want him locking you up when I was trying so hard to believe someone else was responsible."

She heard him coming toward her. She stiffened, but didn't turn. If he wanted to shove her out the window, here was his chance. She closed her eyes and bit her lip when his hands closed on her shoulders from behind. Then he turned her to face him, his eyes, for once, windows to the turmoil inside him. Emotion roiled in their melted-chocolate depths. But what kind of emotion? Regret? Longing? Anger? Hatred? God, how she wanted to believe in him! Would he tell her now that it wasn't him? That she'd been right to believe he could never hurt her? That he—

"How…much do you remember?"

Disappointment hit her with the force of a wrecking ball. She blinked as if she'd been slapped, and let her gaze fall to the floor. "Only that. Whatever other secrets you're keeping from me are still safe."

He frowned.

"There are others, aren't there, Dylan?"

"You can't expect me to tell you your life story within a few days, Cait. You'll know everything, in time."

"Unless I don't have time."

"You really *do* think it was me." He caught her face

between two hands, tipping it up until his eyes could drill into hers. "So which theory are you buying? That I killed Sandra because she wanted to jump my bones, and I wasn't as hot for her? Or did I mistake her for you in the darkness?"

She felt her lips tighten, and tried not to let her features twist in misery. Despite her efforts, a tear slipped through, and trailed slowly down her face.

"Damn you, Caitlin." His palms on either side of her face holding her still, he brought his lips to hers. He kissed her hard, his lips moving against hers in an assault as his hands tilted and tipped her head to fit her mouth to his.

She hated it, and she loved it, and she'd craved it for what seemed like always. In spite of herself, her arms twined around his neck, tightening until they ached. Her body pressed itself to his, and her mouth moved rapidly. When his tongue thrust, she suckled it with a vicious hunger, then dipped her own into his mouth, until his joined hers in a desperate, urgent battle. His hands lowered, wrapped around her, held her tight. They pressed to the small of her back, and then her shoulders, and then her buttocks, and then her thighs. Her fingers clawed and twisted in his hair, and her breaths came in ragged, violent spasms.

His hands came between them, forced their way up to the neck of her gown, gripped and tugged and tore, and all the while he was feeding on her mouth, her tongue. But then his attention altered, and his lips dragged hotly down over her chin, across her throat. He took her breast like a madman, a starving man devouring his first crumb of food in days. He sucked hard, making her whimper with mindless need. Making her clutch at his hair as he bit and tugged just until she felt pain, then licked and sucked until she writhed with pleasure again. Small sounds escaped her throat, begging sounds, that only enraged him further.

Holding her to him, his hands at her back, his mouth at her breast, he began moving backward, dragging her with him.

Then he was turning her, pushing her. Her back sunk into the mattress. His body pressed it deeper. His hands twisted and yanked at her panties, while his mouth moved back to hers. She moved her legs, lifted her hips, to help him, and the scrap of nylon slipped to the floor. She snagged the hem of the tight black T-shirt he wore, and tugged it upward, her hands skimming his muscled back, his shoulders, before pulling the shirt over his head.

His flesh was hot against hers. *She* was hot. Burning up with mindless, senseless need. His big arms encircled her waist, holding her tight to him, making her feel small and delicate as he ruthlessly plundered her mouth.

Then he tore himself away. All at once, she lay alone, completely exposed to him, and he stood beside the bed, yanking at the button of his jeans, his blazing eyes moving up and down over her body. She instinctively tried to pull the tattered edges of her nightgown together, but he lunged, gripping her wrists, stopping her.

"Don't."

She met his heated gaze, held it. He pushed the soft gown from her shoulders, pulling her up a little as he did. Then he let her lie back, and he tossed the garment to the floor. He knelt on the bed, and he pressed her thighs apart. His gaze burned her there, and then his fingers parted, and probed and pinched, all as he watched.

She moaned. It was too much. He still wore his jeans, though the fly gaped open, and she could see the curling, dark hairs there. She was fully exposed, more fully exposed than she could remember ever having been. He was kneeling over her, staring at her so intently, it burned as his fingers tormented her without mercy. He spread her folds, sunk his fingers into her. Against her will, her hips rose to meet them. His gaze seemed to darken, and he groaned deep and gruffly.

His fingers pulled back, but he still held her open, spread wide to his probing eyes. Then, suddenly, he bent over her, swooping down like a hawk diving on its prey. She gasped when his mouth touched her, his lips, his tongue. His mouth attacked her until she whimpered with passion, until her entire body trembled like a leaf in a strong wind, and until she'd have done anything he asked of her.

Then he stopped, leaving her completely insane. He stood only long enough to shed the jeans, and then he was back. He knelt, straddling her waist, staring down at her as she panted and twisted with agonizing need. His hands gripped her head, lifted her. His arousal stood before her, thick and hard. His hands were shaking as his fingers moved in her hair, urging her closer.

She opened her mouth and took him into it. He growled her name and his hips moved slightly. She sucked, and tugged him, and wanted to take in more than she possibly could. Then he withdrew, and pressed her back down to the bed.

His hard body lowered on top of hers. His arousal nested between her thighs, nudging her, testing her. She bent her knees and opened herself to him. Her hands glided down his back to grip his hard buttocks and pull him to her.

He answered her unspoken request with a single, powerful thrust. He sunk himself inside her so deep and so hard that she cried out. And then he drew back and stabbed into her again, and again, until her mind spun out of control. On and on he took her, until she clung to him, cried his name and exploded in sensation.

He thrust into her once more, and stiffened, holding himself there, pulsing inside her. She shuddered, and closed her eyes. Dylan slowly relaxed, the bunched muscles in his shoulders lost their tension, the air spilled from his lungs. He slipped off her, onto his side, and he searched her face.

Caitlin felt like crying. It hadn't been a fantasy. His touch held the same magic she'd felt in her mind. It was real, the passion that sizzled between them. She swallowed hard, closed her eyes and rolled away from him. She felt the morning sun slanting through her window, warming her face.

"You'd better go now," she said softly.

"Why?"

She said nothing, only bit her lip and prayed he'd leave before she cried in front of him.

"Are you having regrets, Caitlin? Are you going to pretend you didn't want this just as badly as I did?"

She shook her head. "I wanted it. The same way I wanted to walk along the cliffs the other night. The same way a drug addict craves his poison."

He was silent for a moment. Then she felt the bed move as he rolled over and sat up. "So, I'm your poison. Is that what you believe?"

"It doesn't matter what I believe, Dylan. I'm stupid where you're concerned, like a moth battering my wings against clear glass to get to the light on the other side. Only I'm going to beat myself to death, and the light is just an illusion."

"I still want you, Caitlin. That's no illusion."

"Physically." She sat up, too. Then stood, her back to him. "It's not enough." She reached for the bathroom door, unconsciously stiffening her spine. "I need to shower. I'm going out this morning."

She heard him turn toward her. "Out where?"

She lifted her chin, opened the door, stepped onto the threshold. "I want to have a talk…with my lawyer." She licked her lips. "I think it's about time, don't you?"

Before he could answer, she took another step, and closed the door behind her. She turned the lock, then twisted the knobs until rushing water drowned out the sounds of her sobs.

Sandra's body had been taken to the medical examiner's office. She had to be autopsied, it was required when someone was murdered.

Dylan would have liked to think she'd just fallen down the stairs. Barring that, he'd like to believe her killer had known who she was before he'd pushed her. But she'd been wearing Caitlin's unmistakable scarlet robe, and the halls at night were pitch-black.

Dylan wasn't blind. He knew there was something going on between Thomas and Genevieve. He also knew Henri had the hots for Caitlin, and he was equally certain, no matter what else Caitlin might have done in the past, that she'd never reciprocated the feeling.

Could Henri be acting out of anger over her rejection of him? Or was it Thomas? He could have had a motive to kill either Sandra or Cait. Sandra, to free himself so he could pursue Genevieve. Cait, to avail himself of the money in her will. And Genevieve…she was such a secretive little thing. Might she have pushed Sandra, knowing full well who the victim was, just to get Thomas all to herself?

Dylan pushed a hand through his hair. This was getting him nowhere. What he'd like to do, what he ought to do, was to take Caitlin the hell out of here. Get her somewhere safe until he could figure this out.

As if she'd go anywhere with him. She thought he was the one out to murder her. And right now, his wife was at her lawyer's office, putting the final touches on their pending divorce. And there wasn't a damned thing he could do about it. He'd already signed everything that needed signing.

But that was before, dammit!

He stalked into the living room, and found Ellen there, rocking Lizzie. He sent his aunt a smile that was forced and tight. "How's she doing?"

"Just fine, boy. No more signs of that fever. I've taken care of babies before, you know."

He nodded distractedly, and paced past her to gaze out the window, into the driveway. His car was there, as well as the old pickup he sometimes used for business, hauling lumber and supplies to smaller job sites. Cait must have taken a cab.

"She hadn't ought to be wandering around town on her own, Dylan."

He blinked and let the curtain fall over the glass.

"Somebody wants to hurt her." She shifted Lizzie from one knee to the other, and rocked a little faster as the baby started to fuss. "You're letting your emotions cloud your judgment, boy. Get on the ball."

He gave himself a mental shake, realizing she was right. Despite what his wife thought of him, and what that did to his insides, Cait was out there, alone and unprotected. A walking target.

He bent low to kiss his aunt's wrinkled cheek on his way out.

Cait sat in the cab, clutching the sheaf of papers in a white-knuckled grip. The visit to the lawyer had gone roughly. He'd been furious at what she wanted to do, considering all the time and effort he'd spent on her case. Caitlin had drawn herself up to her full height and stared down her nose at the man behind the desk. In a voice she thought the old Caitlin had probably used often, she'd reminded him that he worked for her, and would be paid the same fee, no matter what the results. He'd grumbled, but accepted her decision.

She glanced up at the back of the driver's head. "You know this area pretty well?"

"Born and raised. What do you need to know?"

She warmed to his smile and friendly eyes. "There's a little bit of beach, completely surrounded by craggy rocks in sort of a horseshoe pattern. Very private. You know it?"

Glancing over his shoulder, his smile grew wider. "Sure. It's only ten minutes away."

True to his promise, the cabby pulled off to the side of the road beside a steep drop, a short time later. He pointed. "Right down there. There's a path, see it?"

She looked where he was pointing, and spotted a worn

track through the tall grass. "Yeah. Thanks." She fished in her pocket for a twenty, and handed it to him.

"Don't you want me to wait?"

She shook her head. "Eden's not far, and it's a perfect day for a walk, don't you think?" She'd call another cab when she was finished here. She wanted solitude, time to think.

"If you're sure." He took her money, and she got out of the car. She stood for just a second as he pulled away, then started down the path. At its end, she found the little cove she'd remembered, just as she remembered it.

Waves lapped gently at the white sand. Caitlin toed off her shoes, peeled off her socks and tossed both aside. She dug her toes into the warm sand and closed her eyes. It felt good here.

She stripped off her jeans, feeling no embarrassment at doing so. Her T-shirt was long, so she was decently covered. She wanted to feel the sun on her legs. She wanted to feel warmth, to counteract the coldness she'd felt emanating in waves from that house. And the coldness that seemed now to have spread over her, through her, until her very soul was encrusted in ice.

She'd had what she'd been driving herself crazy longing for, so why was she still so frustrated? She'd had sex with Dylan. It had been hot, frantic, almost violently intense sex.

But it hadn't been lovemaking. She'd wanted to make love with him. She'd wanted it slow, and languid, and emotional. The way it used to be between them. The way her snippets of memory told her it had always been.

Unable to resist the lure of the water, she moved toward it. She stepped into the cool, frothy sea and it lapped over her ankles. She walked out farther and the waves licked higher, embracing her shins, her knees, her thighs. She dove into the bracing cold, the shimmering blue, and swam beneath the surface, farther from shore. She broke the surface when she ran out of air, flipping her head backward so the sun blazed on her face. She stroked away, exerting herself full force, swimming hard, as if she were being chased by sharks, then turning and starting back again, just as fiercely.

Her lungs burned and her heart thundered in her chest. The muscles in her arms and legs burned with the effort after a while, but it felt good. Just pouring everything she had into physical exertion, forgetting everything else. Just for a tiny, safe space in time, losing herself in the burn, the effort.

But it couldn't last. She knew she had to get back to the house, back to the husband who didn't love her, and never would. Back to the elderly aunt who thought she'd ruined her nephew's life, and to the brother who resented her. Back to Lizzie. The poor little thing didn't have anyone now, except for Thomas, and he was awkward and uncomfortable with her.

And me. She has me.

Just thinking of the baby made her ache inside. How could she come to care so much for a child she'd only known a few days, a child that wasn't even hers?

She paused in her mindless stroking and tread water. It didn't matter how, it only mattered that she loved Lizzie. She knew she ought to leave that house, but she wasn't going to. She missed the baby, even after only a few hours of separation.

She stroked toward shore and emerged dripping, panting, her body heated despite the cold water dripping from it. Rivulets ran down her legs and she belatedly wished she'd brought a towel. But how could she have? This hadn't been planned. She'd come here on impulse to see...

The half circle of ragged stone rose up before her and she stopped. Then, slowly, she moved toward it. She didn't even have to look for the spot. She found it as if by sheer instinct. She walked right to the stone face and ran her fingers over its warm surface, feeling the deep ridges carved there. The heart. Her initials. Dylan's.

As she stood there, her fingers caressing the spot, she

recalled the warmth; the protected, loved feeling that had
flashed through her memory each time she'd envisioned their
lovemaking. And the lack of it during their encounter this
morning. A pain like nothing she'd dreamed of reached out
to grab her and held her in its grip. She lowered her head.
Tears burned her eyes, and her throat tightened until she could
barely breathe.

Give in to it. You're alone here. No one to see you.

She nodded her agreement with the voice of her own
reason. She *was* alone. God, she was so alone.

She sank slowly to the sand at the base of the rock, and
drew her knees to her chest. The flood of emotion came the
instant she'd locked her arms around her knees. Not silent
tears. There was no dignity in the way she cried. No pride,
no control. She sobbed out loud and moaned as the pain
knifed through her. Her tears ran like endless fountains and
her entire body trembled violently. Spasms ripped through her
chest, as if they'd split her breastbone in half.

"Caity…"

She looked up fast at the hoarse voice. Dylan stood
between her and the sea, between her and the path. She
cleared her throat. "What are you—"

"I followed you."

Fear rippled over her spine, jelling the tears that remained
in her eyes. She remained sitting there in the sand, looking
up at him. "Why?"

Through her blurred eyes, she saw the brief flash of pain
in his face, but it was just as quickly concealed. "Not to
murder you, Cait. I got worried. I just wanted to make sure…"
He sighed hard, shook his head. "I waited outside the law
office and followed the cab."

So he'd been here the whole time, watching her?

She brushed her fingertips over her eyes and fought the lingering sobs that tore through her sporadically, against her will.
"Why did you wait so long to come down here?"

"I wasn't going to come down at all." He moved forward, dropping to his knees in the sand. His hands reached out to cup her face, but she pulled free, and turned her head.

"Leave me alone."

"I can't. Not like this. Cait, I didn't tell you about the divorce because I didn't want to confuse you any more than you already were. I'm not the one who pushed Sandra down those stairs. I'm not the one who tried to kill you."

She faced him then, searching his eyes with hers. "Why now? You wouldn't deny anything before. Why are you bothering now?"

"It's important now."

She shook her head. "You're wrong. You have it all backward. It might have mattered before. It doesn't matter at all now." She stood and brushed the wet sand from her thighs and backside. She moved past him, to where she'd tossed her purse on the sand. She bent to pick it up, then pulled the folded papers from inside it. When she turned, he was behind her. She handed them to him. "It's over, Dylan."

He frowned down at the papers in his hand. She thought his lower lip trembled once, but she couldn't be sure. "No matter what's written here, it's not over. Not until you understand—"

"You're the one who doesn't understand. Read them, Dylan. Sign them, and you're free."

"I already signed—"

"Not this agreement. Look at it, will you?"

He nodded, unfolded the sheets and studied them for a long time. She stood and watched the emotions crossing his face, and tried to identify each one. Surprise? Shock? Sadness? Anger?

When he looked up again, his eyes were carefully blank. "You don't want anything?"

She shook her head. "Nothing. Not a dime. And I had the deed to the house transferred to you, too. I don't want it. I don't want anything that was hers—mine—before. I want to start over. And I hate that place."

"The old agreement?"

She reached into her bag and pulled out the official-looking envelope with the original divorce papers inside. All contained Dylan's signature. "I have both copies. Mine, and my lawyer's, right here. I knew you wouldn't trust me enough to take my word for it." She pushed the envelope into his hand. "Tear it up. Burn it. I don't care. It's up to you. I'm sure your lawyer will be happy to add his copies and yours to the bonfire."

Dylan shook his head. "Why?"

She shrugged and shook her head. The finality of handing those papers to him hit her and she felt tears threatening again.

"It was wrong. That first settlement was the act of another woman. Not me. It was just never my money. It was hers. It just felt…wrong."

"No." Dylan grabbed her purse and shoved both sets of documents inside, then tossed it to the sand. "You're taking away my motive. You're afraid I'm going to kill you, so you're taking away my motive." He stalked away from her, pushing a hand through his hair.

"I'm trying to make things right," she called after him. "I just want to cut my ties with the woman I was. I want to start over, try to build some kind of a life. Dammit, Dylan, I'm giving you what you wanted!"

He whirled to face her. "It was never what I wanted."

"Don't…" God, she couldn't stand for him to give her even a hint of false hope, not now. "Look, at least this way, if the killer succeeds, you won't be a suspect."

"Oh, thank you all to hell." He approached her, gripped her shoulders. "And what if the attempts just stop now, Caitlin? What are you going to believe then?"

"Does it really matter? Do you really care what I believe?"

He did. He knew it right then, and it hit him like a mallet between the eyes. He cared a lot what she believed—too much.

He saw the strain in her eyes when they met his, but she only bent to pick up her jeans and shoes, and her purse. She thumbed the strap of her bag over her shoulder, and carried her shoes dangling from one hand. The T-shirt she wore was soaked, clinging. It molded to her shape, and despite everything else he was feeling, he was aroused. He wanted her. He always had. It had been the one constant in their ever-changing relationship.

She walked in silence up the steep incline, over the path. He glanced back down the path, at the spot where they'd first made love, and wondered how much of it she recalled. Did she know how good it was, even then? How explosive? Did she realize yet, that she could bring him to his knees with a touch of her lips? Of her hands? That she'd driven him to the brink of insanity this morning? Had it been as good for her? He needed to know.

"Caity?"

She looked at him, eyes wide, searching.

"This morning—"

"I don't want to talk about this morning." She averted her eyes.

"You going to try to pretend it never happened?"

"It shouldn't have happened. It can't happen again. It won't." She closed her eyes, shook her head slowly.

He gripped her arm, pulled her around to face him. "It could. It could happen right now."

She opened her eyes. He saw moisture gathering there.

"It could," he insisted. He gripped her other arm, and drew her closer. She planted her feet, held herself away. "You want it, too, Cait. What are you so afraid of?"

"That you'll destroy me." She closed her eyes as the tears spilled over. "It wouldn't take much more, Dylan." The last sentence was a whisper, and a plea.

He let her go.

* * *

She was on her back, with the most horrible pains trying to crush her, like steel bands around her abdomen and back, tightening, crushing, squeezing. Her head swung back and forth on the pillows and someone ran a cool cloth over it. She wanted to cry out, but couldn't catch her breath to do so. And the pain that took her breath away went on and on and on.

And then it was gone.

She sat up, gasping. Her face damp with sweat, her hair clinging to it, her eyes wide and unfocused as she scanned the blurry room. Dylan was there. Standing in the shadows, grim-faced. He held the baby in his arms, wrapped in a white receiving blanket. Caitlin lifted her arms toward him. And slowly, he moved forward.

He lowered the bundle into her arms. Caitlin cradled the child close, but frowned at its minuscule size. So small, so feather-light. And not moving. Not moving at all.

She parted the folds of the soft blanket, and looked down. The baby's skin was thin, translucent, and tinted a ghastly blue. Caitlin's hand touched the tiny cheek, and she recoiled at its feel. Unreal, unresponsive, dead.

Another pair of hands came—not Dylan's—to take the child from her arms. She clung, but they pried until her weak grasp gave way. "No," she begged, her voice choked, desperate. "No, please, don't take him away… No!"

But the stranger's hands, holding the lifeless infant, vanished into the mist. And Caitlin screamed aloud, her grief a living force in her soul.

She sat up in bed and reached for the lamp, knocking it over in her haste. It crashed to the floor, shattering, but she barely heard the sound. The panic ran like ice water in her veins as she staggered from the bed, lunged for the door. Glass razed her bare feet, but she was beyond caring.

She wrenched the door wide and ran through the hall to the nursery. She tore that door open and left it gaping as she reached for the crib, clutched it with trembling hands, leaned over it and willed the thundering in her heart to quiet.

Her hands shook, but she found Lizzie's rounded form beneath a light cover. She touched the warm, plump cheek with a forefinger, and Lizzie instinctively turned her head toward that touch, her lips smacking in her sleep.

Relief washed through her, transforming her muscles from tautly stretched wire to quivering, useless jelly. She sank in a heap to the floor at the side of the crib.

She heard the footsteps in the hall, her name being called. She saw the light spilling in from the nursery's open door. And then she was lifted in Dylan's strong arms, cradled close to his hard chest, held tight, her face pressed to the crook of his neck where his scent enfolded her.

"All right. It's all right, I have you. You're safe."

Her arms slipped around his neck, and she clung to him, crying harder, recalling the silent devastation she'd seen on his handsome face in the dream.

"What happened?"

She shook her head, but it moved very little. "Nothing." Her throat was painfully tight, too tight to speak more than a word or two at a time. "Bad dream."

But it wasn't a dream, was it? It hurts too bad to have been just a dream.

"You scared the hell out of me, Cait. The lamp in your room is smashed all to hell. There's blood in the hall all the way from your room to the nursery. Tell me what happened."

He was carrying her the wrong way, and she realized he was heading not to her bedroom, but to his. The light there was blazing, and he lowered her to the bed. He stood over her, wearing only his brief underwear that fit him like a second skin. "You sure you're okay?"

She closed her eyes. He looked so worried, as though he'd really been afraid for her. How could he look like that and not love her? How could he look like that and want her dead?

"I…cut my foot, I think. That's all."

"The lamp?"

She nodded as he bent to examine her foot. It was beginning to throb, and she could feel the blood that coated it now. She fought to control her breathing, to stop the sobs that sporadically rocked through her. She brushed her face dry with palms that were sweaty, and too warm. "I knocked it over."

He swore softly, left her there and walked into his bathroom, returning in a moment with his hands full of paraphernalia that he dumped on the foot of his bed. She saw tweezers, a roll of gauze and a tube of ointment, some tape. Without a word, Dylan sat on the bed's edge, and pulled her foot into his lap. Slowly, painfully, he began removing bits of the broken lamp from the sole of her foot.

When she winced, he stiffened. "Sorry. I think I got it all." He smeared ointment over her cuts, his fingers so gentle on her skin, they could have been caressing her instead of ministering to an injury. He wrapped her foot in gauze, taped the dressing in place and stood again, pushing a hand through his hair.

She sat up. "Thanks. I was clumsy—"

"You were terrified. Are you sure no one—"

"It was just a bad dream."

He nodded, searching her face with eyes so intense, she felt them cutting through her. "So you said. You want to tell me about it?"

She bit her lower lip. She couldn't tell him. Not now, not yet. Not until she was sure. She couldn't say the words out loud that would make that heartache real. God, but it already was real, wasn't it? It was tearing her apart inside, even now, with that one, devastating image. The baby, *her* baby. Her son, and Dylan's, lying lifeless in her arms.

She shook her head, stifling a new flood of tears. "I don't remember."

His eyes narrowed, but he nodded. She knew he didn't believe that, but he wasn't going to push. She started to get up, but Dylan's hands came to her shoulders. His touch wasn't firm, but tentative, light as a whispered promise, ready to lift away from her at a moment's notice. "Stay, Cait?"

The look in his dark, glittering eyes made her shudder inside. "Stay?"

Chapter 12

"Yeah. Not so I can murder you in your sleep, and not so I can ravage you, either. I won't touch you unless... unless you ask me to. I just want to know you're safe. Stay here tonight."

Here. In his bed. In his arms? She closed her eyes and nodded once. It did no good to question his motives. She wanted to be here with him, wanted it badly. Too badly to ignore, or even to deny.

She was grieving, suffering from a loss they must have shared, if her suspicion that it was more memory than dream was an accurate one. She needed to be held, to be comforted. As he pulled back the covers, peeled them from beneath her so she could slip under them, then slid in beside her, she knew she wanted this. Just to sleep in his arms, feel his heart beating close to hers. She wanted to lie close to him all night, with his scent filling her nostrils. She was stupid to put herself through it, stupid to let herself wallow in his presence. It only hurt her more deeply than ever. But she lay down beside him, anyway. She'd lie close to him tonight. Just that.

Not just that. More. Much more.

He reached for the lamp and snapped it off, plunging them into darkness. Then he lay still, on his back, not touching her. Drawing a breath, Cait rolled onto her side. She rested her head on his chest, and let her arm fall around him.

He stiffened. "Caity…"

"Hold me, Dylan." Her voice broke when she said his name.

His arms came around her, hard and fast. She felt his strength. His smooth, broad chest beneath her head, the taut heated skin touching her cool cheek. She turned her head slightly and pressed her lips to it, not caring that it might not be wise, only knowing that she wanted this man, even more than she had before. He wanted her, too.

He had the divorce papers. She'd given him his freedom, and she sensed it would only be a matter of time until he took it and ran with it. He'd be out of her life soon, leaving her with nothing but a single, vibrant memory of his passion, his touch. It wasn't enough.

She slid her leg over both of his, bending her knee, lifting it up over his body. She kissed his chest again, her lips brushing his nipple, and she heard him swear hoarsely. He gripped her shoulders and lifted her from his chest. "What the hell are you doing?"

There was anger in his voice, but desire in his eyes, glittering up at her even in the darkness. She felt its proof, pressing hard and insistent against her thigh. She moved her leg over him, gently. "Make it like it was, Dylan." She bit her lip when tears threatened. "Make it like it used to be."

His hands tightened on her shoulders. There was a moment of hesitation, a moment when she was terrified he was about to turn away from her. Then he drew her downward until his lips could reach hers. He kissed her long and slow, suckling her lips, tracing their shape with his tongue, nipping them. She opened her mouth to him and his tongue plunged inside her mouth to taste every part of it. Deepening the invasion with every second, he took from her, and he gave to her. His hands threaded in her hair, then danced down the column of her neck. His thumbs pressed little circles under her jaw, then his lips replaced them, so gently her throat tightened.

He moaned deep in his throat, and she moved over him more completely, until she straddled his powerful hips, bringing his hardness against her burning need. She rocked against him, and he trembled. She let her hands roam his body. She pressed her palms to the muscled wall of his chest, kneaded his shoulders, learned his shape all over again. She ran her hands up and down his arms, back and forth across his back. She kissed his face, his chin, his neck.

His hand left her back and she heard the snap of the bedside lamp. She opened her eyes to see the light falling on his face. She searched his burning eyes.

"I want to see you, Caity. I love the way you look."

She nodded. She understood his need. She wanted to see him, too. To see the sensations pass over his face, through his eyes, to see the beautiful shape of him. To burn his image as she held him inside her one last time, into her heart, her soul, her memory. She'd never forget this night. Never.

She sat up, still straddling him, and the covers fell away behind her. He wanted to look at her.

She caught the hem of the nightshirt she wore, and lifted it, tugging it over her head, tossing it to the floor, keeping her gaze on his face all the while. His eyes darkened, slid slowly away from hers, downward, and fixed their attention on her breasts. His hands moved up over her back to her shoulders, and he drew her forward, lifting his head from the pillows at the same time. He captured one yearning peak in his mouth, and he sucked her hard, hungrily, using his teeth, worrying her flesh, nipping it until her head fell backward and her loins ached with wanting him. He released her only to move to the other breast, laving it with his tongue until it responded, then punishing it for the offense with his teeth and lips.

He caught her hips in his hands and lifted her from him. She braced her knees on the mattress as he shoved her panties down. One hand dove between her thighs, cupping the mound of curls. Then fingers parted, explored, pleasured her. He found the tiny nub that was the center of her desire, and ran the pad of his thumb over it. She shuddered and caught her breath. He pinched it between thumb and forefinger, squeezing, rolling, torturing her. She whimpered and all at once his free hand caught her chin, tipping her head down.

"Open your eyes, Caity. Look at me, let me watch you."

She did as he asked. She'd do anything he asked at that moment. And his deep, dark eyes stabbed into hers just as his fingers stabbed into her center. He slid them in deeper, then pulled them out again, watching the responses in her eyes.

She reached down between them, finding the waistband of his briefs, thrusting one hand beyond it. She held him, her grip tight, but trembling. He was like iron coated in silk. She squeezed and moved her hand up and down his turgid length, then up again until her fingers teased at his tip.

"Oh, yeah," he moaned.

She lowered her head to his chest, and worried his nipples just the way he'd done to hers. And then he was gripping her again, rolling her over, peeling her panties away and kicking free of his briefs all at once. He settled himself on top of her, nudging her thighs apart with his, positioning his need at her moist opening.

He entered her hard and fast and deep, groaning as he did. He gripped her buttocks in both hands, and drove himself to the very hilt, holding her hard against him, refusing to back down even when she stiffened, pressing harder, forcing her to take all of him.

He watched her face as she slowly relaxed, adjusting to her

body's fullness, to the feel of him stretching her to his shape and size again. And as soon as she did, he knew, and he withdrew, slowly, until she was all but empty, before thrusting himself into her again. He set the pattern, and the pace continued. Deep, hard thrusts. Slow, mind-altering withdrawals. He kissed her hands, her fingers, one by one. His lips traced a path over her forearms, making her tremble. Then his mouth dampened her shoulders, then her neck, and her ears. It was as though he wanted to taste every inch of her.

The force behind the thrusts grew stronger, harder, and faster with each stroke.

Her hips rose to meet his, her fingers dug into his shoulders. It was as if she were riding a hurricane, she thought vaguely. She felt possessed by him, filled with him and surrounded in him, all at once, and she moved without pause or forethought or planning. She moved according to her body's demands and the ones she could sense from his. And then he drove every thought from her mind as her entire body tightened until her muscles tried to tear from the bones.

Release pummeled her, exploding inside her. She clung to him as her body convulsed around his, and she cried out his name on a voice ragged and broken. He stiffened, plunging again, holding her hips to his. "Caity," he whispered, and then he collapsed atop her, panting, damp with sweat.

He lay there for a long time, his heart rumbling against her chest, his sweat dampening her body, mingling with her own, his breaths heating her skin as they slowed. He lifted his head after a long moment, when their lungs were functioning normally and their bodies began to cool. He searched her eyes, utter longing in his. He started to say something, then shook his head and rolled off her. He cradled her to his chest, held her in arms banded with steel, held her close, and warm and safe against him.

She cried softly, and silently, so he wouldn't know. This was what she'd wanted. She felt cherished, just as she had in her memory flashes. The sad part was, it wasn't real. But she could pretend. Just for tonight, she could pretend.

When she awoke, he was gone.

Dawn hadn't yet painted the horizon. But she was too restless to lie in bed. There was so much to say. She needed to find Dylan, to beg him, if necessary, to give their marriage one more try. She wanted to tear up all of the divorce papers and start over. She wanted the cherished feeling he'd given her last night to live on and on. She wanted it to be real. She was determined to *make it* real.

She threw back the covers, got up and found her nightgown and panties on the floor. She pulled them on, then smiled as she spotted the roll of gauze and tube of ointment on the floor, recalling the tender way he'd cared for her wounded foot. She bent to pick them up, and reached for the tweezers, too. Then she carried the lot into the bathroom and opened the medicine cabinet to replace the items inside.

She set the gauze on a shelf, then froze as her gaze fell on a small, brown glass jar. She blinked at the words on the label, not willing to believe what she saw there.

"Pure ground carob."

"No." She stared at the bottle as though it might leap up and grab her, and backed away from the cabinet. "No, it can't be…"

God, the tenderness she'd felt in his touch last night, the sweet anguish in his eyes, the yearning…had it all been an act? One big performance to convince her once and for all that he was innocent? Could he have faked the passion, the affection, that she'd felt surrounding her all night long? She didn't want to believe it.

Maybe it's time you stopped believing what you want to believe, and start seeing what's staring you in the face.

Tears blurred her vision as she closed the cabinet and walked back into the bedroom. He hadn't returned. She stole in silence into the hallway, tiptoed along its dim length until she heard him, crooning a soft song, his voice deep, trembling, beautiful. "Good night, sweetheart." She caught back a sob that leapt into her throat, and slipped nearer, peering through the open doorway into the nursery.

He walked slowly, barefoot, his calves naked beneath the hem of a terry robe. He cradled the tiny baby on his shoulder, patting her back with his huge hand. He sang very softly, and Lizzie, wide-eyed, seemed to be hanging on every note. He turned to pace the other way and Cait saw his face. His eyes were red, and there were marks on one cheek that looked like the tracks of hot tears.

She backed away slowly, bit her lips as her own eyes filled. How could she make sense of him? Of the tender man she saw holding Lizzie, of the man with the powder that was poison to her hidden in his medicine cabinet?

Blinded by tears, she made her way back to his bedroom. What other secrets was he hiding here? The keys to her past? His hidden motive for wanting her dead? She was tired of waiting to find the answers. She couldn't wait anymore.

He wouldn't come back any time soon. Lizzie was wide-awake, and it would take a while to get her back to sleep. Caitlin went to the dresser, opened the drawers, pawed their contents. She found nothing but clothes. She turned to the closet, and rummaged inside it. Nothing. Just more clothes, shoes, suits. A briefcase.

She drew it out, and lay it on the bed. She tried the snaps, half expecting it to be locked. It wasn't, and inside she found only papers pertaining to the business. Drawings. Blueprints. Invoices. Nothing to do with her.

She closed it and slipped it back into the closet. Then she spotted the fireproof security box on the top shelf. She reached for it, glancing over her shoulder toward the door as she did.

What if he returned, caught her snooping? What would he do then?

It didn't matter. She had to try. She drew the heavy box down, set it on the floor near enough the bed that she could shove it underneath if she heard him coming. She closed the closet.

The box was locked and she felt deflated. Then she saw his jeans from the day before hanging over the back of a chair. She went to them, searched the pockets and found a key ring. There were many keys on it, but it didn't take long to spot the small one that fit the lock. She sat on the floor, and opened the box.

There were photos. Dozens of them. Snapshots of her, in her youth. Pictures of the two of them together, mugging for the camera. She looked at all of them, blinking constantly to keep her eyes clear enough to see. They seemed so happy. So in love.

She found their marriage license. A large manila envelope held it, along with more photos, encased in a leather-bound album. Their wedding pictures. Her dress was off-the-shoulder, ivory-toned, spilling over with lace and pearls. She'd worn a sprig of baby's breath and yellow roses in her hair, carried a bouquet of the same in her hands.

She flipped through the album slowly, her heart aching for what they'd had, what they'd lost. There was a fat man in a dark suit, nearly bald, with hard, glassy blue eyes. He must have been her father, but she found no sense of recognition stirring inside her. Then she found the one of the woman. She looked just like Caitlin. Same auburn hair, only shorter, and permed in kinky curls to frame her petite face. Her green eyes held some secret pain, some deep sadness that belied the smile that curved her full lips. She didn't look old enough to be Caitlin's mother. But she knew that's who she was seeing right now. And her fingertips brushed over the troubled face.

God, she didn't remember her own mother! But she felt something, a pull, a heartache. A longing.

She closed her eyes, and then the album. There would be time to learn about her mother later. It was too late to mend the break she sensed in their relationship. Her mother was gone, dead and buried.

She set the album aside and continued pawing through the contents of the box. Her hand froze, her fingers tingling, when she picked up the envelope buried at the bottom, beneath titles to cars, and countless other documents.

Trembling for no reason, she opened it, and found inside the very item she'd most dreaded seeing. Across the top of the document, she read the words, Certificate of Fetal Death.

She caught her breath in her throat and tears stung her eyes. She swiped them away and forced herself to read all of it, the clinical, cold facts that told her she and Dylan had had a son. A tiny son, who'd weighed just over two pounds. Cause of death was listed as extreme prematurity. She blinked at the date. January 8th. Just over eight months ago. Her heart twisting, she scanned the page, and found the child's name. David Dylan Rossi.

So they'd named him. And if they had, then they'd probably buried him, as well. Where? Desperately, she reread the lines, but found no clue. Oh, God. She fought her shaking hands and replaced the paper in its envelope. But it wasn't empty. She shook out the folded card that was still inside. It read, In Memoriam. David Dylan Rossi. She found the name of the cemetery there, along with the date of his stillbirth and burial.

"My baby," she whispered, holding the card to her chest. And this was all she had of him. This, and the memory. It had been a memory, not a dream. A nightmare memory of the day she'd lost her child. And she knew, as surely as she knew anything, that losing the child had devastated her, that she'd been sure she could never survive going through it again. And that was why she'd been so afraid of getting pregnant. God, she'd been a fool.

She replaced everything else in the security box, but kept the card. She locked it, replaced it in the closet and returned the key ring to Dylan's pocket. Then she paused and took the keys back out. She needed to go there, she realized. She needed to see where her son rested. Yes, there were other things that must be done. She had to confront Dylan about this, and about the carob powder she'd found in his medicine cabinet. But first—before she could even think of anything else—she had to find her baby.

And she had to do it alone.

She found a pad and pen on the dresser and scrawled a note to Dylan. "I need to be by myself, to think. Please understand." She signed her name at the bottom, and left the note on the bed, then crept through the halls to her room, not making a sound, still clinging to the card that bore her son's name.

She set the card and the keys on the nightstand, avoiding the broken glass from the lamp while she dressed in jeans and a sweatshirt. She tugged a brush through her hair and snapped it into a rubber band.

She slipped on her shoes, quickly grabbed the keys and tiptoed out, locking the bedroom door from the inside and pulling it shut after her.

She paused at the top of the stairs, recalling the horror of seeing Sandra's broken body at the bottom. But she forced herself to move down them, through the foyer and then out the front door.

She got into Dylan's car, inserted the key, but didn't start the engine. She only turned the key enough to release the steering wheel, then shifted into neutral and coasted as far as she could down the drive. Only then did she start the car, and put it in gear. She flicked the headlights on when she reached the road.

She drove slowly, feeling her way. She hadn't driven a car since the accident, and it was terrifying to do so now. But she had to. She had to see…

She knew where the cemetery was. She'd passed it yesterday in the taxi. And she found it again with no trouble, despite the darkness. She pulled the car to the side of the road and shut off the engine. She left the keys in the switch, in her hurry to find her son.

The wrought-iron gate stood slightly crooked, like an aged sentry who put duty before comfort. It was closed, and a chain was wrapped around the bars with a padlock for a pendant. To prevent vandalism, she assumed. It had been open when she'd passed it by day. She moved through the damp, scraggly grass, along the short brick wall that surrounded the place, and easily climbed over it. It was really rather silly to have a padlocked gate when the wall was so easily scaled. She dropped to the ground on the other side, then just stood amid rows and rows of markers.

The night wind ruffled her hair. It smelled of fresh flowers, and old ones, and of the sea. Crickets chirped incessantly. The moon's whispered glow slanted into the place, making odd-shaped shadows around the stones. But the moon hung low in the sky, and soon it would disappear entirely. There were a few huge trees, looming like guardians of the dead.

She belatedly wished she'd brought along a flashlight. How would she ever find little David here?

But she began at the first row of markers, barely able to discern the names engraved in the stone in the pale moonlight. And she moved quickly, from stone to stone, searching, her heart breaking into millions of tiny bits. And when she finished with one row, she moved to the next.

It took the better part of an hour to find it. The marker was longer than it was high. The front was adorned with a tiny, sweet-faced angel, kneeling with hands folded in prayer. It read, Our Beloved Son, David Dylan Rossi. Fresh flowers covered the grave. Lilies, pale blue carnations, baby's breath for the baby who'd never drawn one. And yellow roses.

Caitlin ran her hand over the face of the cold stone, her fingers tracing the letters of his name. The pain was too much for anyone to bear and still live. Too much. She sank to her knees, pressing her face to the stone, giving way to the tears she'd cried too often lately. And then she sank lower, until her body was pressed to the fine, new grass that covered her child. She pushed her face into the moist, green blades, and sobbed as she never had before.

When the tears finally began to subside, she sat up again, shakily. She gathered the yellow roses to her breast and bent to inhale their scent. Who'd put them here? Dylan? God, was this as painful to him as it was to her? Why hadn't he told her? Why keep something so vital a secret?

Thinking of Dylan reminded her how long she'd been here. Though time had passed without her awareness, she knew she'd been gone a long while. The moon was gone now. Soon the sky would begin to lighten with the approaching dawn. She wanted to get back before anyone realized she'd gone.

She got to her feet, surprised at the weakness her crying had left in her. She shouldn't be surprised, she supposed. She hadn't been eating right, or getting much sleep at all. Her body needed some TLC, or she'd end up in worse shape than she'd been before.

She walked, dragging her feet, back to the short wall. Then stopped, turning abruptly. She'd heard something, some sound or movement behind her.

She scanned the darkness, senses alert, her pulse accelerating to a constant thrum in her ears. But every shadow could have concealed some waiting evil. There was nothing distinct. Fear shivered up her spine and she climbed over the wall, and hurried to the car. She got in, locked all the doors and reached for the switch, to turn the key.

Only the keys weren't there.

She frowned hard. *I know I left them in the switch. Didn't I?*

Maybe not. She'd been upset, not thinking clearly. She checked the pockets of her jeans and felt nothing. Oh, hell, could she have dropped them when she'd climbed the wall?

Or when she'd lain prostrate on the ground, sobbing for her lost baby?

She glanced uneasily through the windshield, eyes straining. She saw no one. She was alone with her grief and her fears. She unlocked the door and got out, starting back for the cemetery. She stooped near the wall where she'd gone in and felt around in the grass, to no avail. Then she climbed over and repeated the vain process on the other side. Nothing. Sighing, she made her way back to the headstone. If she didn't find the keys there, she'd have to retrace her steps through the entire place as she'd searched for the grave. But as she approached her child's grave site, a slow, smooth motion caught her eye. She squinted in the darkness.

A length of rope dangled from a huge tree, a hangman's noose at its end. She froze, stark terror rinsing her in icy water. She screamed in horror and turned to run back the way she'd come.

Something came around her throat, something smooth and firm, and tight, growing tighter with every second, choking off her airway. She grasped at it with both hands, clawing her own skin, trying to get her fingers behind the leather. But the tightening only went on.

She couldn't breathe! She kicked backward with one foot, but connected with nothing. She was dying! God, someone was killing her and she was helpless to fight.

She was dizzy. Huge black spots danced in and out of her vision, followed by bright red ones that seemed like little explosions in her brain. And then utter blackness swallowed her up.

Chapter 13

Dylan had tucked Lizzie in and returned to the bedroom to find Cait gone, and the note on his bed. That she wanted him to leave her alone was clear, but he was uncomfortable with the notion. He told himself it wasn't because he'd so looked forward to making love to her again, or because he'd dreamed for so long of holding her all night long and waking with her in his arms, snuggled against him. He told himself it was just that he was worried about her. She hadn't told him about her nightmare, but he didn't believe for a minute that she'd forgotten it. It was something she was keeping to herself. He tried to respect that, along with her need for privacy, but after an hour of tossing restlessly, he gave in to his greater need to know she was all right.

He pulled on jeans and a T-shirt, and went to her room, only to find the door locked from the inside. So he knocked, and waited.

No answer.

He knocked again, harder this time. "Caity. Come on, answer me. I'll go away if you want, I just want to know you're okay."

Still no answer, and panic began to spread through him. He pounded again. "Caity! Dammit, answer me! Caity!"

When he only heard silence, visions of her lying in a pool of blood on the floor assaulted him. He took two steps backward and kicked the door open.

She wasn't there. The room looked the same as it had earlier. The lamp shattered on the floor. The bloody footprints on the carpet. Then he spotted the little card on the nightstand and his heart flipped over. He picked it up, knowing already what it was.

He closed his eyes tightly. "Oh, God, she knows. But she wouldn't have gone there. Not at night, not alone…"

With dawning dread, he realized that his keys were no longer in his pocket, and when he raced down the stairs to the front door, he saw that his car wasn't out front, either.

But the battered pickup was. He ran to it, jumped in and found the extra key he kept in the ashtray, just in case. The engine roared to life, and Dylan shifted into gear and pressed the accelerator to the floor with his bare foot.

He was driving too fast. He knew he was, but he couldn't slow down. The feeling of impending doom assaulted him with killing force, and the pickup rocked up on two wheels as he rounded sharp curves without letting up. The headlights barely cut through the gloom enough to guide his way as he careered over the writhing roads toward Eden, toward the cemetery where he and Cait had buried their tiny child months ago…the cemetery where she'd fainted in his arms from sheer grief. He couldn't stand the thought of her there, alone, slowly regaining the memory of her most gut-wrenching experience. She couldn't handle it. Not yet, not alone. God, it still twisted *his* insides into knots to go there every week with fresh flowers.

He skidded to a stop when the pickup's headlights glinted off the metallic surface of his car, parked near the cemetery gates. He leapt out, and vaulted the wall.

He saw a flashlight moving through the darkness from the other side of the graveyard. Heard a gruff, male voice call, "What's goin' on out here? Who's there?"

He ran toward that voice, even as he heard the sound of running feet, retreating in another direction. He moved forward, tripping twice, falling down on hands and knees and lunging to his feet just as fast.

The third time he tripped, it was over a woman's still body.

"My God, Caity!" He gripped her shoulders, shook her gently. Then he saw the belt wrapped around her slender throat, and his heart tripped to a stop in his chest. He snatched the damned thing away and pulled her to him, holding her gently, rocking her, murmuring her name over and over. "Don't die, Caity, not now. Please, not now."

"Let go of that woman, mister."

He lifted his head, only to be blinded by the beam of a flashlight aimed directly at his face.

"She's my wife. Call an ambulance for God's sake, she's dying!"

"Already did that, when I heard the screams. Po-lice, too. So why don't you just stand up, nice and easy, and leave her be till they get here."

Dylan only shook his head and clutched her more tightly.

"Leave her be, mister. I got a twelve-gauge pointed at yer head, and I'd hate to have to use it."

Dylan stiffened, but he lowered her to the cool grass, and looked up, squinting in the beam of light. The light moved then, and caught a noose swaying slowly in the breeze, hanging from a tree right above him.

"Yer one sick son of a bitch, you know that?"

She was lying on a hard surface, in a small, enclosed place. Strangers hovered over her. A mask covered her face, bathing her nose and mouth in cold, sterile-smelling air. Her throat hurt. Her lungs burned. Her head throbbed.

"She's coming around."

"Mrs. Rossi. Mrs. Rossi, can you hear me?"

She nodded at the fresh-faced young man who leaned over her. He wore white, and beyond the open doors at her feet, she saw flashing lights, breaking the dawn with color. She tried to sit up, only to have the young man hold her shoulders in place. "Take it easy, now. You're going to be okay."

"Pulse is stronger. BP's gaining," another, older man said.

In the flashing light through the open doors, she saw Dylan looking rumpled, in jeans and a T-shirt. He was barefoot, and he stood nose to nose with Detective Barnes. It looked as if they were arguing.

Dimly, she recalled what had happened. The darkness, the noose, the grim certainty that she was going to die when her life was being choked out of her.

Dylan was here. What the hell was he doing here? Oh, God, it hadn't been him. It *couldn't have been* him.

The doors swung closed, and the vehicle lurched into motion.

Broad daylight filtered into her hospital room. She'd been examined, X-rayed, poked and prodded until the doctors were certain she was going to be all right.

Now she lay in the bed, sipping ice cola through a straw, letting it soothe her throat, and watching Detective Barnes pace the room.

"I need to get out of here."

He cocked one eyebrow at her, and stopped pacing. "I was told you'd have to stay overnight for observation."

"No."

He frowned at her, then shrugged. "Up to you, I guess. But not until you tell me everything. And don't leave anything out, Mrs. Rossi. Don't try to protect him anymore. We have him cold this time."

Her heart skipped a beat. "Have you arrested Dylan?"

His lips thinned. "He's being held for formal questioning. His answers at the scene didn't cut it."

"I want to be there."

"What?"

"When you question him. I want to be there. I want to hear the answers." She caught Barnes's gaze and held it. "I *need* to be there."

He was silent for a long time. Finally, he nodded. "Need to hear it for yourself, is that it? I can arrange it."

She sighed her relief, and leaned back on the pillows.

"So what happened last night?"

She closed her eyes. "I found out I'd had a child. He was stillborn, in January."

"Your husband hadn't told you about it?"

She shook her head.

"Then how did you find out?"

She licked her lips. "I found the fetal death certificate."

"Ah."

"I wanted to see the grave. I don't know why, I just felt this need to be there, close to him."

"Understandable." He paced again, nearer the bed, then sat in the chair beside it.

"But I wanted to be alone. I left Dylan a note, telling him not to bother me, and then took his car keys. I locked my bedroom from the inside. Then I took the car and drove to the cemetery."

"Anyone follow you?"

She shrugged. "I probably wouldn't have noticed if they had. I was pretty upset."

"I'll bet you were." He leaned forward in his chair. "So you found the place."

"Yes."

"See any other cars there? Anyone hanging around?"

"No."

"So?"

"I visited the grave for a while. I'm not sure how long. Then I went back to the car. Only the keys were gone. I thought I'd left them in the switch, but they weren't there." She sighed, pressing her hand to her pounding head. "I thought I might have dropped them, so I went back to the grave to look for them." She shuddered and closed her eyes tight. "There was a noose, hanging from a tree. I think I screamed, and I turned to run back to the car. But something came around my throat from behind." The horror of that feeling, of not being able to breathe, of certain death looming right in front of her, brought new tears to her eyes. She covered her face with both hands.

"It's all right." A heavy hand closed on her shoulder. "It's all right, you're fine."

She sniffed, lowered her hands and nodded. "That's all I remember. I couldn't breathe. I passed out."

He nodded. "You didn't get a sense of who it was? Did he say anything? Maybe you caught a whiff of cologne, or—"

"No. Nothing." She met his concerned gaze, searched it. "What stopped him from killing me? Why was that awful noose hanging there?"

Barnes shook his head. "My best guess is that the killer planned to make it look like a suicide. Leave you…" He didn't finish.

He didn't have to. "Leave me hanging from the tree above my son's grave. Oh, God…" A sob choked her.

"The caretaker lives right next door. He heard your screams. He had his wife call 911 while he grabbed his shotgun and headed out to see what was happening. I figure that your…that the killer stopped what he was doing when the old man called out."

"Thank God," she whispered.

"Mrs. Rossi, when he got there, he found your husband crouching over you. He didn't see or hear anyone else."

A cold feeling chilled her to the bone. "What did Dylan say?"

Barnes frowned and shook his head. "Let's go find out."

* * *

The mirror was two-way, he had no doubt about it. But he didn't really give a damn. "I want to know how she is."

"You answer my questions, and then we'll discuss your wife, Rossi."

Dylan clenched his fists on the surface of the table. "Is she alive?"

Barnes pursed his lips and Dylan felt like bloodying them for him. "Questions first. You want a lawyer present?"

"I don't need a freaking lawyer."

"Good. Sign here." He shoved a form across the table, then took a pen from his pocket and tossed it down. Dylan scratched his name across the bottom, and shoved it back.

Barnes took a long look at it, nodded and leaned back in the chair opposite Dylan's. "So tell me what happened last night."

"I told you at the cemetery."

"Take it from the top, Rossi. I have all day."

Dylan's glare did nothing to erase the smug expression Barnes wore. He'd get this over with so he could find out about Caity. The sooner the better. Dammit, if she'd died…he bit his lip at the thought. She couldn't have died. Not now.

"She had a bad dream. I found her crying in the nursery, took her to my room. I wanted her where I could be sure she was okay. Later, the baby was crying, so I got up to check on her. Cait was sound asleep when I left her."

"So far, so good. Keep going."

Dylan sighed hard and fought to keep a rein on his temper. "When I came back, she was gone. She left a note. I'm sure your guys have found that by now."

"Hell, yes. Found a few other goodies in your room, too." He took a plastic zipper bag from his huge manila envelope and dangled it like bait from a hook. "Ever seen this before?"

Dylan frowned and looked at the bottle encased in the plastic bag. "Carob powder?" He felt a chill pass over his spine.

"Have you seen it before?" Barnes repeated, his voice booming.

"No. Where did you—"

"Your medicine cabinet, Rossi."

Dylan nodded. "So, someone's trying to frame me. Isn't that pretty obvious, *Detective?*"

Barnes only eyed him as though Dylan was something bad, as though he were a hunk of rotten meat on a platter. "So you found the note. Then what?"

"I lay in bed for a while. An hour or so. I couldn't sleep without knowing she was okay, so I went to check on her."

"Waited a whole hour, huh?"

"She made it clear she didn't want to be bothered." Dylan shook his head. "You aren't buying a word of this. It's bull, a waste of time. You've already decided I'm guilty."

"That's not my job, Rossi. You went to check on her…"

"The door was locked. She didn't answer. I got worried, kicked it in. Found the card on the dresser and guessed she'd gone to the grave. When I found the car gone, I was sure of it, so I took the pickup and went after her." He shook off the chill of precognition that had swept over him when he'd seen his car parked at the cemetery gate, and eyed Barnes. "How am I doing so far?"

"Word for word what you told me at the scene. Well rehearsed. You're smooth. I've seen smoother."

"Go to hell, Barnes."

"Been there for a long time now, Rossi. Finish the fairy tale, will you?"

Dylan shook his head. "I jumped the wall. Heard the old man call out, saw his light. I heard someone running away, and then I found her."

Barnes nodded. "You said that before, that you heard someone running away. Old man Crandall didn't hear a thing."

"He was running, too, toward me, ready to give me both

barrels of that shotgun he was lugging. He might not have heard the other guy's steps over his own. But I did. Someone ran, toward the east side of the cemetery."

Barnes's eyes were still skeptical. He reached into the envelope again. A bigger plastic bag emerged this time, with a leather belt inside. "Reco'nize this?"

Dylan's neck prickled. He took the bag and examined the belt. There was no sense lying about it. His initials were engraved in the leather. "It's mine."

"Your fingerprints are on it, Rossi. And hers. No one else's."

"I took it off her neck, you bastard."

"How?"

The guy wasn't ruffled, not in the least. Dylan imagined he had lots of experience trying to make people sweat like this. "I don't know. I was scared. My wife was lying there as good as dead. I just yanked it off her, okay?"

"Your prints were here," Barnes pointed to one end of the belt. "And here," he added, pointing to the other end. "Hers were only in the center, where she struggled to pull the thing away as she was being strangled." He stood and walked slowly away, then back again. "Your prints were where the killer would have been holding the belt, Rossi. Where you held it as you choked the life out of your wife."

Dylan felt a fist pummel his gut. "Are you saying…she's dead?"

Barnes only continued staring at him. Waiting for him to break?

Dylan came out of the chair like a shot, reached across the table and gripped Barnes by the front of his splashy print shirt. "Tell me, you bastard!"

The door burst open and two uniformed cops ran through, each gripping one of Dylan's arms and jerking him away from Barnes.

"Cuff him," Barnes ordered, straightening his shirt as if he hadn't a care in the world.

Then a soft cry from the still-open door drew Dylan's gaze. Caitlin stood there in the doorway. Her eyes huge, round, her pupils too dilated to be normal. She stood there, just staring at him, as handcuffs were snapped around his wrists, pulled behind his back.

"Caity…"

She blinked, but kept looking at him from those hollow, haunted eyes.

God, the relief that coursed through him almost made his legs give out. She was okay. He wanted to hold her, to run his hands through her wild hair, to kiss her. But his relief at seeing her on her feet, breathing, was short-lived. Her expressionless face, the hurt and fear he saw etched into it, were like daggers in his heart.

He saw the red marks at her throat, the purplish bruises that were already forming. There were garish scratches on her neck, and he shuddered as he envisioned her clawing at the belt, trying to pull it away. She was pale, too pale, and dark circles under her eyes made her look as if she'd been in a fight and lost.

The cops moved him forward until he stood right in front of her, at the doorway. He wanted to reach out, to pull her into his arms and hold her until that turmoil in her eyes calmed. But he couldn't with his hands cuffed behind him. He wished to hell she would say something. Anything. "Caity—"

"You'll have to step aside, Mrs. Rossi," Barnes ordered, tugging gently at her shoulders until she obeyed. But her eyes remained on Dylan, and his on her. "Dylan Rossi, I'm placing you under arrest for the attempted murder of your wife."

Caitlin's eyes fell closed, not softly or gently. They slammed shut like the doors of a prison, and squeezed themselves together hard. And then the two cops shoved him through the door.

"Don't go home, Caity!" Dylan shouted over his shoulder. "Don't go back there. It isn't safe!" He heard no answer as he was pushed through a hallway toward the back of the building.

Barnes opened a cell, and unceremoniously shoved him through. He closed the door. "Turn around and stick your hands through the bars so I can take the cuffs off."

Dylan did, putting his desperate hurt and paralyzing fear for his wife aside, converting it to anger, which he vented on the man who twisted a key in the manacles at his wrists. "You haven't Mirandaized me, Barnes. Slipping up in your old age?"

The cuffs fell free and Dylan turned to face the man. Barnes slipped a little card from his shirt pocket and stuck it through. "Read that."

Dylan took the card, glanced at it and read the first line. "You have the right to remain silent." He'd shot that one to hell already, hadn't he? And it had probably been a stupid mistake, but dammit, he'd had to know about Caity. He shook his head and slipped the card back to Barnes.

"Understand?"

Dylan looked at him, lifting his eyebrows. "What?"

"Your rights, do you understand them?"

"Oh, hell, yes, Barnes. You really have a knack for communication." Dylan won the stare-down. Barnes's gaze flicked away. Dylan searched the man for a weak spot. "You don't have enough to indict me."

"I think I do." He shrugged. "Either way, you won't be offing your wife today. I'll sleep better knowing that."

"Don't sleep too soundly, Barnes. She still isn't safe. Dammit, it wasn't me, but someone sure as hell tried to kill her. She needs protection."

Barnes's gaze narrowed. "Nice try, Rossi."

"Dammit, I'm begging you. Give her some kind of protection. She's just stubborn enough to go back there today."

Barnes nodded. "Especially if she believes her attacker is safely behind bars. Looked to me like she was finally convinced, Rossi. How'd she look to you?"

"You're enjoying this, aren't you?"

Barnes shrugged again. "Can't help it. I honestly like the

lady. She's got that innocent, trusting quality, makes a guy want to look out for her." He shook his head. "Makes a slug like you want to take her for everything she's got and throw her away. You're a fool, you know that?"

Dylan frowned, wondering at the softening in Barnes's voice, the slightly tormented look in his eyes. "You feel like protecting her, then go for it, Barnes. Look out for her, 'cause you've got me caged up and I can't. She still needs watching over. I swear it."

"You know, you almost have me convinced."

"Did she tell you about the divorce?" Dylan knew he was grasping at straws, but he had to try. "She canceled the old settlement. Had a new one drawn up. She doesn't get a damn thing, now. I have no motive to kill her."

"What, you think greed is the only motive that drives a man to murder his wife?"

"If she dies while I'm stuck here, Barnes, I'll make sure you pay."

"You don't scare me, Rossi."

"I'm the one that's scared here. Dammit, she's a walking target. Will you think about that? What if you're wrong, huh? What the hell is going to happen to her then?"

Barnes frowned through the bars. "You're damned convincing, I'll give you that." He turned to walk away from the cell, handcuffs dangling from his fingers.

"Assign a man to watch her, Barnes. If you have one decent cell in your body, protect her!" Dylan shouted after him as he got farther away. "Suppose you have the wrong man, Barnes! Suppose the real killer gets to her while I'm here. You gonna be able to live with that? Are you? Barnes!"

Barnes didn't answer, only kept strolling down the hall as though he were taking a walk through the park.

Chapter 14

"Cait, God, I'm glad you're back." Thomas hugged her hard, but Caitlin remained stiff in his arms, feeling shell-shocked.

"Police have been here, snoopin' all over the place. That Barnes, he's a corker," Ellen snapped. "Said you were in the hospital, but wouldn't say why. Time we called, you'd checked out."

Caitlin freed herself from her brother's grip, and faced the older woman. How on earth was she going to tell her that Dylan had been arrested?

"You look ill, so pale and weak. You need to eat and rest, *non?*" Genevieve hovered with a worried expression. "I can get something for you—"

"No, Genevieve. I'll be fine, really." Her gaze moved around the living room, where they'd all gathered, but she didn't see Lizzie. Henri lurked in the arched doorway that led to the library, just watching, silent.

"What happened last night? There was another attempt on your life, wasn't there, Cait?"

She met her brother's concerned eyes, thinking his fear for her sounded genuine, and simply nodded. She hated suspecting he—or any of them—could be capable of murder. But if Dylan wasn't guilty, then someone else was. She'd only come back here to find out who…and for Lizzie.

His gaze narrowed, moving over her body as if in search of her injuries, then stopped on her vividly bruised throat, and widened. "Oh, my God."

"It isn't as bad as it looks."

"Where's Dylan?" Ellen demanded. "He took off outta here last night like his tail was afire, just a short while after that other car roared away. Made enough racket to wake the dead, that one did."

Caitlin closed her eyes tight. "They've arrested him."

Thomas froze, his eyes the only part of him that moved at all, and then, only to widen.

Caitlin dragged her feet as she made her way to the sofa, and sat down. "I went to the cemetery last night, to see my son. I guess Dylan came after me." She bit her lip hard, tasting blood on her tongue. "Someone tried to strangle me there, and then the caretaker came out to find Dylan bending over me."

"Did he do it, Cait?" Thomas sat beside her, gripped her hand in both of his.

"I was unconscious. I never saw—"

"But what do you *feel?*"

She shook her head slowly. "His fingerprints were on the belt that was twisted around my throat," she whispered, her voice straining painfully just to do that much. "The caretaker didn't see anyone else."

"But did he do it?"

She broke then. Sobs racked her frame, jerking her body with each assault, and she bent nearly double, covering her face with both hands. "I…I don't know."

"Damn fool girl!" Ellen's voice sounded close to Caitlin, and she felt her head jerked up by a cruel hand in her hair.

Thomas leapt to his feet, gripping Ellen's shoulders in a firm, but gentle hold. "Let her go! I know this is tough for you to take, Ellen, but—"

"The man's so in love with you, he doesn't know which way is up! And what does it get him? You're poison to him, Caitlin O'Brien. I always said you'd ruin him someday and now you've gone and done it!"

"Ellen, I—"

"And you're bound to stand by and watch him prosecuted for this. It's gonna kill him."

"Better him than my sister, Ellen."

"It wasn't Dylan who tried to wring your neck, girl, but it should'a been. He'd have left you long ago if it hadn't been for that baby. Him and his pipe dreams that it would change things, that you two could start over. He should have left then."

But he hadn't, Caitlin whispered to herself. He hadn't, and there were eight months between the stillbirth and the car accident. Why? She swallowed hard. No one could answer that question but Dylan.

"I won't see him tried for this, Caitlin," Ellen shouted, though she was standing so close, Caitlin could see the depth of each wrinkle in her face and the deep brown of her eyes. It was a little surprising to realize how very beautiful her eyes were, even now. So dark and deep. So like Dylan's. "I won't stand for it. I'll kill you myself first!"

The older woman turned to stalk out of the room, toward the stairs.

"Ellen, wait. You can't just condemn me like this when I—" Caitlin got to her feet and followed on Ellen's heels as the old woman kept on going. "Ellen, I'm the victim here. I'm the one who—oh, for God's sake. Where are you going?"

"Upstairs. Got some calls to make. A lawyer, and then my

nephew, if they'll even let me talk to him. If not, I have a few things to say to that Barnes character." She struck off up the wide stairway, and disappeared into the hall.

Caitlin let her chin fall to her chest as all the air left her lungs. Thomas's hand on her shoulder gave little comfort. "You'll be okay, sis. I'll help you through this. I gotta say, I can't believe that Dylan…" His voice trailed off, and he shook his head. "I just can't believe it."

Caitlin was having trouble believing it herself. "Where's Lizzie?"

"The nursery. Having a nap, last time I checked."

Caitlin nodded, and gripped the banister in one hand. "I have to be with her for a little while. I need…"

"It's okay. I know."

She blinked fresh tears away as she stared up at her brother. "Don't ever forget how precious she is, Thomas." Then she turned and dragged one foot after the other, up the stairs. Part of her wanted to go to Ellen's room, to try to convince the woman that she wasn't out to destroy Dylan. But she knew it would be of little use.

She brought the baby into her room, and spread a blanket on the floor for her to lie on. Lizzie kicked her feet, and thrashed her arms, cooing and spitting and sticking out her tongue, as her wide eyes fixed first on one strange object, then another. Caitlin spread toys all around the baby, then got down on the blanket herself to play.

And as she did, shaking rattles to capture Lizzie's attention, letting the baby reach for them, seeing her huge blue eyes reflect joy and innocence and acceptance, Caitlin recalled the way Dylan had looked as he'd held Lizzie last night. Patiently, he'd paced the nursery's length, rubbing and patting her little back, snuggling her close to him. And singing.

"You wouldn't believe it, would you, Lizzie?" Cait lay on her side, her head close enough so Lizzie could catch handfuls of her aunt's hair and tug and twist it. "If you could talk, you'd swear your uncle Dylan was the most gentle man on the planet. You'd never doubt him…"

A small hand smacked against Caitlin's cheek repeatedly as Lizzie made gurgling sounds.

"…the way I have."

She sat up slowly, wrapping the baby up in her arms and holding her close. Lizzie chewed on Caitlin's chin. "It wasn't him, was it, Lizzie? It couldn't have been. And if it wasn't, then it had to be someone else. Someone else left this house last night after I did, followed me to the cemetery and…"

Her face fell, and she held Lizzie at arm's length, as the baby laughed out loud and kicked wildly. "Oh, but they couldn't have. Ellen was awake, and she said she only heard two vehicles leave, last night. First mine, and then—"

Cait blinked. "No. She *heard* two vehicles, but three drove out of here last night. She never heard me. Remember? I coasted the car all the way to the end of the driveway before I started it up, and then eased my way onto the road. No one could have heard me leave. There was someone else."

She lowered Lizzie to the blanket again. Lying beside her, with her head pillowed by a silky brown teddy bear. "Dylan is innocent," she whispered. "The question is, what can we do to prove it?"

Barnes led a team through the cemetery as soon as he'd closed the cell door on Rossi. There was something about this case that was bothering him. From day one, he'd been half-convinced Rossi was trying to kill his wife. But now that he'd locked the guy up, he wasn't so sure. He shook his head, and told himself not to lose his objectivity. It was tough, though. He wanted to protect Caitlin Rossi, and to catch the slug that was trying to hurt her more than he'd wanted anything in a long, long time.

He wanted Rossi to turn out to be innocent, because he

could see how much Caitlin wanted it. The way she felt about the guy just about glared from those green eyes of hers. He knew she'd be devastated to find out her husband was capable of killing her. Now, he was probably letting that wishful thinking cloud his judgment, because there was no evidence that Rossi was anything *but* guilty.

Still, there'd been something in Rossi's eyes when he'd begged him to put a tail on his wife, to protect her. Fear. Desperation. Sincerity. Frustration. All of it. Not a hint of cunning, or the whisper of deceit.

And that was why Barnes had dragged the forensics boys back here again. Rossi had said he heard someone running away, toward the east side of the boneyard. When Barnes thought about that, he realized that if another vehicle *had* been parked on that side, neither the victim, the suspect nor the witness would have been in a position to see it there. So he'd sent a car out to keep an eye on the Rossi house, and on Caitlin Rossi in particular. And he'd brought the crew to look for evidence of a fourth person here last night.

But after an hour of combing the place, they had little more to go on. The roadside was gravel, not a good receptacle for tire tracks. And the grass in the cemetery itself was too dense and close-cropped to pick up footprints.

Barnes was about to give up. He didn't want to believe Rossi was lying, but there was no evidence here to suggest he was telling the truth. Then one of his men yelled, and Barnes jogged toward him.

When Barnes reached him, Melbourne was picking the scrap of material from the brick wall with a pair of tweezers. He held it up for inspection, then dropped it into an evidence bag.

"What do you make of it?" Barnes asked.

Melbourne straightened his glasses, holding the bag in front of them and squinting at it as if he could read words written across the material inside. "It hasn't been here long. Two days at the most. A few hours at the least. The sun and rain would've faded some of this color if it had been out here longer. See? It's really vivid red."

"What'd it come from?"

Melbourne shrugged. "Could be just about anything. We'll run some tests on it, see if there's a hair, or a skin cell or a drop of blood, maybe sweat or saliva if we're lucky."

The square of cloth was uneven, and not more than three by four inches in size. Barnes wasn't hopeful. Then again, Rossi hadn't been wearing anything red last night. Neither had his wife, nor Stanley Crandall, the caretaker.

She woke with a start, ashamed to have been sleeping so deeply when Dylan was sitting in a jail cell somewhere. Still, she supposed she'd be able to think more clearly now than she could have before. She'd been exhausted, and from the looks of the dim sky, she'd slept several hours.

Lizzie was still snoozing peacefully. The baby had a habit of sleeping the afternoon away. Storing up her energy to keep every adult in the house up all night, Caitlin theorized.

She got up, realized she was still wearing the jeans and sweatshirt from the night before, and thought longingly of a long bath and a hot meal. She conceded to the bath, and put a clean white muslin nightgown on. She intended to go down to the kitchen, fix herself a snack and plot her next move.

She tiptoed past Lizzie, stepped quietly into the hallway and then to the stairs. She was barefoot, and made little sound as she traversed the hall, and descended the stairs. The chill house was quiet, and the living room dim. Light spilled from the library door, though it was opened only a crack. She heard muted voices, padded footsteps, a clink of ice against glass. Caitlin stopped in her tracks. Her lack of sleep these past few nights, or the past few missed meals, must be dulling her senses. She'd come down here wondering how she could prove Dylan innocent. It followed then, that someone else was guilty of trying to kill her. Of murdering Sandra. Someone in this very house. That hadn't changed with Dylan's arrest.

A chill snaked up her spine. Part of her wanted to turn and run, but she refused to heed that part. She needed to know the truth.

Slowly, Caitlin moved toward the doorway.

She heard Genevieve softly whisper, "Thomas, why? I love you, you know that."

"I just can't live with the guilt anymore, Genevieve. This is wrong. It's always been wrong."

Genevieve, assuming he'd meant guilt about cheating on his wife, Caitlin surmised, sighed loudly. "How can it be wrong, when we love each other, Thomas? When is love wrong?"

"What I did to Sandra was wrong, dammit!"

Caitlin shivered violently.

"You never meant—"

"No, Genevieve. It's over. Don't make this any harder on me than it already is. Please. Just accept it. I have to focus on Lizzie now, try to be a good father to her, try to atone—"

"You are a fool to throw me away, Thomas O'Brien!"

Genevieve exited the room, slamming the door behind her, and came face-to-face with Caitlin. Caitlin swallowed her shock, and her fear. She felt a wave of pity for Genevieve. She was so quiet, so delicate-looking. It was awful that she'd been hurt. But God, she should have known better than to involve herself with a married man.

Caitlin put a hand on Genevieve's shoulder. "I'm sorry, Genevieve. If you want to take some time off, you know, think things through, I won't mind a bit."

Genevieve dipped her head, focusing on the little red cloak draped over her arm, rather than looking Caitlin in the eye, now that Caitlin obviously knew about the affair. "That is very kind of you, *madame*."

Genevieve sniffed. "I think I would like to lie down for a while, if you don't need me."

"Go ahead. Oh, and Genevieve, if you hear Lizzie crying, would you just give me a call? I hate to leave her alone in my room, but I need to talk to my brother."

Genevieve nodded, and smiled softly. "Do not worry. I will watch over little Lizzie for you."

Caitlin watched Genevieve ascend the stairs, then faced the library door again, biting her lip. Aside from Dylan, Thomas was the one person with the most to gain by Caitlin's death. He'd inherit half of her estate, which he probably felt he was entitled to, anyway. He'd also had a motive to kill his wife: his affair with Genevieve. Besides that, it seemed pretty clear that the guilty party not only wanted Caitlin dead, but Dylan convicted of the crime. And she'd heard with her own ears her brother's words about "showing" Dylan, teaching him a lesson.

But she'd never dreamed he'd meant anything like this. Her own brother! She'd just been beginning to feel some kind of bond with him. Could he really want her dead?

She looked up at the library door again, and suppressed a shiver. Was it wise to confront him now?

She licked her lips, stiffened her resolve. She couldn't let cowardice keep her from learning the truth. Henri and Genevieve were both within shouting distance. And there was the police cruiser, passing out front every few minutes like a shark circling its next meal.

Thomas was pouring whiskey into a shot glass when she entered, and she was painfully reminded of the night she'd walked in to see Dylan holding that same bottle. She missed him, she realized slowly. Missed him, hell, she ached for him.

But first things first. "Hello, Thomas."

He turned, startled, slopping a few drops from the shot-glass onto the back of the hand that held it. "Caitlin."

She stayed a good distance away from him. She was still afraid, and not even her own mental reassurances that she was safe, dulled that fear. He wouldn't hurt her with witnesses so close, or with the police keeping such a close eye on the house.

"I think it's about time we had a talk. Don't you?" She tried to sound calm, but her voice trembled slightly.

He nodded, took a deep swig of whiskey and smacked his lips. "I'm not going to deny it. It's pretty obvious you overheard the whole thing. I've been a real bastard, Cait. I wanted so much…" He looked at the floor and shook his head.

"You wanted it all. With me dead, you'd inherit half of my money. With Dylan in jail for killing me, you'd probably end up with his share, as well."

She watched his face as she delivered her accusation. His head came up, his eyes widened and his skin paled. "You really believe all that?"

"What else am I supposed to believe?"

He frowned, shook his head. "Cait, I don't want to believe it was Dylan any more than you do, but for God's sake—"

"It wasn't him, Thomas. He wouldn't hurt me. He wouldn't hurt anybody."

"And you think *I would?*" He slugged back the rest of his drink, slammed the glass on a stand, and the sound reverberated through her nerve endings like an electric shock. "I'm your *brother!*"

"And you resent me for inheriting from our father when you didn't." She forced herself to go on, to carry this thing through and learn the truth. "You resent that I selfishly refused to share what I got from him, and to tell you the truth, I don't blame you for that." A lump leapt into her throat. "But it wasn't worth killing for, Thomas. My God, your own wife—"

"I didn't kill Sandra!"

"You thought she was me!"

"No!"

"Thomas, I just stood outside this door and heard you say you felt guilty for what you'd done to her."

He lifted his hands, palms up, and gaped, shaking his head

in confusion. "I *do* feel guilty. For having an affair. For being a lousy father to Lizzie and a worse husband. I feel guilty for what I've been planning…"

"To murder me and frame my husband and take everything we own? Is that what you've been planning, Thomas?"

His eyes turned accusatory and he lunged at her, gripping her wrists before she could back away. Her heart skidded to a stop and she prepared to cut loose with a scream that would bring someone running.

"I can't believe what I'm hearing! Dammit, Cait, all I was planning was to buy enough stock to force Dylan to make me his partner."

She blinked, and closed her gaping mouth. "Wh-what?"

Thomas eased his grip on her forearms and shook his head sadly. "Hell, I can't blame you for thinking the worst of me. I've been acting like an idiot. Blaming you for our father's rejection of me, hating you for having money when I didn't. Just like I blamed Sandra for making me marry her when she got pregnant. I felt trapped. I only wanted to get free. I didn't know how good I had it until she was gone." He lowered his eyes, turned and sunk onto the sofa as tears shimmered in them. "She deserved better than me, better than what I gave her."

Caitlin was shocked. She moved to the sofa, sat down beside her brother, touched his shoulder lightly, still uncertain. "Go on, Thomas. Explain this to me."

He sniffed, met her eyes. "Dylan only hired me because of you. He resented it, and for a long time, he never noticed I was actually doing a good job. I think he expected me to be a freeloader. I really do. I worked my butt off for him, Cait. I wanted more than I had and I was willing to pay for it."

He shook his head. "He promoted me a couple of times, sure. But never let me show him what I could really do. I thought if I bought enough stock to put me in a position of authority, he'd have to see. So I've been putting money aside, buying small chunks of stock whenever I can afford it. I knew he'd resent it at first, but I thought…hell, I don't know. I thought we'd end up working together, as equals, mutual respect and all that bull." He shook his head.

He stared into her eyes, and she felt him willing her to believe. "Cait, I was planning to divorce Sandra. I thought I wanted to be with Genevieve. I even told Genevieve about my buying the stock, and becoming Dylan's partner some day."

She didn't say a word, just sat there, wishing she could believe him.

"God, I can't believe you think I could actually try to kill you. Cait, we haven't been close in a long time. And I may have resented you and let myself become filled with bitterness and jealousy, but I never hated you. I swear it."

She wanted to believe him, but…

"If it wasn't you, Thomas…then who?"

He shook his head. "I don't know. I wish I did."

Caitlin didn't know what to believe, or whom. It was late. She wanted to be alone, to think through everything he'd told her, to come up with an alternative suspect, rather than believe one of the men she loved wanted to kill her. She just couldn't believe it of either of them. Beyond the library windows, night had fallen. Caitlin glanced out, then faced her brother. "I'm going to bed. I have a raging headache."

"For what it's worth, Cait, I don't think it was Dylan. Not really. At first, I was just too shocked to think about anything, but now—" He shook his head. "You're right. He wouldn't hurt you."

"Thanks for that, but it isn't exactly a relief. It means that the real killer is still free to try again."

She hugged her brother, felt his shoulders tremble beneath her light touch. Then she rose and walked on suddenly leaden legs out of the library. She wanted to get back upstairs to her room. She'd imposed on Genevieve long enough. The woman was heartbroken, she didn't need to watch a baby on top of all that.

But when she entered her bedroom, Lizzie wasn't there. Nor was Genevieve. Caitlin frowned for just a moment, then shrugged. Genevieve probably took her to the nursery for a fresh diaper or a clean outfit. She bent to pick up the little toys from the blanket on the floor. Then the pillows, and the blanket itself. She gathered her own discarded clothes from earlier, as well. Someone, probably Genevieve, had long since cleaned up the broken lamp. Other than that, though, the room was really in a clutter.

She frowned as she reached for the last item on the floor, and as she picked it up, she recognized Genevieve's hooded cloak. She smiled and still held it in her hands when she heard the shrill ring of the telephone on the stand beside her bed.

Thomas would get it, she thought, folding the cloak over one arm and heading for the door. But it shrilled again, and then again. Why wasn't her brother answering on the library extension?

Frowning, Caitlin picked up the receiver. "Hello?"

"Dammit, I knew you'd go back there. Why didn't you listen to me, Cait?"

"Dylan?" She was shocked, and glad to hear his voice. God, there was so much she wanted to say to him. She had to tell him that she believed in him, had to tell him that—

"Lock yourself in your room and wait for me. Don't let anyone else in. You hear me?"

"Dylan, what—"

"They found something, a scrap of red cloth at the cemetery, that proves someone else was there last night. They're releasing me. Look, it's complicated. I'll explain it all later, just do as I say. Are you in your bedroom now?"

"Yes, but—"

"Go right now and lock your door. Please, Caity."

"But Dylan, I don't under—"

"Will you try trusting me just this once, for God's sake?

You want to hear it from Barnes? It wasn't me, Cait, and you have to—"

"I kn—"

"Go and lock yourself in. Now, Cait."

"All right." She set the receiver on the stand, and turned to go to the door. Dylan was scaring her, and she wanted to know why. The urgency she heard in his voice had her hands trembling as she reached for the door, and she inadvertently let Genevieve's cloak slip to the floor. Shaking her head at her own nervousness, she bent to pick it up.

And then her blood slowed to a thick, jelled stop in her veins and her head swam. A tiny square with jagged edges gaped in the red material.

They found something, a scrap of red cloth...

"My God. She has Lizzie!"

Chapter 15

She never returned to the phone. Dylan couldn't help but fear the worst as he and Jack Barnes sped through the night.

"That red scrap of cloth has three pieces of vital evidence on it, Rossi."

Dylan had demanded a detailed explanation of the evidence that had cleared him, even as Barnes's car roared through the night away from Eden, and toward Caitlin.

"One was a hair, and the boys in the lab have already determined that it came from your wife's head. That proves that the person who left the scrap of cloth there had contact with her. The second was a microscopic droplet of blood, and the type doesn't match yours, or old man Crandall's, or Caity's. That proves the person wasn't you. There was a fourth person in the cemetery last night, Rossi."

"You said three pieces of evidence," Dylan said softly, to fill the silence with something besides this gnawing fear for Cait. "What was the third?"

"A partial fingerprint. Slightly smudged, but we might still be able to use it."

"What about the blood? Can't you do DNA testing, or something, to identify the killer?"

"That would only work if we had a suspect to compare it to. And it would take weeks, Rossi. The ball's rolling, but I'm sure as hell hoping we have the bastard behind bars long before the results come in."

"And what do we do now?"

"We make sure Caity's okay. Then we work our tails off. I'm not planning to sleep until we get to the bottom of this."

Dylan's eyes narrowed. "Why?"

Barnes shrugged. "She's special. If you haven't figured that out yet, then you need some serious help."

Caitlin tore through the corridors to the nursery, knowing already that she wouldn't find Lizzie there. From there, she moved to Ellen's room, but no one was inside.

She raced down the stairs, shrieking for Thomas, running to the library and skidding to a stop in the doorway when she saw him, lying facedown on the floor, a gaping cut in the back of his head, thick, crimson blood coating his neck. She took a single step toward him when she heard Ellen's hoarse cry. "Damned if I'll let you— No!" And then a yelp like that of a wounded animal.

Caitlin forced herself to leave Thomas there, silently praying he'd be all right, and turned to race toward the front door where Ellen's cry had originated. She held the white nightgown up to her knees as she ran.

The door yawned wide. Ellen was pulling herself to her feet, staggering forward, and a car stood running, doors open, in the driveway.

Cait caught up to Ellen, saw the way she was limping. "Ellen, are you—"

"Stop 'em! Caitlin, they've got Lizzie!"

Caitlin gasped, and looked toward the car. Henri was just getting into the front seat. In the glowing panel lights, Caitlin saw Genevieve, with a wriggling bundle on her lap. She had no idea what was going on, but it didn't matter. She launched herself toward the car, bare feet bruising as each running step landed on loose stones. She gripped the open driver's door even as Henri began to pull away, reaching to shut it as he did. She was forced down into the gravel, but her hands gripped the handle tighter. Stones tore through the nightgown, clawed her flesh as she was dragged over the driveway.

And then, abruptly, the car stopped. She heard feet crunching gravel and looked up to see Henri standing over her, and in his hand, a black, evil-looking handgun. It was over, she realized. The smell of exhaust fumes, the sounds of the engine, and of the crickets chirping in chorus would be the last things she'd ever experience.

"Get up."

She blinked and struggled to her feet, shaking all over, her gaze darting past him into the car where Genevieve sat holding Lizzie in the passenger seat. The night wind cooled her sweat-dampened face, and made the muslin gown ripple. Her knees screamed in pain where the gravel had scraped them raw.

"Go on back inside, Caitlin."

She frowned. His French accent was gone. "Where—where are you taking the baby?"

"She's gonna be just fine, long as you and your husband pay what we'll ask for her. If not…" He shrugged, leaving the implication clear in her fevered mind.

"But why?"

"After all this work, you don't expect us to walk away empty-handed, now, do you?"

She didn't understand. She had no idea what he was talking about. She only knew she couldn't let them leave here with Lizzie. She wouldn't. "Dylan won't pay for someone else's child." She shook her head hard. "He won't, I swear it. This is all useless."

"You will, though."

She shook her head. "I won't. I can't. I lost my money, all of it. I signed a new divorce agreement, leaving Dylan everything, even the house. I was going to go away, start fresh." She sought Genevieve's gaze in the car's dimly lit interior. "You heard me say I didn't want the money, or anything that was hers...mine...before."

Henri, or whoever he really was, frowned, and shot a glance toward Genevieve.

"She might be telling the truth." Genevieve's cold glare raked her. "But I doubt it."

"It's true, I swear it. Look, take me, instead. Dylan would pay to get me back."

"Nice try," Henri said. "But why would he? He only wants to get rid of you."

"No, that's not true. He'd have to pay to get me back, it would ruin his reputation if he didn't. Besides, he doesn't hate me. He wouldn't want to see me dead." She saw that they were considering her words, and she rushed on. "It won't be easy to hide with a baby. She'll be so much trouble. She's been sick, remember? So fussy. Keeping everyone awake nights, crying every couple of hours. And there are diapers and feedings, and bottles to wash. If you take me, it'll be easier. Hell, I can wait on you. Think of the irony. The mistress serving the servants. Just leave her here. I'll come with you."

Right on cue, Lizzie began to squall. She twisted and writhed in Genevieve's lap, and made enough racket to wake the dead.

The car bounded over the driveway, headlights cutting through the darkness. They illuminated a hunched form, and the car skidded to a stop. Barnes jumped out, gun in his hand. Dylan ran forward as Ellen scooped the screaming baby up from the gravel. Ellen was crying, as well, when Dylan reached her.

"Ellen, are you—"

"Fine. And so's the little one." She shook her head. "Thomas needs an ambulance, though." Barnes was instantly reaching back into the car, gripping the mike mounted to the dashboard, barking orders.

"What about Caity?" Dylan felt himself tense as he awaited the answer.

Ellen chewed her lip. "They took her, boy. Henri and Genevieve. They were trying to take off with Lizzie, and Caitlin...she stopped them." Ellen bounced the baby up and down in her arms to soothe her crying. "I never saw anything like it. She grabbed on to the car door and they dragged her right down the driveway. Then they stopped and that French-man pointed a gun at her. But she got up and started arguin' and beggin' them to leave the baby. She told 'em to take her, instead. And that's what they did."

Dylan swore, and Ellen looked at her nephew intently. "I couldn't have stopped 'em. I was wrong about Caitlin, Dylan. She's got guts like a lion's got teeth. I'm sorry."

The paramedics tended Thomas on the library floor, while Dylan paced. Thomas refused to be taken to the hospital, despite the fact that his head could use a dozen stitches. Someone had clobbered him from behind with a heavy brass lamp. He was lucky to be breathing. Barnes had set up road-blocks, but he'd grimly predicted they would do little good. He said he had a feeling these people were pros. Cold-blooded criminals who'd done this kind of thing before. Otherwise, they'd never have managed to avoid the squad car that had been patrolling the area. He had men working on that angle back at the station, comparing the facts in this case with others like it via the NCIC computer network. But finding a match would take time.

He'd also predicted the pair hadn't just taken Caitlin on a lark. They would want something, probably demand something, for her return. And he was right.

The call came at midnight. Dylan waited for Barnes's signal before picking up. He was to keep them on the line for the tracers. But they were one step ahead.

"We have her. We'll kill her. One million, Rossi. By this time tomorrow night, or she's dead."

Barnes had told Dylan what to expect, but hearing the words was like a knife in his heart. He swore he felt his blood cool to a frigid chill. The man on the phone sounded nothing like Henri. "Let me talk to her."

"Just get the money."

"Not until I hear her voice," Dylan insisted. "How do I know she's not already dead?"

"Listen close, then."

Dylan closed his eyes as Caitlin's scream filled the phone line. They'd hurt her. His fear, his sick worry changed form and solidified into rage. The bastards were going to pay for this.

"Good enough?" The voice he barely recognized came back. He could still hear Caitlin sobbing in the background.

"Don't hurt her. I'll get the money."

"Good."

Barnes was making a stretching motion with his hands. He had to keep them on the line longer. He couldn't fail Caity now. "Uh, where should I bring it?"

"I'll call you tomorrow night. Same time. And tell the cops they're wasting their time. I know how long it takes to trace a call." The loud click in his ear told Dylan they'd hung up. He shot a glance to Barnes, who only shook his head.

"Damn!"

Henri turned off the cellular phone, glanced menacingly at the stubby black stun gun in his hand and then smiled at Caitlin. She couldn't move. She lay on the tilting, swaying floor, where she'd hit hard, every muscle limp, trembling. If he came at her again with that snapping, crackling menace, she wouldn't be able to get away.

But he didn't. He flicked a button and put the thing in his shirt pocket. Then he bent, gripped her shoulders and hauled her to her feet. "Sorry. But your hubby wanted to hear your voice. Think you yelled loud enough for him? Hmm? I do. He sounded damned frantic before I hung up. Guess you were telling the truth about that much, anyway. He doesn't hate you."

She closed her eyes as he shoved her into a padded seat. She heard his footsteps retreating. He trotted up the shallow steps, through the open hatch and onto the deck. Then the hatch slammed down.

He wasn't Henri. It was as though a different being had come in and taken over Henri's body. Not only had his accent vanished, his entire manner was altered. The way he walked, moved, his facial expressions. He was no longer the devoted servant, or the hopeful admirer. He was mean, angry and ruthless.

But why? My God, why had he changed so drastically? And Genevieve. She seemed like a street thug now, instead of the sweet, timid woman Caitlin remembered. Why was she doing this? She'd worked for Caitlin's parents…

"I'm leaving, Scott. I know all about you and our maid…"

Her mother's voice, twisted with pain, came to her like a ghost from the past. Caitlin was eighteen, and had left for school, but had forgotten her American history textbook, and returned for it. Only to hear things she wasn't meant to hear. Learn things she'd never wanted to know.

"…and the other women, too. I know about all of them. I'm leaving today."

Caitlin burst into the den, where her parents were talking. Daddy stood, pacing the gray pile carpet, his face tormented. He turned abruptly at her sudden appearance. Mother remained sitting, stiff-backed, in the Queen Anne chair.

"It isn't true, Mom. Daddy would never—"

"*Caity, what are you doing here? This wasn't meant for you to—*"

"*It's a lie!*" Caitlin screamed the words at her mother. "*You're making it up—or, or, someone else is telling you things that aren't true. It's a lie, isn't it, Daddy?*"

She turned her tear-filled eyes toward her father whom she adored beyond reason. He moved toward her slowly, not easily, due to his rounded middle. "Of course it isn't true. Your mother is just upset, Cait. Go on to school now, and all this will be settled by the time you get home—"

"*No, it won't.*" Sarah O'Brien rose with liquid grace. "*You're practically an adult now, Caity. You're old enough to draw your own conclusions. I won't beg you to believe me. I'm leaving. I'll be gone when you get home today. If you want to come with me, you're welcome…*" She paused there, huge brown eyes searching Caitlin's, with no trace of hope in them. "*But I don't imagine you do.*"

"*How can you do this? How can you break up our family this way?*" Caitlin wailed and cried and threw a fit, but her mother only shook her head slowly.

"*It wasn't my decision, it was his. I have no choice about it. I love you, Caity.*"

Caitlin blinked at the sudden onslaught of memory. It was like a riptide, dragging her out to sea. There was so much going on, so much she ought to be thinking about, doing, planning. But all she could do was remember that final confrontation between her parents, feel incredible remorse over her own choice to believe her lying father. God, she'd worshiped that man.

She turned her mother's accusations over in her mind now. She knew they'd been true. She wasn't certain how she knew it or when she'd learned it. It must have been later, because she'd certainly been in denial then.

I know about you and our maid.

Genevieve had worked for them then. But so had a half-dozen other women, most of them young and attractive. And even if Caitlin had believed her father had been sleeping with one of them, she would never have suspected Genevieve. Genevieve was her friend, even though she only remained with them for a few months. She'd moved to another job shortly after the divorce. Caitlin hadn't seen her again until years later, when she'd been looking for domestic help in her own household, and Genevieve had shown up at her door with her charismatic brother in tow.

"How do I know all this?" She shook herself, shook off the lingering effects of the paralyzing jolt of electricity that had so recently hammered through her body, and tried to analyze her newfound knowledge. She didn't remember the pertinent facts in a flashback or a visual image playing in her mind, the way she did that conversation between her father and her mother. No, she just *knew*. The information simply surfaced in her mind like a buoyant object released from underwater. Suddenly, it was just there.

And what else?

She searched her mind for more of the jigsaw pieces of her past. They were there. She could *feel* them there, just out of reach. Their familiar auras reaching out to her, teasing her, luring her, taunting her. God, she wanted her life to be whole again.

But first and foremost, she needed to be sure she would *have* a life. And that meant putting her past out of her mind, and concentrating on survival in the present. Regardless of what was motivating Genevieve and Henri, the dilemma was the same. She was their prisoner, their captive, and she had serious doubts they intended for her to leave their imprisonment alive.

Especially when Dylan refused to come across with the money. Because he wouldn't pay it. He couldn't. He didn't have that much money, and there was no way he could come up with it in time. The only way Dylan could get that much cash would be to put the business up as collateral.

And that was out of the question. He'd built that company from the ground up, and he wouldn't risk losing it to save the life of a woman he hated. Oh, he'd try to get her back. Caitlin had no doubt about that. He'd have every cop and private investigator he could get on her trail. He'd agree to pay the ransom, and he'd try to get her out alive. Because he was her husband, and he seemed to take that role seriously. He was a man of honor. He wouldn't let his worst enemy die if he could do something to prevent it.

The problem was, she didn't think he could prevent it. Not this time.

And she wouldn't want him to lose his business to save her. It was too great a price to pay for a woman who'd hurt him the way she had. She wouldn't allow it.

She wanted to get away on her own, just to be sure Dylan wouldn't do something foolish. She got to her feet. They hadn't tied her up. She was only locked into the cramped living quarters of a boat. It was a small space, lined on one side with a pair of wooden cupboards, above a two-burner propane cooking center, and a minuscule sink that could have been straight out of a child's playhouse. Below that, more cupboards. On the port side, a high bunk that was now folded to lie flat to the wall. Below was a table and two bench-type seats. Toward the bow, two more bunks, and in the stern, a tiny door that led to a bathroom smaller than a bread box.

She explored the entire area in a matter of minutes. In the bathroom, no hair spray or razors she might use to defend herself. Damn. She searched the galley and found the barest food supply in the cupboards and a little more in the twenty-four-square-inch refrigerator. She checked cupboards, then the two drawers that slid open after a bit of tugging. She found a small, sharp steak knife with a serrated edge. Her fist clenched around its plastic, fake wood-grain handle.

The hatch was flung open with a loud bang that seemed to

rip through her nerves with an edge more jagged than the blade in her hand. She whirled, closing the drawer and slipping the knife into the folds of her nightgown, still holding it as inconspicuously as she could manage, just as Genevieve reached the lowest step and met her gaze with a curious, suspicious stare.

"What're you doing?"

Without the French accent, her voice wasn't sultry, it was coarse. She sounded rougher than sandpaper. "Nothing. I...I was hungry."

Genevieve's eyes narrowed, scanning the cupboards behind Caitlin. "Si'down. You eat when we do."

Caitlin nodded, and hurried back to her former chair. Genevieve passed her on her way to the cupboards, to whip them open and scan the contents. Caitlin stiffened when Genevieve opened the drawers. Would she miss the knife? God, what would she do if she knew Caitlin had taken it?

Genevieve closed the drawer at last, and turned toward Caitlin. The suspicion was gone from her eyes. She hadn't missed the knife.

"Your hubby is going to pay up. You won't be here long."

"How long?"

Genevieve shrugged. "Thirty-six hours at the outside."

"And if he doesn't get the cash?"

"He will. They always get the cash, honey. He's scared out of his mind right now. He'll come through, don't you worry."

Caitlin frowned. "You talk like you've done this before."

Rather than ashamed, she looked proud. Her chin rose a little. "That's 'cause I have."

"How many times?"

Her delicate brows rose. "You really wanna know? You talkin' kidnappings?" Caitlin nodded, feeling as if she were talking to a stranger, a street thug in tight black jeans and a skimpy purple bustier. Her accent sounded like Brooklyn. "You're the fourth."

"And all the others paid?"

"Every nickel. An' we got away clean every time. I tol' you, we're pros."

"And the other…hostages. You released them unharmed?"

Her lids lowered to half mast. "Yeah. Sure we did." She poked a hand into a high cupboard and retrieved a pack of cigarettes. She shook one loose, caught it from the pack in her lips and pulled it slowly out. She held the pack toward Caitlin, but Caitlin shook her head. Shrugging, Genevieve tossed the pack down, and twisted a knob on the stove. She turned, putting her back fully to Caitlin, and bending low to light the cigarette from the burner.

Now, Caitlin thought. Just get up, take the knife and jam it into her back. The thought made her stomach turn. She didn't move, and then Genevieve was facing her again, sucking on the filter, holding the slender white cylinder between two fingers tipped in elaborately decorated nails, and blowing the smoke slowly out.

"Why were you trying so hard to kill me?"

She wasn't aware she was going to ask the question. When it came out, it surprised her, and apparently, it surprised Genevieve, as well.

"You sure it was me? What makes you so certain it wasn't your lovin' man all along, hmm?"

"It wasn't Dylan."

Genevieve tilted her head, and shrugged. "Bigger payoff. You underground, him in jail and your brother wrapped around me like a clinging vine. We could have had it all."

"You and Henri?"

Genevieve threw back her head and laughed, a guttural, throaty sound. "It's Hank. And I'm Jen. I have about as much French in me as a two-dollar bottle of wine, Madame Rossi." She affected her old accent with the last two words, and laughed as if she hadn't had such a good joke in a long time.

Caitlin just shook her head. "That's quite a leap, from kidnapping to murder. And such a convoluted plan. What made you think it would work?"

Genevieve—Jen—narrowed her eyes and sent Caitlin a silent message.

"My God, you've done that before, too?"

She drew again on the cigarette, blew smoke rings and shrugged. "Didn't say that."

Caitlin frowned, the scope of their plotting hitting her hard. "How long have you been…" She didn't know what word to put at the end of the sentence. "Were you…even when you worked for my father?"

"Your parents' marriage was in trouble. It was all over the social grapevine."

"And those are the kinds of households you like to get into, where the marriage is in trouble?"

"You're putting words in my mouth, honey."

"And you were planning the same kind of thing with my parents?"

"I managed to get your old man in the sack when it looked like they might patch things up. It was easy to make sure she found out about it. The stupid bitch walked out without a fuss, though. Didn't demand even a nickel. That screwed things up big-time. I mean, your old man had no motive. Who'd believe he'd done it? And then the old bastard fired me before I could think of an alternate plan. He didn't want his little girl to ever know about our fun and games. God, you were blind to that sleaze-bag. Thought he made the world and everything in it just so you'd have a nice place to live, didn't you?"

Cait swallowed hard. "For a while."

"Yeah. The sweet little princess found out what a bastard her old man really was…and then she turned into a frog."

Caitlin frowned and searched the woman's face. "What do you mean by that?"

Jen shook her head, her short, slick hair not moving. "Nothin'. I wasn't around then. I'm just repeating what I heard. When I left your daddy's house, you were a nice kid. I even liked you, as much as I like anybody. When I met you later, in your own house, you were an arrogant bitch. I guess after your mother offed herself and your idol got knocked off his pedestal, you lost your innocence, hmm?"

Caitlin shook her head, eyes wide, searching inwardly to make sense of all this. "I don't know."

Jen glanced down at the glowing end of the stub she held, dropped it into the sink and rinsed it down the drain. "Yeah well, neither do I." She nodded toward the bunks in the stern. "You might as well get some sleep. Nothing's happening tonight."

Cait shook her head. "I'll never sleep."

And she didn't. She was sure they were going to kill her, anyway, when they got the ransom, no matter what they said. Jen wouldn't have admitted to so many other crimes if she planned to leave her alive to testify against them.

Jen went above and Caitlin laid on the hard little bunk, and tried not to listen to the sounds overhead, a short time later. Sounds that made her sure they were not brother and sister.

Dawn. All night they'd worked, staying in touch with the station by phone and sending files back and forth. Dylan slugged back so much coffee he was practically floating in it. He drank it mindlessly, just to have something to do with his hands.

And then he heard Barnes say softly, "We have a hit."

Dylan spun to see Barnes scanning the screen of his computer. "Tell me."

"Nine years ago, a couple name Hank and Jennifer Korbett were employed in the Garner household, in Bangor, Maine. They'd been working there for a little over a year, when Mrs. Garner was murdered. Hit and run. Her husband's car. They were in the middle of a divorce at the time. She'd been pushing for a big settlement, and that was his motive. He was tried and convicted in the death of his wife."

"But it wasn't him, was it, Barnes?"

Barnes shook his head. "Before his mother's body was cold, the surviving son, and heir to everything, Preston Garner, married Jenny Korbett, the family maid. A week later, his body was found in a ravine. All his accounts had been drained, and Jenny and Hank had disappeared. The partial print we found on that scrap of cloth belonged to Jenny Korbett, alias—"

"Genevieve Dupres," Dylan muttered.

"She's not even French. They're both from Brooklyn."

"So they've been planning to murder Cait, and pin it on me."

"Looks like," Barnes replied. "Then Jenny would marry Thomas, get him to put her name on his accounts, which by then ought to have included all of your wife's money. Then he probably would've suffered the same fate as the Garner kid."

"But it didn't work. Cait didn't die."

"Don't feel too relieved, there's no doubt in my mind that they have an alternate plan. They have a list of priors as long as my arm. Lots of cons, three kidnapping charges—Maine, Boston, Jersey. Their mugs have been on display in every post office in the Northeast. But they were both blond and from Brooklyn. No one was looking for a dark-haired pair of French siblings. They've never been brought to trial. They're wanted in eight states for various crimes. Three of them are murder charges."

"Which three?" Dylan knew just by the way Barnes's gaze fell. "The kidnappings, right? They killed their hostages, whether the ransom was paid or not, didn't they, Barnes?"

His lips tightening to a thin line, Barnes nodded once.

Chapter 16

Dylan couldn't stay at home, restless, powerless. Guilt-ridden. The thought that he'd ever believed he could be better off without Caity in his life kept haunting him. Was some greater force trying to show him exactly what hell that would be, or was it one of those cases where you got what you wished for, and regretted it for the rest of your life? It didn't matter that she didn't love him, didn't trust him, didn't want to be with him. All that mattered was that she live. She deserved to live. If he had to lose her, if he'd already lost her, he'd find a way to deal with it. But not like this. He wouldn't lose her like this.

He huddled with Detective Barnes—Jack, now—in front of his desk at the station, and together they pored over the histories of Jenny and Hank Korbett, charge by charge, case by case, hour after hour, amid the strong aromas of coffee, the ringing of phones and the tapping of fingers on keyboards.

Dylan swilled his fourth cup of strong, mudlike coffee, and

went over the list of assets Jenny had wound up with after Preston Garner's death. She'd managed to liquidate 1.5 million in stocks right after the heir's murder. An estimated 250,000 in cash, once she'd closed out all the accounts. A Mercedes and a Vette, both brand-new. A cabin cruiser, and a half-dozen pieces of art worth a cool 750 grand if she could hawk them.

"You suppose they sold all this stuff?"

"What?"

"Paintings, cars, boat. If they did, they should have been rolling in money. Why risk it all for more?"

Jack shrugged and sipped his cold coffee, grimacing. "Greed. The cars turned up in Jersey. A few of the paintings have been recovered, as well, but not all."

"And the boat?"

Jack shook his head. "Nope, not a sign of it."

Dylan's lips thinned. He closed the folder, and reached for another, hoping to find some clue that would help him get Caity out of the Korbetts' hands and back home, safe, with him.

Instead, he found only a grim trail of death behind the two, littering their path like bread crumbs. In all three kidnappings—the little girl in Cape May, New Jersey, the old man stricken with Alzheimer's they'd taken from his rich family in Bar Harbor, and the new young bride of a business tycoon in Boston—the hostages had been killed. All in the same horribly efficient manner, even though the ransom demanded had been paid. A single bullet, fired at close range, dead center of their foreheads. The thought of Caity, looking down the barrel of that gun, knowing she was about to die, gave him anger, fury that knew no bounds. He'd kill them if they hurt her. He'd kill them.

"Rossi?"

Dylan blinked and faced Barnes.

"You okay?"

He shook his head. "Far from it."

"Well, it's almost nine. You ought to talk to the bank, confirm the details of the ransom."

Dylan nodded, but his eyes strayed back to the folder on the desk. "They killed the others. The families paid and they killed them, anyway. We both know that."

"I know, Rossi. But knowing that, maybe we can strike a better deal. Get them to bring her to us, and trade even up, instead of arranging a drop."

Dylan shook his head. "You don't believe that any more than I do."

The look in Jack's cornflower blue eyes was enough to confirm it without words, but there was something else there, too. A determined stubbornness that wouldn't be banked by the fear. "We'll get her back alive."

"I wish I could be as sure of that as you are."

"I'm not sure, just damned determined. I like your wife, Rossi. She reminds me of someone…someone I knew once. I've been a cop a long time, but I've never wanted to protect a victim the way I want to protect her. And I've never wanted to collar any two-bit slug the way I want to collar these two. It's gonna happen. Count on it."

Dylan tried to believe in the light he saw in Jack Barnes's eyes, but found it difficult. He shook his head. "I don't know. It's like—" His throat closed off. "Dammit." He blinked and averted his face.

"I know what you're going through, Rossi."

"The hell you do."

A heavy hand fell on his shoulder. "My wife…I lost her two years ago. I *know.*"

Dylan looked up slowly, saw the brittle, sad smile of encouragement. "Maybe you do." He sighed, a short, shallow rasp. "Dammit, Jack, for the past two years, all I've wanted was another chance with her. I prayed and fought and groped for the old Caity, the one I loved. The one I still love. Only I gave up too soon, and when the chance finally came, I was too freaking blind and bitter to see it. Now she's gone. I had her back and didn't even know it, and now she's gone."

His eyes burned. Oddly enough, he felt no shame at that. Jack slapped his shoulder hard. "Come on, I'll drive you to the bank. We'll talk this through, brainstorm, maybe come up with something. And on the way back, we'll stop for a good solid belt, hmm? I think we both could use one."

"It isn't a belt I need, Jack. It's a miracle."

"Get up." The hands that shook her shoulders were soft, small and brutal. "Get up, Caitlin. It's time for breakfast."

Caitlin blinked reality into focus. She'd been engrossed in a dream so vivid, it was hard to believe it hadn't been real. She'd been with Dylan, on that beach in the cove, with nothing between their heated bodies but gritty sand and salt-water. And he'd told her that he loved her. That he'd always love her, no matter what.

A tight fist squeezed her heart, and the tears wrung from that organ leaked into her eyes, filling them. She shook herself, and sat up. She was still wearing her torn, dirty night-gown. The knife tucked in the waistband of her panties had made for a restless night. But she'd have slept little, anyway. Barefoot, she got up, and moved toward the table.

"Not there," Jen said, her voice sharp and too loud. "The stove's on the other side. There are eggs and cheese in the fridge. Get to it. We're starved."

She glanced at the woman, saw the hardness in her eyes and understood. She recalled her own words about the mistress serving the maid. Genevieve must have liked the idea. Seen it as poetic justice. Well, okay. She could deal with that. "Can I use the bathroom first?"

"Make it quick."

Caitlin nodded and closed herself in the tiny cubicle. She quickly searched the inside of the minuscule medicine cabinet there, but found only aspirin tablets, sun block and an anti-septic ointment. No sleeping pills. Nothing that she might slip into their damned breakfast to render them harmless while she tried to escape. She emerged frowning, disappointed, grimly certain her time on this planet was nearing its end.

She couldn't remember the last time she'd told Dylan she loved him. She'd wanted to say it when they'd made love, when he'd held her so tenderly in his arms. But she hadn't. God, why hadn't she? She might never get the chance again.

She moved to the fridge and found the eggs and the cheese. She cracked the fragile shells one by one, and dropped their contents into a bowl. Her heart sinking lower with every stroke, she stirred.

"I'm willing to put the business up as collateral."

The banker, Frederick R. Pembroke, leaned back in his chair. "You don't own the entire company, Mr. Rossi."

"Fifty-one percent is well worth what I need."

Pembroke nodded, and fingered the few threads of oiled-down, dark hair that were combed to cover the bald spot in the middle of his head. "I'm aware of that. And I'm sure the loan can be approved, but to get you this amount of cash by the end of the day will be tricky."

Dylan shot to his feet. "Listen, you pompous little twit, my wife—"

Jack gripped Dylan's arms just as he would have reached across the desk to choke the man. Pembroke had jerked backward, slamming the chair and the back of his greasy head into the wall behind him.

"Mr. Pembroke, a woman's life is at stake here. I'm willing to personally guarantee this bank that the money will be repaid, if that's what it takes, but we need the cash today."

"Or they'll kill her," Dylan said. The words were low, soft and steady. "Make no mistake, Pembroke, they'll kill her."

"Surely that's an exaggeration."

"These people are wanted in connection with several other murders," Jack said calmly. "They have nothing to lose."

"And if she dies because you refuse the money, I'll come

back here, Pembroke," Dylan told him, standing straighter, shaking Jack's restraining hands from his shoulders.

"Easy, Rossi." Jack glanced across the desk. "Can you do it or not?"

Pembroke drew a series of short breaths, his eyes darting around the office, anywhere but on Dylan's face. "I'll try. We have two other branches in nearby towns. I ought to be able to get the cash between the three."

"How soon?" Dylan wanted to walk out of here with the money right now.

Pembroke glanced at his watch. "Before closing, certainly. I'll call you when you can pick it up."

Dylan nodded, yanked a business card from his wallet and tossed it onto the desk. It had his home, office and cell numbers. "If I don't pick up, you can reach me at the police station."

He turned and stalked out of the banker's plush office. He wanted to kick something, or slam the door so hard, the bastard's false teeth would rattle. But he didn't. He stalked all the way to Jack's car, and got in.

"How 'bout that drink?" Jack asked when he slid behind the wheel.

"How 'bout a couple?"

"You want to run home first. Change, shower? You look like hell."

"Screw it. I don't really give a damn how I look right now."

Jack sighed and pulled into traffic. Two blocks down, he turned again, into the parking lot of an apartment building. Dylan had expected a bar, but said nothing. He got out and followed Jack through a foyer, to an elevator. They got off at the sixth floor, and the detective opened a door and ushered him in.

"It's a shack compared to your place, but..."

Dylan walked in, barely noticing the decor, caring even less. He heard the ice chinking into the glasses, the gurgle of liquid. He smelled the whiskey. He saw none of it, though.

He'd paused in front of a framed 8x10 color photo of a woman. A beautiful woman with shining emerald green eyes and long, wildly curling auburn hair. Her chin was pointy, rather than blunt like Caity's, and her nose was slightly larger. Her cheekbones were nowhere near as high, or regal, but there was no mistaking the similarities.

"She was tiny, too. Not short, but just…delicate, slender. I always loved that about her." Jack pressed a cool glass into Dylan's hand.

"Your wife?"

"Yeah. Holly. Perfect name, don't you think? Red and green?"

Dylan nodded. He tore his gaze away from the beautiful face and saw the stark agony in Barnes's gaze. "What happened?"

"Boating accident." He didn't elaborate.

"Here?"

Barnes shook his head. "We were visiting her family in Boston. Got plugged by a yacht full of drunken idiots driving on the wrong side, no lights. The bastards."

Dylan said nothing. Barnes tossed back a healthy slug of whiskey, licked his lips and went on. "I tried to find her. I knew she couldn't swim. Still, with the life jacket, I figured…" He closed his eyes. "It wasn't the water, though. She took a blow to the head on the way in. There wasn't a damn thing I could do for her."

"God." Dylan tilted his own glass to his lips, closing his eyes as the burn moved down his throat, spread heat in his belly. "I'm sorry, Jack." There was something tickling the fringes of his consciousness. Something Jack had said, setting little bells off in his mind, but he couldn't put his finger on it.

"Wish to hell we'd never gone to Boston that summer."

Boston.

"One of the kidnappings happened in Boston, didn't it?"

Mentally, Dylan recounted the cases, the scams, the murders. "Boston, Bar Harbor. Where was the other one? Some cape or other. Dammit, Jack, do you see the pattern?"

The detective blinked and faced Dylan, his gaze no longer blank and stark, but sharp, piercing. "The northeast?"

"The coast. They were all on the Atlantic coast. Everything since the rich couple and their son were murdered has been on the coast. And you said Hank and Jen got a boat out of that one."

Jack whistled, and his nod was quick and decisive. "Ten to one that's where they're holding her. Off the coast on that boat. You ever think of goin' into police work, Rossi?"

Dylan shook his head. "Not on your life. What do we do now?"

The storm hit with a vengeance. The wind moaned and howled around the boat, and the waves tossed it with a violence Caitlin was certain would be the end of all of them. She clung to the bunk, facedown, and tried not to feel the nausea, the dizziness, the stark fear. But she felt it all the same.

"Don't look so damned terror-stricken. We've seen worse."

Hank's words didn't even put a dent in the haze surrounding her mind. She was sick. She was scared. God, she wanted Dylan. Needed him.

Waves slapped the boat, battered it until it shuddered with the force. Thunder rolled over the sea toward them, reverberating through the wood and into her soul.

"Look, maybe we oughta take it in. Tie up somewhere till it passes."

"For God's sake, Jen—"

"It's getting worse," she said in a firm, authoritative voice. "Let's just take it in."

"We weather it. We'll be fine. We get near shore, Jen, and we might be spotted. It isn't worth the risk."

"She's sick."

Hank's gaze moved to Caitlin, and she felt him staring in disdain. "So what?"

Caitlin lurched to her feet, groping for things to hold on to as she made her way to the toilet with the floor pitching beneath her feet. She pulled the door shut and fell to her knees, retching. God, what a time to be seasick. How could she plan or maneuver to keep herself alive when she felt this badly?

When she could stand again, she found a cloth and washed her face. She reached for the door.

"Whadda you care how sick she is? It isn't like she's gonna get better."

"She could."

"Dammit, Jen—"

"She *could!* We don't have to do it that way. Not this time, Hank."

"She knows us."

"So does everybody else in that family. They don't need her to tell 'em who did this. We don't have to do it this time, Hank."

"We do if I say we do. She knows about the boat. They'd be one step ahead of us next time."

"We don't need any next time. We have enough. God, can't we just quit this crap? Settle down somewhere? Rio, like we always planned."

"No. Just a couple more jobs, and then—"

"It's always just a couple more!" The words were shrieked at him, and Caitlin stiffened when she heard the ringing slap of a hand on skin, and Jen's startled cry. "You know what I think?" She was whispering now, harshly, loudly, but the words were punctuated by sobs. "I think you like the killing. I think you enjoy it and I think you only want her dead 'cause you couldn't get her into bed. That thing with the rope and the noose in the cemetery, when you know that's how her mother

checked out—that was just to torture her. Just so you could get
your kicks. You're sick, Hank, and gettin' worse all the time."

"Think what you want, bitch. I'm callin' the shots, and you
better not forget it again. Or maybe I'll be flying to Rio
alone." There was a short pause. "We stick out the storm, and
then we kill her. Enough said."

Jen didn't answer.

"Another damned storm. I hate when it blows up like this."

Her mother's voice seemed to echo from the depths of her
memory as Caitlin huddled on the bunk again later, feigning
sleep amid the tossing waves and howling wind, waiting for
Hank to place the call, praying he'd let her talk to Dylan
before he killed her.

*"But I won't see another one. Thank God for that at least.
I'm through with storms."*

Caitlin frowned as the memory solidified in her mind.
She'd held the telephone receiver in her hand, felt the sweat
of her palm making it slick. She'd slowly gone cold all over
as it clicked and went silent. There'd been something in her
mother's voice.

Caitlin had never believed her, never accepted that what
her mother claimed had been true. Her adored father couldn't
have, wouldn't have done the things she claimed. And if he
was tightfisted after the divorce, it was only because he was
hurt. Mom had ruined their family, torn them apart. Daddy
was angry. That was all.

Still, visions of the squalor in which her mother lived had
haunted her. And now the sound of despair in her voice. She
was alone, in that little apartment. And Caitlin knew she had
to go to her, make amends, try to mend the break in their
mother/daughter bond.

And Dylan was at work, just like always. Aunt Ellen was
already in bed, asleep. So she had to face it alone. She climbed
into her modest car, a Mustang with one black door and one

blue one, and rust spots everywhere, and drove through the deluge, wipers beating helplessly, to her mother.

Caitlin blinked as the memories rushed through her. Something told her she didn't want to know any more, some secret dread that lived in her soul. But she saw all of it, anyway. The dingy hallway, the peeling wallpaper, chipped plaster. She even smelled the mildew, the damp plaster, the rotting wood, as she climbed the dim stairs and knocked on the door of her mother's apartment.

But there was no answer, so she tried the knob. And it gave, and she went inside.

And there was a creaking sound, and she turned. Her mother's body swung very slowly from the end of a rope. Her head hung limp, chin to chest, auburn hair veiling her face. Plaster dust sprinkled from the ceiling into her hair. The light fixture she'd tied the rope to wasn't going to hold much longer.

Caitlin moved forward, slowly, as if in a trance. She reached up only slightly, and touched her mother's hand. It was cool. Not cold. Not yet. The two-hour drive had taken too long. Caitlin should've called the police. She should've called a neighbor. Anything. She could have prevented this.

She backed away, her chest heaving, wanting only to find Dylan, to feel his arms holding her tight, to feel his love surround and comfort her.

But there was something else, a small white envelope with her name scrawled across the front. She picked it up, opened it, and read with tear-blurred eyes.

It was all true, Caity. Oh, I don't blame you for not believing me. I know you love your father. I loved him, too. Don't blame yourself for this. You couldn't have known. It's him. He brought me to this. And I'm only writing to warn you, baby, because they're all the same. No matter how much they claim to love you at first, in the end it's always the same. I see the signs already, for you, my poor, trusting Caity. The late hours, the missed dinners, the nights he doesn't come home at all. He'll take everything you have to give him, Caity, and then you'll end up just like me. Alone. And in too much pain for a human to bear. You'll see.

Prepare yourself, Caity. Don't depend on him for your happiness. Find a way to make your own. Don't give your entire soul to him the way I did to your father. He'll only throw it away. Please, don't let this happen to you.

Don't trust that man with your heart.

The letter hadn't been signed. But it had stamped itself on her heart. And in the morning, when Dylan had returned home after a long night at the office, she found she no longer craved the feel of the comfort his arms would offer. She never even told him about her midnight trip, or that she'd found her mother's body. Or about the note.

Because from that day on, it had become fairly obvious that her mother had been right. The late hours, the all-nighters. He was lying to her. She knew it, and she withdrew from him as much as she could manage. And the coldness she gave began to filter back to her, and the distance between them grew.

And then Daddy died, she thought in silence, and I had his money to cling to instead of my husband. Oh, God, how could I have been so stupid?

"Hank, it's twelve-thirty."

"I know what time it is. I want the bastard to squirm a little before I talk to him. You got a problem with that?"

Cait opened her eyes in time to see Jen shake her head quickly.

"You know, bitch, you're starting to be more trouble than you're worth."

Chapter 17

"They're late." Dylan slammed a fist into the wall beside the window. He'd been staring pensively into the storm-ravaged night, conjuring images of a splintered ship, of Caity's slender hands clinging to a jagged bit of wood until she couldn't hang on any longer. Of her face, pale and nearly lifeless, slipping away beneath the angry sea.

He forced the images away and whirled on Jack. "What the hell does it mean?"

"It means they want to make you crazy. Looks like it's working, isn't it, Rossi?"

"Damn straight it is."

Thomas paced. He'd been pacing for an hour now, and it didn't look as if he planned to stop anytime soon. His path was precise and repetitive and it was driving Dylan nuts.

"Calm down, Rossi. We have their coordinates. They're anchored less that ten minutes out. The Coast Guard's ready to move out the second this storm breaks, and when Hank calls, you're going to buy us enough time to last that long."

Ellen came in, carrying a pot of fresh coffee. She scuffed over the tiled floor looking weary, her housecoat floating just above her stretchy slippers. Jack held up his cup, and Ellen filled it. "Any word yet?"

"Nothing. This brew of yours sure puts mine to sha—" He broke off as the telephone bleated like a lost lamb calling for its mother.

Thomas jerked as if electrocuted, and finally stood in one spot. Dylan lurched for the phone, jerking it out of its cradle hard enough to hurt his arm.

"You have the money?"

"Yes. All of it."

"Very good. Now listen. Here's what I want you to do—"

"No, Hank. You listen. I know who you are, and I know what happened to your last three hostages. There's no way in hell I'm dropping this money anywhere, knowing you'll kill her, anyway."

"You don't have much choice, Rossi."

"I have one choice. I'll hang this phone up here and now. I'm not going to pay you to kill my wife."

There was a long moment of tense silence, and Dylan was terrified Hank would slam the phone down in his ear. Finally, his strange voice came back. "Talk."

Dylan's eyes met Jack's steady gaze. Jack shoved a scrap of paper at him. *Get them out of the water.*

"I want you to meet me…in the parking garage below my offices in Eden. And I want you to bring Caitlin. If I don't see her there, alive and well, then the deal's off. You hear me? We'll trade then. The money for Caity. You can take the cash and go, I won't try to stop you just as long as she's all right."

"Sounds like you have this all figured out."

Dylan licked his lips, swallowed the sand in his throat. "Unless you've already…" He couldn't say it. And he couldn't demand to talk to her, because he was afraid Hank would hurt her again. Make her scream in pain as he'd done last time.

"She's still alive." Hank muttered something, but had his hand over the mouthpiece, from the sound of it. When he came back, Dylan's hopes plummeted. "No deal. Forget it, Rossi. You can do this my way, or I'll off her as soon as I hang up the phone. What's it gonna be?"

"If you don't want to meet there, pick your own place. It doesn't matter where, as long as she's with you." Dylan felt desperation making his palms itch, his hands sweat.

"Bring the money to the cliffs, at dawn. I'll be watching you, so don't bring any cops with you. The first badge I see will be your wife's death warrant. Leave it in that little hollow the tide's made in the stone. You know where I mean?"

"Yes."

"Good. After I have it, after I've counted it, and I'm well out of reach, I'll call and tell you where to find your lady. All right?"

"No, it's not all right, you bastard. How do I know you won't kill her, anyway?"

"You don't. You only know that if the money isn't there, I will definitely kill her. Sweet dreams, Rossi."

He hung up. Dylan growled deep in his throat, tore the phone from the table and smashed it onto the floor. Pieces flew in a hundred directions.

"My God," Thomas muttered.

"They're gonna kill her. Dammit, Jack, they're gonna do it. We have to move now."

"Rossi, the storm—"

"They're out in it. They're still afloat. Dammit, Jack, we can't wait. You know it as well as I do. We have their location. It's time to move in. You can either come with me or I'll go by myself, but I'm going out there."

Hank slung the phone across the table, and rubbed his hands together. "He'll do it. He'll pay. I could hear the fear in his voice. He's already figured it out, you know. He knows about the others. Practically begged me not to…" His voice trailed off, but he inclined his head toward Caitlin.

Jen looked at the floor. "Then don't. We don't have to—"

"We don't need her anymore. The money will be waiting in the morning, and we can take it and go. We don't need her for a damn thing."

"Hank—"

He pulled out his gun, and turned toward the bunk to waggle it at Caitlin. "Come on. We're going up on deck. Get some air."

"No…please, I—"

"Hank, stop it! I've had it with your sick games. I can't do it anymore."

He stood stock-still for a long moment. Caitlin clung to the knife hidden in the waistband of her panties, trembling inside because she knew the time had come and she was sure she wouldn't survive this.

Hank turned to face Jen. "So it's over, is it? You can't do it anymore?"

"I just…I hate the killing. I hate it, Hank. I can't—Hank?"

His arm lifted, and without a second's hesitation, he pulled the trigger. The blast was deafening in the closed-in area. Jen's head slammed backward as if she'd been punched, and then she was on the floor. Caitlin lunged from the bed, no longer thinking her actions through as terror took over. She would be next, she knew. She lifted the knife over her head, and brought it down in a deadly arc. The blade sunk into flesh, scraped against bone, and Hank twisted away from her with the steak knife embedded between his shoulder blades, as the gun clattered to the floor.

"You filthy little bitch!" He reached behind him in a feeble attempt to pull the knife free, but couldn't do it. "You're dead…"

Cait dodged his long reach, her gaze darting from the woman on the floor with the small round hole in her forehead and the unseeing stare in her slowly glazing eyes, and the widening pool of dark red spreading beneath her, to the closed hatch at the top of the steps. She ran toward it, flung it open and emerged into the darkness. Sheets of icy water lashed her body, tore at her face, carried by brutal winds. Waves slammed the boat, rocking it crazily.

There was nowhere to go. She glanced frantically behind her, to see Hank making his way up the steps, hunched over, his white T-shirt soaked in blood, the small woodlike handle protruding from his back. She reached for the hatch, and as she did, he brought up one hand. God, he had the gun again.

The shot echoed through her psyche as she slammed the hatch. Pain sliced into her midriff like a white-hot iron. Falling to the side, she grappled with the latches, hooking them to keep him where he was. Then she dragged herself away, toward the rail, her hand pressed to her side.

She felt the warmth of the blood, saw its dark stain spreading over the nightgown, felt it running down her body, coating one leg as it soaked through the muslin, dripping to the deck. She was going to die.

She clung to the rail, leaning out over the rioting sea as if in search of some trace of hope. Something. Someone.

Dylan.

A muffled crash brought her head around. Then another, and the hatch jumped from the force of it. Then another. He was battering the door with something. It wouldn't hold long. God, what could she do?

Again he hit the door, and again. The wood splintered. She cringed against the rail, moving backward farther from him, knowing there was no shelter, nowhere to hide.

One more crash and the hatch was swinging open. Panting, cursing, Hank emerged. He looked around as the vicious wind pummeled him. He couldn't see her. She crouched in the shadows near the bow, watching, water streaming over her, waves reaching for her as if to pull her into their frigid embrace.

Hank started forward, lifting the gun, his gaze narrow, searching, murderous. He'd find her sooner or later. And then he'd kill her.

Caitlin's hands clenched into fists, one against her bleeding side, the other on the watery deck. She bumped against something. A flotation device attached to the side. Her fingers fumbled to free it, careful not to make a sound. When she had the thing loose, she gripped it in shaking hands, whispered a prayer and threw it toward the starboard side.

The instant the ring landed, Hank fired a shot. She saw the flare of the gun in the inky, watery night. Silently, she crept backward, back against the rail, curving along the port side until she bumped another ring. She threw it, as well, drawing another shot.

"That's four," she whispered under cover of the wind. She'd had a good look at the gun. A better look than she'd ever wanted. A big revolver. And she assumed that meant it only held six bullets. "Two more. God, let me find two more." She scurried backward again, her side pulsing with pain, shivering from the cold wind and the brutal rain. He was coming toward her. She wasn't moving fast enough.

Turning, she gripped the rail and pulled herself upright. Clinging to it, she walked, but something hard tripped her and she fell facefirst onto the soaking deck. A shot rang out at the instant of impact, but she didn't think it had hit her. A swell smashed into the boat, lapping over onto the deck, dumping all over her body before fleeing back into the sea. She heard him coming closer, and dragged herself away. But she couldn't keep this up. The blood leaving her body so rapidly was weakening her, making her dizzy. Her movements slowed, and grew more clumsy and noisy with every inch of progress she made. And her killer was closing in.

"All right, hit the spotlight!"

The sudden illumination of the small boat just ahead

caught Dylan completely off guard. He hadn't even known it was there. The Coast Guard cutter's crew knew it, though.

Dylan stood in the bow, wearing a dark blue rain slicker with the hood thrown back, heedless of the water cascading over his face, running down his neck, soaking his hair. Thomas stood beside him. He squinted in concentration as the spotlight swept over the deck of the smaller boat. Then Dylan saw her, lying facedown on the deck, and he saw Hank, lifting a gun, pointing at the woman the light had just illuminated for him.

Dylan's agonized scream pierced the night, even above Thomas's coarse cry, and the bullhorn-enhanced voice that ordered Hank to drop the weapon or be shot. But Hank didn't, and as the cutter charged the boat as if to split it in half, a shot rang out. Dylan wasn't sure if it came from Hank's gun or one of the officers. He feared the worst, because Hank didn't falter, or collapse, or even drop his gun. He looked at it, then tucked it into his waistband and advanced on Caitlin.

Dylan's heart leapt when he saw her move. She gripped the rail and pulled herself to her feet. She staggered forward, and the spotlight danced on the blood-soaked nightgown, as Hank grabbed her.

"Shoot the bastard!" Dylan shouted, but no shots rang out. They couldn't risk hitting Caitlin. Hank held her from behind. He whirled her around in a slow-motion dance even as he was ordered to let her go.

Dylan gaped in horror as he watched Caitlin being wrenched off her feet, then cried out in stark agony as her body hurtled over the rail and into the angry sea. Hank pulled out the gun again, lifted it toward the cutter and then his body jerked like a marionette on a twitching string, as countless rounds hammered into him. Slowly, he sank to his knees.

Dylan didn't know if he sank any farther, because he was ripping off the slicker he wore, and diving through the space between the deck and the raging sea below.

He heard Jack shouting his name just before his body knifed

into the angry waters. He stroked under the surface, propelling himself onward with every ounce of power he possessed. When he broke the surface, saltwater streaming down his face, into his eyes, he was near the smaller boat. He looked around him, seeing only swelling whitecaps, pelting rain, darkness.

"Caity!" He tread water, scanning the sea in all directions. "Caity, where are you?"

The spotlight moved until he was caught in its glow, then swept slowly past him, searching the water for her. Dylan followed it, stroking swiftly, pausing at intervals to search. He had to find her. She couldn't die. He couldn't lose her. Not again. It would kill him.

He heard the difference in the sounds of sluicing water, and turned to see the lifeboat that was fighting its way toward him. As it drew nearer, he recognized the man in the bow.

Jack leaned out, over the water, pointing, shouting. "Near the stern, Rossi. Over your left shoulder!"

Dylan turned and swam in that direction, but he didn't see her. The swells blocked his view of anything, being down in the water. "She's going down!" Jack roared. "Get that light on her! Can't this thing move—dammit, Rossi…"

Dylan crested a huge swell just in time to see her limp hand let go of the rope it had been clutching, and disappear beneath the black water.

"No!" He drew a deep breath and dove under, angling toward her, and seconds later, his outstretched hands bumped something soft and limp, something that was sinking past them, and they gripped, clung, lifted. He pulled her to his chest as his feet propelled them upward. When he broke the surface, dragging air into his burning lungs, it was with Caitlin crushed to his chest as he held her head out of reach of the angry waters.

He searched her face, pale, milky white in the harsh and erratic glow of the spotlights. Her eyes were closed, her lips, blue-tinted. Strands of her wet hair, dark with seawater, stuck to her face and neck, and she remained motionless, perfectly limp in his arms.

Frantically, he pushed his forefingers to her throat in search of a pulse. But he couldn't be certain the hammering in his fingertips came from the rush of her blood, or the current of his own. He brought her face to his with one hand, fighting to keep them both afloat with the other. He covered her lips with his open mouth, parting them with his tongue. He blew life into her again and again, praying desperately for a response, dying a little with each second that passed without one.

The shouts of men, Jack's louder than any other, grew louder in those nightmarish seconds, and then there were hands groping, and a pair of other bodies in the water. Caitlin was lifted by the three men in the water. Jack and Thomas pulled her gently into the lifeboat, and by the time Dylan hauled himself over the side, the cop was already kneeling beside her, pumping her heart with two hands, counting aloud, blowing air into her lungs. And crying. As he worked, twin rivers formed on Jack's face, and he didn't even try to swipe them away. Maybe he wasn't even aware of them.

He worked frantically, and when Thomas, rain-soaked and utterly silent, moved forward to assist him, Jack waved him away with a short bark of a command.

The lifeboat headed back toward the cutter, slicing the rolling sea. Dylan slumped down beside his still, pale wife. He clutched one of her hands in both of his as a puddle formed around him. "Don't die, Caity. Don't leave me like this."

Thomas sat near her, too, but only stared at her, as though he couldn't believe what he was seeing.

Jack sat back on his heels, his fingers pressing into the soft skin of her throat, his eyes intent. Then he looked across her body, and met Dylan's desperate gaze. "There's a pulse." The words were whispered so softly, Dylan wasn't sure he'd actually heard them. But then Jack cracked a wavering smile and said it again, louder. "There's a pulse!"

She drew a ragged, hoarse breath then, one loud enough for them both to hear. Dylan shook his head in silent wonder. Thomas bent until his head lay flat to Caitlin's chest, to hear her heart for himself. Jack blinked rapidly, seemingly aware all at once of his tear-stained face. He averted his gaze and barked at the men to get their butts into overdrive. Someone began packing the wound at her side, and the lifeboat picked up speed.

She was warm. Wet, but warm. And vaguely aware of motion, as if she were being carried at a high rate of speed by a vehicle that repeatedly *bumped.*

She opened her eyes. Dylan was pacing the little room. Thomas was sitting right at the bedside, and it took her a moment to connect the warm pressure on her hand with the fact that he was holding it in his.

He squeezed it suddenly tighter, looking at her face, and she winced.

"It's okay," he soothed. "We'll be at the hospital soon."

"Oh, God, not again."

Her voice seemed to have magically zapped Dylan from where she'd first glimpsed him, to her opposite side. She turned when he leaned over, gripping her shoulders so firmly, it hurt.

"You're awake. Caity, are you all right? How do you feel?" His dark eyes scanned hers with more fear than she'd ever seen in them.

"I'm hurting," she whispered.

His eyes fell closed and his lips thinned.

"Thomas is crushing my hand to sawdust, and your fingers are digging pits in my shoulders." Both grips immediately eased, and Dylan's eyes flew open. "You guys don't have to hold on so tight. I'm not going anywhere."

Dylan sat gingerly on the edge of the bed. His hands slid beneath her shoulders, and he lifted her gently, slowly, until her head was cradled on his chest, his fingers gently threading through her hair. "Damn straight, you're not going anywhere, baby."

She brought her arms around him, and held him as tightly as her pitiful amount of strength would allow. "I have so much to tell you."

"Maybe…maybe I ought to leave—"

"No, Thomas. You need to hear this, too." She released Dylan, though reluctantly, and slid herself higher on the bed, stopping in midmotion at the stabbing pain in her side. The gunshot wound. She'd forgotten. Dylan stacked pillows behind her and eased her upper body onto them. His touch was so tender, so careful, it nearly brought tears to her eyes.

Thomas touched her face. "You're pale."

"Lost a lot of blood," Dylan added.

"I'm fine. My side aches like hell, but—"

"You were shot," Thomas explained.

"I know I was shot. You think I'd forget something like that?" She made the words teasing. "What about Henri…I mean, Hank?"

"Dead."

She closed her eyes and shook her head. "Genevieve, too. He shot her. They've done this before, you know—"

"I know, honey. I know. Jack Barnes filled me in. But all of that is over now. It's over. All I'm worried about now is you."

She lifted a hand to his face. "Don't be. I'm going to be fine, I can feel it. And…and I remember now."

Dylan's brows rose. Thomas leaned forward. "Your memory is back? All of it?"

She smiled at her brother. "Most of it. There are less gaps, and I think they'll get smaller as time goes on. But even if they don't, it doesn't matter. I know what I need to know. I know why I became what I was, why I treated you—" she looked from Thomas to Dylan "—both of you, the way I did."

Thomas nodded. "I already know. It was because of our father." His face tightened as he spoke. His eyes filled with pain, and anger. "You worshiped him, Cait. When you were finally forced to realize that everything Mom said about him was true, you were so disillusioned, you couldn't trust anyone again. Especially not men."

"That's a lot of it, but not all of it." She closed her eyes as the horrible memory threatened to engulf her as it had before. "That night, when our mother…" She shook her head. "She'd called me, and sounded so strange that I was worried, so I drove over there."

She opened her eyes to see Dylan's widen with concern. "It was storming, and you were at the office. I went alone. And when I got there, she was…it was already…done."

"*You* found your mother?"

"Hanging from the ceiling," she finished for him. "And right at her feet, there was a note with my name on it. A note telling me that all men were like my father, and that if I wasn't careful, I'd end up alone, just like her. She said that you'd start spending more and more time away from home, with work as your excuse…"

"And I'd already started doing just that," Dylan whispered. "But Caity, it *was* work. I swear it to you—"

"Shh. I know that…now. Then, I…" She grasped his hand. "We were so new, Dylan. I was still insecure, and you were so wrapped up in the business. I guess I started to believe her."

"And I knew you were keeping something from me. I sensed the walls you were putting between us, and I retreated even more."

She nodded, and turned toward her brother. "I wasn't right, Thomas. My mind just…*wasn't right*. Seeing Mom like that did something to me. It was like I started clinging to the money and the things it could buy, because it was the only thing I trusted, the only thing I dared to hold on to. Can you understand that?"

He nodded. "It's okay, sis. Honestly, I was an idiot to let the inheritance come between us—"

"I was the one who let it come between us. But that's over now. Everything I have, I want to share with you. It's only right, the way Daddy should have done it in the first place."

Thomas's face clouded. "He never really cared about me. I don't want anything that was his. I might have resented that he left it all to you, but I never wanted it. Can *you* understand *that?*"

She bit her lower lip, thinking. "Then it's Lizzie's. I'll put your share into a trust fund for her. Is that an acceptable solution?"

He smiled and nodded. "As long as you'll stay in her life…hers and mine. You're a lot more important to her…to both of us…than your money is."

She leaned forward and hugged him, tears blurring her vision. "My brother…I love you, Thomas."

"Me, too," he returned, hugging her back a little too hard. When he straightened, he brushed at his eyes with his knuckles. "*Now* I'll get out. You two need some time."

She met Dylan's gaze and held it as Thomas left them alone. "I'm sorry," she said softly.

"For what?" He seemed truly puzzled.

"Not loving you enough, not trusting you enough back then. If I'd come to you, told you what I was going through… God, all of this could've been so different."

"It doesn't matter."

She bit her lips, her eyes filling. "Yes, it does. Because you loved me once. I remember that, too, and I remember how wonderful it made me feel. But I ruined that love with my fears and distrust. I killed it, and now, you can't bring it back, even though I love you with everything in me."

"You do?"

She searched his face, misery gripping her heart. "I do. More, even, than I did then. It's not a little-girl love anymore, Dylan. It's real, and deep, and old, and ageless. And even if we have to be apart…" Her words stopped on a sob.

"Caity, I—"

"No, let me finish because this might be important, later. I hope…those precious times we had together…I hope there's a baby. And not because I want to replace the one I lost, or because I want to try to use it to cling to you. But because I want at least one part of you that I will always have near me. Your child, and I'd give it all the love I have for you inside…because it has to go somewhere. There's too much of it to hold back. And I—"

"Caity, let a guy get a word in, will you?"

She went quiet, sat utterly still while his fingers slipped into her hair, lifted it away from her head, sifted it. "I hope you have a baby, too."

"You do?"

He nodded. "But don't be too disappointed if you're not pregnant. Because if it didn't happen last time, it will next time, or the time after that, or…" He smiled down at her. "You get the idea. Because I'm not letting you go, Caity O'Brien Rossi. I love you. I never really stopped, that's why it hurt so much to think you didn't love me back."

She closed her eyes as all the air left her lungs and the weight of the world seemed suddenly to lift from her shoulders. "Say it again, Dylan."

"I love you, Caity. I always will. No matter what."

* * * * *

REGARDING REMY

USA TODAY Bestselling Author

Marilyn Pappano

MARILYN PAPPANO

has spent most of her life growing into the person she was meant to be, but she isn't there yet. She's been blessed with family—her husband, their son, his lovely wife and a grandson who is almost certainly the most beautiful and talented baby in the world—and friends, along with a writing career that's made her one of the luckiest people around. Her passions, besides those already listed, include the pack of wild dogs who make their home in her house, fighting the good fight against the weeds that make up her yard, killing the creepy crawlies that slither out of those weeds and, of course, anything having to do with books.

Prologue

In his twelve years as an FBI agent, Remy Sinclair had lived a charmed life, but on a chilly New Orleans Saturday night, it almost came to an end. Lying facedown on the ground, he felt his clothing grow damp. From the puddles that dotted the ground? he wondered. Or from blood?

He knew he'd been hit, had been hit bad. He'd heard Michael's shout and Valery's scream…. Funny. Michael was part of his backup, but his cousin wasn't supposed to be here. She was supposed to be safe and under armed guard back at Michael's apartment. She wasn't supposed to see this, wasn't supposed.

Oh, God, the pain was so intense, burning and tearing, that it was hard to sort out exactly where it was coming from. His arm, he thought, and his leg and chest. The Kevlar fibers of his bulletproof vest had protected his chest…unless the bullet had been armor-piercing. But wouldn't he be hurting a hell of a lot worse if it had pierced the vest? Or was it even possible to hurt much worse?

He didn't want to find out.

He shifted, just a slight tensing of his muscles, and gritted his teeth on a curse. Oh, hell, yeah, his leg had been hit. It was useless. The only way he was going anywhere was on a stretcher. Please let it be an ambulance stretcher, he silently prayed, and not the coroner's. There were arteries in the leg, weren't there? A man could bleed to death getting shot there, couldn't he? Oh, God, he didn't want to die here. He didn't want to get Falcone badly enough to die for him. He didn't want to leave Michael…Smith…Valery…his parents…

The sounds around him—a few last gunshots, shouted commands, the clatter of metal against concrete—faded, came back, faded again. He hurt so badly that his throat clogged with tears. Every breath was painful, every sensation agony, every nerve raw. Maybe Falcone's men *had* been using armor-piercing ammo. Maybe that was why he couldn't breathe.

Maybe he was dying.

No, damn it. He wouldn't die. He couldn't. There was too much left to do. He had to see Falcone in prison. To make up the last fifteen years with Valery. To resolve the problems between him and his parents. God, there were so many things he'd never done. He had never fallen in love, had never gotten married, had never settled down and had kids. He had always thought there would be plenty of time for that later.

But maybe there wouldn't be.

Maybe not now.

"Remy!"

The voice sounded distant, although he sensed it came from somewhere nearby. Forcing his eyes open, he saw that he was right. Michael was kneeling beside him, bent low to see his face in the dim light—and damn it, yes, that was Valery right behind him.

Michael reached out and touched him, Remy knew, but he couldn't feel it. There was too much pain.

"The ambulance is on its way. You're going to be all right."

Now Michael had his hand. Remy could see it, could feel the tremors—his own? Or his friend's? This had to be bad for Michael—a replay of the night nearly a year ago when his partner had been killed—and he tried to reassure him. "I'm okay," he whispered, the effort to speak making his chest hurt even more. He even managed a faint grin. "I guess I'm slowing down a bit."

"Don't worry about it. Just be quiet until the ambulance gets here."

"Val… Tell Mom—" He broke off and squeezed his eyes shut on a new wave of pain.

Valery was crying. It was Michael who answered. "You'll have plenty of time to talk to her yourself. I'll call your folks as soon as we get to the hospital." He gripped his hand tighter. "You're going to be all right, Remy. Damn it, you're going to be all right."

The fierceness of his tone brought Remy another faint smile. Who was he trying to convince? Remy…or himself?

Far off in the distance he heard sirens. He wished he could roll over, wished he could ask Michael to check his vest, to make sure that the slug was embedded in the Kevlar and not in his chest, but he couldn't find the breath to give voice to the request. He couldn't find the strength to withstand the pain of movement.

All he could do was hold on tight to Michael's hand and pray.

Oh, God, yes, he could pray.

Chapter 1

It was funny how quickly things could change.

Only this morning Susannah Duncan had awakened in her own slightly lumpy bed in the slightly shabby apartment she shared with her brother, and tonight she was going to sleep in an elegantly beautiful, straight out of *Gone with the Wind* Southern mansion.

Only last week she had been a perfectly average, perfectly unremarkable woman, a nurse whose life was noticeably lacking in many things but not decency, pride or honor. Today there was nothing average or unremarkable about her. Nothing decent or proud. Nothing honorable.

Funny.

But she felt no urge to laugh.

She might never laugh again.

She stood underneath a live oak so massive that a number of its limbs required man-made support where their sheer weight pulled them back toward the ground. She knew how that must feel to the tree. Sometimes she thought *she* would bend and break under the weight of her own burdens. Her guilt. Her shame.

Resting her arms on one thick branch that dipped low, she cushioned her chin on her hands and studied the house before her. Belle Ste. Claire. The name was beautiful, the house even more so. It was Greek Revival in style, white, with eight square columns on each side and across the front, with forest green doors and shutters, a herringbone-patterned brick gallery encircling the first floor and a matching balcony upstairs painted pale gray on the floor and paler blue on the ceiling.

It had been in the Sinclair family for nearly two hundred years, had been built by the first Sinclair to come to Louisiana from France. It faced the Mississippi River, where that Sinclair and those who followed had built their fortunes in shipping and sugarcane. They weren't in the shipping industry any longer—or sugar, either, for that matter—and hadn't been in this century, but they still held their fortunes. Generations of prudent investments had seen to that.

She had driven up to Belle Ste. Claire this morning with Valery Navarre. Although a native of New Orleans, Valery had spent much of her life at this gracious old home halfway between New Orleans and Baton Rouge—had lived nine years of it here. She loved the place and had been more than willing to share her memories and knowledge of it. It had taken only a few questions from Susannah to keep the conversation flowing for miles. By the time Valery had realized that they'd talked about nothing but Belle Ste. Claire and Belclaire, the tiny nearby town named for it, they were only a few miles from their destination. She had sheepishly apologized, had lamented the loss of an opportunity to get to know Susannah better.

Which was exactly what Susannah had wanted. She had enough to do in her four weeks here. Making friends wasn't part of her job description. It was a complication she couldn't afford.

With a sudden shiver, she realized that the sun was setting

on the far side of the river. It was time to go inside. Time to start dinner. Time to return to work.

It was time to face Remy Sinclair again.

Straightening, she ducked under the branch and started toward the gallery. The grounds spread for acres in all directions—yellowing grass, flower and shrub beds, plantings of fragrant vines, and all of it shadowed by hundred-foot-tall pines, magnolias and giant live oaks. The house sat square in the center, strong for all its grace, built to last an eternity. It had provided shelter and comfort for two hundred years and, with a little care, would continue to do so for the next two hundred.

And right now it was providing shelter to Remy Sinclair, the man who had hired her as his nurse, cook and driver for the next month. The man who was her only reason for being there. The man who was the key to her, and her brother's, future.

Thoughts of her brother—named Lewis for their father, but called Skip since he was a baby—and his future, if he even had one, brought her another chill, one that settled way down inside her, one that she feared she would never be completely free of. She hadn't seen him in nearly a week, not since she'd gotten a call from some lawyer who'd told her about a job she was going to apply for—who had told her in chilling detail what would happen to Skip if she didn't get it. Three months ago, fresh from Nebraska and naive as hell, she would have found the call totally unbelievable, would have shrugged it off as some prank in terribly bad taste.

But three months ago she hadn't known the extent of the trouble Skip had gotten himself into.

Now she knew, and the lawyer had made it perfectly clear exactly what she had to do to get him out of it. It wouldn't be such a hardship, he had told her. Belclaire was a lovely little town, Belle Ste. Claire a beautiful house. The salary was generous for only four weeks' work. It would be a nice break from the stress of her job as an emergency room nurse, a nice break from the city and from worrying over her brother. *He* would take responsibility for her brother for the next few weeks, he had ominously promised.

No, living here and working for a recuperating FBI agent wouldn't be such a hardship, she agreed silently, bleakly, as she climbed the seven steps to the gallery.

It only meant selling her soul.

And that wasn't such a high price, was it? Not when she would be getting her brother's life in return.

And so she had applied for the position, and she had gotten it. If only Remy had refused to hire her. If only he had looked at her the way her ex-husband had, the way other men often had, and found her lacking. Then she could have called the lawyer, could have said, "I did my best, but it wasn't enough." Surely, if he knew anything at all about her, he would have believed her. Never being enough—pretty enough, smart enough, ambitious enough, talented enough—had been the story of her life. Surely he wouldn't have allowed any harm to come to Skip when she had *tried* to comply with his orders. Surely he wouldn't have punished her brother for her failure.

But Remy *had* hired her. After interviewing a half dozen other nurses, he had asked her a few questions, then offered her the job, just like that. She had never gotten any job so easily.

She had never needed any job so desperately.

She had never wanted to be rejected so desperately.

The steps she had climbed led straight to ornate double doors, and she stood there a moment. Generations of Sinclairs had greeted their guests at this formal entrance. Standing there now in the quiet dusk, she could easily imagine herself into the past, watching carriages turn in the gate down by the river, passing between brick columns and along the shell driveway to discharge their passengers at the foot of these steps. It all would have been very genteel, very gracious, very Southern.

But she no more would have belonged here at any time in

the past than she did today…except possibly during the Civil War, she mused, when traitors and betrayers had insinuated themselves into all sorts of places where they had no rights.

The guilt she'd been living with the past week settled heavier on her shoulders. Betraying the trust placed in her and endangering the life of a patient under her care—that was what Skip and his problems had brought her to. God help her.

God forgive her.

Turning abruptly, she started around the house to the side entrance near where her car was parked. More than an hour had passed since Remy had fallen asleep on the sofa; if he wasn't awake yet, he likely would be soon. She should have stayed inside, close at hand, but she'd felt the need to be up and about. She had needed a moment's fresh air. A moment's escape.

She had needed a moment away from him.

She opened the screen door, then the door, and closed them both quietly behind her. With any luck she could slip past the open door of the parlor where she'd left Remy. With any luck she could delay further contact with him until it was absolutely necessary. She could—

"Susannah."

She started guiltily, her muscles tightening, her face flushing. Forcing in a deep breath, she turned toward the voice, toward the softly lit parlor.

He was standing beside the sofa, leaning on his crutches in exactly the way he'd been shown not to. He hadn't been awake long—he still had a childlike, drowsy air about him. She wondered if he had called her, if he had been annoyed that she hadn't been available to cater to his needs. She regretted spending the last hour outside, regretted that she hadn't started dinner sooner, that she hadn't taken advantage of his nap to unpack his bags. She should be better at this servant role, she silently chastised herself. After all, she'd played it often enough for her father and Skip, especially after her mother's death, and she had lived it through her entire four-year marriage to Guy Duncan.

And she couldn't afford to lose this job. Whatever it took to please her employer was exactly what she had to do, including being at his beck and call.

Clasping her hands together, she moved into the doorway. "Tell me what you need and I'll get it for you," she offered, keeping her voice even and smooth, hiding her nervousness.

He gave her a crooked grin that was faintly abashed. "I believe I can handle this on my own."

Responding with a fading smile, she took a step back as he started toward her. It took him a few moments to navigate the parlor and the half dozen feet of hallway to the small bathroom. He wasn't particularly adept with the crutches yet. Yesterday was the first time he'd been allowed to use them and, according to Valery, after sixteen days of bed rest, he'd been so delighted to be mobile again that he had overdone it. His wince with each step supported his cousin's conclusion.

Susannah sympathized with him as she continued down the hall to the kitchen. Depending on the injury, using crutches could be more painful than the injury itself. The strain on the hands, arms, shoulders and back was tremendous, and only a few weeks ago, Remy's left arm had been subjected to a gunshot wound. The bullet had left a relatively clean trail with nothing more than soft tissue damage that was healing nicely, but the wound was still tender.

His other injuries had been both less and more serious: a fist-size contusion on his chest, where his bulletproof vest had saved his life, and a through-and-through gunshot wound of the right thigh. There had been no internal damage from the contusion, but the bullet in his leg had torn through the femur. The resulting compound comminuted fracture had required open reduction with internal fixation—opening his leg in surgery and putting the bone back together with a titanium plate and screws. Now he wore a hip-to-toe cast and was under strict orders for absolutely no weight-bearing on that leg for at least two weeks. If he wanted a full recovery, the strict use of crutches was mandatory.

Which was why *she* was here. He could have managed his convalescence with the other two injuries. They probably wouldn't even have slowed him down. But the severity of the leg wound, the cast and the crutches made him less than agile. They made her services necessary.

After washing her hands, she turned her attention to the contents of the refrigerator. Remy's parents, the current owners and residents of Belle Ste. Claire, had left only three days ago on a long-awaited trip to Europe. They were celebrating their fortieth anniversary, Valery had told her, and would be gone for a month. They, too, had made Susannah's services necessary. They had wanted to cancel the trip, again according to Valery—had wanted to stay here and look after their son themselves, but Remy had refused. They had been planning this trip for a long time; rescheduling, especially on such short notice, would have been a travel agent's nightmare.

Marie Sinclair had been a busy woman in the past week, Susannah thought as she began removing items from the refrigerator. Not only had she packed and gotten ready for a month abroad, but she had also prepared the house for Remy and Susannah's arrival—had seen to it that the unused servants' quarters were cleaned and aired out and the refrigerator well stocked. She had left Susannah notes explaining where any given item she might need in the next month was located, along with names and phone numbers for their housekeeper, local repairmen and neighbors and a detailed copy of their itinerary. And that was all in addition to spending the majority of her time at her son's side in the hospital.

Down the hall the sound of the bathroom door opening was followed by the slow shuffle and squeak of rubber-tipped crutches on the highly polished wood floor. Still hidden behind the refrigerator door, Susannah hoped Remy was going in the opposite direction, back toward the parlor, but it was a futile hope. The steps were definitely coming closer. Her fingers tightening into a fist, she waited until he stopped before she finally straightened and closed the refrigerator door.

"What's for dinner?"

She glanced at what she'd gathered on the counter: lettuce, cucumbers, carrots and an onion, along with a neatly labeled foil packet of chicken from the freezer and a handful of the potatoes piled nearby in a metal colander. "Fried chicken, mashed potatoes and gravy and salad…unless you don't eat fried food."

"Of course I eat fried food. Don't you know the first rule of Southern cooking? If it ain't fried, it ain't done."

Smiling faintly, she placed the chicken in a sink of cold water to thaw, then started opening drawers, looking for a knife and a vegetable peeler. With a backward glance over her shoulder, she made a suggestion for her own good as well as his. "Why don't you go back into the parlor where you'll be comfortable? I'll bring you some tea, and you can watch television, and when dinner's ready—"

"I've seen more television in the last two weeks than in the last two months combined. I'll be comfortable here." Balancing on his crutches, Remy pulled a chair from the table. Once he was seated, he used his good foot to maneuver a second chair into place in front of him, then raised his right leg to the seat. That done, he closed his eyes for just a moment, letting weariness wash over him, soaking into his muscles, claiming his entire body. All those days lying on his back in the hospital, he had anticipated the time he could be up and about whenever the mood struck him. Well, the time had arrived and, frankly, he couldn't think of anything more appealing than lying on his back in bed. He moved so clumsily that his thigh throbbed, and the cast chafed around his toes. His left upper arm twinged from time to time around both the entrance and the exit wounds, and the crutches hurt his shoulders, arms and hands.

Added to all that was his wounded ego. He wasn't used to being so awkward and graceless. He wasn't accustomed to revealing his helplessness and weakness to anyone.

Especially to anyone as cool, quiet and controlled as Susannah Duncan.

He had first seen her over two weeks ago in the emergency room the night he'd been shot. He remembered how calm she'd been even though chaos surrounded them. He remembered how gently she had touched him. Mostly, though, he remembered her eyes. Other than a doctor's blinding look with a penlight, no one else in the ER had met his gaze; no one but Susannah had made that small human contact with him. He had known when she did that he was going to be all right, had known it with a certainty that had eluded him until then.

They hadn't actually met until she'd come to his room a week ago for the job interview. Michael, who'd been visiting, had wanted time to check out her background and her references, but Remy had offered her the job on the spot. It had taken him maybe a moment to make up his mind; from the time she'd walked into the room and he had recognized her, he'd known she was the one he wanted. The few questions he'd asked her had been for Michael's benefit. Impulse had told him that she was the one, and instinct had backed it up.

Like any good cop, he trusted his instincts.

Settling his crutches against the table, he focused his attention on Susannah, rinsing vegetables at the sink. In spite of their few meetings and spending the better part of today here together, he hadn't yet learned much about her. She was thirty-one—that nugget had come from Valery—and had been living in New Orleans only a few months. She was single and had nearly ten years' nursing experience. She was pretty, although no great beauty. She wasn't the sort of woman to turn a man's head…unless he was looking for more than just a pretty face, unless he was intuitive enough to understand that what she could offer was far more important than beauty that would fade with age.

What else did he know about her? That she had lovely auburn hair and the gentlest hazel eyes he'd ever looked into. That she wasn't too tall, wasn't too thin. That she carried about her a comforting air that said this was a woman who could make everything all right—like a mother, he thought, although there was nothing motherly about her. He knew that she had a healing touch. That she was usually calm, serene and unflustered.

And he knew that she was troubled. There was a wariness and something more—a dispiritedness—in her eyes that hadn't been there two weeks ago.

Maybe it was just the strange situation they found themselves in—two strangers suddenly living together in very close quarters. Belle Ste. Claire was a large house, but she had to remain accessible to him, which meant staying nearby. It meant sleeping in the servants' wing, just off the kitchen and right across a narrow hallway from his own room, and sharing a bathroom with him. And while the house wasn't exactly isolated, it was a little remote. The nearest neighbors in either direction were more than a half mile away, and Belclaire, three miles east, was no more than the proverbial wide spot in the road: a gas station, a post office, a mom-and-pop grocery and a nothing-special café.

Or maybe that look had to do with her reason for leaving New Orleans to come here. Maybe whatever had driven her to take a leave of absence from the hospital, to temporarily give up her job, her home and her friends in the city and come here to live a quiet, dull life alone with him had put the sadness in her eyes. Maybe the end of a relationship? A breakup with someone important?

He could consider the possibilities all night—puzzles and

mysteries fascinated him—but he would save the guessing games, he decided, for later. For when she wasn't around. For when he wasn't more interested in talking to her than in speculating about her.

"What do you think of the house?" he asked her.

She tested the sharpness of the knife blade with the tip of her thumb before glancing not at him but in his general vicinity. "It must have been a wonderful place to grow up."

"It was...for the most part." He had plenty of good memories of his childhood here at Belle Ste. Claire, but none at all of his teen years, and after that... He'd been barely twenty-two the night his father had told him to leave their home and to not return until he had become someone his parents could be proud of. He had stayed away for fifteen years. Until today. "Valery says you come from up north."

"Except for Florida and Texas, everything is 'up north' from here."

"Where in particular up north is home for you?"

"Nebraska."

She was a long way from home, he acknowledged— longer, even, than the miles accounted for. From the Great Plains to the Big Easy. From dry, dusty farm and ranch land to heat, humidity and pure decadence. Thinking back to an old favorite childhood movie, he murmured, "'Gee, Toto, I don't think we're in Nebraska anymore.'"

"Wrong state." She turned from the counter to face him, her expression coming dangerously close to a smile. "It's 'I don't think we're in Kansas anymore.'"

"Oh, pardon me," he said dryly. "So what brought you to New Orleans?"

The hint of a smile disappeared, and he could see more than a little tension in the way she clasped her hands together. "I always wanted to live there."

"Why?"

"It's a beautiful city." Once again she was looking only

vaguely in his direction. Except for that one brief moment when she'd corrected him, she hadn't gotten close to making eye contact with him this evening.

"Did you have friends there?"

"No."

"Had you ever visited there before?"

She shook her head.

Getting information out of her was like trying to interrogate a suspect who knew his lawyers were going to get him out before you even finished the paperwork. Luckily for him, he was patient. He could get to know her one piece of reluctantly offered information at a time. "So you woke up one morning back home in Nebraska and said, 'I think I'll get dressed, have some coffee and move to New Orleans.'"

She sighed softly—he saw the movement rather than heard it—then began the task of making ice tea. "Actually, I ran into my ex-husband and his new wife one time too many and said, 'I think I'll move to New Orleans.'"

"You were married." Why did that surprise him? Most people did get married. He had always planned to do it himself someday…although after getting shot, he'd decided that someday was going to come soon. There would be no more putting things off until tomorrow, as he'd done all too often in his personal affairs. Not when he knew too painfully well that tomorrow didn't always come.

But it wasn't Susannah's having been married that surprised him. It was her being divorced. What man in his right mind, once he had her, would let her go?

"How does the joke go? I was married…but my husband wasn't." This time her sigh was audible.

"I'm sorry."

"So was I, for a very long time."

"And now?"

She didn't answer. She simply went on with her work. He didn't ask the question again. He didn't have the right to probe into an area so obviously painful, at least, not until he knew her better. Much better.

And he had no doubt that day would come.

"So…" He returned to their earlier conversation. "You moved to New Orleans, found a place to live, found a job. Is it everything you thought it would be?"

"Absolutely," she replied with a smile—nothing dazzling, just a sweet smile of pleasure that brought such life to her face that, on second thought, Remy decided, it was pretty damned dazzling after all. Her ex-husband must have been a fool to let her get away.

"Before you came here, had you always lived in Nebraska?"

She nodded.

"I've never been there. What's it like?"

"Kansas," she replied immediately.

He laughed. "I wasn't too far off then on my misquote, was I?"

Slowly she ventured across the room, taking a seat across from him. "Nebraska's a nice place. The northwestern part of the state, where our farm is located, is pretty sparsely populated. We have cold winters, hot summers and beautiful springs that are much too short."

"Do you miss it?"

"No." As if she immediately regretted the answer, she made an impatient gesture. "It's my home, and my family and friends still live there. For those reasons, I do miss it. But I left there with the intention of never going back for more than occasional visits."

He wondered if he was putting her answers together properly, if he was reaching the correct conclusion. She had left her home, family and friends and intended never to return. She had traveled hundreds of miles to a strange city in a place where she knew no one, and she'd done it because of her ex-husband. Was *he* the reason for the despair in her eyes? Had she come here hoping to put him behind her, hoping to start a new life? Had she reached the conclusion after a few months of trying that it wasn't working?

Was she still in love with the guy?

Sometime he would find out—not tonight, not next week or probably even the week after that—but sometime.

Before she left here, he intended to know everything there was to know about Susannah Duncan.

It was nearly ten o'clock that evening when Susannah finally escaped to the privacy of her bedroom. She wasn't used to going to bed so early—she ordinarily worked the three-to-eleven shift, went to bed around two or three and got up about eleven in the morning—but she had to adapt her hours to match Remy's, and he, after refusing any help from her, was settled in his room.

Closing the door quietly behind her, she kicked her shoes off, pushed them underneath the bed, then sat down to remove her socks. These servants' rooms were nothing compared to the family bedrooms upstairs, but she had lived in worse. The room was a nice size and furnished with mismatched pieces: an iron bed painted white and made up with plain cotton sheets, a scarred oak dresser with an oval mirror that reflected a wavy image, an armoire that had seen better days and a small writing desk and straight-back chair in some dark wood she couldn't identify. The walls were painted white, the woodwork stained dark and there were two windows on the south wall, wide and covered with simple white curtains that hung café-style from wide-spaced tabs.

In her half day here, she had already left her mark on the room. There was a basket of bath supplies on the dresser, a twig wreath decorated with silk flowers and ribbons hanging from a nail in the wall, scented candles in brass holders on various pieces of furniture and a free-form sculpture she'd picked up of bubbles suspended in glass.

She'd brought two other things from the apartment she

shared with Skip, but they weren't for display: a family photograph to remind her why she was here and the phone number, already memorized, for the lawyer in New Orleans who had sent her here. They were hidden away, wrapped inside a dark plastic bag and tucked at the back of the armoire behind her other shoes.

Leaning across the bed, she turned on the bedside lamp, then shut off the overhead light. She was tired—she'd been up late last night, packing for this move and dreading it—but she didn't think she could sleep, not yet. Still, she undressed, draping her jeans over the desk chair, tossing everything else into the wicker laundry basket in the corner, brushed out her hair, then pulled on a pale green nightgown. Sliding into bed and beneath the covers, she shut off the lamp and settled in, pretending that this was the end of a normal day, that nothing was wrong. She pretended that she wasn't in a strange house with a strange man, that she wasn't taking advantage of his misfortune, taking his money and betraying him and herself at the same time.

She pretended that she didn't hate herself for what she was doing.

The moon was bright tonight, giving the white curtains a ghostly luminance. She wished she had opened them, wished she could see whatever was outside her window. When she had first moved to New Orleans, it had taken a while to adjust to the city lights and noises after years on the Crouse family farm. Now here she was, back out in the country, where the only light was moonlight, where the only sounds, other than an occasional car on the road, were nature.

And Remy. Across the hall his bed squeaked. When she looked toward the door, she could see the thin line of light that came from his room. Had he gone to bed early this evening merely so she could, or was he in the habit of reading or working in bed? She imagined that in the next few weeks, she would find out. After all, that was part of what she was here for—to learn his habits. His routine.

It was harmless information. What would it hurt if she passed on to the lawyer what time he got up and what time he went to bed? What time he ate his meals and how he spent his afternoons? Whether he had company and when and who?

Harmless information, she insisted to herself. Believing it was the only way she could live with herself.

But she didn't believe it.

Not for a minute.

Again, his bed squeaked, and there was a muffled thud, followed by a curse. Crutches hitting the wooden floor. It was becoming a familiar sound. It would serve him right if she put them someplace out of reach until morning, but of course she couldn't do that. What if he had to get up during the night? He had to have access to them, clumsy though he was with them.

There came another quiet curse, and she pushed the covers back and reached for her robe, hanging over the iron headboard. Tugging it on, she tied the belt at her waist, then opened the bedroom door.

His door was open. His bed was placed the same as hers: in front of the door. All told, less than fifteen feet separated them—a fact that didn't make her comfortable.

He was sitting up in bed, pillows behind his back, the sheet pulled to his waist. Seeing her, he smiled ruefully. It was sweet and charming, and she couldn't begin to deal with it. "Sorry I disturbed you."

He had righted one of the crutches, but the other had fallen out of reach. She bent to pick it up, leaning it against the first one. "That's what I'm here for. Do you need anything? Medication, a snack, something to drink?"

"No, thanks." He closed the book that had been open on his lap. "You don't normally go to bed so early, do you?"

When he fixed his gaze on her, she wished she had pretended not to hear the disruption in here.

She wished she had pretended to be asleep.

God help her, she wished he wouldn't look at her that way.

Brushing her fingers nervously through her hair, she answered his question with one of her own. "Why do you ask?"

"You were working evenings the night we met. If you were back in New Orleans, you wouldn't even be home yet."

That was true. Back in the city, she would leave the hospital a little after eleven. She would go home to an empty apartment, and she would wonder where Skip was, would worry over what he was up to. Most nights she would be asleep before he finally wandered in, and if he did come home while she was awake, they would argue about his friends, his activities, the aimlessness of his life.

Thoughts of her brother inevitably led to thoughts of that damnable lawyer, so she put him out of her mind and concentrated instead on the first part of Remy's comment. "We didn't exactly meet that night in the ER."

"Yes, we did."

"Do you know how many patients we get in the emergency room on a typical Saturday night?"

He grinned. "You remember me whether you want to admit it or not."

Guiltily, she looked away. He was too appealing, damn it, and too willing to trust her when she didn't deserve it.

Moving away from the door, she picked up the clothing he'd worn earlier, a pair of black sweatpants roomy enough to accommodate his cast and a red T-shirt. She folded them carelessly and left them on the bureau top, then placed his single tennis shoe in the armoire with the others. "What makes you so sure of that?" she finally asked when there was nothing left to do.

"Women tend to remember me," he replied confidently.

No doubt they did. He was tall, nicely muscled, had blond hair and gorgeous blue eyes, was too handsome for his own good, and he knew it. But that brash self-assurance was part of his charm—that, and the certainty that he was a good guy. Decent. Fair. Nice.

Returning to lean against the door frame, she folded her arms across her chest. "You're right. I do remember you. You were the third gunshot wound we'd gotten that night, and you bled all over my scrubs."

"How inconsiderate of me."

She studied the bruise, in healing shades of yellow-gray and green, on his chest, then hesitantly asked, "Do you always wear a bulletproof vest when you're working?"

"Not in the office. But if I'm going out in the field, you can bet I've got my Second Chance on."

"It certainly gave you one." The bruise was dead center in his chest. Without the vest, he surely would have died. If she had seen him at all at the hospital, it would have been too late. She would have regretted it, would have thought it sad that the patient had died so young, would have thought it unjust that one of the cops had died when so many criminals lived. She would have grieved for him for a moment or two.

Then, when the next patient arrived, she would have forgotten him.

"Why the ER?"

"Why the FBI?"

"I like arresting people."

People like Jimmy Falcone. Trying to arrest him had almost gotten Remy killed.

People like Skip.

Oh, God, people like *her.*

"I answered. Now it's your turn."

She shrugged restlessly. "I used to believe I could make a difference."

"You don't believe that anymore?"

She shook her head. "Innocent people keep dying. Drunks keep driving drunk. Punks keep robbing for drug money. Crooks keep shooting and stabbing and beating and maiming their victims. Users keep overdosing." Again, she shrugged; then, changing the subject, she gestured toward the nightstand. "If you'll turn on the lamp, I'll shut the light off so you don't have to get up later."

He did as she suggested, and she flipped the switch, then turned away. She made it to her door before he spoke.

"Susannah."

She swallowed hard. A million people had called her by her first name, but no one had ever made it sound quite the same way he did. Soft. Sweet. Gentle. Slowly, blinking hard against the tears that threatened, she looked back.

"You shouldn't stop believing," he said quietly, intensely. "That night… You made a hell of a difference for me."

Before any of the warnings swirling around in her brain could tumble out, she slipped into the quiet, dark safety of her own room. There, chilled once again all the way to the bone, she lay underneath the covers, staring dry-eyed and empty into the night, and whispered three silent, desperate pleas.

Don't trust me, Remy.

Don't be grateful to me.

Please don't take me on faith.

Because doing any of the three would be a mistake on his part. A mistake he might not live to regret.

Chapter 2

Remy awoke early Wednesday morning, before the rising sun had brought more than a touch of color to the eastern sky. Despite the less-than-familiar surroundings, he was immediately alert, immediately aware of where he was.

Home. He had lived in a variety of places over the last fifteen years—a college dorm room and an apartment shared with the three best friends a guy could ask for. He had lived in Virginia while attending the FBI Academy and had called a number of apartments and condos his own after returning to New Orleans for assignment. But none of those places—whether temporary or, like the place he was in now, relatively permanent, whether cozy or cramped, shared or solitary, Spartan or luxurious—had ever been home. That name, that feeling, was forever reserved for Belle Ste. Claire.

He had loved the house for as long as he could remember, had missed it during his fifteen-year exile as much as he had ever missed any person in his life. Sometimes it had haunted him, along with the fear that he would die without ever seeing it again.

Two and a half weeks ago, lying on the wet pavement in more pain than he'd believed possible to endure, he had thought he'd come close.

But now here he was, back home again. This servant's room, unoccupied for as long as he could remember—while his mother had always had help around the house, it had never been of the live-in variety—was a far cry from the elegance and grace of the bedroom upstairs that had been his for the better part of twenty-two years, but it was still home. It was part of Belle Ste. Claire, and it was his for the next month.

His and, to some extent, Susannah's. She would finish his unpacking later today, would be cleaning in here and generally helping him out. She would have as much access to his room as he would.

As if cued by the thought of her, from across the hall came the beeping of her alarm. He wondered why she was getting up at six forty-five. They hadn't discussed a schedule yet, but apparently they needed to. When she was already accustomed to working the evening shift and would, when she finished here, return to those hours, there was no reason for her to make major changes in her schedule just for him.

Although he could think of a few other changes he wouldn't mind her making just for him...such as becoming softer again, regaining the serenity the last few weeks had taken from her and losing the wariness that kept her at arm's length.

Her alarm went off again, this time followed by the sounds of movement filtering through her closed door. He thought of her as she had looked last night here in his room—her hair falling in loose waves to her shoulders, the plain white terrycloth robe so long that it had practically covered her bare feet, the bit of drab green nightgown showing at the neck of the robe. With her coloring, he wouldn't dress her in white or pastels; he would choose jewel tones—emeralds and rubies, sapphires and deep, rich amethysts. He would also do away with the ponytails and braids she showed such fondness for—perfectly reasonable hairstyles, he acknowledged, when you wore a uniform and worked in an emergency room, but just as perfectly unnecessary here.

Especially when Susannah with her hair down was so much softer. So much more appealing.

When her door opened, he grew still. He slept with his own bedroom door open—the better for the cop in him to hear any out-of-the-ordinary sounds—but she didn't glance his way. She glided down the hall, a wicker basket over one arm, her long white robe and soundless passage giving her an other-worldly quality so fitting in the ancient house.

A moment later the gurgle and splash of water filling the tub reached his ears, and he felt a stab of longing sharp enough to hurt. The longing wasn't for Susannah—although that was coming; it wouldn't take many more hours in her company to turn interest into desire and desire into need—but for the bath she would soon be indulging in. Ever since he had awakened after his surgery to find himself wearing a bulky, itchy, scratchy cast, he'd had visions of soaking away all his aches and pains in a long, relaxing bath. Every time he'd endured a sponge bath given by someone entirely too young—and entirely too female—to suit him, he'd entertained fantasies about a big, deep tub, a locked door and water hot enough to steam.

Maybe in four weeks. If his leg had healed enough, if the cast could be removed, then he could take the longest, hottest, steamiest bath ever. Then he could do a lot of things.

Then he would no longer need Susannah.

Maybe.

While she was occupied, he sat up and carefully swung his legs off the mattress. The wood floor was cold beneath his bare foot, but Susannah had insisted on removing the bright braided rugs his mother had scattered around, deeming them a threat to his less-than-stable gait. Taking his crutches from their niche, he used one to nudge the door shut, then slowly pushed himself to his feet. For a moment he simply stood there next to the bed, stretching, tensing and easing muscles. He was a little stiff, a little sore, but all in all, he felt fine.

His first steps, from the bed to the dresser where a few of his clothes had been unpacked and put away, were easy, almost smooth. There, balancing carefully, he stripped off the gym shorts he had slept in as a concession to Susannah and pulled on the sweatpants he'd discarded the night before. When he moved from there to the armoire for a T-shirt, he felt the discomfort begin—mild twinges in his shoulders and upper arms, tenderness across his palms. His mouth formed a grim line as he stuffed the shirt between one hand and the crutch's grip and limped his way back to the bed.

After more than two weeks of bed rest, boredom and pain, he had thought that being allowed the mobility of crutches and getting discharged from the hospital he so disliked were the answers to his prayers. He hadn't realized there would still be so much pain. He hadn't understood that these first few days on crutches weren't going to be easy—or particularly mobile. He hadn't quite understood that being discharged from the hospital didn't mean he was well again, didn't mean everything was back to normal.

He was disappointed, he admitted as he sat down, his breathing a little heavier for the exertion. Until he grew used to the crutches and his palms callused over, until his body adjusted to compensating for his bad leg, life was going to remain tough. He was going to continue being clumsy and awkward. His body was going to continue to let him down, putting his weaknesses on display for the world to see. He was going to continue to need Susannah's help more than any grown man should.

As he pulled the T-shirt over his head, that last thought

almost made him smile. Some clouds truly did have silver linings, and Susannah, it seemed, just might be his.

The house was quiet as he hobbled out of his room and down the hall to the kitchen. He didn't bother with any lights but took a seat at the table, facing the bay window and the lightening sky. He hadn't seen a sunrise or paid attention to a sunset in longer than he could remember. They were both on the mental list he'd compiled in the hospital of things he wanted to do now that he'd been given a second chance. It wasn't a long list, and some of the items on it, like those two, were simple, easily fulfilled and crossed off.

Some were major.

He had wanted to bring an end to his estrangement from his parents, and that had been accomplished. They had spent much of the past few weeks at the hospital with him. While nothing could ever replace the fifteen years they had lost in their feud, while there were still some awkward moments, some resentment and leftover anger, at least they were speaking. At least they were all willing to work at resolving the problems that had driven them apart in the first place.

He wanted to make things right with Valery. His cousin had been one of the most important people in his life, and he had missed her friendship, her love. He wasn't sure he would ever earn those things from her again—he had hurt her badly, maybe too badly to be forgiven—but at least she was no longer afraid of him. She was willing to get to know him again, willing to explore whatever relationship they might manage after all these years.

And the big one, the one that would surprise everyone who thought they knew him, the one that would astonish every single woman he had ever gone out with, every woman to whom the only commitment he'd ever made was no commitment at all: he wanted to get married. He wanted a wife, a family, a house with a mortgage, a big yard, bikes in the driveway and dogs underfoot. He wanted the kind of normal, everyday home life that most people took for granted. He wanted someone who would be happy to see him when he came home at night, someone who would miss him and worry over him when he was gone. He wanted to know that someone's life was richer, happier, because of him.

He wanted to love someone and be loved in return. Like his parents. Like Valery and Michael.

He had come too close to death. He wanted to make the most of the life he'd been given, and love, a wife and kids were the best, the surest, way to do that.

Way down deep in his gut, he suspected Susannah was the place to start.

He wasn't young enough, romantic enough or foolish enough to believe in love at first sight. He knew all too well that most relationships grew from friendship or were stirred by lust. He knew there had to be something beyond desire, knew respect, understanding and genuine caring had to develop.

And he knew to trust his instincts. Whenever he met a woman, he usually figured out pretty quickly what, if any, role she would play in his life—whether they would remain acquaintances, become friends or lovers. He could generally predict the course of a relationship right up front. He usually knew who was going to be important to him and who wasn't.

That Saturday night in the emergency room, he had known that Susannah would be important. She had touched him, had connected with him, at a time when he had desperately needed such contact. Even if he had never seen her again, he had known intuitively that he would never forget her face, her touch, her serenity.

Had her applying for this job been fate or sheer luck? He didn't know and didn't much care. Maybe if she hadn't applied, he would have continued to find fault with all those who did. According to Michael, he'd turned down some highly qualified nurses. Maybe eventually he would have sought out Susannah, would have offered the job to her and no one else.

But, for whatever reason of her own, she *had* applied. Call it fate. Luck. Destiny.

He smiled faintly. He was sitting here in an unlit room, watching the sun rise and contemplating his future with a woman he barely knew.

Who said he wasn't young enough, romantic enough or just plain foolish enough?

Susannah dried the mirror with a towel, then drew a comb through her hair, pulling it straight back from her forehead. This morning's long bath had been a luxury, one that she wouldn't be able to indulge in most days because of time limitations, but she'd felt the need this morning to get herself into the best frame of mind possible before facing Remy. After a less than restful night, she needed all the relaxation, all the soothing, she could get.

After slipping into her robe and belting it, she gathered her bath things, replacing them in the wicker basket. There was plenty of room in the bathroom to store them—a long counter, shelves on the wall, a cabinet underneath the sink—but she felt uncomfortable leaving her toiletries behind. There was something too intimate about placing her shampoo and conditioner on the counter beside Remy's, something too personal about her razor and shaving cream sharing shelf space with his. Maybe she was being silly, but transporting everything back and forth in the long-handled basket allowed her to maintain some sense of distance between Remy and herself.

And she desperately needed that distance.

When she opened the door, the steamy warmth of the bathroom quickly dissipated in the chill air. She shivered but didn't move immediately. Instead, for a moment she simply stood quietly and listened. There were no windows in the hallway or the bathroom, but morning light filtered in from Remy's room and, at the opposite end of the hall, the kitchen. She wondered if he was awake yet, wondered how much solitude she had left before he claimed her time.

Then she heard the noise in the kitchen—she thought it was an impatient sigh. Was he already up and waiting for her, eager for his coffee and hungry for his breakfast? Did he normally get up early, or had she awakened him with her bath?

She hurried to her room, dressing quickly in jeans and a thin cotton sweater. After taking a moment to apply a little blush and eye shadow and another to pull her hair back and secure it, she slipped on her shoes, then headed for the kitchen with a none-too-quiet—and none-too-eager—sigh of her own.

He was sitting at the kitchen table. Last night he had watched her from there while she fixed dinner, had insisted on eating there, too, the two of them together, and he had watched while she cleaned up afterward. Sharing meals was one thing—one of many, she was afraid—that she hadn't quite been prepared for. She had hoped to keep their relationship strictly professional, employer to employee. Growing up in a house this grand, he was surely accustomed to having servants, or a full-time housekeeper at the very least. He had to know how to treat them, how to keep them in their proper places, how to be friendly but never familiar. She had counted on that treatment to make the next few weeks bearable.

But if last night was any indication, he had no intention of treating her like an employee. Not once had he been aloof or distant. When she had tried to inject some professionalism— in politely trying to usher him out of the kitchen or in assuming that he would take his meal in the family dining room while she ate in the kitchen—he had simply, naturally overruled her.

And now here he was, waiting once again. Watching once again.

"Good morning," she greeted him as she crossed to the sink. The first order of the day was coffee—as if she wasn't already jumpy enough—and breakfast, for an already-nervous stomach.

He murmured a response, but didn't turn to face her. She glanced over her shoulder once to see what held his attention outside, but saw nothing other than a dilapidated barn and the sun breaking above the tree line to the east. She'd seen plenty of sunrises back in Nebraska. At home on the farm, she had been up, dressed and cooking breakfast by four-thirty most mornings. During the four years of her marriage, she had continued to rise early, simply because Guy had. That was part of the reason she had requested the evening shift when she'd started at the hospital in New Orleans. There was a whole other world out there, one that she had missed for the better part of her life, and she had wanted to know what it was like.

After three months, the best thing she could say about nightlife was that it gave her an excuse for her nonexistent social life. When she worked five nights a week, including most Saturdays and Sundays, no one was surprised at her lack of dates. It was just as likely that she didn't have time, the reasoning went, as that there was simply no one interested.

Not that she was looking. If she had finally learned one thing from her marriage to Guy, it was that she didn't need a man in her life. She didn't need the criticism, the sly taunts, the snubs and subtle insults. The best sex in the world wasn't worth being made to feel inadequate the rest of the time. It wasn't worth hurt after tiny hurt. Sharing her life with a man who had no respect and little fondness for her wasn't better than being alone.

At this point, she wasn't sure if she ever wanted to get married again, wasn't sure if she ever wanted children. That had been one of her goals since she was a child herself—to be the sort of loving and giving mother that her own mother had been. To have at least three kids, maybe four or even five, and help them grow from cuddly babies to mature, responsible adults who could make any parent proud. But right now she wasn't sure she wanted that. She had helped raise Skip after their mother had died, and look how immature, how irresponsible, he had turned out. He was twenty-three years old and still relying on big sister to get him out of trouble. She wasn't sure she had any mothering left in her to give. She wasn't sure she had the strength to be responsible for another life, to shoulder the obligations and demands of marriage and motherhood.

She wasn't sure, but she thought she might be completely satisfied spending the rest of her life alone.

Even if it did sound like an awfully lonely way to live.

Once the coffeemaker was filled and running, she turned to Remy. Sunlight was reaching through the window now, turning the blond of his hair to gold, a rich, burnished shade that reminded her of the wheat fields back home under the strong plains sun. He was a handsome man, if a person cared about that sort of thing. She noticed, but she didn't care. Guy was a handsome man, too—all tanned and chiseled and perfect on the outside, all empty, weak and petty inside. Skip was also handsome, in a softer, younger, less formed sort of way. Like her ex-husband, her brother lacked all the stronger qualities that made looks unimportant.

But Remy didn't.

Just as she started to look away, he twisted in the chair and their gazes met for the span of a second, maybe less. It was enough to see that his expression, while not including a smile, was pleasant enough. Harmless enough. But looks could be deceiving. Remy was strong, tough. Even temporarily impaired as he was, he could be dangerous.

Her own looks were deceptive. When he gazed at her, he surely saw what most everyone else did: a plain, uninteresting, modest little mouse of a person. He saw no cause to worry for his safety. He certainly didn't see a woman capable of bringing him harm, of fooling him, of betraying him.

He didn't see a woman who just might destroy him.

"How did you sleep last night?"

She opened the refrigerator and removed a package of bacon and a carton of eggs. "Fine, thank you," she lied. She had lain awake most of the night, looking at her future and at herself and hating what she saw. "How do you like your eggs?"

"Scrambled is fine. It didn't bother you—being in a strange place?"

"No, not at all." After taking a bowl from the cabinet, she cracked a half dozen eggs into it, added a little milk and seasoning, then whisked them until the yolks broke and blended. She put them aside and set the first strips of bacon to sizzle in a skillet before forcing herself to speak, to step into her nurse's role and deal with her patient. "How do you feel today?"

"Sore" came his immediate response.

"That's to be expected."

"Not by me. I thought getting out of the hospital meant all the pain would be gone."

"It doesn't go away that easily." Leaving the stove, she crossed the few feet of tile to the table. "Let me see your hands."

He obediently offered them to her, palms up. If he'd been any other patient—if he'd been *just* a patient—she would have had no qualms about taking them, about holding them in her own hands while she examined them. As it was, her hands were less than steady as she reached for first his left hand, then his right.

His skin was smooth, unblemished except for the small, raw places across the middle. These hands had never done any physical labor, had probably never done anything more arduous than grip a tennis racquet—or a gun. She had more calluses from her years of helping out on the farm than he would ever see.

The smell of bacon on the verge of burning gave her an excuse to abruptly drop his hands and return to the stove.

"You're going to get blisters on your palms," she stated matter-of-factly. "They'll make using the crutches even harder. I'll add another layer of foam to the handgrips, and I'll pick up some gloves while I'm in town today."

"Why do you want to go to town?"

"Because we need milk and a few other groceries. If there's anything in particular you'd like to eat in the next few days, let me know and I'll get it."

"I'll come with you," he announced.

She risked a look at him over her shoulder. "That's not a good idea."

"You don't know your way around Belclaire."

Her look grew a few degrees drier. "Your cousin drove through town with me yesterday. There are a few blocks of houses and one block of businesses. I don't think I'll get lost." After she'd turned back to the stove, she casually added, "Anyway, I wasn't planning to go to Belclaire. I thought I would drive back to New Orleans."

"Why? You can get all the groceries you need right there in town."

"But I can't get foam rubber and biking gloves there." And she couldn't go unnoticed there. She knew towns like Belclaire. Nebraska was full of them—little places where a stranger in town was worthy of scrutiny, even if he was simply buying gas and passing on through. If there hadn't already been rumors about the Sinclair son coming home to recuperate from his wounds and bringing a live-in nurse with him, it wouldn't take long for them to start. It wouldn't take long at all for her to be identified as the nurse.

And today she needed to go unnoticed. She needed to make a phone call. She needed to check in with the lawyer.

With Jimmy Falcone's lawyer.

"Baton Rouge is closer."

"But I don't know my way around Baton Rouge."

Remy's smile held more than a hint of triumph. "That's

why I need to go with you." After a moment, his smile shifted, becoming a charming grin. "Come on, Susannah, I've been cooped up inside for two and a half weeks. It's about to drive me nuts. I won't insist on going in the store with you and slowing you down. I'll just go along for the ride." Sensing that she was weakening, he saved his best appeal for last. "What if I stayed here alone and something happened? What if I needed you and you weren't here?"

After a long silence, she faced him again, coming to set a platter of crispy bacon on the table in front of him. "You don't need my permission," she said quietly, meeting his gaze fully, unwaveringly, for the first time that morning. "You're in charge here."

Meaning she would let him accompany her because she had no choice, because he was, after all, paying her salary. His victory was hollow...but it was still a victory. He was going along—and he was going to enjoy it. He was even going to accept the challenge of making *her* enjoy it.

He munched on bacon while she cooked the eggs. When she brought them, disproportionately divided between two plates, to the table, he ate heartily while she picked at her own food. She hadn't had much of an appetite last night, either, he had noticed. Nerves, he decided. She wasn't yet comfortable with him. If she didn't settle down soon, he might have to reconsider her suggestion of last evening—that they take their meals separately, the way an employer and his employee should—just to keep her from wasting away.

Or he would have to help her settle down.

"You drink too much coffee," he remarked as he finished off the last strip of bacon. He was still on his first cup, heavily sweetened and diluted with cream to disguise the taste, while she was finishing her third.

"I like coffee. It keeps me going."

"You'd do better to get your energy from food rather than caffeine."

The look she gave him was steady enough to make a lesser man back down.

Not so Remy. "Let's talk, Susannah."

"I thought we were."

"Let's talk about business." As he watched, she stiffened and withdrew a little inside herself. He went on, keeping his voice level, his tone casual. "We never really discussed what this job would entail, beyond the basics. I don't expect you to stay quietly in the background until I snap my fingers. I don't expect you to keep to a schedule or to get up early and have breakfast waiting when I awaken. I don't expect you to behave like a servant, and I don't intend to treat you like one."

"So what exactly do you expect?"

He ran his fingers through his hair, remembering as he did so that he had forgotten to comb it this morning. That reminded him that he hadn't shaved yet, either, or subjected himself to the dubious pleasure of a bath—a sponge bath, at least until he was able to stand long enough without his crutches to manage a shower. He must look pretty scruffy, not a bad accomplishment for someone who'd been buttoned-down and spit-polished for the better part of his professional life.

"I don't know," he responded with a shrug. "Someone to make the days easier and the nights warmer?"

That brought a flare of color to her cheeks and made her gaze snap up to meet his. Before she could speak, though, he raised his hand to silence her. "Since you obviously don't like that idea, how about just keeping me company? Take care of the things I can't handle, help me out when I need it and be a friend when I need that."

"You're looking for a companion."

He didn't like the way she said the word. He didn't need to know exactly what it meant to her to know that it wasn't quite what he wanted. Her inflection made that clear. Of course, "friend" also fell far short of describing what he wanted from her, but it was the only word he could think of right now that wouldn't scare her back to New Orleans. "A friend," he argued.

When she responded, her tone was both prim and disdainful. "You don't *hire* friends."

She had him there. He had plenty of friends—had been lucky enough to have three of the best friends in the world, friends of the sort that money could never buy. There was Michael, the Arkansas farm boy turned New Orleans cop. Funny…with his small-town, agricultural background, he and Susannah shared more in common with each other than either of them did with Remy, but Michael hadn't wanted him to hire her, at least not without thoroughly checking her background, and Susannah had seemed even more uneasy with Michael than she was with *him*.

There was also Smith Kendricks, an assistant U.S. Attorney based in New Orleans. He was a little more distant than Michael or Remy, a little less demonstrative, but no less important in their small family. There was nothing he wouldn't do for one of them, nothing he wouldn't give if only they asked.

And there had been Evan Montez. Ten months had passed since Evan's death, but a small, vicious wrench of pain still accompanied every thought of him. A detective with the New Orleans Police Department and Michael's partner, he had died doing the job he'd loved—upholding the law, catching the bad guys and making the world safe for innocent little girls and wounded partners. It was small consolation that the man who killed him, the man who had kidnapped that one innocent little girl in particular, had also died. It hadn't comforted Evan's widow. It hadn't lessened Michael's guilt over surviving when his partner had died. It hadn't eased Smith's or Remy's grief.

No, Susannah was right. You didn't hire friends, particularly not of the quality he was used to.

But you also didn't tell a skittish woman with shadowy

hazel eyes, a bad marriage behind her and a serious case of nerves that you were looking for a wife and you thought maybe—just maybe—she was the one.

"All right," he said, giving in. "You can be my companion." Just as she started to visibly relax, though, he added, "And I'll be your friend."

She stacked their dishes together, laying the silverware across the top plate, then got to her feet. "Thank you, but I have friends already. I'm not in the market for more."

Her rejection had been polite, even gentle, but firm. Remy listened to it, considered it and decided to disregard it. It was entirely possible that his instincts were wrong this time—rare, but possible. Hadn't he been way off on the Falcone case? Hadn't he thoroughly misjudged his partner on that case? Hadn't he damn near paid for it with his life? It was possible he was wrong about Susannah, too. Maybe he had simply gotten fixated on her because he had been so very frightened and she had been so very reassuring. Maybe fate, luck or destiny had never intended the connection between them to extend beyond those few moments in the emergency room. Maybe this link he felt with her was all one-sided, born of his gratitude for her cool composure when his world had been turned inside out.

And then he looked at her and rejected all of his logical arguments. There was something between them. Maybe he was reading it wrong. Maybe it wasn't the forever-and-ever something, but it was there just the same. It was worth exploring.

In the awkward way that he was coming to hate, he pushed his chair back and maneuvered up and onto his crutches. "I'm going to clean up and change, and then we'll head into the city. Okay?"

Susannah simply shrugged. He could see she wasn't happy about it. Did she want to escape his company so badly? But she obviously wasn't going to argue with him. He wished she would. Giving in as easily and as completely as she had hinted too unpleasantly at submissiveness, and while he wanted a great many things from her, that wasn't one of them.

He hobbled to the door, then abruptly turned toward her again. "I told you what I wanted from our arrangement. What about you? What were you expecting?"

"I expected to do the job I was hired for," she replied in a curiously flat tone. "To provide whatever assistance and care you need over the next month. As far as specific details, I assumed you would fill me in on those as they came up."

She wasn't being entirely truthful—his cop's instinct told him that—but that was all right. One of these days she would come to trust him.

He could wait.

As soon as the breakfast dishes were done, Susannah retreated to her room, closed the door behind her and exhaled heavily. The muscles in her neck ached, and there was a throbbing starting somewhere deep behind her eyes that threatened to become a first-class tension headache. If she hoped to survive her time here in reasonably decent physical condition, she was going to have to find an outlet for this stress. She had to find a way to deal with Remy without making herself sick.

He was still in the bathroom down the hall. While she was cleaning the kitchen, she'd heard occasional splashes, muttering and curses, but she hadn't knocked at the door, hadn't asked if he needed assistance.

She had been afraid he just might say yes.

Removing the clasp from her hair, she got her hair dryer and brush from a drawer and set about drying her hair. It was thick, dry on top, still heavy with dampness underneath. Someday she would cut it, she promised herself, would choose some short, sleek, carefree style, something like Valery Navarre wore, something better suited to New Orleans and its heat and humidi—

Abruptly she cut off the thought. She didn't need to worry about finding a hairstyle more suitable for New Orleans' climate. She couldn't possibly return there when she completed her job here. She couldn't continue to live in Remy's city, in Jimmy Falcone's territory. She couldn't go back to the job she loved at the hospital, couldn't return to the apartment she shared with Skip, other than to pack up their belongings. She would take him home to Nebraska, she decided. Back home on the farm, he would have to look longer and harder to find trouble to get into. Back home, he would have their father, their uncle, cousins and friends to help keep him in line.

And once he was safe there, away from the city's temptations of easy money, glamour and excitement, she would find someplace new for herself. Someplace where she didn't know a soul. Someplace where no one could ever make a connection between her and New Orleans, where no one had ever heard of Remy Sinclair or Jimmy Falcone. Someplace where she could lie to everyone, including herself, and try to create a new Susannah Duncan, one she could live with.

Once her hair was dry, she went to the mirror sitting atop the dresser to brush it. The image that greeted her there made her stand motionless for a moment. The mirror was old, probably a hundred years or more, and the reflection looking back at her was distorted, full of ripples and waves, a carnival fun-house version of herself that was both familiar and alien.

Since coming to this house, since taking on these two similar but very different jobs, since agreeing to sell out every principle she'd ever held, she had found a stranger, a Susannah she didn't know at all, taking over her life. It seemed fitting, she thought with a choked-back laugh, that she now faced an image of herself that she barely recognized. So fitting.

And so damning.

"Hey, Susannah." Remy's call was followed by a tap on

the door. "Can you come over in a few minutes and see if you can find where Valery hid my shoes?"

Shaken out of her stillness, she slowly drew the brush through her hair. "All right," she replied, her voice little more than a whisper. He heard her, though. The sound of his unbalanced gait withdrawing was proof.

She gave him his few minutes, plus an extra or two while she pulled her hair back, before slowly opening her door. His door was already open, and he was sitting on his unmade bed, fastening a watch around his wrist. He had changed from black sweatpants to red, from a plain white T-shirt to one advertising a ten-kilometer run last fall. His hair was damp and combed carelessly back, and his jaw was clean-shaven, with a small bloody nick on one side.

Already he looked tired.

Her first impulse was to suggest again that he remain here—not so that she would have the freedom to make her phone call in complete privacy, but because he obviously needed rest. Sixteen days was a long time to stay in bed; his body needed time to adjust to the demands of being up and about again. He needed to take things a little slower, a little easier.

But he would merely overrule her again, and she couldn't even convincingly argue the point. She knew how tedious bed rest could be, especially to a man as active as Remy. She completely understood how anxious he was to be in control again, to make his own choices again.

He'd been digging through the bags she hadn't yet unpacked and had located a pile of socks. Valery had packed for him; Susannah had met her yesterday morning at his apartment to pick up both her and the bags for the trip up here. His neighborhood was old and gracious, the apartments also old, sprawling, situated on lush grounds. She had gotten a glimpse inside the door of gleaming wood floors and high ceilings, of elaborate woodwork and a polished stair rail curving toward the second floor, and she'd been impressed.

Then she'd seen Belle Ste. Claire.

The two homes had encouraged her hopes that she could keep things on a strictly professional level between them. A man who had grown up here in what was nothing less than a mansion, who now lived in a place so dramatically different from the small apartment *she* could afford, surely had to have at least one snobbish, smugly superior bone in his body.

But if he did, it was the one he'd broken. He'd already made it clear, both with his words and, more importantly, with his behavior, that he intended to treat her not as a servant or employee, but as an equal. As a companion. As a prospective friend.

That knowledge hurt Susannah, somewhere way down inside. He didn't deserve her deceit, and she didn't deserve his friendship.

Even though some small part of her wanted it.

Pulling a tissue from the box on the night table, she offered it to him. "You're still bleeding," she said, releasing the small froth of white as soon as he took it.

"I haven't cut myself shaving since I was seventeen," he grumbled as he pressed the tissue to his jaw.

"You haven't tried to do it balanced on one leg and a wooden stick before…have you?"

His laughter erased the sourness from his expression. "No, I can't say I was ever that dumb. If you could just find a shoe for me…"

She bypassed the suitcases he had already rummaged through and moved on to a nylon duffel. It was filled with magazines and books, notebooks, stationery and pens.

"I told Valery to bring whatever I might need in the next month," he remarked from the bed where he was watching her. "It looks as if she didn't leave much behind."

The last bag, pushed half under the bed on the opposite side, was also a duffel and, judging from the variety, was the last one his cousin had packed, the one that had gotten all the last-minute choices. Lifting it to the bed, Susannah pulled out a pile of mail that had accumulated during his hospital stay, a couple of jackets, three single left shoes and, from the very bottom, a leather holster and a zippered nylon case. The case was triangular, black and surprisingly heavy for its size, and for a moment she simply stared at it.

For a time Skip had had the same thing at home: a gun rug, he'd called it when she had confronted him with it. Finding it in his room—complete with a semiautomatic pistol and an extra clip of ammunition inside—when she was putting away the clean laundry had frightened her more than she'd ever been frightened before. It was one thing for Remy Sinclair, a responsible adult and FBI agent, to have a gun at home, but another entirely for her immature baby brother. She had caused such a commotion that Skip had promised to take the gun back to wherever he'd gotten it that same day. She didn't know if he had or if he had simply found a better hiding place.

He'd made so many promises.

And he hadn't kept a single one.

Well, she had made a promise, too—to their mother, only minutes before she died. To their father the day she'd set out from Nebraska for New Orleans. To her brother and to herself. She had promised that she would look out for Skip, had promised that she would help him and take care of him, had promised that she would protect him from harm, even when the greatest harm that threatened him was of his own making. She had promised, and she would keep it.

No matter what it did to Remy.

He was watching her now with an absorbed look, a curious sort of scrutiny, that reminded her uncomfortably that he was a cop. After a moment, he leaned across the bed and pulled the case from her hand. "Do you know what's in here?"

She didn't answer, didn't look at him.

He unzipped the case and opened it flat for her inspection.

She risked only a quick glance, only enough to see that there was, indeed, a pistol inside, very similar to but somehow even deadlier-seeming than the one Skip had had. Nestled on the corduroy lining beside it was an extra clip. "This is a ten-millimeter semiautomatic," he said quietly. "I keep it fully loaded, with one round chambered. When we go out, I'll carry it. The rest of the time, it'll stay in the nightstand drawer. You leave it alone, all right?"

She nodded dumbly.

He withdrew the pistol and rezipped the case, then claimed the holster from her. "I'd think, growing up in the country the way you did, you'd have at least a passing familiarity with guns."

"I have a healthy respect for them," she corrected him as she turned away, folding the empty duffel and laying it on top of the dresser.

"Good." In the mirror she caught a fractured glimpse of his wry smile as he rubbed the bruised area on his chest. "I wish more people did."

While he began the task of putting on one sock and shoe, Susannah started neatly refolding some of the clothing scattered around the bed. She had unpacked the smallest of his bags last night after dinner and should have completed the job, but he'd insisted it could wait until today. As soon as they got back from town, she promised herself.

When he was ready, she followed him from the room, confirming with a quick glance back that the pistol was gone from where he'd laid it on the bed. Tucked somewhere underneath the T-shirt and fleece jacket he wore? "Are you expecting trouble here?" she asked, pausing in the hallway before ducking into her own room for her purse.

He glanced back at her over his shoulder. "Trouble?" he echoed, sounding too innocent and surprised to be believed. "At Belle Ste. Claire?"

The idea, she thought, seemed somehow obscene. According to Valery, the house had survived the Civil War unscathed.

It had withstood the Mississippi's flooding and the occasional hurricanes and tornadoes that happened along. It was a safe place, a secure place.

At least, it had been until yesterday. Until they had opened the doors to *her.*

She got her things from her room, then caught up with him at the side door, where he offered her a set of keys. As she locked up, he gestured toward the back of the house. "The garage is back there. The round key unlocks the side door. You'll have to try the keys. I don't know which set goes to which car. You can take your pick."

Susannah's nerves tightened fractionally. "Why can't we take my car?"

"Because I don't think both the cast and I can fit in your front seat—at least, not comfortably. Besides, I told you when I hired you that a car would be provided for you. There's no reason for you to use your car to run my errands."

Although she would have liked to argue the point, she didn't, because he was right. Her car was a good little car—with the emphasis on little. To get the kind of mileage she'd wanted and the price she'd needed, she'd had to compromise on something, and size had been it. "Wait here," she instructed, starting down the steps and across the driveway.

The lock on the side door turned easily. There was a light switch right inside, along with a button for the automatic garage door. She pressed both, then circled the Cadillac for the Buick on the other side. The color was a rich burgundy outside, a subdued shade inside. The seats were leather, luxurious and soft, and the interior smelled of a woman's fragrance, something unfamiliar to Susannah, rich and appealing.

She started the engine, adjusted the driver's seat for more leg room and the mirrors for better visibility, then slowly backed out of the garage. The car was a far cry from the '63 Chevy truck that she'd learned to drive in or even from her own little blue sedan parked outside. How nice it must be, she thought without any real twinge of envy, to have money. It was an experience she would probably never know. She had finally finished paying off her school loans, only to find that her income could barely keep even with Guy's outgo. The year following the divorce had been better for her, but then she had come to New Orleans and had found herself providing the majority of Skip's support.

Someday she would be responsible only for herself and only to herself. That was a promise.

And Susannah Duncan kept her promises.

She pulled up close to the house to save Remy as many steps as possible. Although she got out of the car to help him down the steps, he ignored her and started down by himself. Hovering nearby in case he slipped or lost his balance, she silently counted each of the steps—five, six, seven—until he reached the bottom. A fine layer of sweat glistened across his forehead, and pain-etched lines crinkled the corners of his mouth as he drew a deep, frustrated breath. After a moment to catch his breath, he glanced at her, almost smiled and faintly murmured, "Damn."

In another few minutes, he was settled as comfortably as the cast would allow and they were on their way. Other than giving directions to the interstate, he remained silent for the first portion of the trip. Maybe this wouldn't be so bad, she thought, concentrating on traffic and the soft sounds of jazz flowing from the speakers.

Then he broke the silence. "Tell me about your family."

Her fingers tightened around the steering wheel. "My family?"

"You know—mother, father, sister, brother. You do have a family, don't you?"

"Yes, I do."

"So…?"

"So I have a family back home in Nebraska, running the farm."

"You're not very good at this small-talk stuff, are you?" he asked, his tone mildly amused. "It works like this. I ask you questions and you answer them, and then you ask me questions and I answer. That way we learn something about each other so we're not strangers anymore."

She resisted the natural urge to smile at his teasingly patient explanation. "All right. What about your family?"

"It's not your turn, but I'll answer anyway to show you how it's done." He paused, glancing out the window for a moment, then began. "My father is a lawyer, like me, and my mother is involved in every charity within a hundred miles. They've been married forty years next month. I'm their only child, and I've been a great disappointment to them in one way or another more than half my life."

His words made Susannah uncomfortable. That was more than she'd wanted to know…and yet she wanted to hear more. She wanted to know how a man as bright and accomplished as he seemed to be—a lawyer, for heaven's sake, and a federal agent in addition to that—could possibly be a disappointment to anyone, most especially his parents. She wanted to know how a man as damn near perfect as he seemed to be could have even a vague acquaintance with the feelings of inadequacy that she'd lived with most of her life.

But he was staring once more at the scenery passing by, saying nothing. Feeling compelled to respond, she lamely murmured, "I'm sure you're mistaken about that."

He looked at her, catching her gaze for an instant before she hastily turned back to the road. The expression in his blue eyes was grim and unforgiving. Of his parents? she wondered. Or of himself? "They asked me to leave their home. They told me not to come back until I had become a son they could be proud of. We didn't speak for fifteen years." A hint of self-directed bitterness crept into his voice. "No, I don't think I misunderstood."

She'd heard enough, she silently warned herself. That little pang of sympathy that clutched at her meant she'd heard too much. She didn't want to continue this conversation. She didn't want to hear one more word for the rest of this trip.

So why did she find herself, only a moment later, quietly saying, "Tell me what happened"?

Chapter 3

Remy continued to gaze out the window. He liked wintertime in the south. There were always blasts of cold weather, enough to remind you that it was winter, but nothing cold or interminable enough to prompt vows of moving to a warmer climate. A number of trees lost their leaves, so there were the new buds of spring to look forward to, but just as many stayed green so that they avoided the starkness of barren forests. You could even find flowers in bloom, if you looked, every month of the year.

Tell me what happened. Was she interested or simply making conversation? He could turn to his left, could study her face and her eyes, but he wouldn't find any more of an answer there than he did in the scenery outside the window. For a woman with such expressive eyes, she was good at revealing next to nothing.

Tell me what happened. Drawing in a slow breath, he did just that. "I assume Valery told you that she had once lived at

Belle Ste. Claire." From the corner of his eye, he saw her hair swing with her nod. "Her father is my mother's brother. When his wife left him, she left Valery, too. She didn't want…I don't know—didn't want to be a wife, didn't want to be a mother, didn't want to make any more sacrifices. I guess she assumed that my uncle would take over, would fill the void she left in Valery's life, but he didn't. If she wasn't going to be responsible anymore, then damn it, neither was he. Since he couldn't just abandon Valery, he brought her to Belle Ste. Claire. He just showed up one day with her, with everything she owned packed in a couple of cardboard boxes, and he left her there without apologies, without any promises, without even a goodbye."

More than twenty-three years had passed since that day—a lifetime, Remy thought—but his memories were vivid. He remembered how surprised he'd been to come home from school in the middle of the week and find his cousin there. He remembered how the matter of her parents' divorce hadn't struck him as important at all. His parents were happily married; so were his grandparents, his other aunts and uncles and all the other adults he'd known. He hadn't understood the ramifications of a divorce, hadn't realized that it meant anything at all to him beyond the fact that he wouldn't be seeing his aunt Trish anymore, which had been fine with him because she'd never been one of his favorites anyway.

His parents had explained over dinner that evening that Valery would now be living with them, and he remembered how intensely and how immediately he had disliked the idea. He and Valery had been good friends, even if she was three years younger and something of a pest. She could throw as good as any eleven-year-old boy, could slide into base better than most and could trade wisecracks and insults with the best of them. All in all, for a girl, she wasn't half bad, and he liked it when she came to visit or when he spent time with her in the city.

But he hadn't wanted her living in his house. He hadn'

wanted her to be a closer part of his family. He hadn't wanted to share his parents, his home or his life with her, not on a full-time basis.

"I wasn't particularly happy about having her move in." That was an understatement. He had been so dismayed by his parents' announcement that he had argued the matter with them right there in front of Valery. Already teary-eyed and distraught over the upheaval in her life, at his display of temper, she had burst into tears and run from the room, and he had been sent to bed without dinner.

That had been the first time his refusal to accept and welcome his cousin into the Sinclair family had gotten him punished, but it hadn't been the last. The last time had cost him, and the price had been dear: he had lost the very family he'd been trying in his own selfish way to hold on to. He had lost fifteen years of his parents' love and respect. Fifteen years of being able to go home. Fifteen years of birthdays and holidays, of having a place he belonged and people he belonged with.

"As far as I was concerned, we didn't need her. We didn't have room for her. We'd gotten along perfectly fine as a family for fourteen years without her. If she needed a place to live…well, hell, that was *her* parents' responsibility, not mine. Let them provide for her." His laughter was short and sour. "I was a selfish kid."

Susannah glanced briefly in his direction. "You liked your life the way it was, and you didn't want it to change. That's not so selfish."

She spoke with the sort of knowledge that came from experience, which raised about a dozen questions in his mind. What was it about her life that had been changed against her will? Her marital status? Had she been happy with her marriage, unaware that there were problems until they could no longer be surmounted? Or had she known the problems were there but opted to ignore or tolerate them rather than give up the life she had become comfortable with?

Rather than ask questions that he suspected she wouldn't answer, he went on with his story. "My parents thought that because Valery and I had gotten along well before the divorce, eventually I would welcome her into the family and we would go back to being friends, that we would become...I don't know, pseudosiblings. Valery thought so, too, and she tried to make it happen, but I refused. I resented every bit of attention, every ounce of affection, Mom and Dad gave her. I hated that they treated her exactly the same way they treated me—as if she were their own child and not some niece whose own parents hadn't wanted her. I devoted most of my energy in the next eight years to shutting her out, to never letting her forget that she wasn't a Sinclair, that she didn't really belong.

"And then I found out something that my parents, and most of the adults in the family, had known all along, something that they'd kept hidden from all of the kids but especially from Valery and me—that she really wasn't part of our family. Her mother had already been pregnant when she met and married my uncle. And during one particularly angry argument with my parents, I brought that fact up, not knowing that Valery was standing outside the door listening."

He knew Susannah was smart and compassionate, knew that she would understand exactly what effect such knowledge had had on his cousin, but he continued anyway, sparing himself nothing. He didn't shy away from letting her see exactly how selfish, how jealous and immature and bitter he had been. He wanted her to know. He wanted to be honest about his biggest shame.

"Both of her parents had abandoned her, and her best friend—that was what she always called me—had turned his back on her when she was only eleven. For all those years the only constant in her life was the family—my parents and all the Navarres. They meant everything to her. And I took that away from her."

"And so your parents asked you to leave."

He still remembered the sick feeling inside when he realized that Valery had overheard, when she had walked into his father's study and he'd seen the hurt and disillusionment on her face. He still remembered the deep gut-wrenching fear that his father's anger had stirred. He and George Sinclair had had more than their share of father-son disagreements—most of them over Valery and Remy's treatment of her—but he had never faced such rage. He had turned to his mother—disappointment was her specialty; it seemed so often he had disappointed her—and he had known then, in one brief moment of emotionless clarity, that his relationship with them wasn't going to survive. For eight years he had been pushing, fighting, trying to force them to choose between him and Valery, between their only child and this girl who was no relation to them at all, and finally they had made their choice.

They had chosen her.

He had gone away, feeling as hurt and abandoned as Valery must have when her parents had left her. He had been angry with himself for being so careless, for hurting Valery, for repeating something he'd never intended her to know, for forcing the issue and losing. He had berated himself for being unable to get past his jealousy, for being unable to make even a token acceptance of her, for being so selfish and so immature and so stubborn.

But, somewhere deep inside, he had still blamed Valery herself. If only she hadn't done whatever she'd done to cause both her parents to not want her, if only she had never come to live with *his* family, if only she hadn't been so damn needy...

If only his parents hadn't preferred her to him.

It said something for the man he was, Susannah thought grimly, that something he'd done half a lifetime ago still held such power over him. The fact was there was nothing so out of the ordinary about his resentment toward Valery. It seemed to her, in fact, that his parents had gotten just what they'd asked for: they had wanted Remy to treat Valery like a sister.

Well, sibling rivalry seemed as accurate a description for the behavior he was describing as anything else.

Even that last part was worthy only of a little regret. So he'd blurted out something Valery wasn't supposed to know. It was a fact of life—people lost their tempers and said things they were later sorry for—but it was rarely a great tragedy. It wasn't worth an estrangement between parents and son. It certainly didn't call for a fifteen-year exile.

Besides, wasn't there an old saying, something about eavesdroppers never hearing anything good about themselves?

No, if Remy wanted to know shame, guilt and regret—*real* shame, the unforgivable kind, guilt you never recovered from—he should step into her life for a few hours. He should make this phone call she would soon be making.

"So…" He sounded more cheerful, but his expression didn't match. "Your turn now. What about your family back home on the farm in Nebraska?"

Silently she apologized—to her father, her brother and to Remy himself—for the lies she was about to tell. Then she shrugged and told them anyway. "There's just my father. My mother died when I was fifteen."

"Are you an only child, too?"

"Yes."

"Were you lonely growing up?"

"Not at all. Daddy farms with my uncle. Richard and his family have a house there, too, so I had my cousins around. The oldest two boys work with Daddy and Uncle Richard now and have places, and families, of their own on the farm."

"What was the best thing about growing up on a farm?"

She considered the question for a mile or two. There was much to recommend farm life, if you didn't mind hard work and gambling your livelihood on the whims of the weather. She'd been given more responsibility and at an earlier age than most of her friends in town. She'd been driving a tractor and that old Chevy truck for years before her friends were finally able to get behind the wheel. She had learned a respect for the land and the people who worked it, had learned a respect for life. She'd grown up with good, hardworking people, had grown up with a work ethic and a value system that she had thought would stay with her forever.

"I miss the innocence," she said at last. "Life was simpler in that time in that place. We worked hard, but we still had time to play. We took care of the land, and it took care of us. We treated people and their property with respect, and they did the same in return. We never had a lot of money, but we never went hungry and we never had to worry about being homeless. We had family, friends and good neighbors. There was never any trouble you could get into that you couldn't get out of, and there was always someone there to lend a hand."

"And yet you left with the intention of never going back for more than occasional visits. Why?"

Because Skip, who had come south to New Orleans to go to school and to work, was doing neither. Because he wasn't mature enough to be completely on his own. Because he needed someone looking after him, someone to gently nudge him back into school, to help him stick with a job.

And because, as she had admitted last night, in the past year she'd seen way too much of Guy Duncan and the woman he had left her for, the woman he'd been having an affair with months before he'd finally moved out. Because he had taken such delight in his snide little put downs, in his public snubs and deliberate little cruelties. Because she had needed to put him and what he had done to her pride—to her ego—behind her before she could face whatever might be ahead.

"It was time," she said simply. That was as true as any of her other reasons. Nebraska was a perfectly fine place for people who wanted to be there, but she had been searching for something else. She had needed a new life, new confi-

dence, a new start. She had needed to see other places, to do
other things, to experience other walks of life.

She had needed to be more than the woman she could be
in Homestead, Nebraska.

The answer seemed to satisfy him—or, at least, to give him
something to think about—because he remained silent until
they reached the outskirts of Baton Rouge. There he advised
her to take the next exit, then directed her to a shopping center
where she could find the items she needed.

She parked a fair distance from the front door of the busy
variety store. "Do you need anything?" she asked as she un-
buckled her seat belt.

"I suppose coming in with you is out of the question."

"I suppose so."

"Let me give you some money—"

"We'll settle up later. I'll make it quick." Before he could
say anything else, she left the car, slinging her purse strap
over her shoulder, and set off across the parking lot,
weaving between parked cars until she could no longer feel
his gaze on her back. That one small freedom brought her
a sigh of relief.

The strip shopping center was nearly a block long. She
could probably find both the gloves and the foam rubber in
the variety store, but she wasn't wasting time looking. She
would get the gloves there, she decided as she approached the
main door, and then walk to the fabric shop for the foam. It
was at the opposite end, behind Remy, and there were at least
three pay phones that she could see between here and there.

She took only a few moments to select a pair of gloves,
then got a roll of adhesive tape on the way out. Not sparing
even a glance for Remy a few aisles over in the car, she
headed for the fabric store, where she bought a length of one-
inch-thick foam. As she started back, though, her steps slowed
and grew less purposeful, especially as she approached, then
passed, the first pay phone. And the second.

It was now or never, she thought as she drew even with the third phone. Stopping, she fumbled in her purse for change, then silently ran through the number she had memorized a week ago. Still, for a time she just stood there, numb and cold, before taking the first of the steps that would carry her to the phone. The second step was harder, the third damn near impossible.

Oh, God, she couldn't do this! She couldn't call that slimy lawyer, couldn't tell him any of the things he wanted to know. She couldn't help him or his sleazy boss in what they were trying to do. She couldn't betray herself this way. She couldn't betray Remy.

And then she thought of Skip, safely in the care of the lawyer and, therefore, his boss—safe as long as she cooperated. As long as she did what they had instructed her to do. Safe as long as she didn't let him down.

Going cold inside, she took the last step. She picked up the receiver, dropped the coins into the slot, dialed the number and listened to the rings, followed by a greeting.

"This is Susannah Duncan," she said, her voice steady and unrecognizable. "I'd like to speak to Mr. Carlucci."

Across the parking lot, Remy was slumped in the passenger seat, which he had reclined to a reasonably comfortable position, and using the outside mirror to follow the progress of a blonde two aisles behind him. "You're easily bored, Sinclair," he mumbled as he adjusted the mirror for a better look. "Lucky for you *and* Susannah, you're also easily amused."

The blonde was just his type—pretty, petite and oh, so consciously feminine. The first thing she'd done after parking her car was check her hair and makeup in the rearview mirror; first thing after exiting the car, she had adjusted her slim skirt and snug sweater, then brushed her fingertips across her hair. She walked with a slow, deliberate grace, and he would bet she talked that way, too—a lazy, honeyed Southern drawl that could turn a man to stone. She was a beautiful woman, and she made the most of it.

In contrast, Susannah seemed hardly even aware of her appearance. If asked the color of her eyes, she would probably say mostly brown and drop it at that, leaving out all the subtle shadings, the soft browns, dark golds and muted greens. If pressed for an opinion on her own prettiness, she would likely reply acceptable. If asked to judge her effect on men—on this man in particular—she would probably say negligible.

And, oh, how wrong she would be.

The blonde reached the sidewalk that ran in front of the shops and turned away from the variety store. Tilting the mirror as far as it would go to follow her progress, Remy found the rear view as interesting as the other angles…at least, until she passed a pay phone, a pay phone where Susannah was making a call.

Slowly he straightened in the seat, returning it to its upright position, and twisted around until he had an unimpeded view. The woman's back was to him, but it was definitely Susannah. He recognized the faded jeans, the pale pink sweater and the rich auburn hair. He recognized the sense of familiarity that struck him each time he saw her anew.

Who was she calling, and why was she calling him or her from a pay phone? Didn't she have a cell phone? And he had explained when he hired her that she should consider Belle Ste. Claire her home. She was welcome to have her mail delivered there, to give the phone number to her family and friends and to have visitors, and she had accepted his offer with a solemn nod. Only now that he knew her a little better, he suspected that nod hadn't been acceptance, but simply acknowledgment. She had understood his offer, but hadn't been sure she would take him up on it.

So who *was* she calling? A friend? He knew she'd made friends—other hospital employees—in her short time in New Orleans because Valery had talked to a few of them after he had hired her. Maybe a boyfriend? He had asked a few questions about her marriage, but he hadn't asked if she was involved with another man. He hadn't even considered it. He had simply assumed that any single, attractive young woman who was willing to leave New Orleans to live with him at Belle Ste. Claire for an entire month had to be unattached. After all, what kind of man would quietly accept such a separation from the woman he was seeing?

Or maybe it was simply business. Maybe there'd been some loose end she hadn't been able to tie up before leaving the city yesterday and she didn't want to pay the roaming charges for a call from her cell.

But why couldn't she make a simple business call from the house? In fact, why couldn't any of those calls be made from home? There were at least a half dozen telephones in the house, and he would gladly give her the privacy—well, not gladly; he was too nosy for that, but at least without suspicion—to make whatever calls she needed.

Her call lasted only a minute longer. After she hung up, she simply stood there for a moment, her head bowed, her shoulders rounded. Bad news? Remy wondered. A less-than-pleasant conversation with a disagreeable boyfriend? Whatever the cause, she looked even wearier than he'd been feeling lately.

Then the moment passed. She straightened her shoulders, raised her head and started toward the car. Slowly he turned around, resettling in the seat, and waited for her to reach him.

The air inside the car cooled a few degrees when she opened the door. She tossed her purse and one bag in the back seat, then offered the second bag to him. "Try those on for size."

Inside the small plastic bag was a pair of black biking gloves. He looked at them skeptically. "I'm barely walking. It'll be a while before I feel like getting out the old twenty-one speed."

She simply looked at him, not even tempted to smile.

He opened the package and removed both gloves. Even those small movements made his hands ache. His fingers were sore and swollen, and in addition to the places where his palms were blistering, small bruises were forming, he noted as he cautiously wriggled one hand into the fingerless glove. The fit was snug, the nylon and suede soft—and the thick padding across the palms was heavenly.

"When you ride a bike," she explained, "depending on your position, you can put a good deal of weight on your hands. You grip the handlebars in pretty much the same way that you hold onto your crutches, so the glove's padding is already in the right place. It won't stop your hands from hurting, especially these first few days, but it *will* help."

He pulled on the second glove, then adjusted the Velcro closures across the back. "Not bad," he remarked, flexing both hands before grinning at her. "They teach you this in nursing school?"

Darned if she didn't smile back. "No. I learned that at home when my—" Her words stopped abruptly, her smile disappeared and she looked at him with an expression that, after twelve years with the FBI, he recognized all too well: guilt. He could see it in her eyes, could feel it in the car—hell, he could damn near smell it. She felt guilty about something, but what? Something she had done or hadn't done? Something she had said, something she had tried and failed at?

Like marriage? *I learned that at home....* Her ex-husband was back home, with his new wife, and he was part of the reason Susannah was here. Had she learned the trick with the gloves from him? Was she trying to avoid talking about him? Did it still hurt to even think about him?

"Susannah? Are you all right?"

She looked away then, turning to stare straight ahead. "Of course." Her voice was chilly, tautly controlled, and her jaw was clenched tightly enough to hurt.

"Are you sure?" When she didn't respond, he hesitantly reached across the seat, touching his fingertips to her jaw, intending to turn her gently toward him. But the instant he made contact, she cringed—*cringed,* for God's sake, as if his touch was unbearable—and shrank away from him.

He drew back, fastened his seat belt, then folded his fingers loosely together in his lap. His right hand rested on his cast, and for a moment he simply stared down. It was stupid to take her rejection so personally, but, damn it, it *felt* personal. He wouldn't have hurt her. He had never been rough with any woman except an occasional suspect who interfered or resisted arrest. He had just wanted to touch her, had just wanted her to look at him.

For a long time she sat without moving; then, peripherally, he saw her reach for her seat belt. A moment later the engine purred to life, and she pulled out of the parking space. The only errand left to run was the grocery store. He didn't bother pointing out to her that they had passed two in the last couple of blocks before reaching the shopping center. He trusted that she had noticed them.

Neither of them spoke until they were at the grocery store. Then she finally faced him, her expression remote and as wary as ever. Now there was something else, too: regret. "What kinds of food do you like?"

"I don't eat liver or fish except catfish. Other than that, I'm easy to please." As an afterthought, he added, "I'd like some orange juice."

She nodded.

"And strawberry ice cream."

Another nod.

"And rice. Spicy foods. Barbecue. And I don't like pork."

"Not even bacon?"

"Of course I like bacon. It's hardly the same as pork chops or ham. And I like sausage."

"Spicy sausage?"

This time it was Remy who nodded.

"What about sweets besides ice cream? Do you like cakes, pies, cookies, candy?"

"Carrot, pecan, chocolate chip and pralines." He hesitated, then offered, "It'll be easier if I go with you."

She patted his hand, an awkward little touch where the black nylon stretched across his skin, then hastily left, closing the door with a muted thud behind her. This time he didn't watch her go.

Instead he reached down and, although it was too late, he slowly peeled off each of the gloves and stuffed them inside his jacket pockets.

By seven-thirty that evening they had eaten dinner, Remy had returned to the parlor to watch television and Susannah was just finishing up in the kitchen. She glanced around as she dried her hands on a towel, thinking about what she had accomplished that day. She had finished unpacking all of Remy's things and carried in and put away all the groceries. She had baked a carrot cake and frosted it with real cream cheese frosting, had cooked dinner and talked with Remy and had even stolen away for fifteen minutes for a solitary walk around the grounds at dusk.

And she had talked with Nicholas Carlucci.

She shared the national prejudice against lawyers in general, and she disliked this lawyer in particular. He was one of those people who cared nothing about the law, about the courts or justice. His decision to earn a law degree had been motivated by financial gain and a seriously undeveloped sense of ethics. He had learned to manipulate the system to benefit his clients and himself, and justice be damned.

He was polite. Smooth. Polished. He hadn't hesitated in telling her right up front that he was enormously successful at whatever he set out to do. In her case, what he was doing— for the time being at least—was watching out for her brother.

But if she failed, if she let them down, he could destroy Skip as easily as he was now protecting him.

She hadn't had much information to offer him today, but he had insisted on regular calls, from pay phones if she could manage it. He had asked a few questions about the house, about Michael Bennett and Valery Navarre's visit yesterday—while Valery had ridden up from New Orleans with Susannah, Michael had picked up Remy at the hospital and brought him—and about Remy's parents' vacation plans. He had told her that Skip was fine, that her brother was enjoying his stay at Mr. Falcone's house and that he wanted to hear from her again in three days' time.

She hadn't told him anything important, she reminded herself.

Not a single thing.

Laying the towel aside, she thought longingly about her bedroom, only a few feet down the hall and the only place in the entire house that—so far, at least—offered any measure of privacy from Remy. But when she moved away from the counter, she turned toward the parlor instead.

Of all the rooms in the house, the parlor was her favorite. The others, even the bedrooms upstairs, were decorated with an eye toward history, with antique furniture, silk wall coverings and valuable old rugs, but the parlor was meant for comfort. It smelled of furniture polish and hothouse flowers, of rich old leather and cinnamon potpourri. The furnishings were inviting: overstuffed pieces with tons of pillows, tables that didn't mind a scratch or two, footstools that you weren't afraid to put your feet on. There was a big leather recliner that had definitely seen better days—Mr. Sinclair's, she wagered—and a barrel chair that looked just about perfect for curling up in with a book or needlework.

Remy was sitting on the sofa watching television, a newspaper open but ignored in his lap, his cast propped on the coffee table. As she passed the recliner, she took a pillow, then lifted his foot and placed the pillow underneath to protect the tabletop from fiberglass scratches. He gave her a sleepy sort of smile of thanks, one that made her stomach flutter all out of proportion to the deed.

Sleepy was not sexy, she sternly admonished herself as she settled in the barrel chair. Oh, but in his case, it was—hair tousled, body relaxed, eyes hazy and soft and mouth softer. A sleepy Remy was more appealing than any other man she'd ever seen.

But she couldn't afford to find him appealing. If she couldn't afford to be his friend, she certainly couldn't afford to even think about being anything else.

God help her, she hated this job. She hated Carlucci and Falcone. She hated herself, and sometimes—she whispered a silent, shameful prayer for forgiveness—sometimes she even hated Skip.

"Anything in particular you want to watch?" Remy asked, offering her the remote control.

She shook her head.

"I don't guess you see much evening television with your schedule." He laid the remote aside. "You're not missing a lot."

"Your job's not usually nine to five, is it?"

"That depends on my caseload."

"Do you do the same kind of stuff all the time, like narcotics or vice?" She knew little about law enforcement, and what she knew was probably inaccurate, since it came from television and movies. Back home, Homestead was too small and too quiet to have a police department of its own; whatever crimes committed there were few and far between, were rarely more serious than teenage mischief making and were investigated by the sheriff's department.

"I work organized crime, which these days can include a little bit of everything."

Organized crime. It sounded so ominous, so threatening.

The first time she had heard Jimmy Falcone's name, she hadn't known that he *was* organized crime in New Orleans. Law and order and criminal justice hadn't held much interest for her. She rarely watched the local news, and although she read the newspaper each day, she merely skimmed or skipped those sorts of stories completely. It was just coincidence, she supposed, that she had read or heard something about Jimmy Falcone and the corruption that was his business only a day or two before Skip had mentioned his new job and his boss, Mr. Falcone.

She had asked Skip about Falcone, and he had brushed her off. The man's reputation was undeserved. Yeah, some of the people who had once worked for him had taken some less-than-legal shortcuts, but it had been without Mr. Falcone's knowledge, and once he had found out, he'd gotten rid of them, had fired them right away. Skip had talked his way out of it and she had let him, because she'd had other things on her mind. Because, deep in her heart, she had remained convinced that her brother—while a little wild, a little reckless and a whole lot irresponsible—would never do anything really bad. He might drink a little too much, might pick a fight with the wrong guy, might create a public disturbance, but he was just a high-spirited kid. He would never do anything *really* illegal. He wasn't a crook, wasn't a thief or a thug or worse.

Good Lord, she had been naive.

Even now she didn't know exactly how Skip was involved in Falcone's business. All she knew was that her little brother, the brother she had practically raised, the brother she had promised to always take care of, to always protect, had become someone she hardly knew. He had become someone who would carry an illegal weapon. He had become someone who saw nothing wrong with earning large sums of money for doing very little work for a man who controlled half the money-making crime in the city.

All she knew was that Nicholas Carlucci was promising one of two outcomes to Skip's situation. If she cooperated, sometime within the next month, her brother would be allowed to leave New Orleans, with no threats hanging over his head, free for her to take home to Nebraska. But if she didn't cooperate, Carlucci would see to it that Skip went to prison for a very long time...or worse.

Susannah always kept her promises.

Nicholas Carlucci had assured her in a voice that had left her shaking with fear that he, too, always kept his promises.

Realizing that Remy was watching her, waiting for her to continue their conversation, she gestured toward his cast. "Why did you get shot?"

His mouth thinned, and his eyes turned hard. "Because I trusted the wrong person."

A shiver rippled through her, and she moved uncomfortably, trying to contain it. When she responded, it was in a thin, small voice. "I don't imagine you make that mistake often."

"No, I don't. It won't happen again."

You're wrong, she wanted to warn him. *It's already happening again. You're trusting me when you should lock me away with all the rest of the criminals.* But she simply clasped her hands tightly together to hide their trembling, and she quietly asked, "What happened?"

Remy studied the remote for a moment before pressing the button to mute the sound. Where should he start? How much did she want to know? More importantly, how much did he want her to know? Anything that might boost her interest. Nothing that might give her cause for concern. Everything that could help her come to trust him.

He turned on the couch so that he was facing her, then leaned forward to slide a pillow underneath his foot. Before he managed, though, Susannah left her chair and arranged the pillows so his cast was at just the right elevation for comfort. He could have done it himself, he thought with a faint smile.

But there was something awfully sweet about her doing it for him.

"Do you remember the Simmons murder in the Quarter last month?"

She was back in her chair again, her feet tucked beneath her. "I remember hearing about it. I didn't pay a lot of attention."

"The guy was walking down the street, talking to a woman he'd just met, when two of his buddies drove up, got out of their car and blew him away. The dead guy was one of my informants, and the woman who witnessed his murder was my cousin, Valery."

"Interesting coincidence," she murmured.

"We, the FBI, thought it *was* just coincidence at first. Valery worked in the Quarter. She always left work at the same time every afternoon, always walked the same route to her car every day. It was just bad luck and timing, we thought, that she was there the day Nate Simmons got killed."

"But you were wrong."

"We were wrong. Simmons knew he was part of a scam— he was a con artist by trade; he could smell a game a mile away. He was supposed to meet Valery that day, was supposed to walk down the street with her, was supposed to run into his buddies. Unfortunately he didn't know the rest of the plan. These guys killed Simmons but left Valery unharmed, the best witness the police could ever ask for. She was standing only a few feet from the two men. She got a good look at them, could describe them perfectly. She even heard them mention the name of the man who had hired them to kill Nate, and she had a damned good reason to repeat the information to the police. But she didn't."

"You," Susannah guessed. "They said you were the one who had hired them."

Nodding, he thought back to that Monday afternoon last month. It hadn't been so long ago, but it seemed like forever. He hadn't been hobbling around in a cast then. He hadn't had any contact with his parents or Valery in years. He hadn't known that someone he trusted was going to betray him. He hadn't known he would soon come too terrifyingly close to dying.

He hadn't known Susannah even existed.

Or maybe he had. Maybe he hadn't known her face or her name, but had known the woman, the spirit, the soul. Maybe that was why he'd felt such an immediate connection to her a few weeks later in the emergency room.

Putting those thoughts aside, he continued with his story. "It was a setup from the start. I was conducting an investigation into Simmons's boss's activities, and I was getting close. All it would take to get me pulled off was even a hint of impropriety. Being implicated in the murder of my own informant could have ended my career. The bastard figured that if he could get rid of me, the case would be turned over to my partner, who just happened to be on his payroll. He assumed that, with our history, Valery would be more than happy to bring me down, but he didn't count on family loyalty. She wasn't convinced that I was guilty, and she wasn't going to ruin my reputation until she *was* convinced."

He broke off for a moment to study Susannah. She seemed more distressed by his tale than the facts warranted. Concern for *him* certainly wasn't responsible for that look in her eyes. Maybe innocence was. Growing up on a farm and living a small-town Nebraska life weren't enough to prepare her for the crime, the lack of caring and the violence that were part of life in a big city. No doubt she'd heard plenty about violence before leaving the prairies behind, but what was it she'd said today? *I miss the innocence. There was never any trouble you could get into that you couldn't get out of...*

"Once we figured out what was going on, we made a deal with my partner. He'd get me hooked up with Jimmy Falcone—his boss—and he wouldn't spend the rest of his life in prison. He arranged the meeting, but it turned out that he was more afraid of Falcone than he was of us. He warned the bastard away, and he shot me." He shook his head, still disbelieving even after all this time. "My own partner shot me."

"So Nate Simmons was a sacrifice to Jimmy Falcone's ambition and greed." Her voice was flat, as if she found the very words too repulsive to say with any degree of comfort. "What happened to your partner?"

"He's in jail, awaiting trial. He's considered too big a flight risk to allow bail."

"Is he going to testify against Falcone?"

Remy shook his head again. "He's afraid. People like Falcone…their influence extends everywhere. Even into the jails."

"What about Falcone? Did you arrest him?"

His grin was rueful. "We're working on it—or, at least, the agents who replaced my partner and me are. The man's slippery, and he's smart, and he inspires tremendous loyalty. The night I got shot, we made eight arrests, but not one of them will implicate their boss in any way. Plus, he's bought himself one of the best damn lawyers in the state of Louisiana. Nick Carlucci knows the law inside and out. He's as slick and as sly as the best of them."

"What about Valery? Will she testify against Falcone?"

"She'll testify against the men who killed Simmons, unless they cut a deal first, but she doesn't know anything firsthand about Falcone."

Susannah picked up a needlepoint pillow that his mother had made and signed and stroked her fingertips lightly across the textured surface. "It must have been terrible for her… seeing someone murdered."

"Yes," he agreed grimly, thinking back to the only time in his career when he had watched someone die. "It was. But—if it's not wrong to look on the bright side—because of it she met Michael, and they're getting married as soon as my parents get back from vacation."

"Considering your…" Still studying the needlepoint, she borrowed his earlier word. "History, does that bother you?"

He did consider it for a moment. He'd grown up a lot since that last angry night here, a lot more than the passage of time could account for. Much of his maturing had come in the last ten months, starting with Evan's death. In less than a year, he had lost one of his three best friends. He had watched Michael damn near drink himself to death in a futile effort to ease the pain, the sorrow and the guilt. He had gone through the Simmons case, had coped with his concern for Valery's life and with his partner's betrayal. He had faced his own mortality.

Did it bother him that, after taking his place in his parents' affections, Valery had now taken precedence over him with his best friend? "No, not at all. She's good for Michael. She brings him peace, a reason to believe, and he makes her feel loved. They're both happier than I've ever seen them."

No, far from being bothered, if anything, he was envious of Michael and Valery. He wanted what they had, wanted to share that same sort of love, devotion and commitment with someone. He wanted the future they were facing together: the family, the promises, the years and the undeniable assurance of a lifetime of love.

And he had no doubt that he would find it. Maybe with Susannah, maybe not.

But he *would* find it.

Chapter 4

Sunday was a beautiful day, sunny and warm, a late-winter reminder that spring was coming. Back home spring was Susannah's favorite season because it meant the long, harsh winter was over. She had loved the weeks of snow and ice when she was a kid, but found them less than enthralling as an adult. The hard weather and slick roads had bothered her so much more each year that, last November, she had said a prayer of thanks as she'd driven away from Homestead that she wouldn't be enduring them again. She had refused to even bring her heavy winter clothing with her. Sweaters and a jacket or two had gone into her bags, but the down-filled coats, the gloves and scarves and the warm boots had stayed behind, boxed up in the attic at the farm.

Down here, she speculated, spring couldn't be too different from winter. The temperatures would be warmer—although they'd had plenty of December and January days that were shirtsleeve weather—and there would be more flowers in bloom, although she had already spotted the delicate blooms of wood violets and yellow jasmine, and the honeysuckle was fragrant outside her bedroom window. The change in seasons here would be subtler, more gradual, lacking Nebraska's drama. The world would slowly become greener and warmer, and then one day they would wake and it would be summer.

She regretted with a deep sigh that she wouldn't experience a Louisiana summer.

"If you're bored, you don't have to stay out here."

Rolling her head to the side, she looked at Remy. It had been his idea to come outside this afternoon, to find a sunny spot on the lawn and soak up a few rays. They had brought books—his a murder mystery that Valery had brought from home, hers a history of Mardi Gras from his parents' library—and he had made his way with more grace and assurance than any man on crutches ought to have to one of the few places in the side yard where the giant oaks and pines allowed the sun to reach the ground. It had taken her only a moment to bring chairs from the gallery, wooden ones painted hunter green, along with a small table he could use as a hassock, and they had settled in to read.

"I'm not bored. I'm reading," she replied, fully aware that the book had slipped halfway off her lap at least thirty minutes ago while she had contemplated any number of lazy thoughts.

"You can't learn about Mardi Gras from a book. You have to experience it."

She didn't point out that if she were back in New Orleans instead of here with him, sometime in the next few weeks, she would be doing just that—would catch at least one of the parades, would spend at least a few hours in the Quarter soaking up the atmosphere and being generally overwhelmed. "I didn't realize that technically Mardi Gras refers only to Shrove Tuesday and that all the festivities leading up to it are actually part of Carnival instead." She gave him a smug look. "So I *can* learn from a book."

"Yeah, but being there is a lot more fun." He paused, then offered, "You can go back for the last couple days of Carnival if you want. That's when they have the big parades, and you'll probably be ready for some time away by then."

His suggestion held a certain appeal, Susannah silently acknowledged. But if she got away from him and Belle Ste. Claire for a few days, if she was out of Nicholas Carlucci's reach for forty-eight hours… Who knew? She just might give in to her cowardice—or would it be courage?—and run away and hide. She might abandon Skip to his fate. She might save Remy from his.

She smiled faintly, politely, in rejection of his offer. "It'll come around again next year." But she wouldn't be there to see it. She would be in a quiet corner of some anonymous city, someplace where it didn't get cold in winter, where a person didn't know her neighbors and didn't make friends. In a place where she could forget—no, not forget, but could live with who she was and what she had done.

She would never forget.

Closing the book, she stretched her legs straight out in front of her, then let them dangle over the broad arm of the chair. "You don't seem particularly fascinated with your book, either."

"I figured out who done it and how by the end of Chapter One."

"Must be an occupational hazard. I think cops would find mysteries too easy and would read something totally unrelated to work."

"My reading material usually *is* work—reports, investigative notes, criminal histories. I don't have much time for fiction."

Her next question slipped out before she realized it. "Why did you join the FBI?"

"Didn't we have this conversation before?" he asked with a wry grin. "Because I like to arrest people."

"You didn't have to go to college and law school to do that.

You could have just gotten a job with the local county sheriff's department."

"Parish," he corrected her. "Down here we have parishes instead of counties."

She didn't miss a beat. "With the local parish sheriff's department. Why spend seven years in school, only to become a cop?"

"I didn't plan it that way," he admitted. "I went to college because all Sinclairs go to college, and I went on to law school with the intention of becoming a lawyer like my dad. By the time I started my last year, Michael and Evan—he was one of our roommates in college—were already working for the NOPD, and Smith, our other roommate who was also in law school, already knew he was going to be a prosecutor somewhere. They got me interested enough to follow along, only I didn't want to be a city cop and I sure as hell didn't want to spend my life in courtrooms, so I went with the bureau instead."

"Do you ever regret it?"

"No."

"Not even the night you got shot?"

He shook his head.

It must be nice, she thought, to be so certain. She'd made few choices in her life that she hadn't had doubts and regrets about. Going to school, being a nurse, getting married—even the divorce had been a major indecision for her. Even though it had been Guy's choice, she could have made it difficult for him, and a part of her had been tempted. A part of her had actually wondered, back in those bleak days, if maybe a bad marriage was better than no marriage at all, if maybe a husband who felt little liking and no respect for her was better than no husband at all. She had wanted to be rid of him as much as he wanted to be gone, but she had been afraid—of admitting failure, of being alone, of facing their families and friends on her own, no longer as one half of a couple, no longer Guy's wife, but the woman he had left. The woman he had been so publicly unfaithful to. The woman who couldn't hold on to a man.

Thank God she had regained her sanity—and her dignity— and had let the divorce proceed without objection.

"So you're never going to practice law, like your father," she said, getting her thoughts back in line.

"I can't say never. I don't know what might happen in another ten or twenty years. I *can* say I don't plan to. What about you? Are you ever going to quit nursing?"

"I don't plan to."

"Not even when you get married again and have kids to raise?"

"I don't plan to do that, either."

He studied her for a moment, his gaze steady and intense enough to make her want to squirm. When he finally broke his silence, his voice was quiet and edged with sympathy. "Was it that bad?"

She pretended ignorance. "What?"

"Your marriage. Was it bad enough to scare you away from trying again?"

She didn't have to answer. She could ignore his question or simply tell him that she didn't want to discuss it, and he would let it drop. He was too polite, his manners too deeply ingrained, to insist.

But he was also curious—he'd made that clear their first evening here. And wasn't it only fair, since she was the one who had turned the conversation to a personal level, that he be allowed to ask questions, too?

"I consider my marriage a learning experience," she said at last.

"And what did you learn?"

"That the institution of marriage is largely overrated. That people you think you know can surprise you. That, while it may be true that someone else can't be responsible for your happiness, he can sure as hell be blamed for your misery."

The words hung between them, caught in the ensuing silence, spoken without overt anger or cynicism but brushed with bitterness at the end, Remy thought. He had lived with the feeling for so long himself that he would always recognize it, and he would always remember the other emotions it encompassed: resentment, animosity, hopelessness and pain. Always pain.

After a moment, he responded, keeping his voice carefully neutral. "Those are some interesting lessons."

She simply shrugged.

"They raise a hell of a lot more questions than they answer."

"I get the impression everything raises questions with you."

He acknowledged that with a nod. "But to show you how considerate I can be, I'm not going to ask you to go into it further. Just tell me one thing." He looked away, following the progress of a car as it traveled along the highway out front. When it had rounded a curve and disappeared from sight, he returned his gaze to her. "Do you have regrets?"

"About the marriage?"

"About the divorce."

"Do you mean am I sorry he left me?" She drew a deep breath, then blew it out. "I would like to have been the one doing the leaving and not the one left behind. For the sake of my ego, I would like to have been the one who initiated the divorce. But would I undo it if I could? Would I go back if he'd have me? No." For a moment she looked as if she wanted to say something more, but she settled for repeating and qualifying her answer. "No, I wouldn't. Not ever."

He had assumed, upon learning their first night here that she had been married before, that ending the marriage had been her decision. What man in his right mind, he had wondered, would be fool enough to let her go? Only Duncan hadn't *let* her go; he had pushed her away with both hands. *He* had walked away from *her*.

Why? What had there been about this quiet, pretty, intelligent, gentle and capable woman that he hadn't liked? Exactly what had he been looking for that Susannah couldn't provide? Maybe Duncan had liked his women dumb, brassy and flashy. Maybe he resented a woman who was brighter than he was.

Or maybe he had taken whatever it was he wanted from her, and then had discarded her for someone else. Hadn't she said that part of her reason for moving to New Orleans had to do with seeing too much of her ex-husband and his new wife?

"I plan to get married," he announced, tilting his head back and studying the thin, stringy clouds in the sky.

"You've never been married?" She sounded as if she were asking against her will. Because she was asking only to be polite? Because she disliked the subject? Because she wasn't interested?

Or maybe because she didn't want to be interested but was?

He preferred that last possibility himself. "No. First there was law school to get through, then starting the job with the bureau. After that…I always thought there would be plenty of time to find someone and settle down. There wasn't any rush. I could always do it next year."

"And then you got shot in the chest and realized that next year might not come." The cynicism that had been missing from her voice earlier was there now. "So now you want to do all the things you'd been putting off until later. Life offers no guarantees, so you'll go for whatever you can get."

"You're too young to be so cynical, Susannah," he said, his tone a mild rebuke.

"Marriage is too important to be taken so lightly," she retorted. "You don't wake up in a hospital bed and say, 'Gee, I may not live to see forty-five, so if I want to get married, I'd better do it now.' You don't get married for the sake of having done it. You do it because you've fallen in love, because you can't imagine living without this person, because she completes who you are, because there's an emptiness to your life that no one can fill but her."

"So you do have a romantic streak hidden somewhere inside. I was beginning to wonder," he teased. After a moment, though, his smile faded. "I'm thirty-seven years old, and I've never married. It's not because I haven't had the opportunity. There have been women, but none that I want to wake up with five years down the line, and certainly none I can imagine spending the rest of my life with. You know those pictures you see sometimes in the newspaper of little old gray-haired couples who have been together fifty and sixty and even seventy years? *That's* what I'm looking for. Getting shot didn't make me decide to get married for the sake of being married, but it did make me rethink my priorities. It made me reconsider what's important in life."

"And you consider marriage important." She shrugged as if the conversation now bored her. "Well, good luck. Because you know those little old gray-haired couples who have been together fifty, sixty and seventy years? They're getting harder and harder to find. Marriage is no longer a commitment in our society. It's a short-term affair."

"Not to everyone." But, no doubt, he thought grimly, that was all it had meant to her ex-husband. She had wanted the fifty or sixty years, the commitment, but he had only been interested in the affair. Now she was determined not to give anyone else the chance to change her mind.

She didn't yet know how persuasive *he* could be.

Knowing instinctively that they had covered the subject as thoroughly as Susannah intended to at the present time, he let his attention drift from her to the grounds. His mother had always had help with the house, but the yard had been a family job. The azaleas, numbering well into the hundreds and some of them taller now than Remy, were his father's pride and joy, and the flower beds and vines—wisteria, honeysuckle and jasmine—were his mother's responsibility. He supposed that now they hired someone to help with the acres of mowing that had once been *his* job. At his apartment in town, he had a handkerchief-size patch of lawn with an azalea or two, a dogwood, a crape myrtle and the kind of lush, thick grass that couldn't be grown underneath the shade that covered most of this lawn, and the management company hired someone to come in and take care of everything so all he had to do was admire it.

He had hated the mowing when he was sixteen and eager to be off with his friends. Now he kind of missed it.

"How does it feel to be home?"

He glanced at Susannah and grinned. "A little strange with Mom and Dad gone."

"Valery said they wanted to cancel their trip and stay here, but you refused."

"They'd been planning it for a long time. After all, how often does a fortieth anniversary come along? Besides, we had two weeks in the hospital to get caught up on the last fifteen years, and we'll have plenty of time to visit when they get back."

And, he had to admit, he'd had other, more selfish reasons for encouraging them to continue with their vacation as planned. He hadn't wanted to share his first visit home with anyone else. Susannah didn't quite count; after all, the place was new to her. She didn't have any memories of it, good or bad. It didn't represent anything to her. He had wanted the house to himself, had wanted to indulge only his own memories.

And then there had been Susannah. With his parents here, he would have no need of her care. He would have missed out on the long hours they'd spent together, on the conversations and the simple pleasure of sharing her company. He would have missed out on getting to know her. He would have missed out on starting to care about her.

A car on the highway drew his gaze as the driver slowed, then pulled to the shoulder of the road. Tourists, he thought, as the woman in the passenger's seat raised a camera and snapped off a few pictures from inside the car. "Belle Ste. Claire has never been open to the public," he remarked, "except for an occasional fund-raiser for one of Mom's charities. But that's never stopped people from pulling off the road and taking pictures. When I was a kid, we used to find strangers wandering around the grounds, and I remember coming home from school one day and there were people up on the gallery, peeking through the windows."

She lazily turned her head to glance at the couple before they drove on. "It's an impressive place," she murmured. "You grew up here. It's all very familiar to you. It's *home*. But most people will never know what it's like to live in a house like this. It's so gracious and elegant and grand. They like to look. They like to wonder, to pretend, to fantasize."

To fantasize. Over the past few days he'd been developing a few fantasies of his own, but they had nothing to do with the house. No, his fantasies could take place anywhere or nowhere. They didn't involve elegance or grandeur, but in a sense—spiritual almost—they had a great deal to do with *home*.

They had a very great deal to do with Susannah.

With a sigh that sounded like regret, she got to her feet. "I need to start dinner and run a few loads of laundry. Do you want to stay out here a while longer?"

Of course not. He wanted to follow wherever she went. Laundry, cooking, cleaning—he'd discovered a fascination in the most mundane of chores when she was the one doing them. He could watch her do nothing for hours and never be bored. He could do nothing with her for hours or, better yet, he could do with her all the things his fantasies were built on. Like touching. Looking. Undressing. Getting familiar.

Getting intimate.

"I'll come in. It's going to get cooler as the sun starts

going down." His voice was huskier than it should be, but she didn't seem to notice.

Standing up from the low, slanted seat had been so easy for her, a smooth, graceful flow of movement. Damn this cast, it was awkward as hell for him…at least until she took his hands in hers and pulled.

Susannah almost always regretted acting on impulse, and she knew the instant she touched him that she would regret this. But there was no way to help him up without touching him, no way without getting much too close.

By the time he was on his feet, they were indeed close. So close that to see his face, she would have to tilt her head back and look up. So close that she could smell the fabric softener that scented his T-shirt. So close that she could feel his heat and imagined that she could hear his heartbeat, although it was really probably her own, erratic and rapid, echoing in her ears.

Once he was steady on his feet, she would let go, would back away and retrieve his crutches. She told herself that. But once he was steady on his feet, *he* let go and instead skimmed his hands along her arms until they rested on her shoulders.

"Susannah."

She swallowed hard. She couldn't pretend the huskiness in his voice was normal.

"You know I'd like to kiss you."

Her response was little more than a frightened plea. "No."

"No, you don't know? No, I wouldn't like to? Or no, I can't?"

"You don't… I… You can't."

Bit by slow bit, his hands moved, sliding across the thin cotton of her shirt, inching up until his palms cupped her cheeks, until his fingers were gently stroking her jaw, raising her head, lifting her face to his. "You have to know that I would never hurt you."

She forced a deep breath, then another. Feigning the calmness that had long since forsaken her, she met his gaze.

"Is this part of the job, Remy?" she asked in a soft, blunt voice. "Is this part of what you expect from a companion?"

She saw the surprise in his eyes, saw the denial and the faint flare of hurt that she had even asked; then his expression subtly shifted, emotions taking cover behind shadows. "What if it is? What if keeping your job here means accepting this? What if this is one of those specific details you thought I would fill you in on as they come up?"

He was bluffing. She knew it as surely as she knew anything. Remy Sinclair was a handsome man. He was charming, sexy, came from a genteel background, had an advancing career and the promise of fortune in his future. With everything he could offer a woman, he had no reason to resort to blackmail. All he had to do was pick up the phone, make a call or two, and he could have his choice of women up here from New Orleans within the hour.

He had no reason to resort to *her.*

"I'd say one of us got a bad deal," she said, her voice even, her tone noncommittal. "Either I hired out cheap…or you're not getting what you paid for."

His smile was grudging. "Any price you might ask would be too cheap."

"Any price you might pay would be too much."

He chuckled. "You're a hard woman, Susannah."

That was one of the insults Guy had thrown at her from time to time. She was hardheaded when she was too stubborn to give in to him on some minor issue, hard-hearted when she wouldn't let him sweet-talk his way out of trouble, and just plain hard when he was looking to undermine her self-esteem. Men liked their women soft and sweet, he would remind her. They liked women who knew how to act like women, women who were feminine and seductive, tenderhearted and malleable. They didn't much care for hard, tough bitches.

But, search as she might, she couldn't find any insult in Remy's use of the word. He just seemed amused, but kindly so—not in the cruel, calculating way that Guy had always found her amusing.

She raised her hands to his forearms, intending to push his hands away, slip free and get his crutches for him before fleeing to the house. But her focus was so fully on her own intention that she overlooked his...until his mouth touched hers.

The kiss lasted only a moment, only long enough to stun her, to make her go utterly still, barely breathing, her heart barely beating. It was a moment of surprise, unexpected and brief. It was a moment that never should have happened. A moment that ended way too soon.

Then he released her, taking a hobbling step back, reaching for his crutches while she stood motionless. His gloves were fastened around the foam-padded grips; she was vaguely aware of the ripping sound as he pulled the Velcro apart, then tugged each glove on and refastened the hook-and-loop closures. When that was done, he looked at her again. This time there wasn't a hint of amusement or teasing in his expression. "I don't know whether you prefer games or seduction or honesty, Susannah, but I prefer the honest approach myself. I'm a patient man, and I'll give you all the time you need. I'll also give you a fair warning. That kiss was just the first. I want a lot more from you than that. I want more than companionship, more than friendship. I want intimacy. I want whatever you have to give. I want it all."

Feeling as if the ground were slipping beneath her feet, she took a few awkward steps away until she bumped into her chair. She took cover behind it, holding tightly to the curved wooden back for support. If he had given her a chance to choose between games, seduction and honesty, she would have told him that she, too, preferred honesty.

But his next words still would have knocked her for a loop.

She had no right to speak of honesty, not when her very presence in his life was the worst of deceptions. Not when her every word or action was a lie. Not when her lies were likely to cost him his life.

And she had no right to want his kisses, his companionship or his friendship. She had no right to even think—as some small, buried part of her was doing right now—about intimacy with him. She had no right to want whatever he might give before she destroyed him.

"You don't ask for much," she said, her voice small and cold because the place it came from, her heart, was small, tight and cold.

His smile was faint and crooked as he shook his head. "I'm asking for everything."

"Which amounts to just about nothing. I don't have anything to give, Remy."

"I think you do." He lifted one hand as if to touch her again, but the distance between them was too great. With obvious regret, he let his hand fall to rest again on the crutches. "I have a better opinion of you than you have of yourself."

"That's because I know myself. You don't."

"You're wrong. I know enough to know that I want you."

She smiled at that, striving for disbelieving but achieving something more along the lines of thin and hurtful. "Call your girlfriends in the city. Get one of them to drive up for the night. She'll take care of you more willingly and more capably than I ever could."

"This isn't about sex, Susannah," he said irritably. Then, when she gave him a skeptical, raised-brow look, he grudgingly grinned. "Well, of course it's about that, too, but not *just* that. I'm talking about a relationship, about a future, about making something together, something that lasts."

Pain, emotional in origin but very real all the same, twisted deep in her stomach. "But *I* don't want those things—not with you, not with anybody, not ever."

"I don't believe you."

She forced herself to shrug casually. "You have that right."

"Yes, I do," he agreed softly. "And I have the right to want you anyway. I have the right to try to change your mind. And now that you've been warned, I have the right to try to seduce you."

"And *I* have the right to say no." She tried to sound forceful and strong, but in her own ears, her words sounded more like a plea.

"Of course. Always." He started toward the house, but when he was about even with her, he stopped and faced her again, delivering his final warning in a husky voice with a sweetly confident smile. "*If* you can."

Susannah remained where she was long after he was gone, her fingers clenching the wood so tightly that they went numb. God help her, this was a complication she didn't need, one she couldn't even begin to afford. For all her talk, she knew she was a weak woman. She knew she could be seduced by sweet kisses and sweeter words. She knew she would sacrifice pride, resolve and dignity for an hour or two of believing that she was loved. Guy had taught her those lessons on a humiliatingly regular basis.

He had also taught her how easily she could be shattered by sweet lies.

And every feminine instinct in her said that Remy's lies would be the sweetest—and most devastating—of all.

Forcing her hands to release their grip on the chair, she picked up their books, then slowly turned toward the house. Remy was already inside, their conversation probably already put aside, his thoughts directed elsewhere. And why shouldn't they be? After nearly three weeks of recuperation, he was well enough to crave activity but not quite well enough to seek it out. He was bored, restless and looking for some entertainment. For all his talk of honesty, of a future and something that would last, he was simply looking for someone to fill his hours, to—how had he put it?—to make the days easier and the nights warmer.

He was looking for a good time.

She had already been Guy's good time. She couldn't go through that again.

It was funny. As different as Remy and Guy were, their approaches were unnervingly similar. She had first seen Guy at a party, had noticed time and again that he was watching her from across the room, until finally he had come over and introduced himself. It had been a charming introduction, one that had mentioned honesty, destiny and marriage all in the same line.

And she had fallen for it. Innocent, naive and incredibly flattered by his attention, she had believed everything he'd told her. She had believed him for the five months they'd dated and the four years they were married. She had believed that he was interested in a future together, one that would last. That he loved her. That he intended to keep the vows he made to her in church. She had believed his apologies every time he'd hurt her, every time he'd spoken carelessly or cruelly, every time he had treated her without consideration. She had believed that the first affair she knew about truly was the first, had believed his promises that it would never happen again, and when it had happened again—and again—she had believed those apologies, those promises, too.

She had been a trusting fool. But, as she'd told Remy, she considered her marriage a learning experience.

And the best lesson she had learned was not to be so trusting.

Oh, she believed Remy when he said he wouldn't hurt her—at least, not unless he discovered her real reason for being here. He wouldn't deliberately hurt her, but he didn't know, in spite of his protests, who he was dealing with. He didn't know that Guy had already destroyed whatever defenses and protections she'd ever had. He didn't know how easily he could destroy whatever was left. He didn't know that *she* was here to help destroy him.

The parlor was empty when she passed it on her way down

the hall, but she could hear Remy's voice from one of the more distant rooms—Mr. Sinclair's study, she thought, one of three rooms on the first floor that had a phone. She wondered if he was taking her advice and making a date with one of his lady friends in New Orleans. She hoped he was.

Even if the mere thought made her ache inside.

Leaving the books on the kitchen table, she gathered the dirty clothes from their rooms and carried the two baskets to the laundry room. It was located off the kitchen and past the pantry in a small room that had once been a screened-in porch. The screens had been replaced by tall windows, but the same white boards that sided the house formed the interior walls, and the original floor of dusty red brick remained.

After sorting the laundry and starting the first load, she returned to the kitchen to make dinner. Remy's voice still filtered down the broad hallway, a low murmur, the words indistinguishable from this distance. If she were doing her job the way Nicholas Carlucci wanted, she would sneak down the hall and hover outside the study. Remy was still slow, still noisy, with his crutches. She would have no problem, once his call ended, in retreating to the kitchen before he made it to the study door, none the wiser.

But she didn't slip down the hall. She continued chopping vegetables for a quick-cooking stew, listening to his voice and the occasional sounds of his laughter and wishing that she could simply disappear off the face of the earth.

She browned chunks of beef in a deep pot, added cans of broth and water, tossed in the vegetables and seasoned them. Then, with one quick check on the laundry, instead of returning to the kitchen, she slipped out the door and started across the lawn.

Her usual work schedule kept her on her feet for such long hours that regular exercise was the farthest thing from her mind, but in her days here, she had developed a fondness for late-afternoon strolls around the grounds. It was time away from Remy, time to relax and regain a little of the equilibrium that she always lost around him. It was a chance to appreciate being in the country—to hear the birds' songs, to watch the small changes each day as winter gave way to spring and daffodils sent up new shoots and barren trees began forming buds, and to listen to the traffic on the Mississippi River, unseen on the opposite side of the tall levee that fronted the road.

It was an opportunity to escape.

The grounds were enormous, measurable in acres rather than footage. Across the front a tall iron fence separated the lawn from the shoulder of the road. The spikes were eight feet tall and were broken up every twelve feet with a tall, square column of brick. She found the fence itself and the sheer length of it impressive, but it was the wooden fence across the back that captured her fancy. Once upon a time it had been painted white, possibly when Remy was a child, and been maintained in a long, straight row. In recent years, though, it had been allowed to begin a slow and graceful decline into disuse. Boards had fallen to the ground, posts leaned at precarious angles and vines overgrew entire sections. Such disrepair would never be tolerated on the farms she knew back home, but she found something soft and appealing about it here.

She had completed one circuit of the grounds and was beginning another, approaching the stately front fence again, when she noticed the car sitting on the shoulder a few yards down. It was an unremarkable car—a year or two old, four doors, a dusty shade of gray, with a man behind the wheel and a woman in the passenger seat. It looked like any of a hundred other cars that might pass this way every day, someone going to evening church services or returning home from work at one of the riverside factories, locals on their way to town or a relative's house, tourists seeking one last look before dusk....

Tourists. *Belle Ste. Claire has never been open to the public...but that's never stopped people from pulling off the road and taking pictures.* She'd had only a glimpse of the people and the car that had prompted Remy's comment earlier this afternoon, but that glimpse certainly seemed to match this car. That woman had been blond, too, and Susannah distinctly remembered the bright red of her jacket.

What kind of tourists, she wondered, feeling the evening's chill for the first time, would still be hanging around? Why would they be parked a short distance down the road, apparently just watching the house? And why, as she watched them, did they finally decide it was time to go, to start the engine, make a U-turn and head downriver toward New Orleans?

Maybe the sort who worked for sleazy lawyers. Maybe Carlucci didn't trust her. Maybe he had someone keeping an eye on her while *she* kept an eye on Remy.

She walked right up to the fence, curling her fingers around one rusty bar, staring hard after the car until it was gone from sight, its brake lights a hazy red glow in the gathering dark. Carlucci—if he was, indeed, responsible—needn't worry. She had made promises, and she would keep them. While she wasn't one hundred percent certain that he and his boss would keep their promise—that when she was finished here, she could take Skip away from Louisiana with no threat or danger hanging over him—she *was* certain of something else.

They *would* keep the other promise they'd made if she failed.

They *would* see to it that her brother faced prison for the rest of his life.

Prison…or worse.

"So everything's okay up there?" Michael made a question out of something he was trying to present as a simple statement and making Remy grin in the process.

"I'm fine. Susannah's fine," Remy replied, swiveling his father's chair so he could see out the window. He had seen Susannah pass by a while ago on her evening walk, strolling along at a leisurely pace, occasionally stopping to examine something more closely. It had been many long years since he'd taken the time to enjoy a simple walk…but he intended to do just that soon. In another week or so, if his leg had healed enough, the doctors would let him trade the crutches for a cane. Then all he would have to do was persuade her to let him join her.

He could manage that.

"So we'll see you Tuesday," Michael was saying. "Do you need anything from here?"

"A muffuletta, maybe, or a little shrimp Lafitte," he replied with a wry smile. Whatever Susannah was fixing for dinner smelled wonderful, but the mere mention of his two favorite dishes could still make his mouth water. "No, I don't need anything. Listen, you guys come by the house and we'll go out for lunch before you head on up to Arkansas."

After settling on an approximate time, they said their goodbyes, and he turned his attention fully outside. Susannah was in sight again, this time at the southernmost corner of the yard. She was standing still, gazing at something outside the fence. All he could see there was a flash of silver. A car, he realized as the driver turned across the road and headed in the opposite direction. A neighbor stopped to say hello, maybe, or a tourist asking for directions.

She stood there by the fence for what seemed like forever before finally turning and heading straight back toward the house. She moved so gracefully, so naturally. Although she had chosen city life over the country, she was obviously very much at home out here. He could easily see her on a farm— competent, efficient, serene and in control…and breaking all the farm boys' hearts.

Except it was *her* heart that had gotten broken up there in Nebraska and, damn that ex-husband of hers, she was determined not to risk it happening again.

So somehow he would have to convince her that he was a better man than her ex. That—in this respect, at least—he shared her talent for healing. That one bad relationship didn't automatically condemn her to another. That mistakes she had learned from didn't have to be repeated.

He had to convince her to give him a chance. Just a chance. Everything else would follow from there.

Her path to the back door took her past the study windows, then out of sight. For a moment he was content to remain where he was, to give her a few moments of peace without him. It wasn't long, though, before *she* sought *him* out.

She signaled her presence with a tap on the half-open door before pushing it back and stepping inside. "Dinner will be ready in about ten minutes."

Stretched out comfortably in the leather chair, he turned to face her, acknowledging her announcement with a nod, then waited for her to take flight right away. When she didn't, he gestured with one hand to the chairs opposite the desk in a silent invitation. Surprisingly she accepted it, venturing farther into the room, seating herself almost primly in the oldest and shabbiest of the three chairs. It was also, Remy knew from experience, the most comfortable.

"This is my father's room," he remarked. "When I was a kid, he spent hours in here every evening. When the door was open, anyone could come in. When it was closed, only an emergency or an act of God—or an occasional act of defiance—could get us in."

"It's a comfortable room," she murmured, then frowned. "Not comfortable, exactly. Comforting."

He nodded in agreement. There was a certain comfort, a coziness, to be found within these four walls. It wasn't the faded or, in some places, ragged air that said the room was well used, or the homey touches—family pictures, old heirlooms, small treasures. It was the feeling of life, of continuity, the connection between the past and the present. "This chair belonged to my grandfather. The desk was *his* grandfather's.

Other than the phone, I don't think anything ever came in here new. It was all passed down from some relative or another."

After a moment's silence, he picked up a framed photo and studied it. "When I was a kid, I used to come in and sit in that chair you're in and just watch my dad work. I admired him. I wanted to be just like him when I grew up. We used to fish from the levee out front, hunt in the woods out back and play football and baseball out in the yard. He was a busy man, but he almost always made time for me."

At least, until Valery came.

He looked at the photograph a moment longer before leaning forward and offering it to Susannah. He was about seventeen in the picture, Valery around fourteen, and they were both scowling. His parents stood between them, his mother nearest him, his father beside Valery. *They* were both tense. "Somewhere around here Mom has an entire photo album of pictures like that. You didn't see too many smiles or displays of affection in the Sinclair family during those days."

"I imagine you were pretty typical of families with teenagers," she replied, her gaze on the faded picture. "We have some pictures at home—" Abruptly she broke off and leaned forward, passing the frame back to him. "Kids don't always get along," she went on at last. "With each other, their parents or anyone else. It's part of growing up."

What did those last remarks have to do with her family pictures at home? he wondered. As far as that went, what did *her* family pictures have to do with *his* family problems? She was an only child, and her mother had died when she was fifteen. Her father was the only one left for her to not get along with, and somehow he couldn't imagine her ever showing the slightest disrespect to her father.

Setting the questions aside, he returned the picture to its place. "That was Michael on the phone earlier. He and Valery are going to Arkansas Tuesday—he's taking Valery home to meet his family—and they're stopping by here for lunch. Do you mind?"

She shrugged. "It's your house."

"And your time."

Another shrug. "Is there anything special you'd like me to fix?"

"No. We're going out. All four of us," he said, clarifying his answer, stalling the protest he knew she was about to make. "It'll only take an hour or two. You'll enjoy it." A break in routine wouldn't hurt either of them, and he really did think she would enjoy a little time with Valery. His cousin wasn't the most outgoing person in the world, but she had gotten on the phone long enough to inform him that she really liked Susannah. That was high praise from a woman who, in her entire adult life, hadn't gotten close to anyone other than Michael.

He was looking forward to the visit himself. Back in the city, he usually saw Michael and Smith three or four times a week; when their schedules interfered with that, they checked in regularly by phone. He missed his friends' company, missed their presence in his life. Of course, with Michael getting married soon, their friendship would change, would have to alter and adapt to include Valery.

It would be good practice for when *he* got married and brought his wife into the circle.

A glance across the desk at Susannah showed that she was none too anxious to be brought into anyone's circle of friends. "Don't fret over it, Susannah," he said, his tone deliberately mild. "I'm not asking you to make friends or anything vile like that. I'm just asking you to have lunch with my friends. Do you think you can survive that?"

She gave him a dry look. "I think so."

"Good. They'll be here around eleven o'clock Tuesday morning. That will give you more than—" he glanced at his watch and did some quick figuring "—forty hours to disguise that reluctance in your eyes."

After another long, steady look, she got up and started toward the door. "By the time you hobble into the kitchen, dinner will be on the table," she called over her shoulder. "Try not to let it get cold."

Chapter 5

As the clock down the hall struck the first of eleven chimes Tuesday morning, Susannah laid down the small sewing scissors she'd been using and studied her handiwork. The cut she'd made across the right leg of the jeans was crooked, and the hem hastily secured with a long, running stitch, but for short notice—and for someone who had never displayed much skill at sewing—it was satisfactory work.

On the fourth chime, she shook out the jeans and rose from the table, heading for Remy's room. When he had mentioned that he'd like to have a pair of the jeans Valery had packed for him altered to fit over his cast, she had offered, maybe with just the slightest bit of reluctance, to do it for him. She hadn't been thrilled by the idea of using scissors and a seam ripper to take out the long, double-stitched outer seam all the way from hip to hem, but she had learned at a very young age that every job included some tasks she didn't like.

But Remy had had other ideas—better ideas, she secretly

thought. Don't waste time removing a seam that would later have to be replaced, he had advised. Just cut the leg off so he could get the jeans on. Then, when the cast came off in another month's time, he would get rid of the jeans along with the cast, the crutches and the cane.

So that was what she had done, somewhat inexpertly. It had taken a couple of efforts and a couple of fittings before she had cut away enough denim to allow the jeans to pass over the cast, and then a few minutes' quick sewing to lessen the fraying. Now, just in time for his guests, she was finished.

He was waiting in his room, dressed in a sweater and gym shorts. The beautiful weather of the weekend was gone, replaced by a dreary, grim winter chill that had prompted his desire for jeans. The wind gusting outside would cut right through the cotton sweats he'd been living in. It was also going to turn his toes into cubes of ice, she thought as she handed the jeans over.

"If you don't mind sacrificing a pair of socks, I'll see what I can do for your foot," she volunteered.

"I'd sacrifice my best running shoes if it would keep me warm," he said, accompanied by a gesture toward the drawer where she'd stored his socks.

Crossing the room to the dresser, she tugged open the top drawer and removed a pair of thick, white socks. She was about to turn to leave again when she caught a glimpse of him in the mirror, balanced unsteadily against the bed, pulling his gym shorts down over his hips. Quickly—but not quickly enough to avoid a glimpse of narrow waist and slender hips or the blush that warmed her face—she averted her gaze.

This was silly, she chastised herself. She'd been a nurse for more than nine years. She had seen men in various stages of dress—more men than she cared to count. She saw men on television and in magazine photos wearing much less than Remy wore. It wasn't as if she had so little familiarity with the male form that she should be embarrassed by this particular male form.

But all those men she saw as a nurse had been patients, and Remy wasn't.

And all those men on television and in magazines were strangers. Remy wasn't.

And she wasn't embarrassed by what she'd seen. Heavens, no. She wanted to see more. Wanted to touch. Wanted to stroke, to caress, to explore.

No, she wasn't embarrassed.

She was intrigued. Fascinated.

Aroused.

Drawing a deep breath, she pulled one last sock from the drawer, then went to the armoire to pick out a shoe. She pretended she didn't hear the sounds of Remy dressing as she left the sock and shoe on the mattress, then turned toward the door. "I'll see what I can do with these," she announced, her voice insubstantial as she slipped out.

Back in the kitchen, she forced herself to concentrate on this new task. Curiously, the arrival of their guests—of Remy's guests, she reminded herself—made it easier. Remy insisted that she act as a friend, not an employee, but his real friends, especially Michael Bennett, expected her to act as an employee, a nurse and housekeeper. Susannah knew instinctively that Michael didn't accept her as Remy's friend. Because he was a cop and was suspicious by nature? Because his friend had almost died and Michael was protective of him now?

Or because whatever it was that made Michael a good cop—instinct, intuition, sixth sense—told him that she wasn't to be trusted?

Valery let herself and Michael into the house with her own key, calling out as they came down the hall. "Remy? Susannah? We're here."

Susannah heard Remy approaching from his room as the other couple approached from the hallway. She stayed at the table, her head down, now thankfully occupied with cutting the heavy sock just right...or so, she hoped, it appeared. In reality she was watching covertly as the three entered the room from opposite doors.

Valery released her fiancé's hand to hug her cousin. It wasn't an exuberant greeting, as Susannah might have expected, but a long, silent embrace that said more of her feelings than any words could have. When at last she stepped back, she turned to Susannah and offered her a smile. "It's been…what? A week? And you're still here. I figured Remy would have run you off by now."

The slight smile Susannah had been prepared to offer in return seemed to freeze, then dissolve. Did Valery know something she didn't, something Remy didn't? Had Michael uncovered something about her—maybe her relationship to Skip and his own ties to Jimmy Falcone—that he had passed on, or intended to pass on, to Remy?

Oh, God, had he come here for more than an innocent visit on his way home to see his family?

"That's an awkward remark, Val," Michael said dryly. "Why don't you explain it?"

The other woman laughed. "I guess it did sound kind of funny. I just meant because Remy's such a grouch. He was awfully ill-tempered in the hospital. He has this idea that he ought to be in control, you know. The day he checked out, the staff lined the halls to wish him farewell and to celebrate his release."

The knot in Susannah's stomach slowly started to loosen. "I've had a few patients like that myself."

"But I'm not one of them," Remy challenged, coming to sit beside her. "I've behaved, haven't I?"

If "behaving" meant watching her too often and too intensely, she thought privately. Or being too friendly. Or kissing her. Or bluntly announcing that he wanted to have an affair with her.

Instead of answering, Susannah held up the sock. "Let me see your foot."

"I can do it." He took the cut-down sock from her and bent forward, only to discover what she already knew: unable to bend his leg, he was also unable to reach his toes, at least not well enough to manage.

Slipping from her seat, she took the sock back and knelt in front of him. This was the first time she'd had to help him with any of his clothing since they'd moved in. It helped that they had company and that it was nothing more personal than a sock.

So why did it feel so damn personal?

Circling them to get to the next empty chair, Michael rested his hand briefly on Remy's shoulder. "How are you?"

"I'm fine."

Shifting his dark gaze to her, Michael repeated the question. "How is he?"

Glancing up, she met his eyes for less than a second before looking at Remy. "He *is* fine," she repeated. "His arm is healed, and the bruise from the bulletproof vest is almost faded. He's more or less used to the crutches, and he doesn't have any more bruises or blisters on his hands. If he could get around a little better, he wouldn't have any need for assistance, except for driving."

"So you could go back to your job at the hospital anytime."

There was a challenge in Michael's softly spoken words that made the muscles in Susannah's neck tighten. What did he know? she wondered. What did he see in her that Remy and Valery missed?

"But I can't get around a little better," Remy said, drawing Michael's attention away from Susannah and over to himself. "And I can't drive, I can't cook, my parents said I couldn't stay here alone, and Susannah promised me a full month. Don't give her the idea that I'd let her off so easily."

Keeping her gaze on her hands, she worked the sock into place over his toes, then carefully smoothed the excess fabric inside the opening of his cast. It was difficult to tell whether his foot was cold because her hands were. In fact, there were chills shivering all through her.

Once the sock was in place and she felt reasonably certain of it remaining there, she got to her feet. "I'll get your jacket," she murmured before escaping the kitchen. Down the hall she went first to Remy's room to get the heavier of the two leather jackets that hung in the armoire there, then she crossed to her own room. She was pulling on her coat when Valery joined her there.

"Hi," the other woman said softly.

Susannah straightened her collar, then pulled her hair free. "I hope you don't mind my tagging along. Remy insisted."

"I wouldn't dream of leaving you behind." Valery came a few steps farther into the room, glancing around. "You guys seem to be getting along okay."

"He's easy to work for."

Valery turned from the desk where she was sniffing a fat, vanilla-scented candle. "I bet you half the FBI agents in New Orleans would disagree with you. *I* think he's on his best behavior because he's sweet on you."

Steadfastly ignoring the last part of her comment, Susannah took a moment to run a brush through her hair. Lacking a scarf or cap, she had opted to leave her hair down today to provide some measure of warmth for her neck and ears. And that was the only reason it was down, she reminded herself. Not because, on the few occasions she'd worn it loose, Remy had given her such appreciative looks.

"Remy's a good guy."

Susannah laid the brush down and picked up the leather jacket again. "It says a lot that you think so."

"What do you mean?"

"He told me about when you came here to live and when his parents asked him to leave."

Valery looked surprised. "Did he?" she murmured. "Hmm. That says a lot, too."

She didn't want to ask, didn't want to know…but the question slipped out anyway. "In what way?"

"Remy, Michael and Smith Kendricks have been best friends since college, but until about a month ago, neither Michael nor Smith knew that I existed. You've been here a week, and he's already confided in you."

It wasn't that way, Susannah wanted to deny. There hadn't been anything special or important about Remy telling her his family history. It had just been small talk, an exchange of information, a little "I'll tell you this and you'll tell me that." It was nothing that merited examination.

"It was just conversation," she said at last. "You spend as much time together as we have, and you wind up looking for things to talk about."

Valery gave her a long, disbelieving look, then laughed. "Remy got a little bored, and so he hauled out his biggest secrets for your entertainment. Right, Susannah."

Clenching her fingers tightly together underneath the jacket, Susannah forced a faint smile. "Are you ready to go?"

The hamburgers at Belclaire's only café were thick and greasy, the french fries thin and crispy and the atmosphere undeniably small town. Remy figured he'd seen at least eighty percent of the town's residents in the last ninety minutes and that he remembered every single one of them from his years at home. He and Valery had spent half the meal introducing Michael and Susannah to everyone who had stopped by and fielding questions about his injuries, his stay at Belle Ste. Claire and his parents' trip to Europe.

Now Susannah had slipped off—for a trip to the post office, he had said—and Valery was sitting at the counter, visiting with a high school classmate. Now was his chance to talk, to *really* talk, with Michael. "You don't like her, do you?"

Michael spared him a moment's glance, then looked out the window again. "She seems like a nice woman."

Remy chuckled. "What's that old saying? Something about damning with faint praise?"

"It doesn't much matter what I think, does it? Because *you* like her."

"Of course it matters."

"No, it doesn't. It's gone beyond that for you."

"What do you mean?"

Michael glanced across the restaurant at Valery, and his expression softened. "In the first few days after I met Valery, I would have cared about your opinion of her. You probably could have influenced *my* opinion of her. But after a certain point…I wouldn't have given a damn if you hated her. Don't get me wrong. We've been friends a long time. Along with Evan, you and Smith have been the best part of my life for nearly half my life. It would matter to me if you didn't like Val…but it wouldn't stop me from marrying her next month. It wouldn't stop me from spending the rest of my life with her." He grinned. "It wouldn't stop me from making you spend a good deal of the rest of *your* life with her."

Remy understood exactly what Michael meant and knew, too, that his friend was right. He *had* already passed the point where he could be influenced against Susannah by anything less than hard and fast proof of wrongdoing on her part. Opinions were subjective. He didn't need Michael's or Smith's approval.

He just needed Susannah's.

Still…

"Out of curiosity, exactly what is it about her that bothers you?"

"'Bothers' is a little strong," Michael replied. "It's just feeling that something's not right."

"An instinct feeling or a *feeling* feeling?" Remy knew the question sounded silly, but it was an important distinction. His cousin and Michael shared more than love; they were both more than a little on the psychic side. For Valery, it was mostly minor things—foreknowledge or second sight. She sometimes knew the doorbell was going to ring before it did, knew who would be there before she opened the door. On occasion she knew what a person was going to say before they spoke, knew something was going to happen long before anyone else was aware of it.

She had known that Remy's partner on the Falcone case was going to betray him; unfortunately, she hadn't known in time to warn him.

For Michael, though, it was a lot more than that. He had visions—visual, auditory and sensory—and what he had visions of were people in trouble. His first contact with Valery had been in a vision. Another of his visions had led him and Evan to the kidnapper who killed Evan. If he was having *those* kinds of feelings about Susannah...

"Instinct," Michael replied, easing the tightness in Remy's nerves. "I'm not saying there's something *wrong* with Susannah. There's just something not quite right."

"She got divorced not too long ago," Remy said. "Her husband left her and, apparently, married someone else pretty quickly. He left her thinking she doesn't have anything to offer anyone. She's convinced that she's never getting married again because it's safer that way. If you don't love or trust someone, then you can't get hurt."

"But you can get damn lonely." Michael finished the last of his coffee, then shook his head in dismay. "You never do anything the easy way, do you?"

"Oh, like you found Valery the easy way," Remy scoffed.

"Yeah, but—" Having no argument to offer, Michael broke off with a grin. "I hope she's worth it."

"Valery?"

"Susannah. I *know* Val is. So...is she aware that you've got plans for her?"

"I've warned her."

Michael raised one eyebrow. "Don't you think you'd have better luck romancing her or seducing her?"

"What do you think I was warning her about?"

"Well, the least you could do is make the woman feel enough at home to get her mail there, and maybe give her access to a telephone now and then. It's damn cold to be standing out in the wind while you chat."

Remy pushed back the gingham curtains that blocked his view of the street and followed the direction of Michael's gaze. Indeed, Susannah was standing across and down the street, at one of only two pay phones in town. The wind whipped her hair around her face, and when she turned once to impatiently wipe it away, he saw the stack of mail she held.

Interesting. He had given her the address for Belle Ste. Claire when he hired her, had told her to feel free to have her mail forwarded there. In the week since they'd moved in, he hadn't considered whether she'd done so. She picked up the mail each day—the walk from the side door to the box at the end of the driveway was still too far and, in silty sand and shell, too risky for him to make. She always left the mail on the kitchen table for him to tend to, to separate his from his parents' and to sort through theirs for anything that might require a response before their return. He had assumed that she took her own from the stack before leaving it for him.

But she was having hers delivered to a post office box in town. Was she really so intensely private?

Or was she getting mail that she didn't want him to see?

Right, Sinclair, he silently chastised himself. It wasn't as if he would ever even consider snooping through her mail. He would never do more than maybe glance at return addresses, and since they didn't know any of the same people, what would that tell him? The names of the people who wrote to her would mean nothing to him.

The names of the people—or the person—she was calling from pay phones would, though. Judging from his occasional glimpses of her face, it didn't seem that this call was pleasure Even from this distance he could see that her expression wa stony. He could read the tension in her body, in the way she held her shoulders back instead of huddling as any other person would have done against the wind. He could tell that her voice, if only he could hear it, would be that small, empty, chilling tone that she used on occasion with him.

Suddenly feeling as if he were invading her privacy, he let the curtain fall into place and settled back in his seat. Across from him, Michael had looked away, too, directing his gaze once again toward Valery.

I'm not saying there's something wrong *with Susannah. There's just something not quite right.*

Maybe Michael had more of a point than Remy wanted to admit. Maybe there was more in her background than just a marriage that had ended badly. Maybe her wariness was more than the distrust a woman would naturally feel when someone she loved hurt her. Maybe there was a reason other than her ex-husband for her claim that she had nothing to give *him*.

Maybe something else was going on.

The bell over the door tinkled, and cold air blasted in as Susannah came through the door. Her purse was over her shoulder, the mail she'd been holding a moment ago tucked away inside, Remy guessed. She took her seat beside him in the booth, her clothes cold, her cheeks red, her hair tousled, and reached for her coffee cup with both hands. She didn't drink from it, though, but simply warmed her hands on the heavy pottery.

"I'm sorry if I kept you waiting," she said, not looking at either of them.

"It's okay. We were just waiting for Valery to finish visiting with her friend." Remy turned on the bench so he was slightly facing her. "Did you get what you needed at the post office?"

"Yes. I just had to pick up some stamps and mail a few letters."

Michael's gaze met his over the table, then they both looked away again. After an awkward moment, his friend broke the silence. "I'm going to have to drag Val out of here if we're going to make it to Titusville today. Since you're having a little trouble getting around, why don't you head on out to the car, Remy, and I'll get her and pay the bill?"

Remy nodded and, as soon as Susannah slid out of the booth, got to his feet. She got his crutches from the corner, then held the door open wide for him. At his mother's car, she helped him get settled, then got behind the wheel, starting the engine, letting it warm up.

"Your friend doesn't like me much, does he?" she asked, shivering visibly as the heater blew cold air over their feet and up into the compartment.

"Does it matter?"

"I don't know." She stared straight ahead. "Does it?"

Instead of answering her question, he asked one of his own. "Who were you calling?"

Abruptly she swiveled around to look at him. Her face was pale except for two bright circles of color on her cheeks. That was a guilty look if ever he'd seen one…and after twelve years as a federal agent, he'd seen thousands of them. But why should she feel guilty for making a phone call? At the moment, he could think of only one reason: she'd been calling a man.

A man she was involved with.

A man whom she was giving all the things he had arrogantly expected her to give *him.*

Arrogant. God, yes, he was that. He hadn't even bothered to find out if she was available before he'd announced his intention of seducing and possibly—probably—marrying her. It was no surprise that she'd done nothing to encourage him. The only surprise, in fact, was that she was still around, that she hadn't packed her bags and gone racing back to New Orleans.

Back to *him,* whoever he was.

She hadn't yet found her voice when Michael and Valery joined them. Still looking stricken—and so terribly guilty—

she at last looked away from him and turned her attention to the driving.

It was a quiet few miles back to Belle Ste. Claire. There Michael and Valery refused Remy's halfhearted invitation to come inside. They had to be on their way, Michael insisted.

"Oh, before we go, Remy, I brought you something," Valery exclaimed. She waited impatiently for Michael to unlock the trunk of his car, then pulled a heavy black garbage bag from it. "A few years ago, Aunt Marie was doing some housecleaning, and she gave me a stack of quilts. You know the ones—they used to be four and five thick on the guest room beds. They're family heirlooms and rightfully belong to you, but since Aunt Marie gave them to me, I'm keeping them anyway," she said with a confidence that Remy knew she couldn't have managed too long ago. "Except for this one. I thought you might like it."

She offered the bag to Susannah with a smile that reminded him of the Valery he had loved like a sister when they were kids…before she had come to live with them and he had been expected to actually accept her as a sister.

"Thanks, Valery." Balancing on his crutches, he pressed a kiss to her forehead. "Feel free to enjoy the rest of them with my blessings."

"Thank you." She extended her hand to Susannah. "It was nice seeing you again."

Wrapping her arms around the bag, Susannah accepted her handshake and murmured something in response, then began edging toward the door. She wished she could go inside and go to bed. She wanted to shut the door, draw the curtains, pull the covers over her head and hibernate for the next three weeks. She didn't want to talk, to think or to feel. She didn't want to want, didn't even want to live for the next twenty-one days.

But there was little chance of Remy granting her wish.

Little chance. The phrase described her life and her future. There was little chance of getting what she wanted. Little chance of escaping the guilt. Little chance of being happy again.

There was no chance at all that Remy would ever forgive what she was doing.

She unlocked the door, then held the screen for him. He didn't glance her way as he swung expertly over the raised threshold, then turned into the parlor. Shrugging out of his jacket, he tossed it onto a nearby chair, dropped onto the sofa and let his crutches fall to the floor nearby as he reached for the TV remote.

Susannah hesitated in the doorway, then, using the heavy bag as an excuse, she said, "I'll put this quilt in your room."

She hadn't done more than pivot when he suddenly spoke. "You never answered my question."

Stubbornly she asked, "What question was that?"

"Who were you calling from the pay phone?"

She hugged the bag tighter, making it crinkle. "You sound like my ex-husband," she said flatly. "He thought he had the right to question every part of my life, and because he always lied to me, he believed that *I* lied, too."

"I'm not accusing you of lying."

"But you're suspicious."

"I was curious the first time I asked," he replied, clarifying his answer.

"And now, because I didn't answer right away, you're suspicious."

"Because your reaction when I asked was as guilty as any I've ever seen, and, honey, I've seen a lot." The hostility slowly faded from his expression, from his voice. "If you're involved with another man, Susannah, just say so. I won't fire you. I won't cause problems for you. And I won't come on to you again."

She stared down at the wooden floor. Could it be that simple? Could she lie and say yes, she was seeing someone else? Could she really put an end to his looks and his sweet smiles and the soft seductiveness that accompanied his mere presence with one simple, single three-letter reply?

Could she banish her own yearnings so easily?

It was an easy lie. She said nothing at all, and Remy found his own answer in her silence. "So…tell me about him."

She supposed he was trying for casual interest, but she heard disappointment instead. Dismay. A little bit of wounded ego. She opened her mouth for more lies—damn, she hated dishonesty! "There's nothing to tell. That call was business. It wasn't important, and it's something that I prefer not to discuss. I can handle it myself. I made it from the pay phone because I wanted privacy and because it was long distance and because that's the way I wanted to do it. I wasn't aware that you expected to be keyed in on every aspect of my life while I work here. I wasn't aware—" Breaking off, she drew a deep breath. What she was about to say was unfair, and she had to swallow hard first. "I wasn't aware that you were so much like my ex-husband in that regard."

After a moment to let that sink in, she quietly asked, "Are there any other questions you'd like to ask, or am I free to go now?"

He didn't say anything…oh, but he wanted to. She could see it in his eyes, just as she could read his determination to say nothing in the set of his jaw. What other suspicions was he harboring? she wondered.

And then she remembered: if he had seen her on the phone, then he had likely seen the mail she was holding. She had been nervous when she had opened the creamy white envelope with no return address, had been chilled when she had seen the photographs inside—pictures of her and Remy, sitting in the sun Sunday afternoon. There had been no note, nothing but that little photographic message—warning—that they were being watched. Her name and address had been typed, and the envelope had been mailed locally, postmarked yesterday and delivered to her box today.

So, if he had seen the mail, then he knew she was getting

it delivered elsewhere, just as she was making her phone calls elsewhere. He knew she was being secretive and evasive.

And he knew she had lied in the café when she'd told him that her business at the post office had consisted of buying stamps and mailing letters.

He *knew* she had lied to him.

Feeling sick deep inside, she slowly crossed the room to the chair where his coat was. She picked it up, tucking it under her arm with the quilt, and sat down. "You say I should feel at home here, that for this month, Belle Ste. Claire *is* my home. But I don't feel at home here, Remy. I'm here to work. I'm here because it's a condition of my employment. But it's *not* home. That's why I'm having my mail delivered in town. That's why I make my phone calls elsewhere. If you think that's silly or secretive or suspicious, I'm sorry, but it's what I'm comfortable with."

She waited for some response from him. When none came, she tiredly got to her feet again. "I'll put these in your room now."

After leaving her things in her own room, she went to his and hung up his jacket. She had made the bed earlier this morning, but it was wrinkled again from when he'd waited while she fixed his jeans. She smoothed out the wrinkles, then tore open the plastic bag and slid the quilt free.

Having grown up with hand-pieced quilts by the dozen, she had never placed much value in them, as so many people did. They were special because they had been made by her mother and grandmother and other relatives she had never known, but at the same time, they had been common and undeserving of special attention because she'd had them from the time she was in a crib. To her they had been functional, same as the dresses, rompers and playsuits her mother had sewn for her or the tables, chairs and cradles her father had put together in winter when farm life was slow. They were something for everyday use, not works of art.

Only one quilt held any real sentimental value for her, and

that was the one she had brought with her from Nebraska. It was the last one her mother had completed before she died. It was pieced of three fabrics: squares of a tiny lavender floral print, squares and triangles in unbleached muslin and trapezoids in solid lavender. It had been a gift from a mother to her only daughter, a gift chosen for reasons as sentimental as could be.

This quilt of Remy's, the one Valery had thought, of all those given to her, that he might like, was pieced in the same pattern.

With a soft sigh, she traced over the straight seams. Although the patterns were identical, the differences between her quilt and Remy's were readily apparent. Hers in its soft shades was as feminine as his was masculine. It was done in a rich cranberry, a deep blue that was almost black and a print mixing the two colors with subdued gold. Whoever had crafted his was more of a perfectionist than her mother had been—a corner that didn't quite line up or stitches that rarely came close to uniformity in size had never been of great importance to her mother—and the fabric was undoubtedly of better quality. The three layers of her quilt—front, batting and back—were secured in a simple and easy cross-hatch pattern, while his had been quilted together in an elaborate, time-consuming system of swirls, curlicues and interlocking diamonds.

But hers provided as much comfort to her as his would to him.

She unfolded it carefully, unsure of its age, and smoothed it across the bed, settling it accordion-style at the foot.

When that was done, she returned to her own room, pushing the door until it almost closed, then kicking off her shoes and taking a seat on the bed. Her purse was there where she'd left it. Removing the mail, she settled back to thumb through it.

There was nothing of interest to anyone but her—and Remy, who seemed to be interested in everything. A few bills, a piece or two of junk mail, a letter from her father and those pictures. Those damnable pictures. With a sigh, she swept everything aside and turned her attention to her father's letter.

Lew Crouse wasn't much of a writer—had never had the practice, he'd written to her in his first letter. Except for a brief stint in the army before she was born, he had lived his entire life in the same little corner of Nebraska, within shouting distance of his brother Richard and only a few miles down the road from both of their sisters. He'd known his friends and neighbors for a lifetime, had been best friends with the same man for fifty-one years. He hadn't ever owned a computer—and vowed never to have one.

But, while he wasn't overly comfortable with putting his thoughts and feelings down on paper, he was reliable. His letters came every two weeks without fail. If there was anything new—a rarity, it seemed to Susannah—it came first, followed by a mention of the weather that was so important to a farmer, a few lines about Uncle Richard's family and a hello from some friend or another in town. He always asked after Skip, always remarked how grateful he was that Susannah was looking after "their boy" and always ended with the same somewhat stiff closing. *Love, Your Dad.*

Susannah's smile was teary. Her father wasn't comfortable putting feelings into words, either. She supposed there must have been a time, maybe when she was a little girl, when he had told her straight out that he loved her, but she couldn't remember it. Not that she'd ever had any doubts. He had shown her in every way possible. He'd been the best father a girl could ask for.

But he'd been an even better father to Skip.

She didn't begrudge Skip his favored place in the family. She remembered how desperately her parents had wanted more children, remembered her mother's three pregnancies—two that had ended in miscarriage mere weeks after they'd begun and the third one that had resulted in a premature stillborn daughter. She remembered her mother's hopes as each pregnancy progressed and her father's grief as each one ended. Even though Susannah hadn't fully understood their sorrow, she had shared it.

And then, after they had given up hope, after they had accepted that the daughter they had was the only child they would ever have, Skip had come along. If her mother had been thrilled, her father had been ecstatic. Finally he'd had the child he had always longed for, the son who would follow in his footsteps, who would carry on the Crouse name.

The entire family had adored Skip, had pampered and treasured him. Infractions that had earned Susannah and her cousins suitable punishment went ignored when Skip committed them. His temper tantrums were indulged, his whims catered to. Because his presence in their lives seemed nothing less than a miracle, he'd been treated with too much love and too little discipline.

Would Skip be different today, she wondered, if he had been held to the same standards of behavior that her parents had imposed on her? Would he be more responsible, more reliable, more honest and trustworthy?

Not that she was sure that the person she had become was of any more value than the person Skip was. After all, look at her: she'd had rules, limits and guidelines. She'd been taught the difference between right and wrong, had learned to respect others and the law, had developed values and morals and ethics, and look at what she was willing to do for her beloved brother: she was putting a man's life in danger. She was trading Remy's life for her brother's.

She was going to be responsible for Remy's death.

A soft, choked cry escaped her as she curled into a tight ball and pressed her fist to her mouth. God help her, she couldn't do it.

There had to be some other way, some way to free Skip and protect Remy. Maybe if she confided in him… But he was an FBI agent. He would have no interest in saving, of all the people who worked for Jimmy Falcone, her brother. He would find Skip guilty by association and would direct his energies toward punishing him right along with Falcone.

He would find *her* guilty, too. What was the penalty, she wondered with a shudder, for what she'd done so far? Prison, most likely. The end of life as she knew it.

But she had faced that two weeks ago when Nicholas Carlucci had called her the first time.

Maybe there was some way she could outsmart Carlucci and Falcone. Maybe she could give them inaccurate information, just for the duration of her time here. Once the month was up, it was up, and there was nothing either of them could do to change that. They couldn't expect any further help from her. They couldn't place any further demands on her.

But who was she, a nurse from Homestead, Nebraska, to think she could outsmart one of the best damn lawyers in the state, according to Remy, and the biggest crook in southern Louisiana? Who was she to succeed where others far more capable, far more skilled at that sort of thing—including Remy himself—had repeatedly failed?

She stood little chance at getting away with passing on lies to Carlucci…and very likely might get her brother killed for her efforts.

She could go to the authorities, could talk to Michael Bennett. But he'd made little effort to disguise the fact that he didn't approve of her presence in Remy's life, that he didn't approve of *her.* She might get as far as mentioning Carlucci's or Falcone's names before he hauled her off. She wasn't likely to find any sympathy for Skip or herself from him.

Her best bet, she thought hopelessly, was to quit thinking about it and to do exactly what the lawyer had told her to do. To answer his questions and pass on her little bits of information. To go back to pretending that it was harmless information, that knowing Remy's schedule, activities and movements couldn't possibly be of major importance to anyone. To hiding from the truth and trying to create a version of it that she could live with.

At least until she found a better option.

Remy lay on the couch, the television on but ignored, his gaze fixed on the white cylinder of his cast and his thoughts on the other side of the house in the servants' quarters. Susannah hadn't come back after taking the quilt to his room, but he hadn't really expected her to. It wasn't as if he couldn't get around fine on his own, and if he needed her, he could call. In fact, she would be perfectly within her rights to avoid him the rest of the day. She didn't have to sit down to dinner with him, didn't have to spend the long evening hours with him. She didn't have to have any real contact with him for the next three weeks, even though he had succeeded at badgering her into it for the past week.

You never do anything the easy way, do you? Michael had asked. Sometimes it seemed that was, indeed, the way of his life. Unlike Michael and Evan, he'd had no natural flair for investigative work; he had become the good agent he was through damned hard work, endless patience and never giving up. After fifteen years of stubbornness and foolish pride, it had taken getting shot for him to resolve his problems with his parents. And instead of falling for any number of willing women down in New Orleans, he'd picked the one woman in the state least likely to surrender to his charms.

Had she told the truth when she'd denied being involved with another man?

He couldn't say, because the truth was she hadn't actually denied it. "Tell me about him," he had invited, and she had replied, "There's nothing to tell." She had explained the telephone call and had come clean about her mail, but she had never actually said, "No, I'm not seeing anyone else." He had accepted it as a denial because that was what he'd wanted to hear.

Maybe he had been wrong.

Maybe he should give up, leave her alone and make the next few weeks as easy and uncomplicated as possible for them both.

You never do anything the easy way, do you?

And maybe he shouldn't.

Maybe he couldn't.

He wasn't afraid of hard work. He had immeasurable patience. He was stubborn as hell. And he knew what he wanted.

He knew something else, too: if he accepted that Susannah felt nothing for him, that she didn't share his attraction, if he gave up after so little effort, he would always wonder what might have been. He would always wonder if she had, indeed, been the right woman for him.

He would always regret giving in.

Reaching for his crutches, he got to his feet and headed toward their rooms. His was quiet, the door open, the quilt Valery had brought folded across the bed. Susannah's room was also quiet, the door open a few inches. Through that small bit he could see the corner of the dresser, the desk against one wall and the foot of the bed. He could also see Susannah's feet, tucked underneath the edge of the coverlet. She was asleep, he guessed, judging from her stillness and the utter silence in the room.

As a kid he had sometimes slept in this room when one family get-together or another had filled the upstairs bedrooms with out-of-town relatives, but he hadn't been inside in years longer than he could remember. Since he and Susannah had moved in, it was the only place in the house—in a house where she didn't feel at home—that she could consider her own; she hadn't invited him in, and he hadn't intruded.

He wished he could go in now, wished he could push the door open and sit down on the bed beside her. He wished he could lie down with her, wished he could simply hold her while she slept. For now that would be enough.

For now.

Turning, he made his way back through the kitchen before taking a left down the long, central hallway. The ceiling there soared more than twenty-four feet to the second floor, where a massive chandelier hung centered in a plaster medallion of rosettes, curling leaves and flowing vines. The hall was as wide as the first floor rooms, wide enough to require its own furniture: a sofa and tables in a niche over here, two chairs flanking a gracefully turned table over there and a pair of vases, blue and white, slender and nearly five feet tall, standing one on each side of the front doors.

He loved this house, but he understood Susannah's refusal to think of it as home. It was beautiful, grand and intimidating as hell. Everything about it was just so perfect—the architecture, the construction, the symmetry, the furnishings. He could well understand how someone who hadn't grown up in such surroundings could be made uncomfortable by them. His own mother had felt out of place when she had moved here with his father forty years ago. Marie Navarre had grown up in a perfectly normal family in a perfectly middle-class home. She had known that one day George, as the oldest Sinclair son, would take over Belle Ste. Claire, just as one day Remy would, but she hadn't expected that day to come for years.

Instead it had immediately followed the wedding. Remy's grandparents had retired to a smaller property they owned upriver, leaving Belle Ste. Claire to George and Marie and the family they were expected to start.

As luck—or choice, Remy had preferred to think—would have it, their family had consisted of only the three of them. There would have been plenty of room for his grandparents to live with them at Belle Ste. Claire. He had never questioned why he was an only child, although, as kids, Valery had often teased him that it was because he'd been more than enough. His parents had gotten a taste of what life with him was like and had sworn off having any more kids for fear of getting another just like him.

He wondered now as he rubbed the gleaming stair rail why they hadn't had more children. *Had* it been by choice? Considering the willingness, even eagerness, with which they had taken responsibility for Valery, he didn't think so. How different would he be if he'd had brothers and sisters? Would he be less selfish if he'd had to share his home and his parents with others whose claim on their time, attention and love was as strong as his? Would he be less arrogant if he hadn't lived the first fourteen years of his life as the center of their lives?

Would Susannah find him more appealing, less threatening?

Maybe.

Maybe not.

For a moment he stood at the foot of the stairs, gazing around. It was colder in this part of the house, both in temperature and in nature. The rooms here at the front were rarely used even when his parents were home. The furnishings were more formal, every piece an antique. The chairs weren't comfortable for sitting, the rugs too fragile for everyday traffic. The walls were hung with tapestries, the windows with heavy draperies that puddled on the floor, and over each fireplace were imposing portraits of long-dead Sinclair relatives, a stern-looking, grim-faced bunch if ever he'd seen one.

He hardly even considered the rooms a part of the house. They were always on the tour for new visitors—Valery had taken Susannah through them their first day here—but, other than being opened up and decorated for holiday celebrations, they were otherwise ignored. The housekeeper dusted them once a week and did a serious cleaning periodically, but for all of Remy's life, at least, the living at Belle Ste. Claire had been done in the parlor, the library, his father's study and the kitchen.

And the bedrooms, of course. There had originally been seven of them, but two had been sacrificed in the early part of the century for the addition of modern bathrooms. Of the five that remained, one belonged to his parents, of course, and two were guest rooms. One was kept ready for Valery's visits, and the fifth one… The fifth one had been his.

He wondered how his mother had changed it in the years he'd been gone. What had she done with the things he'd left behind and never reclaimed, all the things he hadn't been ready to part with and yet had had no need, or space, for in school? Knowing his mother, everything was probably packed up in boxes and stored somewhere in the attic, just in case he ever decided he wanted it badly enough to ask for it.

Still, he wouldn't mind seeing for himself.

He gazed up the stairs. They were pretty straightforward— no spirals, no turns, just one long shot from here to the next floor. The day Michael had brought him here from the hospital, he had looked forward to seeing his old room, to sleeping in it. Over the years he had forgotten that this was no ordinary staircase, that it climbed for forever, and he had overestimated his ability with the crutches.

But his mother had planned ahead. She had prepared the servants' quarters for him and Susannah. She had even left a note warning him to avoid these stairs as long as he required crutches. There would be time for reminiscing up there later, she had written.

Listening for and hearing no sound from the back of the house, he carefully swung onto the first step. It wasn't bad. He managed the steps leading to the gallery every time they went out someplace, and he hadn't had a problem yet. These were exactly the same.

There were just more of them.

By the tenth step he was starting to breathe hard.

By the twentieth, the muscles in his good leg were starting to ache.

By the time he reached the top, he needed a moment to sit down and recover from the effort. Fortunately there was a petit-point divan at the top for just that.

Within a few minutes, he was hobbling down the hall toward his room. More recent family portraits were hung on this floor. Here were his grandparents, only weeks after their wedding, and there they were, celebrating their fiftieth anniversary. Next was his own family, the occasion his first birthday. After that, oils and canvas were traded for the ease of photographs. The formality was still there, though, as their close-knit family of three became a fractured group of four. The only decent shots from that point on were individual ones—his high school graduation photo, his parents on their twenty-fifth, thirtieth and thirty-fifth anniversaries, Valery's high school and college graduations. He had missed all those occasions.

He had missed so much.

At the end of the corridor, he paused in front of the last door, balancing on his crutches as he wrapped his fingers around the cool crystal knob. With no more than curiosity and the expectation of seeing something new, he pushed the door open, then stepped inside…and came to an abrupt halt.

A wave of nostalgia, bittersweet and intense enough to hurt, swept over him as he stood there in the dreary afternoon chill. Nothing had changed—not a single thing. His books, including college textbooks that he'd thought worth keeping, still filled the shelves. Photographs and posters hung on the walls, and the letter he'd been awarded for his one and only season on the Belclaire High baseball team was still attached by a tack to the bulletin board.

Slowly he sank onto the bed, its dark green coverlet faded now where the afternoon sun came through the big windows, and he let his crutches slide to the floor. His parents hadn't changed a thing. They had kept Valery's room for her, and they'd kept his room for him.

Finally, for the first time in fifteen years, he truly was home.

Chapter 6

It wasn't difficult for Susannah, when she awoke, to locate Remy: she simply followed the trail of lights he'd left burning. She took her time, though, studying each of the portraits and photographs in the hall, lingering over those few including him, before finally approaching the open door at the end of the hall where yellow-tinged light fell onto the worn rug.

Now she stood there, waiting to be noticed, to be invited in—or out. As moment after moment ticked by without him becoming aware of her presence, at last, she cleared her throat. "I take one little nap, and you go off climbing the stairs you're supposed to stay away from."

He looked up from the book he was paging through—a yearbook, she saw, slender and filled with yellowing pages of black-and-white photos. He didn't offer a welcoming smile. For a moment he didn't do anything at all, but finally he spoke. "Sorry. I didn't hear you."

"Am I intruding?"

"No. Come on in." He turned another page, then closed the annual and set it on the desk. "I just wanted to see what Mom and Dad had done with my room."

"Looks like they left it alone. They must have been hoping for you to come back someday."

"You think so?"

She ventured past him to stand at the foot of the bed. By nature there was something incompatible about fine old furniture sharing space with a very young man's keepsakes, but in this room it worked. Maybe it was the plain lines of the four-poster bed, the dresser and armoire, the desk and the chairs, along with the simplicity of the drapes and bedding.

Or maybe it had nothing at all to do with furniture, drapes or bedding. Maybe it was simply Remy himself—the force of his personality—that made it work.

"I was still living at home when I got married," she said in response to his question. "After the ceremony, I was saying goodbye to my father, and I told him that finally he had a room to convert to an office. He shook his head and told me that he planned to leave my room exactly as it was, in case I ever needed a place to go."

"He didn't have real high hopes for your marriage, did he?"

She smiled wryly. "My father met Guy once and had him all figured out. He tried to warn me, but…" She ended with a shrug.

"You married against your father's wishes? That's not what I'd expect from you."

"I was in love. It makes you do foolish things."

"Are you still in love?"

After a still moment, she turned to study the bulletin board on the wall in front of her. There wasn't much on it: a fifteen-year-old calendar turned to the month of May, a hand-printed list of names and phone numbers belonging mostly to girls, a bumper sticker advertising Louisiana State University, a photograph of a pretty redhead wearing a dark green-and-cream-colored cheerleader's uniform and an athletic letter, a swirly *B,* in the same green-and-cream shades. The letter was dusty, faded and marked with a circle of rust where the thumb-tack pierced it. "What did you letter in?" she asked absently.

"Baseball."

"Were you any good?"

"Yeah. But I only played one year. My parents kept missing games because they were busy with Valery. Their excuse was always, 'We'll come next time,' or 'There'll be plenty of games next season. We'll make it up to you then.'"

"So, to get back at them, you made sure there wasn't a next season."

He looked sheepish. "It sounds pettier now than it did at the time."

Susannah glanced around again. Besides the chair he was sitting in, there was one other tucked into the corner. It was wooden, oversized, the seat polished to the sort of sheen that only years of use could give. She made herself comfortable in it before responding to his last comment. "It doesn't seem petty now. No matter how much your cousin needed your parents, their first obligation was to their own child."

Leaving his crutches where they were, he cautiously moved the few feet to the bed, propping his leg on a pillow. "You didn't answer me."

"Again?" She tried for a faint smile, but it wouldn't come. She didn't feign ignorance, didn't pretend that she'd forgotten the question. "No. The answer is no. I'm not still in love with Guy. I'm not in love with anyone, and I don't want to be. Like I said, love makes you do foolish things, and I've done enough foolish things to last a lifetime."

"Somehow I have a great deal of trouble imagining you behaving foolishly."

"Keep trying. The image will come."

He shook his head. "You know what image I'll always have of you? That night in the emergency room. Everyone was doing something to me, and they were shouting at each other, and I already hurt like hell, and they were making it worse. No one was looking at me or talking to me or even noticing that I was there…except you. You were so calm. So serene."

"Serene," she echoed, injecting skepticism into the word even though his compliment touched her deeply. "That's a new way to describe it. Guy always preferred words like dull. Uninteresting. Boring."

His voice rang with annoyance. "Then Guy was an idiot."

"Careful," she gently warned. "In some ways you remind me of him."

"What ways?"

"Well, there's the superficial. You're both tall, blond, blue-eyed and handsome."

Immediately Remy grinned a charmingly unrepentant grin. "You think I'm handsome?"

"Don't most women?"

"I don't care what most women think. I want to know what *you* think."

"There's that, too," she said thoughtfully. "The ability to say lines like that and actually make a woman think you're sincere. You're both very brash, very confident. You're very certain that you deserve to have what you want at exactly the time you want it. You're both more than a little forceful."

While she spoke, his expression shifted from charming and amused to stony. "And what about our differences? There have to be some."

"I don't know," she admitted. The similarities were easy. They were right there on the surface for all the world to see. But the differences… Oh, she knew they were there. She knew Remy was a better man than Guy could ever hope to be, knew Remy was a *good* man, but differences ran deep. They took time to uncover. They took knowledge—intimate knowledge—to sort through. While she had lived intimately with Guy for four years, she'd been with Remy only a week, and they certainly weren't intimate. They weren't even exactly living together but simply sharing quarters.

But there was one very obvious difference. "I don't believe you would ever be deliberately cruel."

"And he was."

She shrugged. "It was a way to amuse himself when nothing else was going on." Insults, hurts, comments calculated to undermine her confidence—that had been the way of her marriage. He had piled them one on top of another, so subtle at first that she'd been convinced she was imagining them, so skillfully that later she had blamed herself. If she was prettier, she had reasoned, he wouldn't flirt with other women in front of her. If she was more outgoing, he wouldn't snub her when his friends were around. If she was more interesting, he wouldn't neglect her so much. If she was taller, shapelier, more exciting, better skilled, more imaginative or any of a hundred other things, he wouldn't have affairs with other women.

It had taken four years to catch on to what he was doing to her. Four years to see how he was manipulating her, making her take the blame for his failures. Four long, unhappy years before she got smart…and by then, the damage had been done.

At the end, the very end, she had confronted him regarding how badly he had treated her. He had shrugged it off as if the issue were unimportant—as if *she* were unimportant—but, in his own defense, he had replied, "At least I never hit you." As if that counted for something. As if his words hadn't been, in their own way, every bit as painful as a physical blow might have been. As if his restraint was something to be proud of.

"I'm sorry, Susannah," Remy said quietly. "I'm sorry your ex was a bastard. I'm sorry he hurt you and that things didn't work out the way you wanted them to. But, you know, people go through bad relationships, they get over them and they go on with their lives. They fall in love again. They get married again. They find happiness again."

Leaving the chair, she walked around the perimeter of the room, giving a wide berth to the bed where he sat. "You don't have to be in love to be happy. You certainly don't have to be married."

"Logically I can agree with that. Emotionally I can't. I can't imagine finding happiness in a life that you're living alone."

"I'm not alone. I have friends. Family."

"Your family is halfway across the country in Nebraska. So are your friends, except for the ones you've made in the last few months. How can that be enough to satisfy you?"

She came to a stop in front of the bookcase, which held fewer than a dozen books and shelf after shelf of mementos. In a prominent place was a framed photograph. It was different by far from those hanging outside in the hall. There was nothing professional about it, not in the composition, the taking or the framing. It was just a snapshot in a two-dollar frame, but it held the place of honor in the room.

Taking it down, she cradled it in both hands. There were four young men on the steps of a slightly shabby house, the sort that college students, no matter what their background, were always happy to call home. She easily recognized Remy, the fair-haired charmer, and Michael, intense even then. She didn't know enough about either Evan or Smith to decide which of the handsome boys—the tall, serious one beside Remy and the shorter one with the dark mischievous eyes—was which.

In this moment frozen in time, they were all so young, so innocent, each facing a future that was full of possibilities. Now the youth was gone, and so was the innocence, and the future. At least Michael's was full, with his upcoming marriage to Valery. Again, she didn't know enough about Evan or Smith to guess at their futures.

And she knew too much about Remy.

Still holding the frame, she went to the bed and sat down facing him. "Which one is Smith?"

He pointed toward the serious boy, then touched his fingers lightly to the glass over the dark-eyed youth. "And this is Evan. I haven't told you about him, have I?"

"You said he was one of your roommates in college and that he's a cop."

"He *was* a cop. He was a good cop."

There was such emotion in his voice that Susannah knew what was coming, and she knew that she didn't want to hear it. Still, she sat quietly, waited and listened.

"He died last spring. He and Michael were trying to help a little girl who had been kidnapped. Michael went in after the girl, and Evan went after the bastard who'd taken her. She came out of it unharmed—physically, at least—but Michael got shot and Evan—" Breaking off, he sighed. "Risk comes with the job, you know? Criminals tend to be people who don't have a lot to lose. This guy knew that if he got caught, prison would be sheer hell—it usually is for child molesters— so he figured that he'd check out rather than give in. And since he was going to kill himself, hell, why not take a cop or two with him?" Sighing again, he withdrew his hand from the photograph, leaving it unsteady in her hands. "He's the only friend I ever lost. We thought we would be together forever, the four of us. And then there were three."

And soon would there be only two?

Susannah forced the morbid thought out of her mind, forced the guilt back into the darkness where she would deal with it later, and returned to the point she had intended to use the photo to make. "How old is this picture?"

"Eighteen years. That was our sophomore year in college. We'd met the year before when we all lived in the same dorm. That picture was taken the day we moved into that house together."

"Michael and Smith are still your friends, aren't they?"

"Best friends."

"And they've been enough to satisfy you for nineteen

years—or, at least, the fifteen years since you argued with your parents."

"No." He leaned back against the pillows and faced her. "I see the point you're trying to make, Susannah, but you're wrong. They were a very important part of my life. They have been and always will be. But they weren't enough to make up for the things I was missing. One person can't satisfy all our needs. A friend can't make up for the lack of parents or a husband or wife or children. Your father couldn't take your mother's place when she died. Michael, Evan and Smith couldn't replace my parents. Michael, Smith and I couldn't fill the emptiness in each other's lives when Evan died." He paused, then softened his voice as he finished. "And you're never going to be happy with just friends and long-distance family in your life."

She wanted to argue with him, wanted to tell him that he was wrong, but how could she when he was more right than he could imagine? She *wasn't* going to be happy, not here and now and certainly not anytime in the future. Once she'd done the job she had come here to do, once she had safely returned Skip to their father's home, she was going to be so alone. How could she make new friends when she knew how little she deserved them? How could she face her father when she knew how her actions would shame and shock him? Not even her relationship with Skip could survive, not when, for the rest of their lives, she would blame him for what she'd had to do.

She was going to be so totally alone.

And so incredibly unhappy.

Striving for cynicism to ward off the pain accompanying those last thoughts, she asked, "And what do you think I need in my life, Remy? *You?*"

"Don't sound so thrilled by the idea," he said dryly; then immediately that small bit of humor faded. "Are you afraid that this is just a line? That I'm bored and looking for something to amuse myself with? That when the cast comes off and my life returns to normal, I'll no longer need either the amusement or you?" He paused, but not long enough for her to answer. "I would never hurt you, Susannah."

"Maybe I'm afraid that *I'll* hurt *you.*" Her manner was careless and hard-edged, but inside all she felt was the ache. She had thought it bad this afternoon when she had curled up in bed and silently cried herself to sleep, but that was nothing compared to the pain now. "That's a hoot, isn't it, considering who you are and who I am. You could have any woman you want, and I'm supposed to be grateful that for now you've decided you want me. It never occurred to you that maybe I could hurt you."

His smile was fleeting, a little unsteady and a whole lot sad. "Honey, I have no doubt that you could break my heart."

"So go find someone else."

"What if I think you're worth the risk?"

"You're wrong, Remy. I'm not worth anything." She rose from the bed, intending to escape before he could get to his crutches, but abruptly he reached out and stopped her with his hand on her wrist. It was warm where his skin touched hers, soft and nubby where the black glove did, and his fingers were gentle where they held her.

His voice, though, was anything but gentle. "Damn it, Susannah… Is this what he did to you? Is this how your ex-husband amused himself? Telling you that you should be grateful for his attention? Teaching you that you don't have anything to offer, that you aren't worth anything?"

Too ashamed to answer his questions, having no answers that she could possibly give him, she stared hard at their hands, her vision blurred by the tears that burned her eyes. "Please let me go," she whispered. She pleaded.

His reply was every bit as much a whisper, every bit as much a plea. "I can't." But he did exactly that, releasing her wrist, freeing her to walk away.

It took a moment for his action to sink in, took another

moment for her to gather her strength and turn away. But she
made it only as far as the door before he spoke again, his tone
more determined this time, more of a warning.

"I'm sorry, Susannah, but I can't. You're going to have to
deal with that."

Over the next few days, Remy realized that, in a sense, one
of Susannah's fears had been true: he *had* been relying on her
to keep him occupied, to stave off the boredom that accompanied his limitations. Since their conversation in his room
Tuesday afternoon, she had, for the most part, avoided him.
She cooked his meals and ate across from him, washed his
clothes and ran his errands, but she spent no time in his
company that wasn't necessary.

The strain between them didn't seem to be taking much of
a toll on her. Of course, she was keeping busy with her job.
She was taking long walks around the grounds and, lately,
venturing into the woods behind the house where he and
Valery had played when they were kids. She spent the better
part of Wednesday helping Mrs. Holloway when the housekeeper came for her every-other-week cleaning, chatting and,
apparently, enjoying the other woman's company.

She had things to do. All *he* could do was brood.

That was why he'd decided to return to New Orleans this
afternoon. Not to stay, he had explained when he'd seen the
startled look come into Susannah's eyes as he'd made his announcement over breakfast. He had an appointment with the
orthopedic surgeon tomorrow morning; rather than get up
early to make the drive down, he'd chosen instead to go back
today. He had called Michael and Valery, back from their trip
to Arkansas, who had invited him, Susannah and Smith over
for dinner. Then they would spend the night at his apartment,
see the doctor in the morning and, sometime Monday afternoon, return to Belle Ste. Claire.

Susannah certainly didn't seem enthusiastic. It had taken

a moment for that unnerved look to fade, only to be replaced by the distant, troubled expression he'd seen so much of lately and was coming to hate with a passion. That was a good idea, she had agreed in a distant voice, and she had gone off to pack their bags. Now they were in the city, and she'd barely spoken since then.

He would wager half this month's salary that she was planning to ditch him tonight. She would wait until the last minute, he figured, probably until they were standing outside Michael's door, and then come up with some excuse for why she couldn't join his friends for dinner. There would be friends of her own to visit or errands of her own to run and, after all, it wouldn't be an inconvenience to him because his cousin and friends would be more than happy to give him whatever assistance he might need.

But she wasn't going to get away with it.

"Take the next exit," he directed, and she turned her head for a moment to look at him. Dark glasses hid her eyes, but he could feel the cool steadiness of her gaze.

"I remember the way to your apartment."

He would like to think that there was something significant about that. After all, much of the city was still unfamiliar to her, and she *had* been to his apartment only once. But he knew better than to flatter himself. She was a capable, efficient woman who was probably good with directions. "We'll drop off our bags and then go someplace for a drink before we head over to Michael's."

He waited a moment to see if she would put her getaway plan in motion now, if she would display any reluctance to spend the evening with his friends, but she said nothing.

She did, indeed, remember the way to his place. She pulled into the single parking space he was allotted in addition to the private garage where his own car was stored, then got their bags while he made his way over the curb and up a short flight of steps to the square stoop at the apartment's entrance.

The apartments had been built in the twenties, and they had everything more modern places lacked: large rooms, high ceilings, quality work and personality. The floors were cypress or tile; there were large expanses of high-gloss terracotta running through his. The walls were thick, the windows deep-set, and there were steps everywhere. He had lived there so long—and had been fortunate to be in such good health—that he'd practically forgotten the three steps down into the living room, the two steps up to the dining room, the four up into the kitchen.

Susannah closed the door behind her, set their luggage down and gave the foyer a cursory glance. He watched her, searching for some sign of approval, of like or dislike, on her face, but her expression didn't change. Just once, he thought, he would like to see a little sheer, unanticipated pleasure on her face. He would like to see something take her by surprise, something that she liked so much, she couldn't begin to hide it.

Even more, he would like to, if not *be* that something, at least be responsible for it.

"What do you think?" he asked.

Her gaze brushed across him, then skittered away. "It's pretty."

Pretty. The word was universally accepted as a compliment, but it seemed to Remy—at least when spoken in that tone of voice—to be just one more of those damnably bland and meaningless words. Nice. Sweet. Pretty.

"Do you want to go by your place while we're in town and pick up anything?"

That brought her gaze back to him, along with a too-abrupt answer. "No."

"Are you sure? It's not too far from here, is it? Three or four miles?"

She shoved her hands into the pockets of the jacket she wore, then leaned back against the banister. "Three or four miles can be a long, long way."

He supposed that was true anywhere, but especially in New Orleans. Traveling a few miles could take you from gracious, old-money elegance through government-supported projects and back into affluence. Cross one street—the wrong street—down in the Quarter, and you traded historic ambience for a no-man's-land where your life wasn't worth the slug it would take to end it.

"Are you embarrassed by where you live, Susannah?"

Ready with a denial, she opened her mouth, then her face grew red and she slowly closed it again. She turned away from him and stood at the top of the steps descending into the living room, where her sigh seemed to echo from the tile floor to the sparsely decorated walls to the high ceiling. "I'm not embarrassed by it," she said at last, "although I understand why you might think so. It's nothing like this. Calling this place and my place both apartments is sort of like calling a two-foot-deep ditch and the Grand Canyon both holes in the ground. It's a plain, average apartment in a plain, average complex. Nothing fancy, nothing expensive. Fifteen, maybe twenty, years old, a little the worse for wear. It's what I can afford on my salary with my expenses, and it suits my needs just fine."

She faced him then and, for the first time in days, her smile wasn't forced. It wasn't filled with pleasure, either— in fact, it was slightly self-mocking—but it was real. "The apartment and I have a lot in common."

Plain, average, nothing fancy, a little the worse for wear.

Remy covered the distance between them with a few easy paces, then balanced on his crutches in front of her. He lifted one hand to her hair, which was pulled back today and fastened with a plastic clip so that it cascaded down in soft waves, and stroked it gently. "You're not plain, there's nothing average about you, and, honey, we're all a little the worse for wear."

The smile came again, a little different this time, touched

with a hint of longing and the mocking now directed at them both. "Lines, Remy," she murmured. "Those are just lines."

"Truths, Susannah. Someday you're going to recognize the difference between the two." Bracing against the crutches, he placed both hands on her shoulders, then waited for her to step back, to effortlessly glide away from his touch, to do something, anything, to break the contact between them. When she didn't, he slowly drew her closer. At first she was hesitant, and under the circumstances, she had to be the one to move; because of the cast, the crutches and their position, he was physically incapable of it.

One step, he silently pleaded. Just one small step at a time.

Finally, when he was about to give up hope, she took that last step that brought her into his arms. For a moment she remained still and stiff; then, with a soft, weary sigh, she relaxed against him, resting her head on his shoulder, pressing her cheek to his sweater, settling her hands at his waist.

It was a simple embrace—not passionate, not joyful, not sexual in the least. He had experienced more intimate encounters with total strangers in crowded elevators or in a Saturday night throng on Bourbon Street.

More intimate…but not sweeter. Never sweeter.

For a moment he was content to simply hold her and to stroke her hair, the exposed curve of her neck, down her spine. But it wasn't long at all before contentment turned to greed. Holding and touching should lead naturally to caressing, to kissing and more. He wanted more. Always more.

But was she ready to give it?

Was she ever going to be ready?

"I wish I'd met you before he did," he said regretfully. He didn't have to clarify that by "he," he meant her ex-husband. He could feel the tension of acknowledgment ripple through her. Raising both hands to her face, he gently forced her back gently forced her to look up at him. "Want me to make life miserable for him?" he asked with his best grin.

She almost smiled. "He's in Nebraska. What could you do from down here?"

"Plenty. I could call the nearest field office up there and give them his name and address. They would call the local sheriff's department and pass it on. It would be strictly unofficial and off-the-record, one cop doing a favor for another—it happens all the time. Good ol' Guy wouldn't be able to leave his house without getting followed, stopped, warned or ticketed. They would make his life hell."

This time she did smile. "That's harassment."

"That's satisfaction, sweetheart. You deserve that much." He couldn't resist tracing his thumb across the curves of her smile. "Say the word, and I'll make it happen."

Wide-eyed and innocent, she shook her head. "Guy likes to drive fast and reckless. The insurance company had told him just before we separated that if he got one more ticket, they would cancel him. I couldn't be responsible for that."

Remy pretended disappointment—although he'd known, if he had made the offer seriously, what her answer would be. "You're a better person than I am. I'd let the sheriff have him."

His words faded and stillness grew between them as their gazes locked and held. She was a beautiful woman—not merely pretty, as he'd first thought, but quietly, dazzlingly beautiful. When had she changed? he wondered. The answer, of course, was that she hadn't. *His* perception of her had. The more time he spent with her, the better he came to know her, the more deeply he cared for her, the more beautiful she became to him.

On impulse he leaned forward to kiss her. Instinctively—as he'd half expected—she drew back and turned her head so that his kiss, if completed, would graze her cheek rather than her mouth. "Oh, Susannah." His voice was soft, his breath warm and ticklish, sending a shiver through her. "What will it take to convince you to trust me?"

She had no answer—he didn't expect one—but slowly she tilted her head back until her gaze met his again. The position moved her body into closer contact with his, into damned intimate contact, he thought, suppressing a groan even though he couldn't suppress his body's response.

"You've got to help me out here, sweetheart. I feel as if I'm playing a game that I can't afford to lose, but I don't know the rules. Tell me what you want, tell me what you need that I haven't offered, and I'll give it to you."

"Tell me what *you* want," she said quietly, her voice curiously cool when their bodies were undeniably hot.

"I want *you*."

"What exactly does that mean?" Acknowledging his arousal, she gave a tiny little shrug that sent shocks through him everywhere they touched. "Besides the obvious."

He considered all the ways he could answer, weighing the merits of one reply against another. When he finally spoke, his words came haltingly. "From the first time I saw you, I felt…connected to you."

"You were afraid and in pain. Sometimes, in a time of great stress, a person develops an emotional attachment to someone who can help him—a patient to a doctor, a victim to a police officer. It's not an unusual response. But it's not enough to build a relationship on."

"It's not the same, Susannah, and you know it." While stroking her hair, he worked the clip open and pulled it free so that her hair swung loose over his hands. "It's ironic. I *was* afraid that night…but you've been afraid ever since. Look at me, Susannah, and tell me that you don't feel something for me. Tell me you're not curious about what could develop between us. Tell me you don't care."

Stiffening, she pulled away. He couldn't force her to stay in his arms, but he did catch her wrist, holding her close, close enough so he could see the shadows in her hazel eyes. "Tell me, Susannah."

"You want an affair, Remy—"

"Yes," he interrupted. "I do. I don't deny that. Hell, right now I *can't* deny it. I want to make love to you, Susannah. I think about it at night when you're asleep across the hall. I think about it when I watch you work and when you sit in the parlor in the evenings and read, and I damn sure think about it when you take those long baths every morning. I'm a normal, reasonably healthy man and you're a lovely woman, and I would like to spend the next fifty or sixty years indulging my desire for you. Is there something wrong with that?"

"Don't say things like that," she insisted. "You don't know me!"

Giving in to the demands of his leg, he moved back to the half wall that separated the entry from the living room, pulling her with him, and leaned against it. "I know that your ex-husband hurt you tremendously. I know that you're a generous, nurturing woman. I know that you're not as afraid of believing in me as you are of believing in yourself. And I know that there are things troubling you." He smiled faintly. "I also know the important things, Susannah. I know that you have the gentlest eyes I've ever seen. I know that you brighten a room just by walking into it. I know that you have a healing touch. And from the first time I saw you, I've known that you were the woman I wanted—not just for a nurse, not for a friend, not for an affair, but for always."

She shook her head, almost frantic in her denial. "I could be a terrible person. I could have awful things planned for you."

"I've known terrible people, sweetheart, and I've seen awful things. You're not capable of hurting anyone."

"You don't know that," she whispered, "because you don't know me."

"I do know, Susannah."

She tried to pull her arm free, but still he held her. "This is ridiculous. Let me go, please. I need to unpack bef—"

Breaking in, he repeated his earlier request. "Look at me, tell me you don't feel something for me, and I'll let you go."

Her gaze settled somewhere around the waistband of his jeans. "I...don't..."

"Susannah. Look at me."

At last she forced her gaze up until it locked with his.

"Say, 'I don't want you, Remy,'" he demanded, even as he silently prayed for her to deny it.

She didn't say it...but neither did she deny it. She simply said nothing.

"Say, 'I don't feel anything for you.'" *Please, damn you, tell me you do.*

Still nothing.

His voice grew harsh and tight, and his breathing sounded strained in his own ears. "Say, 'I don't give a damn about you, Remy.'"

The gentlest eyes he'd ever seen were also now the saddest. He'd never felt such sorrow...such longing...or such regret. "I'm sorry, Remy," she whispered.

He stared at her a long, long time, until the emptiness growing inside him was complete, until the pain lost its raw edge and the shock began turning everything numb. Finally he released her, and he took a clumsy step away, followed by another. "No, Susannah," he said at last, his voice hollow and unsteady. "*I'm* sorry. I thought... I assumed that anything I felt so strongly couldn't possibly be one-sided, but obviously I was wrong. I am sorry."

He turned away then, feeling aches that he hadn't felt in days as he made his way down the steps and across the living room to the overstuffed sofa. As he gingerly eased down onto the cushions, she came to the second step. "Remy..."

Whatever she was about to say, he didn't want to hear it. Not now. Not yet. "My room is the first one at the top of the stairs. You can have either of the two guest rooms. Go ahead and unpack our bags now." He drew a deep breath that stung.

"Michael and Valery are expecting us about six, so I'd like to leave here around five-thirty."

"Maybe…maybe I shouldn't go."

He smiled mockingly. There was no maybe about it; she *definitely* shouldn't go. He didn't need to spend an entire evening watching her with his friends. He certainly didn't need to see how naturally she fit in, how easily she belonged. But more than that, he didn't need the questions that showing up without her would generate. "They're expecting both of us," he said pointedly. "Be ready at five-thirty."

Then, using a coolly polite tone that he'd learned years ago from his grandmother, he dismissed her as effectively as any servant had ever been dismissed. "That's all for now, Susannah. You can go."

Shortly after arriving at the third-floor apartment overlooking Jackson Square that Valery and Michael shared, Susannah accepted Valery's invitation to step outside to take in the view of St. Louis Cathedral. While the other woman went to get jackets to protect them from the damp evening chill, Susannah left Remy, seated at the dining table, and Michael, cooking their dinner in the small kitchen, and went on out alone. It *was* cool outside, but she swore she would have been just as chilled inside, alone with the two men.

Remy was treating her exactly as she had expected to be treated on her first day at Belle Ste. Claire—as a servant, someone paid to see to his needs, to follow his orders and to remain more or less a nonperson the rest of the time. She had been sure in the beginning that an all-business relationship was exactly what she wanted, but now that she had it, it hurt. It hurt to see that cool impersonal look in his eyes. It hurt to watch him distance himself from her.

Most of all, it hurt to know that he was doing this because *she* had hurt *him*.

And she hadn't even meant to.

He had misunderstood her in the foyer this afternoon. She hadn't been apologizing because she couldn't deny the things he was saying. She had apologized because she couldn't confirm them, because she couldn't tell him that she didn't care. She *did* care, God help her, entirely too much. She cared more than he would ever know.

And she had no right.

A shiver rustling through her, she turned to face the cathedral, lit against the encroaching night, at the far end of the square below. Although she had been a regular churchgoer from the time she was born, it had been shamefully easy not to find a new church once she'd moved here. There had been other priorities in her life—getting a job and dealing with Skip—and a new church home wasn't one of them.

She hadn't even looked. She had known she would never find a church like the one she'd left behind—the one where she'd been baptized, where she had taken part in every Christmas play and Easter pageant in twenty-five years, where she had for a number of years taught Sunday school, where she and Guy had been married. They'd had the same minister her entire life and, it seemed, more or less the same congregation. Oh, there had been marriages and births and deaths, but the heart of the church had stayed the same. More than half the members were related to her in one way or another. Uncle Richard was a deacon, and his youngest boy was the youth leader. Aunt Salley, who lived just down the road from the farm, played the organ, and a cousin on Susannah's mother's side was the pride and joy of the informal choir.

Since she couldn't replace what she'd had at home, she hadn't even tried. It had felt funny at first—awakening on Sunday mornings and not putting on a pretty dress or doing her hair or makeup. A lifetime of Sunday morning services had been a hard habit to break, but she had managed. Oh, she had still tried to follow the teachings and the preachings, had tried to live a good Christian life, and for a time there, as she uncovered the extent of Skip's problems, her prayers had grown more fervent, more impassioned, more regular.

Until the day that lawyer had called.

Although she knew she needed divine guidance and help more now than ever before, she didn't feel she even had the right to pray. She was committing a crime, was conspiring with an evil man to commit an even greater one. Why should God hear her prayers? Why should He care?

"The cathedral is a beautiful place, isn't it?" Closing the French doors behind her, Valery joined Susannah on the balcony, offering her a heavy woolen shawl for protection from the damp evening chill. "Sometimes I go inside and just sit there. It's so peaceful." She pulled on her own jacket, then leaned on the wrought-iron railing. "You look as if you could use a little peace."

Susannah offered her a sad smile. "I could use a new life."

"One away from Remy?" Valery didn't wait for an answer. "You know, Susannah, we've all been kind of enjoying the way Remy's pursued you. Granted, I haven't been around him much in recent years, but Michael and Smith both say this is pretty much out of character for him. He's never been so single-minded about a woman before. They also say it's a sign of how important this is—how important you are—to him. But if you really aren't interested in him, if you don't feel what he feels, maybe it would be kinder for both of you if you made it clear to him now."

On a not too distant street corner, a single horn—a saxophone, Susannah thought—was playing a sweet, rather mournful tune. She didn't know the name, but she'd heard it before. She remembered one line. *Do you know what it means to miss New Orleans?* Oh, yes. She was standing right there in the heart of the French Quarter, in the heart of the city itself, and she already missed it. She already felt the ache that she knew was going to follow her forever.

As the last notes died away in the night, she turned to

Valery. "It's not a question of being interested. There's much more to it than that."

"Do you want to talk about it?"

She missed that, she thought regretfully—talking. Confiding. When she was a girl, she had told all her dearest secrets to her mother and later, after Janet Crouse's death, to her girlfriends. She had cried over the gradual breakup of her marriage with Traci Lynn Williams, the best of her best friends, and she'd made more than a few long-distance calls back to Nebraska to discuss her concerns about Skip with Traci Lynn.

But she couldn't confide in anyone anymore. This time her secrets truly were secrets. Telling them would do more than cost her the respect and possibly even the love of people who had always loved her. Telling, at best, would put those friends in the difficult position of having to choose between protecting a friend and obeying the law.

At worst, it could put their lives in danger.

"I wish I could. But I can't." She held the other woman's clear blue gaze for a long moment, then looked away to the square. "You and Michael have a lovely place here. If you're going to live in New Orleans, I can't imagine a more perfect location."

After another long moment, Valery let the change of subject stand. "I know. We'll both miss it when we move."

"Then why do it?"

"We both want babies—lots of them—as soon as we're married, but the apartment is just one bedroom. Besides, an apartment is no place to raise kids if you can avoid it."

"When is the wedding?" Susannah asked, telling herself that it was all right to discuss marriage, weddings and babies. That twinge around her heart had nothing to do with wanting any of that. It was simply a little sorrow left over from hearing that song. In the right hands, the clear tones of a sax on a cool, foggy evening could turn the cheeriest song in the world into the blues

"A few more weeks. As soon as Aunt Marie and Uncle George get back from their trip."

A few more weeks. Everything would be settled in a few more weeks. She would be gone. She would never see New Orleans or Valery or any of her friends here again.

She would never see Remy again.

Unless...

Unless she found some way out.

Unless she somehow managed to rescue her brother and to save Remy at the same time.

Unless she betrayed Jimmy Falcone.

She pulled the shawl closer, burrowing her fingers into the soft woven fabric. It was an impossible suggestion. Jimmy Falcone had a nasty little way of dealing with people who betrayed him. He made sure they couldn't do it to him or anyone else ever again. He didn't give them a chance to live to regret their deeds.

He simply had them killed.

Life meant so little to him that he'd had Nate Simmons murdered merely as a means of framing Remy. Now, for whatever reasons—because Remy had escaped his trap, because he was still an irritant, because for too long Remy had headed the case against him—now Falcone intended to have *him* killed.

And to accomplish that, he was threatening to do the same to Skip.

And if she tried to stop him, he would simply add her to his list.

God help her, she didn't want to die.

But did she want to live at the expense of someone else's life?

The three soaring spires of the cathedral drew her gaze. Only moments ago she had wondered why God should listen to her prayers; a person committing the terrible sin that *she* was committing wasn't deserving of His attention.

But she had been taught better than that. Saints weren't quite so needy of God's direction.

Sinners were.

And she was sinning in the worst possible way. That meant she probably ranked pretty high right now on the Lord's list of priorities.

Her hands clasped tightly together, she stared hard at the church as she offered a silent prayer, a silent plea for help. There had to be a way to escape this nightmare, hopefully with their lives intact, but she didn't know what it was. She couldn't see any way out, but then, all she could see was her own fear, her own worries. There *had* to be some solution, some way to save both Remy and Skip, some way to stop Jimmy Falcone before he destroyed any more lives.

Failing that, there had to be some way to save Remy. He was the only innocent one involved. Whatever else happened, he had to survive.

Dear God, she whispered silently, he *had* to.

Beside her, Valery stirred, disturbing, then breaking, the tense silence that surrounded Susannah. "Ah, there's the answer to my prayers," she said with a smile. "Now we can eat."

The answer to my prayers. Susannah blinked back the moisture that glazed her eyes. There was no justice, she thought, not when she and Valery could share the same small space, could look at the same church and offer such different prayers.

There was certainly no justice when it was Valery's prayers that brought an answer.

After mouthing one final, silent *please,* she turned to face the brightly lit apartment. The curtains across the wide windows and doors were sheer, allowing a filmy, hazy look inside at the new arrival. He was as tall as Remy and as lean as Michael. Although he was as casually dressed as they were and was sprawled as comfortably as they were around the table, something about him screamed—no, wrong word— something about him *whispered* refinement. Breeding. Pure class. It was indefinable, unmistakable.

Intimidating.

But, curiously, she didn't feel intimidated. "Is that Smith?"

Valery nodded.

"Tell me about him."

"Ah, Remy hasn't filled you in?" Valery considered her request a moment. "Well, his name is Smith Kendricks. You've probably heard of him. No, I forgot, you're a newcomer. Stay around long, and you'll see a lot of him—if not in the headlines, then in the society pages. He's *the* most eligible bachelor in the city for obvious reasons. He's incredibly handsome, sexy as hell and very, very rich with very old money. He comes from back east, from Connecticut or Rhode Island or someplace. I think his family owns New England."

Susannah smiled weakly at that, and it felt surprisingly good. She had smiled so little in recent months and she missed it.

"For reasons that escape me, he turned his back on all those venerable old institutions where people like him usually go to college and came here instead. That's how he met Michael and Remy. He went back to Harvard or another of those venerable old places for law school, then got a job here with the U.S. Attorney's office. He's very bright and very talented. He's already inherited a number of fortunes and has more just waiting for him, and the best part of it, Susannah, is he's such a nice guy."

"Right," she said. "Those are qualities *I* always think of together. Incredibly handsome, sexy as hell, bright, rich and nice." But Remy was all those things, too. He was incredibly handsome and sexy, and he came from money, but he was sweet, nice, charming and thoughtful.

"I know. Isn't it a hoot?"

"Sounds as if he'd be the answer to a lot of prayers. With all that going for him, why isn't he married?"

"I imagine it's difficult to find someone whose bloodlines and bank balances measure up. That seems to be his only flaw.

He chooses his women based on their suitability for a relationship with the heir to the Kendricks empire rather than something as unimportant as physical attraction or compatibility." Valery shivered as a breeze rustled across the square. "In all fairness, I'll also say that he *is* dedicated to his job. Michael says he's the best damn prosecutor around. He believes very strongly in what he's doing."

"And what exactly is that?"

"He prosecutes federal cases, primarily organized crime. When they finally get Jimmy Falcone for the murder that I witnessed and for trying to kill Remy, Smith will take the case to court." The easiness disappeared from Valery's voice and was replaced by a tougher, colder tone. "He'll send the bastard away forever."

Susannah studied him for a long, still moment. A federal prosecutor, scheduled to prosecute Jimmy Falcone if the government ever got him to court. One of Remy's two best friends, one who hopefully wouldn't take an immediate dislike to her as Michael had, and such a nice guy.

Maybe Valery had been wrong earlier. Maybe Smith Kendricks wasn't the answer to *her* prayers.

Maybe he was the answer to Susannah's.

Chapter 7

A blast of cold air swept into the room when Susannah and Valery returned from the balcony. Sitting near the door as he was, it should have sent a chill through Remy, but he already felt pretty damned cold inside. The air temperature outside couldn't begin to compete.

Valery came in first, wearing a welcoming smile and offering a friendly greeting to Smith. Behind her, Susannah took her time, making certain that the billowy curtain didn't get caught in the door as she closed it, before she finally joined them at the table. He wondered if anyone else could recognize her reluctance to be there at all. It wasn't obvious, wasn't anything that couldn't be mistaken for shyness at spending an evening with a bunch of people who were mostly strangers, but he could see it. She didn't meet anyone's gaze, didn't speak unless spoken to, and even though she did join them around the table, she somehow managed to also stay apart. She sat straight, kept her feet together and her hands clasped in her lap.

Valery performed the introductions with little fanfare as she went about setting the table. "Susannah Duncan, Smith Kendricks. Susannah's taking care of Remy until his folks get back from Europe."

"Susannah." Smith leaned across the table and offered his hand, forcing her to also lean forward. When she did, Remy caught a whiff of fresh, cold air, of the sweet, flowery fragrance that clung to the shawl still wrapped around her shoulders and, barely noticeable beneath the rest, her own fragrance—subtle and simple. The mix of scents was appealing. So was her wind-ruffled hair, the pinkness slowly fading from her cheeks and the faint glitter the cold had put into her eyes. The whole damn image was appealing.

There was just one problem.

She didn't want to appeal to *him.*

Damn her.

And damn his own judgment for being so far off. He'd never missed before. He had always known when a woman was attracted to him, when she would welcome his attention. He had never approached anyone who wasn't happy to be approached, who didn't share his interest.

So how had he managed to be so wrong about Susannah?

Maybe she'd been right. Maybe it had been some sort of gratitude complex. Maybe he had fixated on her because she had helped ease his fear and his pain, because she had offered him assurances at a time when he badly needed them. Maybe he was simply grateful to her, and he had let it get out of control.

No way. If he was grateful to anyone in the emergency room, it was the doctors. They were the ones who had spent hours putting his leg back together. They were the ones primarily responsible for his recovery.

Besides, he was a smart man. He could tell gratitude from attraction. He could damn sure recognize desire.

But he had failed to recognize her lack of desire. He had failed to notice that she didn't reciprocate his feelings. Maybe he wasn't so smart, after all. If he was, he never would have forced that scene back at his apartment. He never would have asked her to admit that she didn't care about him if he hadn't believed with all his heart that she did.

A smart man? he thought bitterly. No. Except for her ex-husband, he was the sorriest fool that ever lived.

"Remy."

Susannah's voice, soft and all too sweet, broke into his thoughts. For a moment, he ignored her. In forcing an answer from her this afternoon, he had done more than destroy the future—the fantasies—he had built around her. He had put himself in an impossible situation. He couldn't continue living with her, knowing how she felt. He couldn't pretend that it didn't matter. He couldn't see her every day and know that there was no hope for them.

But how could he let her go and never see her again?

"Quit daydreaming, Remy, and take the food," Valery commanded from across the table. "There are hungry people here."

Finally he focused his gaze on the dish Susannah was offering. Red beans and rice. Michael could cook anything, but he preferred Cajun. Tonight he had fixed a sampling—beans and rice, crabmeat gumbo and crawfish étouffée—with something equally rich for dessert. Ordinarily the mere smell of his cooking was enough to make Remy's mouth water, but tonight he had little appetite.

Taking the bowl from Susannah, he ladled a portion onto his plate before passing the dish on to Smith. He passed the other bowls around as they came to him, ate and even took part in the conversation, but he didn't notice what he was eating. He couldn't remember what was said.

God, he wished he could go home.

Alone.

Before he realized it, the meal was over and Susannah, Valery and Smith were clearing the table. Michael offered him the crutches that had been put in the corner out of the way and suggested that they move to the sofa where he could stretch his leg out.

"What's the problem?" Michael asked once they were settled in the living portion of the large room.

"What problem?" Remy arranged a pillow underneath his foot to protect the coffee table, then leaned back.

"Between you and Susannah."

Somehow he kept his expression even and blank. "Who says—"

"I do. You two haven't looked at each other since you got here. What gives?"

"There's nothing wrong between Susannah and me." And that was the truth. How could something be wrong when there was nothing between them?

"Right. That's why you've been off in another world most of the evening, and she's been afraid to even look up from the table, much less open her mouth."

Remy stubbornly refused to back down from his first response. He had always been honest with Michael, had confided practically everything in him, but he'd be damned if he'd sit here with Susannah across the room and repeat this afternoon's conversation to him now.

After a moment, Michael apparently decided to let it slide. "So you have a checkup tomorrow. What good news are you hoping for?"

"That my leg's healed, the cast can come off and I can go back to work." Then he shrugged and offered a more realistic response. "That my leg has healed enough to bear weight, I can trade the crutches for a cane and can finally take a shower again."

"When is the cast supposed to come off?"

"A couple more weeks."

"And then what?"

And then he had no excuse for having Susannah around any longer.

But that was already true. He had no excuse now. He had never been interested in her nursing, her housekeeping or cooking or driving. He'd never had any interest at all in a paid servant/companion, and that was all she was willing to be. The smart thing to do would be to cut her loose now. Pay her the rest of the month's salary and send her back to the city, back to her apartment, her friends and a new job. Hell, she might not even have to look for a new job; after only two weeks, she might be able to get the old one back.

But he wasn't feeling particularly smart right now.

In fact, he felt pretty damned masochistic.

With a sigh, he turned his attention to Michael's last question. "Then I begin physical therapy to rebuild the muscles in my right leg, I rely on a cane until I can manage on my own, and I go back to work on a limited basis. I have checkups every month for six months, then every three months. The doctor says I'll even be able to start jogging again…oh, after a year or so. And after only one and a half to two years, if everything's okay, they'll put me back in the hospital, open my leg and remove the titanium plate. It's something to look forward to, isn't it?"

Michael ignored the sarcasm that tinged his voice. "You're alive, Remy. That's a hell of a lot to be grateful for."

Immediately Remy felt ashamed of his attitude. He knew how easily he could have died that night, and he knew that if he had, it probably would have destroyed his friend. For months Michael had blamed himself for Evan's death, because it had been *his* visions of the little girl in trouble that had drawn Evan into the case. He hadn't wanted to survive his own injuries, and when he had lived in spite of himself, he'd done his best to drink himself to death.

It had been a tough time for all of them, but Remy and Smith had finally reached Michael, had finally gotten him out of the bottle and brought him—unwilling but coming along anyway—back into the world. Then the visions of Valery had started and, in the end, Remy had gotten shot. If he had died, Michael would have once again blamed himself, and there was no way he could have survived it a second time.

"I know," he said quietly. "And I am damned grateful. I just wish…" Letting the words trail off, he looked away. He'd been given a precious gift—his life—but it wasn't enough. He wanted someone to share it with. He wanted to share it with Susannah, who didn't think that what he had to offer was worth taking.

After a brief silence, Michael spoke again. "I ran into Shawna Warren Friday."

Mention of the agent who had replaced him on the Falcone case lessened Remy's moodiness slightly. Shawna was a good agent, tougher than most of the men in the office and with an IQ that was practically off the charts. He liked her—had liked her enough, in fact, when she was first assigned to the office to spend a few evenings and one particularly memorable night with her before they had both decided that a personal relationship wasn't worth jeopardizing their professional relationship. He couldn't have asked for a better agent to take over his case.

Even if it had—pardon the bad joke—almost killed him to give it up.

"What's going on with her?" he asked.

"She was in her usual bad mood. She asked about you. Said she's not getting anywhere with Jimmy and that, as far as she's concerned, when the doctors let you return to work, you can have him back."

Remy scowled. "So she says. Let me try to take him, though, and she'll bite my hand off at the wrist. I was hoping they'd made some progress against Falcone."

"No, you weren't. You were hoping that things would just sort of idle along until you were back at work so you could bring the bastard down yourself. But you know that's not going to happen."

"I know. I can't be the case agent when I've become part of

the case itself." He shook his head wistfully. "But it would have been nice to be the one to get him and all the sons of bitches who work for him. I'd like to see them all locked up for the rest of their worthless lives and know that I put them there."

"At least you'll know you helped. Probably ninety percent of the evidence you guys have against Falcone is stuff you dug up."

"Yeah, but I'd sure like to supply that last ten percent."

In the silence that followed, Remy's gaze shifted unwillingly to the small kitchen. Valery and Smith seemed to be doing most of the talking, while Susannah quietly washed the dishes that wouldn't fit into the dishwasher. Occasionally bits of their conversation drifted out and across the room, but not enough to make eavesdropping worthwhile.

Occasionally the sound of Susannah's laughter drifted out, too. Had he heard her laugh before tonight? he wondered bleakly. No. All he had managed to coax from her was a rare smile, and even those were usually tinged with emotions other than pleasure.

He had thought her ex-husband or some other problem, maybe whatever had put that sorrow in her eyes, was to blame for the rarity of her smiles. Now he knew it was because she didn't find any pleasure in his company. Because, while he'd wanted an affair, a commitment, a future, all she had wanted was to do her job. Because he hadn't given her the space and the peace of mind to do it.

Setting his brooding aside—after all, he had plenty of time for that back at Belle Ste. Claire—he turned his attention back to Michael. "How did it go with your family and Valery? Did they make any unfavorable comparisons to Beth?"

"Are you kidding? You know my folks weren't too fond of Beth. They weren't happy when we divorced, but it was more because there had never been a divorce in the family before, not because they were sorry to see her go." Michael looked at Valery with a tenderness that Remy envied—rather, what he envied was the fact that Valery always looked back with the same tenderness. "My grandmother adored her," Michael continued, "and she pretty much rules the rest of the family."

"So you've got her blessing, and theirs. Is your father going to conduct the ceremony in his church?" At his nod, Remy chuckled. "Not many people can be married by their fathers even once, and here you'll be doing it for the second time."

"For the last time," Michael corrected, and Remy had no doubt his friend was right. He and Valery would be spending the rest of their lives together.

How long would it take, he wondered, for *him* to find someone to spend the rest of his life with?

How much longer would he have to live alone?

In the kitchen, Susannah dried her hands, then laid the dish towel on the counter. It had been a long time since she had shared a family meal—and even if there were no blood ties here, these people were, undoubtedly, family. Back home such meals had been as regular a part of her life as work on Monday morning and weekends off. Every Sunday after morning services, every holiday, every time a wandering relative passed through town and on any other occasion a person could think of, the families had gathered at one house or another. Being a very traditional bunch, the women had shared the cooking, the child care and the cleanup, while the men had eaten their fill and discussed crop prices, weather and politics. At the time such events hadn't carried any special significance for her; they were just a part of belonging to the Crouse family.

Now she knew how special they were. Now she missed them.

"You like chocolate, Susannah?" Michael asked, joining them in the small kitchen and wrapping his arms around Valery's waist.

"Doesn't everyone?"

"I don't know. Remy only eats it in cookies. Valery, on the other hand, inhales it as if it were vital to sustain life as we know it." He ignored Valery's teasing scowl as he released her, then eased past to the refrigerator. "Go on in and make yourself comfortable, and Val and I will serve dessert."

Susannah saw that Smith had already left and was seated in the chair directly across from Remy on the sofa, where they were deep in conversation. "First, I have to make a call."

"Sure. Why don't you go into the bedroom? It's private."

"Thank you." Picking up her purse and fishing for her cell, she made her way across the living room and into the bedroom, where she closed the door quietly behind her. There was only one chair in the room, placed between the windows, and she headed straight for it. It was big and comfortable, the sort of chair made for curling up and dreaming in.

But she had no time for dreams. Not this evening.

Quickly she opened her phone only to find she had no service in this area. With her restricted budget, she'd chosen a cheap cell phone and plan, not caring at the time that a lower bill also meant spotty reception. Now she wished she'd gone for the top of the line. She had to call Carlucci. Seeing no other option, she picked up the cordless phone that was on the bedside table and dialed the number that had become too offensively familiar to her, asking for the man she had never met face-to-face but had come to hate with a passion. She didn't know if this number reached his home or office, or if possibly his office was in his home. All she knew was that she could use it to contact him anytime, night or day.

Nicholas Carlucci's voice was smooth, charming and underlaid with steel—with threat—as always. If he was annoyed to have his Sunday evening disturbed with business, he gave no hint of it. "I was beginning to wonder when I would hear from you."

"I've kept to our schedule," she said defensively.

"Yes, you have. But you were also told to call when schedules changed."

So he knew they were in the city. She was as sure of it as if he'd come right out and said so. And if he knew, then that meant he was still having them watched. It meant that he already didn't trust her. If she started lying to him now… "I didn't know about Remy's plan to spend the night in town until he told me this morning. This is the first opportunity I've had to contact you."

There was silence on the other end for a long, unnerving moment. Then, at last, he spoke. "Are you staying at his apartment?"

"Yes."

"Is that where you're calling from?"

"No. We're at his friend's place."

"Which friend? Bennett or Kendricks?"

"Michael Bennett." She hesitated. "But Kendricks is here, too. And Valery Navarre."

"What are Remy's other plans for this trip?"

"Just the doctor's appointment in the morning."

"And after seeing the doctor, you'll be returning to Belclaire."

"As far as I know."

"Does it seem to you, Susannah, that he's keeping you in the dark? That perhaps he doesn't trust you with his plans too far in advance?"

Her voice turned haughty and cold. "I'm his employee, Mr. Carlucci. He tells me what he wants me to know when he wants me to know it. If you don't like the way things are going, release my brother and find someone else to help you."

The cynicism that had shaded his voice disappeared, leaving it smooth—oily smooth—again. "Things are going just fine, Susannah. I believe we'll hold on to young Skip a while longer. Mr. Falcone does enjoy his company." There was an interruption in the background, then his manner became all business. "Very well, Susannah. I'll expect to hear from you…shall we say Friday? Unless, of course, something changes before then."

Before he could hang up, she spoke abruptly. "I want to talk to Skip."

"I'm sorry. He can't come to the phone now. Goodbye, Susannah." There was a click, followed by a dial tone.

Muttering a curse, Susannah returned the phone switch to Off, then stared for a moment into the distance. After a time she realized that she was staring at a portrait of Valery, beautiful and as ethereal as any angel. It was the work of an artist passionately involved with his subject—Michael's work. How wonderful it must be, she thought wistfully, to know passion like that.

Remy had offered *her* such passion. If she found some solution to her predicament, and if she could convince him to give her a second chance, maybe she could accept…temporarily, at least. Maybe she could know just once in her life what it was like to experience such ardor. Maybe she could believe in him and, for a time, believe in herself. Maybe she could gather enough memories to last the rest of her life.

Until he found out the truth about her.

Until he knew how she had lied. How she had betrayed him.

Until he started hating her with as much passion as he had ever wanted her.

From the next room came a burst of masculine laughter. She needed to rejoin them, but first there was one more call she wanted to make. This was a familiar number, too—her home number. On the second ring the answering machine picked up. She listened to only a few words of Skip's *We can't take your call* message before pushing the proper buttons to access the messages.

There were only three—one from a friend for Skip, one for her from an X-ray technician at work and a second for her from… She whispered a little prayer.

"Hey, Susannah, I don't know if you'll be checking for messages, but this is the only way I know to get hold of you," came Skip's voice. "I've got to be quick—I don't know when they'll be back. I'm sorry about all this, Suz. I know that's not good enough…I know I really screwed up this time…but it'll never happen again, I swear. I promise, really. When this is over, I'm going home, and I'll never, ever—" Suddenly his voice dropped to a whisper. "Gotta go. Love you, Suz."

Her hands trembling, she pressed the button to replay the last message. When the machine signaled the end the second time, she disconnected and gave a great shuddering sigh. He was her brother, one of the dearest people in her life. She had promised their mother on her deathbed that she would always take care of him, had promised their father that she would look out for him and keep him safe.

Could she really break those promises now? Could she do anything other than exactly what Nicholas Carlucci was asking of her? Could she take any chances at all when, with the slightest slipup, it was Skip who would have to pay the consequences?

Could she trust someone else—Remy, Smith, Michael or anyone—to care about her brother as deeply, as intensely, as she did, to put his best interests ahead of everything else as she did?

She didn't know.

God help her, she just didn't know.

Rubbing the ache that throbbed between her eyes, she wearily got to her feet, putting the phone back into its cradle. She couldn't think about this anymore, and she'd been in here long enough to surely arouse suspicion, at least in Remy and Michael. It was time to return to the living room. Time to pretend that nothing was wrong.

Time to, once again, start living her lies.

Sunday evening had been chilly and damp with fog—suitably dreary for February—but Monday was as sunny and clear as any midsummer morning. Susannah stood at one of the three wide windows in Remy's guest room, gazing out across the grounds. A broad expanse of ground separated his building from the next, and it was heavily planted with trees— weeping willows, crape myrtles, dogwoods and oaks. Shrubs provided natural barriers between neighbors, and bulbs bloomed along the winding sidewalks.

It was a lovely place, she thought with a smile. Three and a half miles and a world away from the apartment she shared with Skip, where the few trees that hadn't been uprooted were scraggly, where not a single flower bloomed and— thanks to the neighbors' kids—where the grass grew best in the cracks of the sidewalks.

She hadn't lied yesterday—for once—when she'd told Remy that she wasn't ashamed of where she lived. Granted, it *was* a world away from his life, but she knew better than to judge people by such things. After all, she'd grown up on a farm, where extra money went to improving the operation, buying new stock, replacing worn-out equipment, hiring extra help or saving for the inevitable bad season. A fancy place to live came pretty low in a farmer's priorities. A house in good repair was enough to satisfy most people she knew—and her apartment, while not luxurious like this place, was in good repair.

It would be different when this was all over. Skip would be back home in Nebraska, their father's responsibility once more, and she would be supporting only herself. For the first time in her life she would be truly on her own. Before her marriage she had lived at home—apartments or rental homes were scarce to nonexistent in Homestead. After the wedding, she had moved in with Guy with the assumption that it would be a partnership, that they would each contribute to the household expenses, only Guy had had other ideas. *She* had paid all the living expenses, including his car payment, and he had spent his money on...

She smiled faintly. To this day, she didn't know where his money had gone. No doubt he had blown much of it partying and playing poker with his buddies, and another substantial chunk had likely been spent on his other women. He liked to impress the women he dated, the way he had impressed her.

After the divorce, she had moved back home, back to the room her father had kept waiting for her, and then she had come to New Orleans. Skip had been more than happy to have her live with him; his roommate had moved out a few months before, and the rent was killing him. She had naively believed his promise that they would split expenses right down the middle. Of course, that was before she had discovered that he didn't have a regular job, that when he was working, he spent his money on things more important—meaning more fun—than necessities.

The day she moved in, he had hit her up for a loan. The rent was past due, as were the electric bill, his car payment and his car insurance. The telephone company was threatening to disconnect the phone, and his long-distance bill—for all those calls to his old buddies back home—was astronomical. "It's no problem for you, Suz," he had said with his most charming grin. "You're so reliable about saving. I'll pay you back, I swear."

I swear. Two of her brother's favorite words. *I'll pay you back, I swear. It'll never happen again, I swear.* And why shouldn't he use them so casually? That was all it took to win forgiveness from anyone in the family—Uncle Richard, Aunt Salley, their father and Susannah herself. They were all suckers for Skip's grin accompanied by an "I swear...."

Look how he had paid her back this time.

With a sigh, she turned away from the window, pulled her robe on and took a large freezer bag from the dresser. Inside were her shampoo and conditioner, toothbrush and toothpaste and a smaller zippered bag containing the bare essentials from her makeup case. She crossed the plush rug and a chilly section of wood floor to the door, then stepped out into the hall just as Remy came out of his room, directly across from hers.

They both stopped abruptly, and she uncomfortably pulled her robe tighter. He was already dressed in sweatpants and a T-shirt. His jaw was clean-shaven, and his hair was slicked back, a dark, wet gold. He looked well rested and handsome. So handsome.

For a moment, she thought he was going to smile, the way he did every morning, but he caught himself and instead simply looked at her. He had, in the past eighteen hours or so, developed a way of looking right at her and straight on through her, as if she were nothing of substance but simply a vague visual disturbance. It made her feel small and insignificant.

It hurt.

Clutching the plastic bag in both hands, she offered him a taut smile. "Good morning."

He didn't speak.

Wetting her lips, she tried again. "I noticed last night that you don't have any food in the house. Would you like me to go out and get something before your appointment, or would you rather stop on the way?"

He looked away then, directing his gaze toward the stairs—no doubt wishing he had escaped down them a moment or two sooner and damning his cast and crutches for slowing him down. "I'm not hungry."

Such simple words to send such a shiver down her spine. She had never heard a colder, emptier voice. "All right. What time do we need to leave for your appointment?"

"Eight-thirty."

"I'll be ready. Do you want me to pack first, or will we come back here before returning to Belle Ste. Claire?"

His gaze flickered across her face, then away again. "Get everything taken care of now. I want to get home as soon as possible." With that, he walked away, easing past her, then carefully making his way down the stairs.

He wanted to get away from her as soon as possible, she

knew. This morning he had to spend time with her—here in the apartment, in the car, at the doctor's office—but back at Belle Ste. Claire, avoiding her would be relatively simple. There were very distinct territories in the old house—family quarters as opposed to servants'. He could go wherever he wanted, while she could, quite fairly, be restricted to the back of the house—the kitchen, the laundry room and her own room. Except for the little tasks of daily straightening and cleaning she had taken on in the parlor, there was no reason for her to set foot in any of the family living areas.

She didn't know if he would put such restrictions on her, although it was only fair if he did. After all, *she* was the one who had wanted a strictly business arrangement. *She* was the one who had insisted there was nothing personal between them. *She* was the reason he felt this need to stay away.

But if he did, if he limited her to her working areas, if he began taking his meals in the parlor or the dining room while she ate in the kitchen, if he spent his long, free hours ignoring her…

It was going to be a very lonely way to live.

At the bottom of the stairs, Remy listened for the soft shuffle that meant she had finally moved from where he'd left her. When he heard it at last, he swung away on his crutches, crossing the foyer to the study. The room was large, high ceilinged, done in dark woods and rich colors.

He realized for the first time that it was very much like his father's study at Belle Ste. Claire. When he had chosen these colors, this furniture, had he subconsciously been trying to duplicate a little bit of home here in his apartment. Possibly. Probably.

He settled in the chair and leaned back. Like his father, he kept photographs on his desk. There was one of himself with his three friends, taken only a few months before Evan' death. A picture of Valery, which was taken a year or two ago obtained by the FBI from his parents when she had disap peared after witnessing Nate Simmons's death. Copies had been distributed to everyone involved in the case, and his had ended up here in a small brass frame. There was a snapshot of Evan and his wife Karen. He saw her around town from time to time, but the basis for their friendship had been lost when her husband died. She had to get on with her life and, he suspected, having little contact with him, Michael or Smith made that easier.

The last frame held a picture of his parents. He wasn't sure how old it was—more than fifteen years. In it his mother's hair was still blond, while his father's was just starting to show a little gray. They had been an attractive couple, and they still were. They had aged well, partly because they had aged together.

He thought of Susannah, who didn't want to grow old with anyone, least of all him, and he felt as if he were already old. But he would get over it, he told himself. He just wasn't used to misjudging a woman. He wasn't used to being rejected by a woman. But he had no doubt he could deal with it, because he was very used to not being able to have what he wanted.

It would just take time.

And distance.

He was still sitting there, doing nothing, when she came looking for him a short while later. He had never known a woman who could shower, dress, fix her hair and do her makeup as quickly as Susannah. He had never known a woman who looked so good.

She wore suede moccasins that were run-down to the point where they were truly comfortable, faded jeans and an ivory sweater with the sleeves pushed to her elbows. Her hair was down, pulled back on each side with a tortoiseshell comb, and her expression was sad. He wished he could pull her into his arms, wished he could hold her there in his favorite chair in his favorite room and simply stroke her cares away.

He wished he didn't have to remember to keep his distance, physically and especially emotionally.

She was carrying both of their bags, small and lightly packed. She set them on the tile before venturing into the room. "Everything's ready."

By that he had no doubt that she meant she had made the beds, straightened the bathroom, repacked every single item she had unpacked yesterday and probably even plumped the pillows on the sofa where he had lain yesterday. Except for the faint scents they would leave behind them—her perfume, his after-shave—the apartment would bear no sign that they'd even been there.

When she didn't say anything else, he gestured for her to have a seat. "How long will this appointment take?" he asked, careful to keep his tone perfectly neutral.

She sat stiffly on the edge of the chair. "If the doctor's on schedule, it should be fairly quick. He'll ask if you've had any problems and get an X ray. If everything looks good, they'll fit you with a boot and a cane. That'll be it."

"A cane," he repeated softly. "My grandfather walked with a cane. I don't think he needed it, though. It was just awfully convenient for getting someone's attention."

She started to smile, but didn't get past the faintest beginnings. A part of him was tempted to go ahead and coax it out of her. The stronger part, the part in charge of self-preservation, knew it was wiser not to try.

"What if everything doesn't look good?"

Gradually she settled back in the chair. "The bigger problems would be with nonunion, meaning the bone isn't healing properly, or infection. I don't think either one would be much of a concern at this point. When they changed the cast before you were discharged from the hospital, the gunshot wound was nicely healed and the X rays looked good. You've followed their instructions, stayed off your leg and used the crutches. You're probably in good shape."

Swiveling his chair just a bit, he shifted his gaze from her to the wall where three framed certificates hung together

One was his college degree. The second was his law degree, and the third was the certificate he had received upon finishing training at the FBI Academy. "What are the chances—" He broke off. The question on his mind had occurred to him not immediately after getting shot—then he had been concerned about whether he would live—but soon after arriving at the hospital. But he had never found the courage to ask it. He preferred to ignore the possibilities, preferred to be optimistic and to believe that everything was going to be just fine.

The closer it came to the time for removing the cast, though, the more often the question popped up, and this morning he was feeling just morose enough to ask it.

Except that he didn't have to. "That there could be a problem?" she asked softly. "It's a possibility. Because of its weight-bearing job, the femur is a nasty bone to break, and your break was particularly bad, with the added complication of the gunshot wound. There's always the possibility of a not-so-good result. But it's remote."

"How remote?"

"I'm not a doctor. I can't give you a definite answer. But your recovery has been normal so far. There's no reason to believe your prognosis is anything less than good." She paused, then added, "There's no reason to think you might not be able to continue working as an FBI agent."

He started to deny it but, of course, that had been exactly what he was wondering about. "You know," he began, his gaze fixed on his degrees, his tone soft and distant as if he were speaking to himself, "when I joined the bureau, I was just looking for a job. I went through the academy with these people who had wanted to be FBI agents all their lives, people who had grown up knowing that was what they were going to do, but I didn't have that certainty, that dedication or zeal. I just wanted a job that would make use of my education, pay a decent wage and maybe someday make my parents proud of me. It's funny. Some of those dedicated people didn't make

it through the academy. Some of them did and have since quit.
But I'm still here. I know now that this is what I want to do.
Always."

He glanced at her, then immediately looked away again.
"I don't know what I would do if I couldn't be an agent."

"You would make use of that education," she replied.
"You've been one of the good guys. Now, if necessary, you
can be a lawyer." He heard the soft creak of the chair as she
got to her feet. "Don't go looking for trouble. All you need
to worry about today is whether you get off the crutches. In
a few weeks you can worry about getting the cast removed
and after that happens, you can worry about how long it takes
for things to start feeling normal again. The time to worry
about any long-term problems is when you find out that you
have them. Not until then."

"That's an easy enough attitude for you to take," he said,
glancing at his watch, then also standing up, though without
her grace. "*You're* not the one who would have to be a
lawyer."

She left the apartment first, carrying their bags and her
purse. Behind her, he pulled the door shut and locked it, then
for a moment simply stood there and watched her. The
sunlight glinting on her hair brought out the reddish highlights
and deepened the faint golden hue of her skin. There was
something about her, something missing in the other women
he knew. Something innocent. Something wholesome.

If this was what growing up on a farm did for you, he
thought with a reluctant smile, then hurray for America's
farmers and every one of their daughters.

By the time he reached the car, she was waiting at his door
to take his crutches. She stowed them in the back seat, then
circled to the driver's side. After he gave her directions to the
medical complex where the orthopedic surgeon's office was
located, the rest of the trip passed in silence. There had been
many silences between them, but none, he thought, as uncom-

fortable as this one. It was because he wanted to talk to her, wanted to share one thing or another with her. Several times he caught himself about to speak, and then he remembered the new order: strictly business.

He'd said more than he should have this morning, but at least it had been medically related. In the future he had to restrict their conversation even more. There could be no more confidences, no more reminiscing. He had to remember that she was his employee. Not his friend. Not his companion. Certainly not anything more intimate.

As soon as she pulled into a parking space in front of the doctor's office building, he unfastened his seat belt. "If you're right and the doctor's on schedule, this shouldn't take long," he said as he opened the door, then carefully swung his leg out. "You can wait here."

Although his back was to her, he could tell that she'd become very still. Then he heard the slithering sound as the seat belt she had already unfastened rewound in its case. "All right," she agreed quietly. She got out of the car anyway, retrieving his crutches from the back and brought them around to him. She avoided looking at him and, after one glance to see that, he avoided her, too.

She hadn't parked far from the door, but it seemed to take him forever to reach it. This was the first time in a month that he'd been allowed to go anywhere without someone at his side. It felt odd.

It felt freeing.

And just a little bit lonely.

Surprisingly, the doctor was on schedule. Not surprisingly, the appointment went exactly as Susannah had predicted. He asked Remy a few questions, sent him off for X rays, told him the films looked fine and had one of his assistants fit him with a boot. Lastly they gave him a cane—simple, wooden, with a rounded handle. When he got home, he thought grimly, he would look for his grandfather's cane; knowing his mother, it was stored somewhere in the house. If he had to rely on an old man's cane to get around, it would at least be a cane with character.

Susannah was out of the car when he hobbled outside, seated on the curb in the empty space beside the car. Abruptly she got to her feet, brushing her jeans off as she rose, and came to meet him. She took his crutches, then matched her pace to his. "Does that feel better?"

"It's definitely easier." He hesitated. "Is my leg supposed to be a little sore?"

"That'll go away in a day or two. Remember, you haven't had any weight on that leg in more than a month. You'll get used to it." She didn't speak again until they were in the car. "Back to Belle Ste. Claire now?"

Two weeks ago, he had been absolutely thrilled by the prospect of returning to Belle Ste. Claire. He had gone with such hopes, such anticipation. If he could go back to Belle Ste. Claire, could once again call it home, then anything was possible.

Even building a relationship with Susannah.

Especially building a relationship with her.

But he'd been wrong.

With a weary sigh, he reclined the seat and fixed his gaze out the side window. "Yeah," he agreed listlessly. "Back to Belle Ste. Claire."

Susannah rarely had trouble sleeping, but after more than four hours of tossing and turning, she was no closer to drifting off than when she'd first crawled between the covers. Finally pushing them back, she pulled her robe on, felt around on the floor for her fuzzy booties and pulled them on, too. Then she quietly slipped out of her room and down the hall. She didn't bother with lights; by now, she knew her way to and around the kitchen with her eyes closed.

At the table she pulled out the chair closest to the window, propped her feet on the sill and gazed out across the lawn.

Moonlight shone on the old barn and the tumbling fence but got lost in the trees behind them. Once the Sinclairs had kept horses and a few cattle, but not in Remy's lifetime. The barn, she knew from her explorations, held a few pieces of ancient farm equipment, some musty old hay and some junk. It really ought to be torn down, the realist in her admitted; it was generations past its prime and no longer served a purpose.

But her romantic side thought that it, like the fence, added a certain charm to the landscape. Someday the honeysuckle and jessamine vines that climbed the sides and wound in through the doors and between the slats would completely cover the building. They would help support it at the same time they overtook it, until one day it would collapse, a heap of rubbish beneath wiry vines and fragrant flowers.

She felt rather like the barn herself—fragile, none too stable, with a tough web of delicate vines pulling her apart even as they held her together. Her promises to her mother and father, her promises to Skip, her deceit and betrayal, Nicholas Carlucci's demands, Remy's offers, Jimmy Falone's evil and her own honor... Everything was wound together to pull her in a dozen different directions—and all of them down. She knew what she should do, what she wanted to do, what she had to do, and she knew of no way to do it all.

Rescue Skip.

Protect Remy.

Save herself.

But rescuing Skip required sacrificing Remy, and saving herself required protecting Remy, which meant sacrificing Skip. There was no way out.

Was there?

How much easier it would be if she could simply turn her back on her brother. He was, after all, twenty-three, an adult by any legal standards. But he was a very young twenty-three—immature, spoiled, irresponsible—and she was, in part, responsible for his irresponsibility. The family had never set any standards for him. They had never taught him to take care of himself. They had failed him in so many ways.

She knew there was a time to stand back, to wash her hands of him, to leave him to sink or swim on his own.

But that time wasn't when he'd gotten himself caught in a life-and-death situation.

He would get one last assist from his big sister, she silently promised, and then no more help. No more advice. No more money. No more support. Nothing but love.

As for Remy, how could she protect him without help? She could watch out for strangers, could keep him close to home, could be alert for anything suspicious, but she doubted that would be enough. She didn't know how Falcone planned to have him killed. It seemed that those people had preferred methods of killing, but maybe that was only on TV. Nate Simmons had been shot at close range walking down a public street in the middle of the day. Remy had also been shot at close range, only at a private meeting on a wharf under cover of darkness. This time they could be planning a drive-by shooting, a bomb, a hit-and-run accident, a break-in, a fire. The possibilities were endless.

The responsibility was enormous—more than she could bear.

Everything was more than she could bear.

Too weary to worry any longer, she drew her knees up and rested her chin on them. She would relinquish half the year allotted her if only she could start this job anew. If Sky wasn't in trouble. If she wasn't deceiving Remy. If she could accept what he had offered.

If things were different, she would have long since left Gu and all his hurts and cruelties in the past.

She would have discovered what it was like to know true passion.

All her old wounds would have healed. All her broken dreams would be mended.

If things were different, she would be facing a future filled with hope, with family, with marriage and children.

She would be well on her way to being in love with Remy.

If things were different…

She smiled tearfully in the quiet, moonlit kitchen. She'd never been one to fool herself. Things *weren't* different and weren't likely to change. The only passion she was likely to find with Remy would be temporary, only until he discovered the truth about her. Her old wounds *would* heal, but the wounds in the making would last forever. There was no hope in her future—and no family, no marriage, no children.

And as for love with Remy…

Only in her dreams.

Chapter 8

He just wasn't cut out for the role he was playing.

By Wednesday morning, Remy knew things couldn't go on the way they were. He couldn't ignore Susannah, couldn't avoid her, couldn't take his meals separate from her. He couldn't live in the same house with her, couldn't sleep across the hall from her, and not acknowledge her presence. He couldn't continue treating her as if he didn't give a damn about her because, whether she wanted him to or not, he did.

He cared too damn much.

When he went looking for her, he found her in the laundry room, seated in an old slatted rocker, placed to take advantage of the morning light coming through the tall windows. Between the sun and the heat from the dryer, the small utility porch was warm, and Susannah, only occasionally rocking back and forth, looked drowsy. Maybe that was because she wasn't sleeping well at night. No matter how quiet she was, he heard her when she slipped from her bed in the middle of the night. He listened to her pad down the hall in those silly furry slippers of hers, heard the scrape of the chair as she sat down at the table and heard her when, after an hour or two, she padded back to the privacy of her room.

Last night he thought that, while she was up, he had heard her crying. He had wanted to go to her, to find out what was wrong, to somehow make it right, but self-preservation had kept him in his room. Middle-of-the-night rejections were hard on a man, especially one whose ego was as fragile as his was right now.

And so he had lain there in the dark, listening and waiting, and after a time, she had wandered back to her bed.

He navigated the few steps down onto the porch with care, then leaned against the washer. Her eyes closed, her hands loosely clasped across her middle, she rocked on, unaware of him until he spoke her name. "Susannah."

Abruptly she looked at him; then, just as quickly, she dropped her gaze in a manner that could be described only as subservient. He hated it. "I'm sorry," she said in that unnaturally quiet voice that was all he'd heard lately. "I didn't hear you."

"I guess this is a comfortable place to be on a cool morning."

She murmured her agreement as she uncrossed her legs and settled both feet on the floor. "Did you need something?"

He walked over to the door, pretending to gaze out across the lawn. In truth, his peripheral vision was focused on her. She was sitting upright now, all the lazy drowsiness gone. He liked her when she was soft and relaxed; she seemed more approachable that way. Now he could fairly feel the tension humming through her, could see it, he thought, in the way she held her head and clenched her jaw…and all because he had walked into the room.

His regret was almost enough to make him walk out again, to leave her to her sunshine and the rocker and the low, hypnotic rumble of the dryer. But he couldn't keep walking away.

After a moment, he turned his gaze outward. "We need to talk, Susannah."

There was a blur of movement—auburn hair, white shirt, blue jeans—as she rose from the chair and opened the dryer door, bringing it to a stop. She removed a selected armload of towels, closed the door and started it tumbling again, then began folding the towels. "You want me to leave."

He turned around, watching her openly now, admiring each efficient move. She gave each towel a shake, then smoothed it out across the top of the washer, folding it in half, then again and again. The scent of fabric softener and tiny particles of lint drifted into the warm air. "No, Susannah, I don't want you to leave," he admitted. "I want…" He thought better of finishing, sighed heavily and went on. "I want to be friends with you."

That caught her attention. Slowly she became still, and even more slowly she turned to face him. She still held a brightly patterned bath towel, and as she brought her gaze to his, she wrapped her hands tightly over and over in the terry cloth. "Friends?" she repeated. "Just friends?"

Damn his ears for playing tricks on him. He could swear that she sounded almost disappointed that that was all he was asking for. "Just friends."

"Why?"

"Because I don't like the way things have been the last few days. I thought it would be easier under the circumstances if we had little contact with each other, but it's not easier. It's just lonely."

She twisted the towel tighter. "It would be easier if you fired me," she suggested, her voice brittle.

"Is that what you want? To be fired? So you can go back to New Orleans and say, 'I did my best, but working for him was impossible'?" He meant his words as gentle mockery, but there was guilt in her hazel eyes. Such guilt. "Who do you need an excuse for, Susannah? Who are you answerable to?"

"No one," she murmured.

He wasn't sure he believed her. It was possible, he supposed, that she merely needed the excuse for herself. She *was* the sort of person who took failure personally, regardless of whose fault it was. Her marriage was proof of that. But he wasn't entirely sure he believed that there was no one waiting for her back in the city. After all, there were those secretive phone calls, and the fact that she paid to have her mail delivered in town when she could have almost as great a guarantee of privacy if it came here.

"Is it the money?" Maybe she thought that, if he fired her, instead of giving her notice, he would pay the remainder of the month's salary. It would only be fair—and it was exactly what he would do. "You'll get the full month's pay whether you're here, you quit, or I fire you."

"Why would you do that?" She sounded not exactly interested, as if she might take him up on it, but rather curious. As if it didn't matter but she would like to know anyway.

"Because the only reason I would fire you is if we can't find some way to get along. And the only reason you would quit is if I make it impossible for you to stay. Either way, I would be at least partially responsible. Paying your full salary would be the least of my obligations."

At last she began unwinding the towel from around her hands. She turned back to the washer and to the folding that awaited her. "I don't want to quit," she admitted in a soft, husky voice.

"And I have no intention of firing you. So that leaves getting along." He joined her near the machines, where a wooden shelf painted white had been nailed to what had once been the house's outer wall. The paint was peeling now, and the wood showed gray underneath, but it was still sturdy enough to support his weight when he leaned on it. "I'll admit, Susannah, that I'd still like to have a whole lot more than friendship with you, but…I'm willing to settle for whatever you want to offer. I don't like the way we've been living. I miss you. I miss talking to you. I miss being in the kitchen with you while you cook. I miss spending evenings in the parlor with you."

She gave him a sidelong glance, accompanied by what might have been a shy smile if it had managed to form. "I've missed you, too."

He couldn't resist his answering grin even as he gently warned, "Careful there, or I might start thinking you like me a little bit, after all—and after you've spent two weeks convincing me that you don't."

After folding one last towel, she turned to face him. For once her gaze was incredibly direct. "I never said that I don't like you, Remy."

His grin disappeared as he straightened and leaned on the cane instead of the shelf. The particular conversation they were discussing had been too painful to take lightly. "I asked you to tell me that you didn't give a damn about me, and you said—"

"That I was sorry."

"Right. Sorry because you couldn't deny it. Sorry because you *didn't* care. Sorry—"

"I said that I was sorry because…I do care and because I don't have the right to. I was sorry because I was lying and I knew it would hurt you and there was nothing I could do about it. I was…I am very sorry."

Slowly he went to stand at the door again. There he stared out a long time, watching birds on the newly budded trees. If he opened the door, he could hear their song, a sure sign that spring with all its lush growth and beauty was on its way.

But he didn't open the door. He concentrated instead on Susannah's answer. He had never heard words both so hopeful and so lacking in hope in the same sentence. In one breath she admitted that she did care for him, and in the next she made it sound as if that caring was inconsequential. She cared enough to not want to hurt him, but not enough to stop herself from doing it anyway. And that last sentence seemed to indicate that nothing had changed.

"Why don't you have the right to care?" he asked at last "Are you married?"

"No."

"Are you in love with another man?"

"No."

So far, so good. Of course, he had already known those answers. Now for the tough one. "Are you involved with another man?"

She sighed audibly over the dryer. "Remy…"

He turned to face her. The sunlight, warm on his back, unmercifully lit her face. She couldn't hide even the slightest nuance of emotion. "Are you involved with another man? Are you seeing someone, dating someone, living with someone? Are you having an affair with someone? Are you some guy's mistress?"

Sighing again, she shook her head. "No."

He believed her. Those eyes couldn't lie. They were too clear, her gaze too direct, too open and honest. "So what's to stop you from getting involved with me?"

Leaving the dryer, she took the few steps necessary to close the distance between them. "Common sense. A sense of honor. You keep insisting that you know me, Remy, but you really don't. Maybe you like what you've discovered so far, but that's not who I am, not entirely. I've done things that I'm not proud of. I've made mistakes. I've created problems. I know myself better than you ever will, and I don't see a whole lot of possibilities here for us."

"That's because your vision is so narrow. You judge yourself more harshly than anyone else ever will. You're not open to a whole lot of possibilities because you're afraid of getting hurt again. I'm not. I would never hurt you, Susannah."

"But I might hurt you," she whispered.

She had warned him of that before. He responded in much the same way as he had then. "Maybe you will, but I'm willing to take that chance. Anything worth having is worth taking a risk. And who knows, Susannah? Maybe we'll surprise you. Maybe we'll fall in love and live happily the rest of our lives."

A fleeting wistfulness crossed her face, convincing him far more than her words that she did care about him, more than she wanted him to know. More, perhaps, than she was even aware of herself. She wanted that, wanted to fall in love and live long and happily.

But she was afraid. "And maybe you'll die, regretting the day we met," she whispered.

"That won't happen."

"It could. You don't know—"

He laid his fingers across her mouth, silencing her. "I'm not a naive man, Susannah. I've seen more bad things, more problems and mistakes and hurts than you could ever imagine. I've seen all the evil one person can do to another. Believe me when I say there is nothing you or anyone else could do that would ever make me regret meeting you."

She pushed his hand away. "You're too trusting, Remy."

His laughter was spontaneous. "I don't believe anyone has ever accused an FBI agent of being too trusting."

"You trusted your partner, and it almost got you killed."

"True. But I won't be fooled again."

Oh, but he would be. He was being fooled right now Susannah thought with an ache around her heart. But at leas he would live to regret it. She would see to that.

She had spent hours last night mapping out her strategy She knew nothing about making deals and even less about ne gotiating with an Ivy League prosecutor who was, according to Michael Bennett, the best damn prosecutor around. N doubt Smith Kendricks played hardball and played to win.

But she had a few things in her favor. Smith and Rem were like brothers—closer, even, than most brothers—an just as she would do anything to protect her brother, so woul he to protect Remy. There was also the fact that she, God hel her, had become a more important part of Jimmy Falcone' organization than her brother had ever been. If she offered herself in his place, surely Smith would agree to let him go. After all, as Skip had told her—and Nicholas Carlucci had verified—her brother had never been involved in any major undertakings for Falcone. Yes, he had committed some minor crimes, and yes, he deserved punishment, but not the long-term prison sentence Falcone had threatened to set him up for.

He certainly didn't deserve to die for his foolishness.

So she would make a deal with Smith. She would make it clear to him that keeping Skip alive and safe had to be as important to the government as keeping Remy safe. She would make him understand that she was offering information against only Falcone, Carlucci and herself—not the three of them, plus Skip.

She would make certain he understood that Remy's life depended on their working together.

She had no doubt that Smith would deal with her. Why shouldn't he? He would be protecting his best friend *and* getting evidence to use against the man he was trying to lock away.

And what would she get?

Skip's safety.

Remy's life.

And a few more days with him.

Carlucci had scheduled her next check-in for Friday. Surely that meant he had nothing planned before then, didn't it? She didn't trust the lawyer to tell her when it was going to happen—she sure as hell didn't trust him to give her any warning so that she could stop them—but surely he wouldn't have planned another phone call if he intended to conclude their business before then.

So she would call him Friday.

After she called Smith.

After she'd shared just these next few days with Remy.

Abruptly she realized that he was watching her, waiting patiently for her. In some ways, he was the most patient man she'd ever known. In other ways, he was as impatient as hell.

He was smiling whimsically when she finally focused her attention on him. "Where do you go when you disappear into your thoughts like that?"

"Just away," she murmured. After a moment, she sighed. "You're a persuasive man, Remy."

"What does that mean?"

"It means I still don't have anything to offer. That I can't promise you won't regret this. That it might wind up costing both of us more than we can afford to pay. But...I do want you. I do care about you." She smiled very, very faintly. "I'm willing to take a few risks."

He remained still and unresponsive for a long, long time. Then, as he took her hands, a slow smile came to him. "Such a romantic proposal, Susannah," he teased as gently as he touched her.

"You said you preferred the honest approach. That's as honest as I can be. If we both go into this with our eyes open...maybe we can both come out of it okay."

"Maybe we can come out of it better than okay," he said, pulling her into his arms. "I'll be the optimist."

And she would be the realist, she whispered silently as she pressed her cheek to his shirt. Of course, it was easier to be realistic when she knew everything she was keeping from him.

He held her only a moment before filling his hands with her hair and tilting her head back. "I haven't even gotten to kiss you yet."

"You kissed me outside that day," she reminded him.

"Doesn't count. That was a pale imitation of the real thing."

A pale imitation? It had left her barely capable of breathing and utterly incapable of moving. It had touched her more sweetly, more deeply, than a thousand of Guy's most passionate kisses. "How about letting me be the judge of..."

Her remark died away unfinished as he covered her mouth with his. A pale imitation? Oh, yes. Who needed breath or the ability to move? Who needed anything more than this—

his mouth on hers, his tongue stroking hers, his body supporting hers?

He kissed her sweetly, gently, then hungrily, his tongue alternately teasing, then satisfying. He stirred her arousal to life with no more than his kiss, without caresses, without tender touches. He heated her blood, made her weak and stole all thought from her mind. All she could do was feel, and all she could feel was need—sweet, fiery, demanding, throbbing need.

There was a time, Remy thought hazily, for finesse, for subtlety, for seduction, but this wasn't it. He was too aroused, and she was too willing. He had waited so long, had wanted so long, and now he craved, could damn near taste, the satisfaction his dreams and his fantasies and her body had promised him. Holding her tight, still kissing her hard, he moved blindly to the side, seeking and finding the old rocker. He sank into it, pulling her with him, settling her across his lap where his erection pressed intimately against her, and he pulled her shirt free of her jeans. He opened the buttons easily and pushed the garment off her shoulders, then dispatched her bra with as little care.

He cupped her breasts in his hands, blindly stroking them, teasing her nipples and making her groan. Ending the kiss at last, he was bending his head to her breast when, with surprising strength, she stopped him.

"Remy, no."

For a moment he simply stared at her, certain he had misunderstood. His heart was pounding, his blood was rushing, his entire body was throbbing. Surely he hadn't heard properly.

But that long look said he had. She sat there astride him, her hair mussed, naked to the waist, her breasts soft and her nipples achingly hard, and with such an exquisite look of regret on her face.

"Remy, we can't…"

Leaning back against the chair, he deliberately stroked his fingertips across her breast, bringing them together on her nipple in a gentle squeeze. The action made her gasp, made her eyes close, made her go all soft and weak right before his eyes. "Don't tell me you aren't interested," he said quietly.

When she looked at him again, she looked drowsy and too perfectly aroused to put up a fuss over anything but stopping. But with a few unsteady breaths, she gathered her strength. "I couldn't lie about it if I wanted to."

"So what's the problem?"

She touched his face, stroking his cheek and along his jaw. "It's me." With an awkward little smile, she started to push away, to climb clumsily off his lap. "I can't talk sitting like this."

He caught her, though, one hand on each of her thighs, and held her, pressed hard against him, for a moment, savoring the pain and the pleasure of being so close…and yet so far. At last, though, he released her, and, taking her shirt, she retreated to sit on the top step leading into the house.

She smoothed the shirt, then slipped her arms into the sleeves and pulled it on. She didn't button it, though. With each breath she took, he could see the full curves of her breasts. When she was still, he could make out the swell of her nipples underneath the fabric. Sitting there like that, her hair needing brushing, her cheeks pink and her mouth obviously well kissed, she presented, he decided, quite possibly the most erotic image he'd ever seen.

After searching for a way to begin, she offered him a faint smile and said, "You've never asked much about my marriage."

"I know the important stuff."

"What's that?"

"I know that your ex-husband lied to you. That he was cruel to you. I know that you're not still in love with him. That you wouldn't go back to him if he asked." He hesitated. "I know that he was unfaithful to you."

"Did I tell you that?"

"The first day. You said that you were married, but your husband wasn't." He scowled as he realized where she was going with this. "He was involved with his new wife before he left you, wasn't he?"

She nodded. "But she wasn't the first. I don't know how many there were. I don't know who they were. I don't know what precautions he took with them, if any at all, but he didn't take any with me. Do you understand what I'm saying?"

With a grin, he used his good foot to set the rocker in motion. "You're saying that if I can't produce a condom within the next few minutes, the fun stops here."

Her responding smile was far less confident and far more regretful as she nodded.

"Hell, sweetheart, the days when I was always prepared ended about ten years ago. If you had asked me at my apartment, I probably could have come up with at least one, but I'm fresh out here." He softened his words with another grin. "I wasn't counting on getting lucky."

"Me, either," she admitted. With a deep sigh, she sat straighter and began buttoning her blouse.

Rising from the chair, he joined her at the door and brushed her hands away. "Let me do that." But instead of fastening the buttons, he slid his hands inside the shirt, filling them once again with her breasts.

"Remy…please…don't…"

"Don't worry," he murmured in her ear, making her shiver. "We're both responsible adults. We won't go too far…" Oh, but it was a temptation. It was tempting just this once to be irresponsible, to forget caution and make love anyway, right here in the warm morning sunshine. But when he had told Susannah that he was willing to take a chance, he had meant with his heart, not his life. Certainly not with her life.

At last he got her shirt done up properly, and he sat down on the step next to her. "How about if I help you fold this last load of laundry and then we drive into town?"

"To Belclaire?"

"Actually I was thinking Baton Rouge."

He looked uncomfortable, Susannah thought, but she completely understood why. She had come from a small town, too—not as small as Belclaire, but small enough that she'd known the salesclerks and owners of every store in town. Small enough that she, too, would have driven to another town to make such a purchase. "All right," she agreed.

"We can have lunch while we're in town."

"Hmm."

"Do a little shopping, maybe even take in a movie."

"Hmm."

"Or…" He gave her a wicked grin. "We could find a drugstore, get what we need, come straight back here and spend the rest of the afternoon and on into the night…"

"Indulging our desire?" she prompted him with a smile. As his expression grew more serious, hers grew more uneasy. "Having sex?"

He cupped his hands to her cheeks and kissed her. It wasn't passionate or heated or teasing. It was a solemn kiss, the sort used to seal a bargain. The sort that often followed promises like "I do." "Making love, Susannah," he replied quietly, intensely. "It will always be making love."

Always. Their *always* was going to last about forty-eight hours. Once she talked to Smith, he would undoubtedly tell Remy everything, and that would be the end for them. It would be the shortest *always* on record.

And she intended to make the most of it.

"Leave the laundry, and we'll go as soon as I clean up."

"You look fine."

She gave him a chiding look. "My bra's on the floor, my shirt's wrinkled and untucked, and my hair needs to be combed."

"So you look as if you've been engaged in a little illicit passion. We're going to buy condoms. We'll look like we need them." Still, he got to his feet and let her get up. "You go on. I'll fold the clothes."

She made it as far as the hall before he called her. "Oh, Susannah? Wear your hair up."

"I thought you liked it down."

"You noticed that." His smile was sweet, charming and, at the same time, sexy as hell. "I think this time I'd like to take it down myself."

With a smile of her own, she went to her room, where she changed into another shirt, this one the color of crimson. After putting on her shoes, she spent the next fifteen minutes fashioning her hair into the most intricate braid she could manage.

When she was finally ready, she found Remy waiting at the kitchen table. He locked up while she got his mother's car from the garage, and then they set off for Baton Rouge, taking the river road instead of the interstate.

"Anything else you want to tell me about your marriage?" he asked once they'd gone a few miles.

"Like what? You know the important stuff, remember?"

"Like why you stayed married for four years."

She flexed both hands around the steering wheel. "I loved him."

"But he treated you badly."

"It was the way he did it. He could be so subtle that, in the beginning, I thought I was just overly sensitive. By the time I realized what was going on, my self-esteem had been worn down to just about nothing." She could smile at the memories now, but three years ago, two years, even one year ago, that had been impossible. "From the time I was a little girl, all I wanted when I grew up was to get married and have a family and be like my mom and dad. Guy convinced me that he was my only chance of having that. That I had to put up with him because no one else would put up with me."

Reaching across the seat, Remy claimed her right hand. "You were a fool to believe him."

"If you're told something often enough, no matter how outrageous or wrong it is, you start to believe it, at least a little. When he left me, I was so afraid of admitting failure, of being alone, of finding out that he was right and no one else would ever want me, that I actually considered pleading with him to stay. He made my life miserable…but I was familiar with misery. I knew what to expect. I didn't know what being divorced and alone would be like."

"What was it like?"

"It wasn't easy. Everyone in town knew about his affairs. They all knew when he didn't come home at night or when he took women to our house while I was at work during the day. I had a lot of support—so much of the town's related to me—but there was a lot of gossip. A lot of whispers and catty remarks. Pitying looks." She had hated those most—the looks. She couldn't endure pity.

"You know, my offer from Sunday still stands. One phone call, and you can spread some of that misery where it belongs."

She thought of Guy on the receiving end of someone else's harassment. It sounded tremendously satisfying, but it wasn't something she needed. "You wouldn't really do that."

"Why do you say that?"

"Because it would be an improper use of your authority."

"What's the good of having authority if you can't use it improperly once in a while?" he replied, then he relented. "You're right. I wouldn't do it…except for you."

Coming into the edge of the city, she pulled into the parking lot of the first shopping center they passed. It was a strip mall, about a block long, very new and generic looking. It could have been picked up and set down anyplace in the country and fit right in.

But it had a pharmacy. That was all that counted.

"Would you be more comfortable waiting in the car?" Remy asked.

She wanted to say, "No, of course not. I'm not embar

rassed." But the truth was she *was* a little embarrassed. It was one thing to talk about making such a purchase. It was another entirely to actually do it. "Yes," she said decisively. "I would."

"Then why don't you pull up to the curb in front? Save me a few steps."

She did as he directed, letting him out, then drumming her fingers on the steering wheel while she waited for him to return. Her stomach seemed to be tying itself into intricate little knots. Nerves. She was thirty-one years old and having a bad case of nerves. Of course, it was one thing to talk about spending—how had he put it?—the rest of the afternoon and on into the night making love.

It was another entirely to actually do it.

But after an all-too-short drive back to Belle Ste. Claire, that was exactly what Remy expected of her, and in her heart, it was exactly what she wanted.

But what if that was one thing Guy hadn't lied about?

What if she disappointed Remy?

She couldn't let herself consider the possibility. She had to believe that what she lacked in skill and experience, she would make up for in sincerity. In genuine affection. In the intensity of her desire.

In love?

She shied away from the thought. It was too dangerous. Considering that, after her phone call to Smith in two days, Remy would surely hate her, that line of thinking was entirely too hopeless. Too hurtful.

She had the rest of her life to be hopeless and hurt.

But only forty-eight hours with Remy.

Remy made his selection from the display near the cash registers, paid a young clerk who popped her gum through the entire transaction, then left the store. He was a little more agile with the cane, but his mobility was still limited tremendously by the hip-to-toe cast. He hoped Susannah wasn't averse to taking the lead, because, quite frankly, he didn't see how he and the cast were going to cope otherwise.

But they would manage. They had to. Otherwise, he just might die of need.

As he approached the car at his usual hobbling pace, he could see her tapping her fingers nervously. Given the circumstances, it was remarkable that they'd gotten themselves to this point. After that conversation Sunday afternoon, he'd been convinced that his chances with her were somewhere between slim and none. After what her bastard of an ex-husband had put her through, it was no surprise that she'd been unwilling to try again, to trust again.

Guy Duncan should be strung up for what he'd done to her. She had been right, on the drive up here, when she'd said that Remy wouldn't misuse his authority to harass Duncan. But it would be only natural, after they were married, for them to take a trip to Nebraska so he could see where she'd grown up and could meet her family and friends. And if he happened to run into her ex while they were there, it would be only appropriate that they exchange a few words. And if most of the words were his, and most of his words were threats... Who could expect less from a loving husband?

"Great, Sinclair," he murmured as he gingerly stepped off the curb. "She agrees to go to bed with you, and you've already got yourself married. One step, partner, remember?" *One small step at a time.*

As she started the engine, he maneuvered into the car; then they pulled away from the curb. Susannah was quiet, and he let her remain that way for the major portion of the drive back. At last, when they were only a few miles from home, he looked at her. "I wish I'd met you when you were twenty."

She gave him a curious glance. "Why then?"

"Because you were young, sweet and innocent. I was twenty-six. I had completed the academy and moved to New Orleans. I wasn't sure I was ever going to make a good FBI agent, I bitterly missed my family and I was much too friendly with far too many women. I could have used someone young, sweet and innocent in my life then."

"You wouldn't have given me a second look."

"Always," he disagreed. "Even if you'd been young enough to land me in jail."

"I was very young at twenty."

He chuckled. "Honey, you're very young at thirty-one."

"I was very naive."

"Some things don't change."

"I was also very idealistic."

He waited until she turned off the highway into the driveway at Belle Ste. Claire before he reached across and drew his fingers lightly along her arm. "I wouldn't have disappointed you."

She brought the car to a stop near the parlor door and turned to face him. "I was a virgin at twenty."

Growing serious, he let his fingers come to rest on her hand. "I would have been honored."

He swore, before she blinked and looked away, that he saw a tear form at the corner of her eye. But it was gone when she looked back. "Guy found it more a chore than an honor."

So much information in such a brief statement. She had remained a virgin until her mid-twenties, when she'd met the man she had eventually married. And after all that waiting, her first time had been less than special. And *he* was going to be only her second lover.

And her last.

He really did feel honored.

"Guy was an idiot." Lifting her hand, he pressed a kiss to her palm, then leaned closer to her. "Why don't we try really hard to see if we can't exorcise him from your memory?" he murmured, brushing his mouth across hers.

She warmed to his kiss immediately, opening to his tongue, raising her hands to his shoulders and drawing him closer. He felt the heat rush through him, from every place they touched and every place they didn't. He felt the blood rush through, collecting, hot and heavy, in the lower part of his body. With one kiss, he was hard, damn, and desperate for relief.

Drawing back, he stroked her hair from her face. "Put the car away later and come inside with me now."

"It'll only take a minute."

A minute. Sixty seconds. He could endure anything for sixty seconds, couldn't he?

Releasing her, he collected the small plastic bag and his cane and climbed out of the car. A walkway of brick laid unevenly in a herringbone pattern extended from the edge of the shell driveway to the steps. By the time he had crossed that distance and climbed the seven steps, Susannah was approaching behind him. She waited quietly while he unlocked the door. For once, he could hold the door open for her—as a gentleman should, his mother would say—instead of struggling through with crutches and cast while *she* opened doors for *him.*

Inside, he turned to lock the door once again. For a moment, the house seemed inordinately quiet; then he heard the ticking of the grandfather clock in the front hallway, the faint hum of the refrigerator in the kitchen and the settling creak of ancient wood somewhere up above.

He could also hear the uneven tenor of Susannah's breathing and the less-than-steady beating of his own heart.

Returning his keys to his jeans pocket, he faced her. Her gaze was directed demurely downward, and her hands were loosely clasped in front of her. She looked impossibly shy, but he had no words that would reassure her. Besides, didn't actions speak louder than words?

Taking both of her hands in his free hand, he gently pulled her along with him as he made his way down the hall, through the kitchen and into the servants' wing. For a moment, he hesitated; then he chose his room. Susannah's room was her only private place in the entire house. Until she invited him in, he couldn't take that from her. Besides, he wanted her in *his* room. He wanted to see her in his bed, wrapped in his quilt, her hair spread out across his pillow.

The curtains were drawn across the windows, but the fabric was sheer enough and the sunlight bright enough that the room needed no additional lighting. It was warm inside and smelled of potpourri, aged wood and after-shave—a good place to be lazy and cozy and intimate on an early spring day.

He came to a stop beside the bed and turned to face her. He had seduced a number of women in his life—and had been seduced, in turn, by a few more. After the first time or two, he had never been unsure of what to say or do, of what approach to take with each particular lady.

Until today.

But then, it had never been so incredibly important until today.

Offering her a sheepish smile, he admitted, "I don't know what to do."

She smiled the dazzling sort of smile that he'd been waiting all his life for, the smile of sheer pleasure that he'd thought he would never see her wear. "Let me give you a few pointers," she suggested, her voice husky, her hands unsteady as they clasped his hand and lifted it to her cheek. "You touch me here…" Pressing his palm gently against her skin, she guided his hand down across her jaw and her throat to her breast. "And here…" Her fingers trembling, she drew his hand slowly across her nipple, so slowly that he could feel it bud and harden beneath her shirt; then, pressing harder, she led him over her stomach, from soft cotton to coarser denim, directing him until his hand was spread flat and low across her belly. "And eventually here…"

Letting his cane fall, he raised his right hand to her breast, covering it, gently caressing it. "Here, like this?" he asked hoarsely. Her only answer was a faint murmur. "And like this?" His left hand inched lower, feeling the heat that radiated through her. "And what do you do?"

"I—" She caught her breath as he lightly pinched her nipple. "I go weak and collapse on the bed and sigh, 'Oh, Remy.'"

He chuckled and wrapped his arms around her, pulling her close. "I like the way you say that."

"Kiss me, and I'll say it again."

He did kiss her then, and Susannah did go weak, reaching for him for support. She supposed there must have been a time when Guy's kisses had affected her so, but she couldn't recall it. She couldn't recall their grandest, most passionate moment even coming close to what little bit she and Remy had so far shared.

When he raised his head and she could at last speak again, she smiled drowsily and sighed, "Oh, Remy."

"Do you ever touch me?" he asked, still playing along with the game she'd started.

"I get to undress you." Summoning her strength, she curled her fingers where they rested at his waist and gathered handfuls of his T-shirt.

"Because I'm clumsy and slow and need the help?" The teasing was still there in tone but not in feeling. She realized it bothered him that he wasn't at his physical best, that his natural grace was overshadowed by the awkwardness of the bulky cast and its restrictions.

"Because it gives me an excuse to see you everywhere. To touch you everywhere. Because, when I'm done and your clothes are out of the way, then you can help undress me."

She pushed his shirt up, drawing her fingers over warm skin. His muscles rippled where she stroked, and his nipples, even though she skirted them, puckered. Pulling the garment over his head, she dropped it behind him, then once again drew her hands over his skin. There was only the faintest discoloration left from the contusion where his bulletproof vest had saved his life. If she hadn't known exactly where it was, she wouldn't even notice the shadow that remained. As for the other injury, there was a reddish-tinged entry wound on the front of his arm, about three-quarters of an inch in diameter, slightly sunken in and healing nicely, and a matching exit wound on the back.

"You're a very lucky man," she murmured, pressing a kiss to the base of his throat.

"I know. No other man in the world has ever done what I'm about to do with you."

She tickled along his ribs and made him squirm. "I'm talking about your wounds. Not many people get shot three times at close range and live to tell the tale."

"A bulletproof vest is a wondrous thing."

Sliding her hands flat across his ribs, she came to a stop when she encountered his jeans. "Besides, are you forgetting that you're not the first?"

It took him a moment to realize that she was referring to his earlier statement; then he grinned boastfully. "Maybe I can't be the first, but I can be the last, and I promise you, sweetheart, I'll be the one who loves you the best." As she had done before, he claimed her hand and, molding it, controlling it, he guided it lower, over his jeans—the waistband, the zipper—and down to his arousal. "Oh, Susannah," he murmured. "See what you do to me?"

She touched him gently, tentatively. He was hard and hot, and she... She felt like that young, naive virgin they had teased about in the car. Her hands felt clumsy, not quite her own, not really sure of what to do or how to do it. Undressing him—that was what she was supposed to be doing. But the metal button on his jeans didn't want to come free. The zipper didn't want to slide down.

"Honey..." His voice was hoarse, thick, as unsteady as her fingers. "Are you doing that on purpose? Because—oh, hell—you're going to finish me off right here if you don't..."

His last words faded away on a groan as she worked open

the zipper, then began peeling his jeans away. Underneath he wore only briefs—and brief was certainly an appropriate description. Aside from the fact that they were cotton and white, they shared nothing in common with the underwear the men in her life had favored.

She knelt in front of him, working his jeans down over his good leg and the cast, following them with his briefs, tugging his shoe off and loosening the straps on the boot. Finally he was naked, and she was still fully dressed, and sometime in the last few minutes she had lost her shyness. He pulled her to her feet again, back into his arms again, and kissed her while she stroked him gently, curiously, greedily, everywhere.

Everywhere.

Desire, barely controlled, strong enough to make him weak, rippled through Remy in ever-widening spirals. He had always enjoyed intimacy before, but he had never really bought into the theory that an emotional connection with his partner could make a good experience better. He'd had great sex with women he'd known he wouldn't see again and lukewarm sex with women he had genuinely cared about.

But he had never experienced anything like this before.

He had never wanted so desperately.

He had never ached so intensely.

He had never craved such torment, had never anticipated such satisfaction.

He had never known such sweet need.

For the second time that day he pulled Susannah's blouse from her jeans and opened the buttons with ease. When she had returned to her bedroom earlier to change for their trip into town, she hadn't bothered with replacing her bra, so when he slipped his hands inside the cool fabric, he touched bare skin. Soft skin. Warm, tantalizing, utterly feminine skin. Her breasts were heavy in his hands, her nipples hard against his palms. When he rubbed them, she shivered. When he lowered his head and sucked one nipple into his mouth, she cried aloud.

"Remy…"

"I know. Help me…your jeans…"

Disentangling herself from his embrace, she removed the rest of her clothing while he settled on the bed. He ripped open the plastic bag from the pharmacy, opened the box and shook out the square packages inside. By the time he'd taken care of that, Susannah was standing beside the bed, naked and nervous and…

He gave her a long, hard look, then exhaled heavily. "You're a beautiful woman."

She smiled hesitantly. When he extended his hand, she took it and placed one knee on the mattress. It barely dipped beneath her weight. When he pulled, she came to him, her gaze locked with his, her mouth steady in that uneasy little half smile.

"I wish I could give you moonlight and romance…seduction…sweet words…" He grinned as he stroked a light, feathery caress from her cheek all the way down to her breast and beyond. "And an able body. I wish I could make love to you the way I want, the way you deserve…but right now I can't. You'll have to… I can only lie on my back…"

Her smile blossomed, sweet and slow, starting in her eyes and lighting her face, dazzling him with its sensuality. "I don't care about moonlight," she replied as she moved into place above him. "Or romance…or seduction. I don't care who does what to whom…as long as we do it together. I care about this, Remy." She lowered her body to his, taking him slowly, painfully slowly, inside her. She was hot and slick and held him tight, so tightly that he swore, right there in the middle of the day in his sun-filled room, he saw stars.

"And I care about this." Leaning forward, bracing her hands flat against his chest, she bent her head to his for a kiss, sweet and breath-stealing.

"I care about this, too." She began moving against him,

withdrawing, then pushing forward, taking him again, all of him, sometimes fast, sometimes slow, but each time creating sensations of pure, raw pleasure.

"But most of all…" She was whispering now, her breathing as ragged as his, her skin growing damp with a flush, her breasts swelling and her nipples drawing up even tighter.

"Most of all, Remy…I care about *you.*"

Chapter 9

Shadows drifted across the walls as, outside, clouds drifted by overhead, occasionally blocking out the afternoon sun completely but more often just filtering it through their cottony edges. Susannah knew it was well past lunch—her stomach told her that—and that they had made an impressive dent in the contents of that small box that had been well worth this morning's drive into the city, but beyond that she had no clue as to what time it was. There was a clock on Remy's side of the bed and the watch on his wrist was only inches from her nose, but she didn't bother to look.

She didn't want to know how many of her forty-eight hours were gone.

She didn't want to face how little time was left to them.

She was lying on her side, her back to Remy. As he'd pointed out, he had to lie on his back, but he still managed to hold her body to his. He still managed to hold her close, his arm curved around her, his hand resting on the swell of her breast. He still managed, every few minutes, to kiss her or stroke her or find some other way to send a shiver down her spine.

Behind her, he yawned, then drowsily murmured, "Oh, Susannah." After a moment, he asked, "When you were little, did the kids ever tease you about that?"

She thought of the old-time folk song whose name she shared, the song she'd heard a thousand times more than was funny. *Oh, Susannah, oh, don't you cry for me...* She faced the prospect of plenty of tears in her future. She would cry for Remy and for herself, for everything they might have had and everything she had cost them.

"Oh, yeah," she replied, focusing on the past and not the future. "I used to plead with my mother to let me go by Susan or Susie, but she refused. She had named me Susannah, and no smart-mouthed little kids were going to change her mind."

"That's because she wanted a beautiful name for her beautiful daughter."

Beautiful. She smiled bittersweetly. "When you say that... can almost believe it."

"That you're beautiful?" He tugged until she rolled over to face him. "I'll tell you often enough in the next fifty years that you'll have to believe it. You'll see it for yourself."

Her desire for that, fifty years with him, was so strong that it made her heart hurt and her eyes tear up. Smiling to disguise it, she asked, "Has anyone ever told you that you're awfully sure of yourself?"

"Maybe a time or two."

"You'll be getting that cast off in a few more weeks, and your parents will be home around then. You'll go back to work and back to your regular life, and you won't need me anymore."

Taking her chin in hand, he forced her to look at him. "My need for you has nothing to do with this cast or my parents being gone," he said fiercely. "I'll always need you, Susannah. *Always.*"

"Remy, you don't—"

"Remember what you told me the other day?" he interrupted. "Don't go looking for trouble. The time to worry about problems, sweetheart, is when you find out we've got them. The only thing you've got to worry about right now is whether or not I intend to let you out of this bed anytime today."

She let him silence her protest because it was easier than arguing with him. Because it was too wonderful a time to spoil. Because the idea of a future with him was too sweet. Because she had never been a dreamer and for two days she wanted to be.

And because reality—with its disillusionment, betrayal, anger and hatred—would intrude soon enough.

Shivering a little, she snagged the quilt folded across the bed with her foot and managed to pull it up to cover them without leaving his side. "Do you know why Valery gave you this quilt?"

He shrugged. "She thought I would like it."

"But do you know why she chose this particular one?"

Another shrug. "The colors are nice. So's the pattern. It's a family heirloom. I don't know."

Leaning on one elbow, she spread the coverlet over his chest, smoothing out wrinkles. "I understand she manages an antique clothing store. Do they sell quilts there?"

"I don't know. I've only been there once, and that was when she disappeared after Nate Simmons was murdered."

"I come from a family of quilters," she remarked with a smile. "My mother quilted, and my aunts and my grandmothers. Life slows down on a farm in winter. It kept them busy, and it kept the family warm on those cold prairie nights. Mama kept her quilt frame in the dining room—we usually ate in the kitchen because it was cozier. She balanced the frame on the back of the dining chairs, and she worked in there for hours at a time. Sometimes one of my aunts or my grandmothers came over and helped, although special quilts—those she was planning to give away—she made all by herself. I used to play in there on the floor underneath the frame, or sometimes I sat in one of the chairs and watched her."

"Did you learn to quilt, too?"

"I always intended to, but I never did. There were chores to do, games to play, friends to visit. Then Mama died, and there was dinner to cook, laundry to wash, a household to run." And a baby brother to help raise. To help spoil.

"You can learn now." He stroked her bare shoulder as she stroked the swirling stitching on the quilt. "You can make a quilt for us."

She knew it was reckless to ask, knew it was a risk she was ill prepared for, but she asked anyway. "And what kind of quilt would you have me make?"

"I don't know. Something with a big heart that says, 'Susannah loves Remy.'"

She had to swallow hard over the lump in her throat to get even the simplest of responses out. "Uh-huh. Sort of..." Forcing a deep breath, she strengthened her voice. "Sort of the fabric-art equivalent of carving initials into a tree, huh?"

His grin was charming. "I could do that for you. My old pocketknife is upstairs, and we have some live oaks out front big enough around to spell out your entire name."

He was too sweet. Too dear. And too right. Susannah did love Remy...even if she never could tell him so.

"Hush," she admonished, shifting slightly so he couldn't see her tears. "I'm getting to the point here."

"I thought you were reminiscing," he teased. "I didn't know there was a point."

"I was, but there is. The point is I never learned to quilt, but I learned a lot about them. I learned how to piece the top and how to secure the layers before they went into the frame. I learned how to choose fabrics and patterns and colors, and

I became very familiar with most traditional quilting patterns. Apparently Valery is familiar with at least one pattern, because she chose this quilt to give to you. I have one in the same pattern at home, one my mother made all by herself."

He was serious now. "A special one," he said, and she nodded confirmation. "These traditional patterns…they have names?"

She nodded again.

"What's the name of this one?"

Turning at last to face him, she whistled a few bars of an old-time folk tune and watched his smile as it grew.

"Oh, Susannah? My quilt is named Oh, Susannah?"

For the third time, she nodded.

He looked as smug as a man could. "You see, sweetheart? It's fate."

"What do you mean?"

"Long before you and I were even born, some Sinclair relative knew that one day one of her descendants was going to have reason to treasure a quilt named Oh, Susannah. We were meant to be together."

Fate. The idea made her want to laugh and cry at the same time. Fate had brought them together, all right, but its form was nowhere near as harmless and sweet as the image of some long-ago Sinclair woman piecing together a fine quilt by lamplight. It was a stupid, twenty-three-year-old kid who didn't have the brains to stay out of trouble. It was a slimy, repulsive lawyer who twisted the law for his own purposes, justice be damned. It was an evil man who thought nothing of destroying human life for his own greed, maybe even for his own pleasure.

"Remy, please don't—"

He cut off her words with a kiss, hard and hot, demanding response, and she gave it in spite of herself. She twined her arms around his neck, welcomed his tongue into her mouth, rubbed her body sinuously against his, arousing him, arousing herself.

Just as abruptly as he had taken her, he pushed her back. For a moment he subjected her to a long, hard look, a look that left her feeling naked in a way that had nothing to do with her lack of clothing. A look that, God help her, could open her soul and see every one of her lies.

And then the chill was gone, and the sweet, teasing, sexy man was back. "What are the chances," he asked with his most endearing smile, "that we could get some lunch, then pick up where we just left off?"

Her breasts were aching, and in that one brief moment, heat and moisture had begun gathering between her thighs. She was surprised that she could want him again so quickly, surprised that her body could take him again…but then, she needed to store up memories—a lifetime's worth. "I'd say they're pretty damned good," she said evenly.

"Good. Would you mind getting me a pair of sweats out of the armoire?"

She wriggled out from beneath the quilt and located her shirt where he had dropped it. It offered some degree of modesty while she opened the cabinet door and fished out a pair of black sweatpants. After handing them to him, she picked up her underwear and jeans and started toward the bathroom to finish dressing there.

Remy waited until she reached the door to speak. He knew what he was about to say wasn't going to thrill her—but damn it, someday it would, so he was going to say it anyway. He wanted her to know. "Susannah?"

She paused, looking back at him.

"Did I remember to mention that I intend to marry you soon?"

Her face went blank. Absolutely blank. "No. You didn't."

"Then consider yourself warned."

Thursday afternoon found them sitting—reclining, more accurately—on the gallery on the sunny side of the house being lazy and quiet and, oddly enough, intimate, although they weren't even touching. This was exactly the sort of idyllic time Remy had been looking for when he'd first made his plans to come home to Belle Ste. Claire to recuperate and exactly the sort of romantic time he had hoped for when he had chosen Susannah to come with him. They had spent Wednesday afternoon in and out of bed and most of the evening stretched out on the sofa in the parlor, a fire burning in the fireplace and the television tuned to some show or another. They had touched a lot, talked a little and said nothing, and it had been the most satisfying evening he could recall.

There was one thing he wished she would mention, though—since she hadn't last night, then sometime today: yesterday's warning. He wished she would say, "Gee, Remy, I'd love to marry you," or "I'm just waiting for you to ask," or even, "I'm not sure that's what I want."

Instead she had said nothing. Right after he'd said it, she had given him a long look, then walked out of the bedroom and down the hall to the bathroom, where she had very quietly closed the door and stayed for a long, long time. When she had finally come out again, he'd been in the kitchen, gathering the makings for sandwiches at the table. She had brushed and rebraided her hair—he'd forgotten his request to take it down himself—and finished dressing, and for the first time in weeks she had looked almost but not quite serene again.

But she had pretended his promise of marriage had never been made.

With a sigh, he thought back to last spring and early summer, after Evan's death, when he'd spent so much time in French Quarter bars—literally hours looking for or sitting with Michael while he drank, convincing him to go home, half carrying, half dragging him out the door. He had put his friend to bed when he could afford the time to sleep it off, had given him coffee and food when he couldn't. Remy had sat with him when he was sick and when he was hung over and had tried reasoning with him when he was sober. The limits of Remy's patience had never been tested before that time, and he had been surprised by how far they extended.

Susannah just might test them even further before he got her to stand up beside him in front of God and their families and make vows of forever.

But that was all right. He could counter every argument she might make. He could eliminate every excuse she might give him. He wouldn't even have to try very hard. "I love you" pretty much took care of everything she might come up with. Someday she would run out of reasons for holding back and she would have to replace her don'ts and can'ts with "I do."

Someday she would find it easier to quit making excuses and start making that quilt with the big heart that said "Susannah loves Remy."

From the wicker chaise longue set at an angle to his, she unexpectedly spoke. "Want to take a walk?"

"A walk?"

"Around the grounds."

He glanced down at the cane leaning against his chair, the smooth silver handle gleaming in the sun. It was his grandfather's and he had found it not buried away in the attic, with only his mother knowing where, but so prominently placed in the front hall that he couldn't help but wonder if she'd left it there, the ebony and silver all brightly polished, specially for him.

"I can do that now," he said, surprised by the realization. He had become too accepting of his limitations in the past month. While there were still things he couldn't do—run, take a bath, drive a car or make love to Susannah the way he would like—there were a few new things he could do, such as taking a shower and sharing an afternoon walk with her.

"Is that a yes?"

He was already on his feet by the time she finished asking. Together they descended the steps and started across the grass. Susannah, her hands hooked in her hip pockets, stayed close to his side, naturally adjusting her stride to his. "Thi is a great yard for kids," she remarked. "I can't get used to these trees. They're perfect for climbing."

They ducked underneath a massive branch of the live oak she was gesturing to. "You can go all the way to the top of that one, and I swear, you can see all the way to Texas," Remy remarked. "If you're reckless or a little adventurous. You, being the sensible sort, probably wouldn't make it more than twenty feet."

"And you, being the adventurous sort, have been to the top and have seen Texas." Trailing her fingers lightly over the bark, she turned in a complete circle around the trunk, disappearing from sight for a moment or two before reappearing. "They're wonderful trees."

"They are that. This one is Claire."

She gave him a doubtful look. "Claire," she repeated. "You named this tree."

"Not me. It's been Claire—actually, La Belle Claire—for as long as I've been alive. I imagine my grandparents named it." He studied her for a moment, reading the good-natured skepticism in her eyes. "Ah, you don't believe me, do you? You wound me, Susannah. I could tell you something totally outrageous, and you would probably accept it as fact. I tell you something perfectly logical—such as that I'm going to marry you or that this tree has a name—and you don't believe me."

"I can see that your definition of outrageous varies significantly from mine," she retorted. "You know, in my part of Nebraska, trees are a little on the rare side. We admire them. We try not to cut them down. We even plant them, water them and nurture them, hoping to get more. We get awfully attached to them. But we do not name them." She gestured to the next closest tree. "And who is this? Thomas? Henry? No, wait. Your people are French. Beauregard? Philippe?"

With a grin, he approached her, not stopping until she was leaning against the trunk of the second tree and he was holding her there with his hands placed on either side of her head. "Don't be silly. This is a magnolia. Who would name a magnolia?"

She raised her hands to his chest, rubbing him through the thin, worn cotton of his shirt. "You Southerners are a strange lot," she teased softly.

"We have our eccentricities."

"And you're proud of them."

"Hmm. I think it'll make for awfully interesting kids—my Southern peculiarities and your Midwestern conventionality."

Her smile faltered at the mention of children. That was all right. He could give her time—a little, at least—to get used to the idea.

"So tell me," she said, her voice soft and as warm as sunshine. "Why does your oak tree have a name but not your magnolia?"

"Actually—" he pressed a kiss to her forehead "—Claire is a live oak, not an oak. There's a difference." His next kiss landed beside her eye. "Claire is a member of the Live Oak Society, which is a collection of live oaks around the state that are at least a hundred years old. It can't very well be listed on the society's rolls as 'the big tree at Belle Ste. Claire,' so someone—"

As he placed his next kiss on her cheek, she took over for him. "Likely your grandparents."

"—in keeping with the name of the house, the family and the town, named it La Belle Claire." He was about to kiss her mouth when she ducked away, sliding underneath his arm. She circled the magnolia, then resumed her leisurely stroll. After retrieving his cane where it had fallen, he went after her, catching up when she slowed to wait for him.

"Will you live here someday?" she asked, looking out across the field where the family had once kept horses. "Like your parents and grandparents and generations of Sinclairs before you?"

"Probably. When we're retired and the kids are grown an

on their own." He grinned at her refusal to react to his assumption that they would still be together when retirement came. "Every morning we'll sit on the gallery and drink lemonade and watch the traffic and the birds and the grandkids, and every afternoon we'll sneak off to the servants' quarters and make mad, passionate love."

Lowering her gaze to the ground, she kicked a pine cone, sending it skittering away. "Remy, please don't…"

"Susannah." He stopped right where he was and waited for her to turn, to come back and face him. She did stop, but she didn't turn right away. "Tell me that the idea of spending the rest of your life with me holds no appeal for you. Tell me that the prospect of being my wife doesn't interest you. Tell me that the possibility of carrying my baby inside you doesn't fill your heart, just the littlest bit, with pleasure."

Finally she did turn, but her expression was so sad that he almost wished she hadn't. "All those things sound wonderful, Remy, but…we can't always have what we want. Sometimes we just have to take what we can get."

"Not in my world."

"Then your world is privileged. But in *my* world—in the *real* world—sometimes you have to settle."

He shook his head. "The night I got shot, when I thought was dying, I looked back at my life and about all I had were egrets. When I knew I was going to live, I swore I would change that. I know now what I want. I want you—*you*, Susannah. Do you understand that? I want to marry you, to have children with you. I want to spend the rest of my life loving you." He looked away, then back at her, finishing fiercely, "And I'll be damned if I'm going to settle for anything less."

"You are the most stubborn man!"

"Damned right I am."

"You *aren't* God. You can't just decide what you want and make it happen."

"Why not?"

She sighed wearily. "Because life doesn't work that way, Remy."

"We'll make it work."

"Some things *can't* work."

In an effort to lighten the mood, he wryly remarked, "You're certainly no optimist, are you?"

"No," she agreed. "I'm a realist."

"That's all right, Susannah." Taking her hand, he gently pulled her along with him. "I've got dreams enough for both of us."

The night was quiet and still. Susannah sat in the barrel chair in the parlor, her feet tucked beneath her, her head resting on one hand, and let her gaze move slowly around the room. What would it be like to live here, to call this place home? To have pictures of her husband, her children and herself on those tables? To make this homey room *her* family room? To gather here on holidays with children and grand-children? To become part of the centuries-old Sinclair family traditions?

It would be closer to heaven than she was ever going to get.

She sighed a little, and her head sank a little lower. From that position it was easy for her gaze to settle on the sewing basket, its lid decorated with intricate cross-stitch, under-neath the chair-side table. Marie Sinclair did needlework, she remembered. Some of her work decorated pillows in here; other signed pieces were framed in the kitchen and the upstairs bedrooms. That basket likely contained her equip-ment—floss, needles, scissors, probably even a few pieces of fabric.

From the sofa Remy switched the television from the movie that had just ended to a program she found interest-ing, then got to his feet. "I'm going to take a shower."

"All right," she murmured, still looking at the basket.

"When I get out, maybe you'll be ready for bed."

"I'm sure I will."

He brought the remote control to her, then bent and kissed her cheek. It was such a natural gesture, so husbandly. It frightened her how easily she accepted it…and how soon she would face a life without such gestures. Without Remy.

When he reached the door, she abruptly spoke his name. "I noticed that your mother does needlework. Do you think she would mind if I borrowed some of her supplies? Just a small piece of fabric and a little floss?"

"Of course not. If you don't find what you need in that basket, she keeps a bigger one on the window seat in their bedroom."

For a time after he left, she remained where she was. Finally, though, she knelt on the floor and pulled the basket out. Inside she found exactly what she needed, including an eight-by-ten-inch piece of linen in a fine ivory shade. Feeling impossibly romantic for an avowed realist, she chose her colors—one the golden hue of Remy's hair when the sunlight touched it, the other to match his eyes, bluer than the snatch of song she'd heard on Michael and Valery's balcony the other night.

She also took out a needle, a threader, a pair of small pointed scissors and—the miracle of modern sewing—a disappearing marker. She had never possessed much artistic talent, but what she was doing didn't require much. It would be a simple, unfinished piece, an apology of sorts that would probably never be accepted.

But she had to offer it anyway.

She worked through Remy's shower, not stopping even when she heard the distant sound of the blow dryer. He wasn't drying his hair, she knew—he preferred to leave it be, even though it meant waking up with some interesting styles in the morning—but rather his cast. The doctor's suggestion of covering it with a plastic bag worked only partially. Remy always completed his showers with damp places on the foot and leaks inside at the top opening of the cast.

When the hair dryer shut off, she smoothed the linen across her lap. She was working without a hoop, so she would have to press the piece when she was done. But even wrinkled and unfinished, it had charm. It wasn't the best embroidery she'd ever done—not surprising, since she hadn't done any at all in more than fifteen years and had never been particularly skilled—but it wasn't the skill that mattered.

It was the sentiment.

Gathering the supplies in the center of the piece, she folded everything together and stored it in Mrs. Sinclair's basket. Then, after shutting off the television and the lamps, she went toward the back of the house, where she met Remy coming out of the bathroom. "Why don't you make sure everything's locked up?" she suggested as she slipped past him. "I'll meet you in your room in fifteen minutes."

Without giving him a chance to reply, she closed the door and began hastily undressing. The bathroom was steamy and smelled of him. Having deliberately left her own bath supplies in her room, she used his—shampoo, shaving cream and even, when she was done, his cologne—so she smelled of him, too, without even getting close to him.

Wearing nothing but a towel, she turned off the bathroom light and stepped into the hall. The only light on was in his room, spilling out through the open door to light her way. She didn't go there, though. Instead she went to her own room, leaving her door open, turning on the bedside lamp. A quick glance across the hall showed that he was sitting in bed, pillows propped behind his back, the quilt pulled to his waist and watching her.

Good.

She sat down on her bed and began smoothing lotion over her left leg, starting low at her toes and working all the way up to her hip, rubbing it in with slow, lazy, long strokes. Afte repeating the procedure on her right leg, she applied a small amount of the cool cream to her face, then her hands.

Another furtive glance showed that Remy was still watching her…and that he was very definitely interested.

Leaving the bed and his line of sight, she dropped the towel across her laundry basket and took a nightgown from the dresser. It was soft, thin and white, one she'd bought on a whim but rarely wore. She wasn't sure why she had even brought it with her, unless maybe the poet's ruffles along the neckline, the billowy sleeves and the yards of flowing fabric had seemed dreamily appropriate for a sojourn in a wonderfully romantic antebellum Southern mansion. In reality, the gown, falling to her knees, was so full, ruffled and flowing that, whenever she tried to wear it, it wrapped itself in a choking tangle around her when she slept.

But tonight it would be on the floor long before she fell asleep.

Taking her hairbrush with her, she moved to stand in the doorway. This time she didn't pretend that she was unaware of Remy watching her. She didn't pretend that being watched, and enticing him in the process, wasn't exactly what she wanted.

She had towel-dried her hair in the bathroom. Now she drew the brush through it, slowly working out each tangle. When that was done, for a time she simply brushed her hair, each stroke drawing back from her face, long and sensuous, each movement causing her gown to shift and swirl, pulling the soft fabric across her breasts and her impossibly sensitive nipples.

At last, when she knew from her brief, but intense, experience that he couldn't get any harder, that she couldn't get any hotter, she laid the brush on the night table, turned off the lamp and slowly crossed the hall that separated them. She placed one knee on the bed, then swung her leg over him and settled across his lap. Her quilt—that was how she'd begun to think of it—was between them, trapping, exchanging their heat, rubbing sensuously over his hard flesh, abrading her tender flesh.

Wrapping her fingers around the iron bars of the headboard, she leaned forward to kiss him—gentle little nips along his ear, his jaw, finally reaching his mouth. He opened to her immediately, inviting her in, and she tentatively accepted. It was a new experience, being the aggressor, one that, with practice, she could come to like. She mimicked the way *he* kissed *her,* exploring his mouth with her tongue, teasing, tasting, before slowly withdrawing.

He started to speak, but she silenced him with a light, fluttery kiss before she leaned aside to reach the nightstand and the small pile of plastic packets there. She tore one open and removed its small coil of latex, then pushed the quilt back and…

And her confidence faltered. Her seduction scene fell apart.

Recognizing the reason for her falter, he brought his hands to hers, guiding her. "Hold it here," he instructed in a voice that was hoarse and sharp with desire, "and put it here…now unroll it…" He groaned. "There."

A soft giggle escaped her. "So much for seduction. I'd never…"

"I know…and, sweetheart, I find that incredibly seductive."

"You do?"

"That I'm the only man you've done this for? Done this to? Hell, yes."

In thanks she gave him a quick kiss, then softly admonished, "Be serious again. I can manage from here on out."

Without further play, she lifted her gown and took him inside her, controlling her movement, sinking a millimeter at a time until their bodies were as closely, as perfectly, joined as was physically possible. For a time she simply sat there, eyes closed, breathing uneven, and felt the changes—the fullness, the heat, the stretching. Then he moved just the slightest bit, and satisfaction quickly gave way to hunger.

For one instant she cursed his cast, cursed that she would never know what it was like to make love with him any other way, cursed that she would never experience the full expression of his passion. Then the instant passed, and she began making love to him. She began loving him.

She took him slow and deep, withdrawing, then returning, feeding her arousal with every stroke. With his hands underneath her gown, he stroked her breasts and her belly and occasionally slipped his fingers between her thighs, helping her, pushing her, guiding her, faster, harder. He was close, she knew from the rhythm of his breathing and the tightening of his body, and she— Sweet mercy, she had gone beyond close. Her lungs were tight, her heart pounded mercilessly and her body had gone hard and quivery with a pure, relentless ache that threatened to consume her.

When it happened, it was sudden, violent in its intensity, painful in its pleasure. The ache exploded from the inside out, stealing her breath, robbing her of her voice, her strength, her soul. It made her tremble and plead, words with no sound, sounds with no meaning.

But it left her with enough awareness to hear Remy's throaty groan. To feel the clenching of his muscles. To feel— sense?—the protected emptying of his body inside hers.

It left her with enough awareness, when he gathered her into his arms, when he stroked and held and soothed her, to hear the low, quiet promise he whispered.

"I love you, Susannah. I always will."

And it left her with enough awareness to literally feel her heart break.

Remy awakened Friday morning to empty arms and an empty bed and a future that couldn't have been more full. He knew Susannah loved him, knew it with a certainty that he couldn't explain. Call it instinct. Intuition. Whatever it was, he *knew* it.

And he knew *she* knew it.

It was just a matter of getting her to admit it.

Then they would get married. Get pregnant. Have the first of at least three or four babies. Begin living the rest of what was guaranteed to be a long and happy life together.

He wondered what she would think of his parents and all the Sinclair-Navarre relatives. They would probably intimidate the hell out of her. But his father—being a typical male— would surely adore her, and his mother, he had no doubt, would, too. Susannah and Marie shared much in common: they were both gentle, quiet, sensible women. They understood family ties and obligations. They gave freely of their time to those who needed it and of themselves to those they loved.

And what would her family up in Nebraska think of *him*? On the whole, he wasn't a bad catch. He came from a good family. He was well educated and had a reputation as a damned tough FBI agent. Even though he'd come into his share of the family money when he was twenty-five, he worked hard and had no intention of slacking off.

Still, there *were* those resemblances she'd said he bore to her ex-husband. And he was a stranger who would be keeping her in a distant city far from the farm where she'd grown up. And after her first marriage, her family would have to be leery about seeing her try again. And the simple truth was he didn't deserve her.

But he could make them promises that Guy Duncan never could have: that he would always love Susannah. That he would always treat her with respect. That he would never be unfaithful to her. That he would never hurt her. That her love and her happiness would always be the most important things in his life.

He was persuasive. Susannah had said so herself. If he could win her over, then he could win anyone over.

But, he reminded himself, he hadn't *quite* finished winning her yet.

Pushing back the covers, he swung his feet to the floor and slowly, with his usual morning stiffness, stood up. He was tired of sleeping on his back all night, and he was damned tired of lying there passively while Susannah made love to him. He wanted to trade positions with her, wanted to cover her body with his, wanted to lean over her while her hips cradled his. He wanted to feel her legs wrapped around his hips, wanted to share the work of their lovemaking as well as the pleasure.

A few more weeks. The words had become a promise. A prayer.

After dressing and a trip to the bathroom, he went in search of Susannah. Her room was empty, the door open, her bed unslept in these past few nights. The kitchen was empty, too, with no sign of breakfast having been started, and the parlor was still and untouched from last night.

But the locks on the door leading to the gallery were undone.

He circled the house, at last locating his mother's sewing basket on a bench on the south side. He stopped at the top of the steps and was staring out across the lawn when a voice called out from above him. "Good morning."

It was the swinging of her feet in midair that gave away her location. With a grin, he moved down the steps and approached the giant live oak, where she sat, her back against the trunk, on a branch some fifteen feet from the ground. She looked so smugly self-satisfied and so damned beautiful that he would give almost anything for a camera to capture the moment. "What are you doing up there?"

"Isn't it a beautiful morning?"

"Louisiana's full of beautiful mornings." After a curious pause, he repeated his question. "What are you doing?"

"I was sitting on the porch—"

"The gallery," he corrected with a grin.

"—doing a little embroidery, and I remembered what you said yesterday."

"I said a lot of things yesterday, ranging from 'I'm going to marry you, Susannah,' to 'I love you.'"

"I'm referring to the conversation where you said I was sensible and dull while you're reckless and adventurous."

"I never called you dull," he argued good-naturedly. "Hell, I never said that *I* was reckless and adventurous."

She gave him a look that was so haughtily superior. "Oh, please…what do you think sensible means?"

"Rational. Reasonable. Logical."

"Predictable. *Dull.*"

"Take my word for it, sweetheart. *Nothing* about you is dull."

She moved from her perch to the next branch below, then to the immense limb, bigger around the middle than she was by at least three times, that sagged all the way to the ground before rising up again. She was right in front of him now and only six feet or so off the ground. "Anyway, I was sitting on the porch—sorry, on the gallery—enjoying the morning and doing some embroidery and admiring La Belle Claire, and I realized that I had never climbed a tree before. I had never been reckless or adventurous. I had never seen Texas before."

"Honey, if that's how you're defining reckless and adventurous," he teased, "then you 'saw Texas' two days ago, when you took a chance with me."

She held out her arms, and he reached above to grasp her around the waist. He pulled, and she leaped—well, sort of slid—and he helped her to the ground. When her feet were safely on firm earth again, though, he didn't release her. "No, Remy," she seriously disagreed. "That was heaven."

His laughter was quick and easy. "Damn, Susannah, I've never met a woman who amuses and arouses me at the same time."

Giving him an innocent look, she stepped closer and rubbed tantalizingly against him. "Are you aroused?"

"Sweetheart, I'm horny as hell."

"Hmm. *I'm* hungry. I was thinking about having a big breakfast and then maybe settling into that chaise longue on the gallery and not moving the rest of the morning."

That held a certain appeal, too, Remy admitted. And, after all, they did have all day.

In fact, they had the rest of their lives to indulge their desire.

Keeping his arm around her shoulder, he steered her back toward the gallery. "Come on, and I'll help you with breakfast."

"I thought you couldn't cook."

"Anyone can fry bacon or scramble eggs." They paused at the bench so she could scoop up the sewing basket, then continued their leisurely walk around the house. "What about your embroidery?"

"Oh, I finished it. It wasn't anything much."

"Do I get to see it?"

She considered it for what seemed an extraordinarily long time before finally looking up at him. "I suppose so. Sooner…" She walked inside the house and straight into the parlor, looking at him over her shoulder as she returned the basket to its place. "Or later."

It was approaching three o'clock when Susannah finally stirred from the chaise longue where she was watching Remy alternately doze and watch *her*. It had been the laziest of days, one that she couldn't bear to bring to an end.

But she had to.

She had to bring everything to an end.

Sitting up, she stretched, then brushed her hair back where it had come loose from its braid. "Hey, Remy?"

"Hmm."

She opened her mouth, but no sound came out. Her throat

had closed in a knot and required a moment's swallow to clear. "I've got to go into town to pick up some things. Do you mind?"

Tilting his head to one side, he opened only one eye to study her. "I take it you're not inviting me to go along."

"No. I thought…" She cleared her throat again. "I'd kind of like to go alone."

She waited for him to protest, but instead he grinned. "You don't have to sound so hesitant, sweetheart. We're not permanently joined at the hip, although I wouldn't object if we were."

Relief washed over her. "Is there anything special you want while I'm out?"

"Nah. Just bring yourself back."

Rising from the chair, she bent and kissed his mouth. It wasn't the sort of kiss she wanted to give him, full of passion and fire and love. It was just a simple goodbye kiss. *Goodbye.* It damn near broke her heart.

"Be careful," he called as she disappeared inside.

She combed her hair and got her purse, with the number she had looked up in Mr. Sinclair's study early this morning, then went out to the other side of the house. Her little car was parked near the back, unused since the day she had moved in here. It seemed appropriate, under the circumstances, that she should drive it today.

The engine turned right over, an amusing little putt compared to the powerful purr of the car she'd been driving. She rolled the windows down, turned the stereo on and drove onto the highway. At the first junction, she turned east toward Belclaire, but when she reached the small town, she kept right on driving. At the interstate, she debated between New Orleans and Baton Rouge, finally settling on the capital city.

She would call Smith Kendricks first, she decided. She would explain her situation, would tell him that she wanted to help, would offer the terms under which her cooperation was available. Then she would call Carlucci, take care of a little shopping, then return home… Not home. Because of what she'd done, it would never be home. Then she would return to Belle Ste. Claire.

By the time she got back, she had no doubt that Smith would have already called Remy. What action would the U.S. Attorney's office and the FBI decide to take? Would they put Remy someplace safe and unreachable? Would they leave him at the house, under protection, and try to catch Falcone's men in the act? If that was the case, would they allow her to remain also, so Carlucci—and, therefore, Falcone—didn't suspect that they'd been double-crossed? Or would Remy hate her too much to let her stay in his precious family home?

And what would they do about Skip? How could they protect him when he was being held at Falcone's house? How could they get him out safely when he was surrounded by people who wouldn't hesitate to kill him if their boss so ordered?

She didn't have any answers, didn't even have any guesses. All she could do was trust that Smith would take care of things. She had to trust that he loved Remy enough to make everything work out right.

Pulling into a shopping center on the outskirts of Baton Rouge, she found a parking space, then hurried to the nearest pay phone. It was the same place, she realized, where she had come to buy Remy's gloves. The same phone where she had called Nicholas Carlucci the first time.

Dialing the number she had written for the U.S. Attorney's office in the back of her checkbook, she charged the call to her credit card. A receptionist answered and switched her to Smith's office, where another woman picked up.

Her voice trembling, Susannah asked for Smith.

"May I ask who's calling?" The woman sounded terribly efficient and tough. Getting around her could be a problem.

"Tell him that it's regarding Remy Sinclair and—and Jimmy Falcone."

"Yes, ma'am. And your name?"

She clenched the phone tighter. No names, she had

promised herself that. Not until she had Smith's promise that
Skip would be protected. "Please." Her voice was little more
than a whisper, nothing more than a plea. "Tell him that it's
very important."

The secretary put her on hold, and she sighed with relief.
There was no way Smith would ignore a message like that,
even if it did come anonymously. And as soon as she got his
promise, she would identify herself.

She would destroy everything between herself and Remy.

She would destroy her future.

After a moment of silence, a voice came on the line, a
man's voice, strong and authoritative. "This is Alexander
Marshall. How can I help you?"

Panic made her hand tremble. "There's been a mistake. I'm
holding for Smith Kendricks."

"Yes, I understand, Miss…" He waited a moment, but
when she didn't speak, he went on. "Mr. Kendricks is in court
this afternoon. I'm his boss, though, and I'd be happy to help
you. Now I understand you're calling regarding Remy
Sinclair. You have some information for us?"

"I have to talk to Smith. I don't—I don't know you. I have
to—" She gulped a deep breath. "When will Smith be back?"

"I really don't know. But anything you tell me will be in
confidence, and I'll pass it on to Smith as soon as he returns."

"No, I'm sorry. I can't—" Abruptly, she hung up. Stupid,
stupid, *stupid,* she berated herself. Why hadn't she considered
the possibility that Smith—a prosecutor, for heaven's sake!—
might be in court today? And why hadn't she come earlier in
the day, so that if he *was* gone, she would have the rest of the
day to call back? This late in the afternoon, he very well
might not even return to the office until Monday morning.

And Monday morning could be too late.

She was a fool to think she could handle this. She
deserved whatever punishment the government chose to give
her, even prison.

She *deserved* to lose Remy.

Bleakly, pulling her credit card out again, she dialed Carlucci's number. Until the end, the call was virtually the same as the others. She told him that Remy had had no visitors, no phone calls, that except for a brief trip into the city Wednesday, he had gone nowhere and done nothing, and he told her that Skip was still fine. She hated the way he said it— *still fine*—as if that condition was liable to change at any moment.

At the end, though, she gathered her courage. "It's been nearly three weeks, Mr. Carlucci. How much longer?"

"Don't be impatient, Susannah. By the time the Sinclairs return from their vacation, you and Skip will be safely home in Nebraska."

"When will we be leaving? Tomorrow? Monday? Wednesday?"

He was silent for a long, cold moment, then he replied, "Call me Tuesday morning, Susannah." He hung up.

Frustrated, she slammed the receiver down with more force than necessary, and returned to her car. She had to buy some groceries, and there surely would be a pay phone at the store. She would try Smith one last time, and if she didn't get him then...

Then she would go back.

And she would tell Remy everything.

Remy was standing in front of the refrigerator, wishing he ad asked Susannah to pick up some beer, when the phone egan ringing. There was an answering machine in his father's ffice that would get it on the fourth or fifth ring, but he eaded that way anyway. She'd been gone a long time for a hopping trip to Belclaire; maybe she'd had car trouble or had otten lost or something else had gone wrong. Whatever the roblem, he didn't want to leave her to talk to an impersonal achine.

The machine picked up before he reached the office; he

could tell by the low tones that it was a man, not Susannah. Before he got close enough to recognize the voice or understand the words, the caller hung up, but only seconds later, the phone rang again.

This time he got it before the machine. He didn't even get out a complete hello before Smith interrupted him. "Where is Susannah?"

Puzzled, Remy eased himself into his father's chair. "What?"

"Where the hell is Susannah?"

"Uh…she went to pick up some things at the store. Why?"

"Do you have your gun up there?"

"Yeah, it's—"

"On you?"

"Of course not. It's in my room."

"Go get it."

"Smith, what's going—"

"*Now,* Remy. I'll wait. And if Susannah comes back while you're gone…don't turn your back on her."

Curious as hell—and wishing his father had a cordless phone like everyone else in the world—he laid the phone on the desk, took up his cane again and went to his room. Once the pistol in its holster was secured to the waistband of his sweats, he returned to the study as quickly as he could. "Okay, I'm back. Now what the hell's going on?"

Chapter 10

It was after five o'clock and growing dark when Susannah let herself into the house and carried two bags of groceries into the kitchen. She stopped at the doorway to flip the light switch with her elbow, then gave a start when she saw Remy sitting there at the table. Was she simply surprised to see him sitting there in the dark? he wondered grimly.

Or was she surprised to see him at all?

She gave him a long, uneasy look—a guilty look. God help him, how many times had he seen that guilt in her eyes and disregarded it? People didn't look guilty for no reason, but he had ignored it, had brushed it off as if it were unimportant.

He was a fool.

After a moment, her gaze dropped to the table and the items spread out there in front of him. There was a small bag—a shopping bag, about the right size for a greeting card, made of a plastic so dark that the first time he'd searched the armoire in her room, he had missed it there in the back. There were the contents of the bag: a sticky note, the kind meant for refrigerators and computers, with a New Orleans phone number and a five-by-seven-inch photograph.

And there was his gun, within easy reach and, right now, lying there pointed at her.

The shopping bags began sliding from her arms. She caught them about halfway to the floor and eased them down, then straightened again.

"Put your purse down, too, and move away from it."

She obeyed him, taking a few steps closer to the table. After a moment he gestured for her to sit in the chair across from him.

"Remy—"

"Why, Susannah?" he interrupted. "Was it for love? Money?"

She laid her hands on the tabletop, her fingers knotted together but trembling a bit anyway. Nice touch, he thought cynically. "There's no money involved."

"So it's love then." He would have preferred money, he realized with an ache. He would have preferred believing that his life—or, rather, his death—was worth money to her to knowing that it meant nothing more than a favor for someone she loved. "He's a little young for you, don't you think?" Of course, with the appetite she'd shown in the past few days, she probably had to take them young. More energy, better stamina—those were probably important qualities to her.

"So you and young Lewis here... Sort of an old-fashioned name, isn't it? Do you call him that or Lew?"

She reached out, and his hand moved closer to the pistol, freezing her in motion. Drawing her hand back, she quietly asked, "Can I see the picture?"

He looked at it a moment, at Susannah, smiling and beautiful and happy, and at the dark-haired young man whose arms were around her, also smiling, handsome and equally happy. It was relatively recent, taken soon after her arrival in New Orleans, assuming that part of her story was true.

Disgusted, he tossed the photograph across the table and watched her catch it just as it slid to the edge.

"How do you know his name?"

"We have a file on Lewis Crouse. He works for Jimmy Falcone...but, of course, you know that." He shook his head grimly. "I have to be honest. I don't know how we missed you, living with Crouse and on Falcone's payroll yourself. We got sloppy. So...you call him Lewis or Lew or what?"

"Actually I call him Skip." She gave the couple in the photo a sad smile, then laid it on the table and looked at him. "Lew is our father."

Remy stared at her. "Lewis Crouse is your brother," he said skeptically. "How does an only child three weeks ago suddenly come up with a twenty-three-year-old brother?"

"I lied to you." Ignoring his muttered curse, she went on. "I thought that, with the trouble Skip was in—with the trouble that *we're* in—it would be best to deny having a brother."

He wasn't sure he believed her, but that could be sorted out later. "So what's the deal, Susannah? You help them kill me— that's easy enough to figure out—but what do you get in return?"

"I get my brother back safe."

"Get him back? From where?"

She drew a deep breath. "For the last month or so, they've been keeping him at Jimmy Falcone's house."

"Keeping," he repeated, "You mean as a prisoner."

"Yes."

He considered the plausibility of that for a moment. It was certainly a prettier tale than he'd expected. It had a much nicer, much more innocent, ring to it than admitting, "I'm conspiring with a known organized crime figure to murder a federal agent because it's how I get my kicks or because my bad brother asked me to or because it's been a slow month in the emergency room with not enough people dying to satisfy me." *He* would certainly rather believe that she'd done all this—come here, betrayed him, put his life in danger— because her brother's life was in danger.

But then, he was crazy in love with her. He would rather believe any story, no matter how outlandish, in which she was acting against her will.

Without waiting to be asked, she began her explanation. Her excuse. "Skip came down here about two years ago to go to school. He had always been pampered at home—smoth- ered, he called it—and he wanted to get away, wanted to get out on his own. I don't know how he got tied up with Jimmy Falcone. I guess he's just that kind of kid...if there's trouble around to be found, he'll find it. I had no idea what was going on when I moved down here. I was eager to get out of Nebraska myself, and when Skip invited me to come down and live with him... It seemed like the answer to my prayers. I could start all over in a new place, but I wouldn't be totally on my own. I'd have family. I'd have Skip."

She closed her eyes for a moment, then blinked them rapidly to control the dampness that had collected. "As soon as I got to New Orleans, I discovered that Skip was in debt, that he wasn't going to school and couldn't—or wouldn't— hold a regular job. His friends were rougher, tougher, than back home, and he was more reckless, more irresponsible than ever. He was getting into trouble and staying out late. And then he got the job with Jimmy Falcone. It seems that after that, all we ever did was argue. I wanted him to grow up, and he was having too much fun playing the tough guy. Then..."

Remy stared at her as she spoke, his expression stony and hard, but inside he felt a strange, almost giddy sense of relief. She was telling the truth. It was in her eyes, her voice, her ex- pression and her gestures. She had lied to him, true. She had betrayed him, when he had sworn that he would never let anyone betray him again.

But she hadn't done it willingly. This was what she had meant all those times she had insisted that he didn't know her at all. When she had said that she didn't have the right to care about him. When she had sworn repeatedly that she had nothing to give, that she was worth nothing. When she had warned that she might hurt him.

I could be a terrible person. I could have awful things planned for you.

And maybe you'll die, regretting the day we met.

She'd been warning him from the beginning, only he had been too intent upon seducing her to recognize it.

Realizing that she had fallen silent, he prompted her. "And then?"

"One day I got a phone call. Skip wasn't home—I hadn't seen him in a day or so, but that wasn't so unusual. When we argued about the way he was wasting his life, he often stayed over at a friend's place a night or two. Anyway, the phone call was from a lawyer named Nicholas Carlucci. He told me that he was Falcone's lawyer, that he knew Skip. He said that he knew the details of every job Skip had ever done for Falcone, that he had documented everything. It was all minor stuff, nothing really bad, but it would be such an easy thing, he said, to make it look worse, to make the police believe worse."

If anyone could build a tight, credible case against a reckless, irresponsible Nebraska farm boy, Nick Carlucci could, Remy acknowledged. If Falcone had used Nick to construct the frame for Nate Simmons's murder around *him,* he would likely be sitting in a cell somewhere right now. "So in exchange for your help, he wouldn't set your brother up for a crime he didn't commit."

He sounded so cold, Susannah thought. It was useless continuing with her explanation. Even if he believed her, which he doubted, he would never, ever forgive her. Still, she did continue, her voice slight and empty of hope. "He told me that you were looking for a nurse to help you out until the cast came off. He advised me to apply for the job and to do whatever was necessary to get it. In the meantime, he said, Mr. Falcone had invited Skip to come and stay with him for a while, and that was where he would stay until…" She paused to recall Carlucci's exact words. "Until the issue of Remy Sinclair had been resolved."

"Why didn't you go to the police?"

"Because he assured me that if I did, my brother would pay, most likely with his life."

"So what were you supposed to do? How far were you supposed to go to protect your brother from his own actions?"

"Carlucci wanted regular reports. He wanted to know your schedule, who you talked to, who you saw, where you went. That's all."

"That's all," Remy repeated scathingly. He pushed away from the table and paced across the room. He didn't forget to take the pistol with him. "That's enough to get me killed."

"I know." The tears that had burned her eyes earlier spilled over now. "I'm sorry, Remy. I'm so sorry."

"So that's who you've been calling—Carlucci. That's why you didn't want your mail delivered here." At the counter, he turned back to face her. "Did he tell you anything? How they plan to do it or where or when?"

She shook her head. "Just…sometime before your parents get back from Europe."

He started to speak, thought better of it and turned away.

"I know it's not enough," she whispered, "but I *am* sorry. I thought—I thought I could take care of everything. I thought I could protect you and Skip and that no one would have to get hurt."

He gave her a derisive look. "And how the hell were you going to do that? Make a deal with Smith? Tell him he could do whatever he wanted to you as long as he let your precious little brother go free?"

She wished she dared reach into her purse for a tissue, but

he was still holding that gun and he still looked so angry. Instead she wiped her cheeks with her hand. "Is that how you found out? Does Smith's office record his phone calls?"

"Technology's a wonderful thing, isn't it?" he replied sarcastically. "Do you know how much trouble you've caused? You called Carlucci from Michael's apartment, for God's sake. The man is part of a major investigation. Do you think the government isn't keeping track of the phone calls he receives? How do you think it looks when the bureau's doing a routine check of all the phone numbers that have made calls to Carlucci or Falcone or any of the others, and they find a number belonging to a New Orleans cop listed there?"

She huddled a little tighter in her chair. Now Michael had a reason other than simply instinct to dislike her.

"They began a background check on Michael—on my *friend*. Do you have any idea how that looks, for a cop to be investigated by the FBI? It's not exactly a career-enhancing move. They began examining *his* phone records, and today they went to court to get a wiretap order so they could monitor *his* calls. Fortunately for him, they had to go through Smith for the court order, and he remembered that *you* were the only one to use Michael's phone that night. Michael verified that, and so did Valery."

"I'm sorry," she whispered helplessly. *So sorry.*

Gripping his cane in his right hand and the pistol in his left, he came back to the table, this time sitting in the chair closest to her. "When Smith got back to his office this afternoon," he continued, his voice empty of emotion, "his boss had something for him to listen to. Marshall had already notified the FBI, and they had already traced the call to a pay phone in Baton Rouge. Interestingly, a few weeks ago a call was made to Carlucci from that same phone on the same day and at the same time that I saw you using it. Everyone already suspected it was you, but Smith was the only one who could prove it. He recognized your voice, and he called me. Damn it, Susannah—"

At that instant, the room fell into darkness, and Remy muttered a curse. Susannah prayed that it was just a fuse that had blown or that the power had gone out everywhere along the highway, but that awful sick feeling in her stomach warned her that wasn't the case.

His chair scraped just a little when he stood up. "Come on," he demanded in the hoarsest of whispers, taking her arm and pulling her with him out of the kitchen and down the hall toward the study. She followed blindly, not familiar enough with this part of the house to find her way in total darkness. He went straight to his father's desk and picked up the phone there, then swore again. "It's dead…and, sweet God in heaven, so are we."

"Maybe it's just—"

He silenced her with his hand on her mouth as the distant almost delicate sound of breaking glass echoed through the house. She couldn't tell where the sound had come from— the darkness confused her, disoriented her—but Remy seemed to know. He began moving quietly, around the desk the chair, the credenza, to one of two French doors tha opened from the study to the south gallery. There wer multiple locks on every exterior door in the house, and he wa in the process of unlatching the second one when footstep sounded in the hall.

Susannah recognized at least two distinct steps, one heav like a boot and the other lighter, stealthier. A man and woman? It had been a man and a woman in that gray car tha Sunday afternoon, taking pictures of them when they wer outside. Could these be the same two?

After an excruciatingly long moment of stillness, Rem opened the third lock, then began easing the door open. Whe it creaked, he stopped immediately; when no one can running, he opened it farther. As soon as the space was wic enough, he slipped outside, pulled her after him, then bega the slow process of closing the door again.

It was quiet outside; just another peaceful country evening. Susannah shivered, wishing for one of the sweaters in her room. She wished for socks, too—her ankles were cold—and for the car keys she had dropped on the kitchen floor when she had dropped her purse.

Most of all, she wished for the power to stop what she had started.

She wished for some way to protect Remy.

She wished she didn't have to die knowing that he hated her.

Her sudden understanding—that she *was* going to die, that Falcone and Carlucci had probably intended from the start to kill her along with Remy—brought with it a sudden calm. Using her free hand, she tried to pry his fingers from her arm. "Let me go, Remy."

He looked at her in the moonlight. "We've got to get away from the house," he whispered. "They'll search some of the rooms, but maybe not all of them. We've got to get to the woods."

"Let me go back inside. Let me talk to them."

"Are you crazy? You can't reason with people like them! They came here to kill us, Susannah—*us,* not just me!"

"I know. But maybe…" Maybe she could slow them down. Maybe she could throw them off track. Maybe she could do something, *anything,* to give him an advantage.

"No. *Hell,* no. You're staying with me." To ensure that, he held her tighter, tight enough to hurt. "We have to work our way around to the back of the house, then use the trees and their shadows to get to the woods. Stay beside me and stay close. Understand?"

She nodded, and he set off, drawing her with him. They practically hugged the outer wall, following it all the way back to the steps that led down to the yard where La Belle Claire grew. They had to step into the moonlight then, and Remy cringed at the thought of how it shone on Susannah's pale shirt and his own fair hair. Quickly, though, they worked their way back into shadows, squeezing between the house and the shrubs that grew around the foundation.

At last they reached the back wall of the servants' wing. It was the easternmost part of the house and came closest to the woods that offered their only hope. It seemed to have taken forever, but he estimated it had been only a few minutes, maybe five or six at the most, since the power had been cut.

Now came the tough part. Now they had to move, quickly and quietly, through moonlight and shadow. Now they had to expose themselves to a high risk of discovery. All Falcone's people had to do was look out the window at the right moment—and they were in a house filled with windows.

He drew a deep breath, then blew it out again. Before leaving the cover the house provided, he looked at Susannah, expecting to see fear, tears, terror. Instead there on that lovely face was the serenity he'd fallen in love with that long-ago night in the hospital. Serenity, damn it. The woman was facing death, and she was doing it with far more calmness than *he,* an experienced federal agent, could dredge up. He would laugh if he weren't so damned afraid.

She looked at him then, and he mouthed, "Ready?"

At her slight nod, they left the safety of the house, hurrying across moonlit grass to the cover of a live oak. This one wasn't as big as Claire, but it was big enough to hide them both on the other side.

They cut a zigzagging trail from one tree to another. If only he could run, they could take a straight shot for the old barn, then veer off into the woods and use these precious moments to put as much distance between them and the house as possible. But he couldn't run. He could only hobble at a moderate pace, and even that was quickly becoming painful. He wasn't kidding himself: if they made it to the woods, he wouldn't be able to go far. But at least he could get Susannah headed in the right direction. At least he could give her a chance to escape. He might even be able to set up an ambush of some sort and, if he was really lucky, save himself.

At last they reached the last tree. A wide clearing stretched ahead of them, lit by the moon and with nothing, not even the faintest shadow, for cover. Remy leaned against the trunk of the live oak, taking his weight off his favored leg for a moment. "Once you get into the woods, there's a trail," he whispered. "It's probably pretty grown over, but you can find it, and when you do, you run like hell. It winds back for a mile or two and comes out on the next road over. When you reach the road, turn left. There are a half-dozen houses just a few hundred feet away. Go to one of them, call the sheriff and tell him to call Michael or Smith. Understand?"

When she didn't respond, he gave her a little shake. "Do you understand, damn it?"

"Yes," she replied with a mutinous scowl.

"Don't worry, Susannah," he said with a grin meant to reassure. "I'll be right behind you." *If I'm not dead.* "Ready?"

Together they pushed away from the tree, trading its safety for the lighted clearing. At about the halfway point, he started to think that just maybe they might make it when, from somewhere up above, a shout—and, God help them, a shot—rang out. "Hey!" a woman called from the second-floor veranda. "They're out back!"

"Go on, Susannah!" he commanded, shoving her in the direction of the woods, but apparently she had other ideas. She knew he couldn't keep up with her in the trees, knew he couldn't outdistance their killers and, damn her, she wasn't going without him. In fact, *she* was the one leading now, the one pulling him straight into the barn.

It was the worst place they could have gone, the first place their killers would look. It was old and musty, big and filled with shapes he couldn't recognize. But Susannah could. She had explored inside during one of her walks, he realized, for she led him straight to the best cover—the only cover—the

old place seemed to provide: bales of hay stacked precari-
ously, one atop another, some only four feet high, others
towering over their heads. Releasing his arm, she wriggled
into a crevice between stacks, then disappeared from sight.

Remy hesitated only an instant, then, hearing a screen
door slam, he pushed through behind Susannah. The bales
were stacked unevenly, some pushed up tight against the rows
behind them, others leaving gaps. It was like a maze—narrow,
winding, the dust overpowering. Dropping to his knees where
there was room, he rounded a corner and found a small
breathing space. Susannah sat there in a huddle, knees drawn
to her chest, head bowed. He settled a few feet away from her,
listened and tried hard not to notice the fine dust that was
clogging his throat and his lungs.

"Check the woods," the woman directed from the clearing.

"They wouldn't go into the woods," disagreed a deeper
male voice. "The guy's a cripple. How far is he gonna make
it in the woods? My money's on the barn."

"There's nothing in the barn except hay and old rusted-out
equipment, and there's only one way out. He'd have to be a
fool to hide in there, and Sinclair's no fool."

"No, but he's got a bum leg, he can't run and he's dragging
the deadweight of a woman around behind him. It's his best
bet."

Remy glanced at the woman he was supposed to be dragging
around with him—the woman who had dragged *him* in here. She
was no more than a pale shadow in the darkness, curled up tight
as if she were trying to crawl inside herself. He wished he could
reassure her, wished he could somehow comfort her, but he
didn't dare speak or even move. Not now, not when the powerful
beam of a flashlight was playing across the interior of the barn.

"Sinclair!" The man's voice echoed off the rafters, then
dissipated in the still night. For a time it seemed there was no
sound at all, then Remy could make out the man's breathing
and, more distant, a car passing by on the highway.

"We know you're in here, Sinclair. There's no way you can get away with that bad leg. Give it up now, and we'll let the woman go."

Although a part of him desperately wanted to believe that was possible, Remy knew the bastard was lying. Falcone had never intended to let Susannah or her brother walk away from this. Their deaths had been part of the plan from the very beginning. Like Nate Simmons, they were expendable, a sacrifice to their boss's ambition.

And this time, Falcone was determined to succeed. He wasn't using his own people. Remy knew them all by sight, and there wasn't a woman in the bunch, which meant he'd brought someone in from out of town. He was paying big bucks for the big guns.

"Come on, Sinclair, don't be stubborn. There's no way you can save yourself…but you *can* save her. Come on out."

What was the worst they could do? Remy considered. Open fire on the bales of hay? Thick as they were, they wouldn't stop the sort of high-powered ammunition these people were sure to be using. There was a slim chance, he supposed, that he and Susannah could survive, but very slim.

If he were in their position, he would save his ammo and take the easy way out: toss a match into the hay, stand back and watch the place go up in flames. As aged as the timbers were, as dry as the hay was, the barn would become an inferno in literally seconds. The best he and Susannah could hope for then would be to succumb to smoke before the flames got them, and that wouldn't be likely.

"Maybe they're not here," the woman said impatiently.

"Oh, they're here." The man sounded supremely confident. "I can smell 'em. Go pull the car up. We can use the headlights to help find them."

What were his chances, Remy wondered, of moving soundlessly with his cast and finding a crack in the stacks of hay that would allow him a view of their hunters? And if he got that view, what were the chances he could take them both out before either of them got any shots off? He was a damned good shot. He routinely spent hours on the range practicing for just such a purpose.

But the targets on the range didn't shoot back.

And these targets would be shooting at Susannah, too.

From outside came the sound of an engine, then light flooded the barn. Hoping their hiding place was more secure than it felt, he took advantage of the increased light to check on Susannah…just in time to see her disappear deeper into the stacks of hay. Damn her, where was she going?

"So what do we do now?" the woman asked after switching off the engine, then rejoining the man in the barn.

"We start pitching hay and see what little creatures come slithering out."

"Don't bother." The voice came from a few feet above and at least a dozen feet away. It was clear, unmuffled by hay and it was definitely Susannah's.

Remy bowed his head against the bale in front of him and whispered a silent prayer, a silent plea. *Dear God, Susannah what have you done?*

Susannah's hands were in the air, shoulder high, her finger spread wide. Blinded by the lights, she could see little—tw shadowy forms, one slender and about her height, the othe bigger, bulkier. She couldn't tell anything about the ca couldn't see their guns, although, of course, they had them

And they were prepared to use them.

"Please don't shoot me," she said, ignoring the bits straw that clung to her hair and clothes, that floated in the a and tickled and itched wherever they touched. "I'm unarme Please don't hurt me."

It was the man who responded. "This little creature's whole lot prettier than the rodent I was expecting," he sa with what sounded like a grin. "Where is Sinclair?"

"I don't know. He wouldn't come in with me. He said it was too obvious." She forced a tremble into her voice. "He said…he said we would have a better chance in the woods, that there's a road back there, and some houses."

"I told you so," the woman muttered.

"So why didn't you go with him?" the man challenged.

"Because he's slow. He can't run with that cast. Besides, it's him you're after, not me. If I stayed with him, you might shoot me by mistake."

The man found that remark worthy of a chuckle. The woman didn't. Ignoring him, she took a few steps forward, partially blocking the headlights' beams. "Come on out here."

Susannah had crawled into a dead end. Now she maneuvered carefully, slowly, lifting herself up onto the bales in front, wriggling and sliding, wasting as much time as she dared. She wasn't sure exactly what she was hoping for—that while she distracted them, Remy would find some way to escape; that she could convince them that he had, indeed, gone into the woods instead and that they could use her to find him; that she might simply give him a little longer to live.

Finally she could delay no longer. She climbed down makeshift stairs of bales and at last stood on the dirt floor in the center of the barn, cold and shivering.

The woman approached her, coming close enough that Susannah could make out her features in spite of the light in her eyes. She was blond, probably in her mid-thirties, really rather pretty. What kind of career choices had this woman made, she wondered, that she found herself in a job where she killed people for a living?

The woman stopped only a few yards—ten, maybe twelve feet—away and raised her right arm, extending it fully. That put the pistol she was holding dead level with Susannah's heart. From that short distance, there was no way she could miss. "You want to watch her die, Remy?" she called. "Because that's what's going to happen if you don't get out here *now*."

Her voice trembling for real this time, Susannah edged a step back. "You can't kill me. I did everything I was asked to. I kept my end of the bargain. I made a deal with Mr. Falcone, and I kept it."

It was the man, still over by the door, who responded. "No, you made your deal with Nick Carlucci. *We* deal with Mr. Fal—"

"Shut up!" the blonde interrupted. "Sinclair, last warning!"

Hearing a scrape of noise off to the side where she had left Remy, Susannah burst into rapid, tearful speech. "I told you he's not here! I want to talk to Mr. Falcone! I did what I was supposed to, I gave Carlucci all the information, I kept quiet and I didn't tell anyone anything, and he promised, damn you—"

"Susannah, get down!"

Remy's warning shout was followed immediately by a thunderous shot as she scrambled for the nearest crevice in the stacks of hay. Amid more shots, she fell to the floor, then began burrowing backward, feetfirst, seeking more cover, not stopping until something blocked her way. Twisting in the narrow space, she turned to see what the barrier was and whether she could work her way around it....

And found herself facing the blonde and one very deadly looking gun.

Dimly she heard a grunt of pain from across the room, heard the sound of weight hitting the floor and a muttered curse. It came from over near the door, she told herself, over where the man had been standing. It wasn't Remy who'd been hurt. It wasn't Remy who'd gone down. She assured herself of that.

She prayed for it.

And her prayers were answered.

"You have me at a disadvantage," Remy called out in the heavy silence. "You know me, but I don't know you."

Down at Susannah's feet, the woman remained silent.

"Your partner's down. Why don't you come on out and let's get this over with."

She still said nothing, but she seemed to be considering her options. It didn't take her long at all to settle on her best hope. With her pistol and the jerk of her head, she gestured for Susannah to get to her feet. Turning onto her stomach, Susannah prepared to do just that. "Remy? It's me. Don't shoot."

Over in the corner Remy listened to her tearful plea with genuine regret. The serenity had disappeared again. She was afraid—afraid for her life—and there was nothing he could do to reassure her. Nothing he could do to help her. "Come on out, Susannah," he said softly.

Crawling to the opening, she slowly got to her knees, then stood up. Immediately rising behind her was the blonde—why wasn't he surprised?—with the barrel of her gun pressed hard against Susannah's back. "You're right, Sinclair," the woman said. "Come on out and let's get it over with."

After a moment's hesitation, he stepped out from behind his cover and gave them a rueful look. "Hell, Susannah, how did you manage to hide where she already was?" he asked, the mildness of his voice negating the rebuke.

"I do my job very well," the blonde answered. "And for the record, Remy, my name is Greta, and I'm from Chicago."

"Why don't you let her go? It's me you're after. You don't want to kill her."

"Yes, I do. She's part of the job."

He flexed his fingers around the grip of his pistol. When your target was using a hostage as a shield, your best shot was a head shot, but Greta was careful. She was a little bit shorter than Susannah and a good deal thinner, and she was keeping Susannah squarely in between them. From this angle, he couldn't get off any sort of shot at all without sacrificing Susannah.

And he wasn't *that* desperate to live.

But he was desperate enough to stall. To hope that

someone had heard the gunshots and called the sheriff. To hope that help would arrive. To pray that somehow, someway, they could find a way out of this.

"Things must be pretty slow in Chicago if you'd come all the way down here to Louisiana to take care of a nurse from Nebraska."

"I wouldn't cross the street to take care of a nurse from Nebraska or her idiot kid brother. Don't be so modest, Remy. You know it's you I'm here for."

"So you kill us, and you go back to Falcone's place and take care of the brother." He regretted saying those last words, regretted the look of sorrow they brought to Susannah's eyes, but he kept it out of his expression. "Then what?"

"I collect the rest of my money and go home."

"Are you sure about that? Jimmy Falcone's developing reputation for not upholding his end of his deals. He made deal with one of his own men a while back to help set me up, and when the guy had done his part, Falcone had him killed. He made a deal with Susannah through Nick Carlucci—and you know dealing with Carlucci is the same as dealing with Falcone—and now he's reneging again. What makes you think he's going to keep his deal with you?"

Greta's laugh was low and husky. "Because I can kill him as easily as I'll kill you."

"Sweetheart, he's got two dozen men around him at any time, any one of whom would be happy to put a bullet in your brain when you least expect it. For all you know, they could be right here, just waiting for you to kill us before they kill you."

She laughed again and shifted just slightly to one side so she could see him better. She was opening her mouth to speak when a single gunshot echoed through the barn. The bullet found its target, entering high in the chest and spinning the woman back and away from Susannah, who shrieked and, for the second time tonight, scrambled away seeking safety.

"Dear God," Remy whispered, stunned, looking abruptly around for whoever had fired the shot.

Then Michael stepped out of the shadows near the door, his expression grim, his pistol in hand.

Remy blew out his breath in a rush. "My God, what are you doing here?"

Holstering his gun, Michael crossed to where the woman's body lay sprawled over a bale of hay. He claimed the pistol she had dropped when she'd fallen, then turned to answer Remy's question. "Smith and I figured this would be a good time for me to spend a few days in the country, while the FBI decided how they were going to handle this new development. I got up here in time to see that you already had some unexpected guests. I called the sheriff from my car. They should be here any minute. I told him to notify Smith. Are you all right?"

"Yeah." He put away his own weapon, found his cane where he'd propped it and limped out into the center of the floor. The man he had shot was coming around now, moaning pitifully as Michael dragged him a few feet closer to the old tractor, then cuffed his wrists to it. The woman… He didn't get close enough to check, but it was a good bet she was dead. Michael was too good a shot, and too good a cop to mess around with trying to wound a suspect when a hostage was involved.

As for the hostage, Susannah was sitting on a bale of hay, her head down, her shoulders rounded, her hands pressed between her knees. She looked utterly lost. Bereft. He sat down beside her, stretching out his leg. "Are you all right?"

For a long time she didn't respond, then finally she raised her head and nodded.

"As far as we know, he's still alive, Susannah. When these two don't come back tonight, Falcone will know they've failed. With you and me both still living, it'll be in his best interests to keep your brother alive, too. He'll be all right."

Her gaze held his a long time, searching, then she

nodded again, accepting his assurances, just not terribly re-
assured by them.

"Are you sure you're okay?"

One more nod.

"Then what the hell were you trying to do, surrendering
like that?" he demanded. "Are you crazy?"

The blankness in her soft hazel eyes was replaced by
surprise, then shock, then anger. "I was trying to give you a
chance to do something!"

"By turning yourself over to them? By letting them take
you hostage? For God's sake, Susannah, you could have
gotten yourself killed!"

She raised her chin stubbornly and replied in her chilliest
voice, "Better than getting you killed." Getting to her feet, she
crossed the room, pausing only briefly in front of Michael.
"I'm sorry for the trouble I've caused you." With a glance
back at Greta, she added, "Thank you."

Then she stalked out of the barn and into the cold night air.

In the silence that followed her leaving, Michael looked at
Remy, out the door into the darkness, then back at Remy.
"Whatever she did must have worked. You were both still
alive when I got here."

"What she did was reckless. Crazy."

"People in love do crazy things." Michael waited. "You
going after her?"

Remy sighed. "Yeah, I guess I am." Outside, sirens sounded
and a combination of red and blue lights lit up the night. The
sheriff and his deputies had arrived, along with an ambulance.
"Can you deal with them for me?" he asked Michael.

There was little for the newcomers to do. The ambulance
crew could attend to the gunman and verify that Greta was,
indeed, dead, and the sheriff could secure the scene, but the
investigation would be handled at the federal level. No doubt
a team of FBI agents was on its way up from New Orleans
even now.

He didn't have to go far to find Susannah. She had stopped at the nearest tree outside, the same live oak where, such a short time ago, he had instructed her to head into the woods—just moments before she dragged him into the barn. He could admit now that her choice had been better. Handicapped as he was, he surely would have gotten trapped in the woods, with no place to hide and little hope of Michael finding him before it was too late.

She was leaning against the trunk, her arms crossed tightly over her chest. He wished he had a jacket to give her; failing that, he wished he could draw her into his arms and see if they could generate some warmth together. But she looked so fragile, so brittle, as if she couldn't quite bear being touched.

Taking up position beside her, he watched as a growing number of people milled around the old barn. "Thank you."

"For what?"

"Giving me a chance to do something."

She didn't respond. For a long time she just stood there, little shivers rippling through her. Then she spoke, soft, sad and distant. "I'm sorry."

This time it was his turn to ask. "For what?"

"All this. Everything I did. Those people. Tonight."

"You're not responsible for all this, sweetheart. Falcone had it in for me long before either of us knew you existed."

"I'm sorry for my part in it. I'm sorry I didn't tell someone sooner. I'm sorry things went so far." Her voice quavered then. "I'm so sorry."

Remy watched as yet another car pulled into the driveway. It was a sedan, clearly marked by its antennae as a government car, and driving it was Shawna Warren. Other agents would be arriving soon, along with Smith. It was time for him to go to work, but not without one question. "Susannah?" He felt rather than saw her look at him. "Can you tell me one thing? Your brother…is he worth what you did here?"

She looked away again, and tears made her voice thick.

She took so long to answer that he had already started to turn away when finally she spoke. "No," she whispered. "He isn't."

Hours passed before quiet fell over Belle Ste. Claire again. Susannah had been questioned by Smith and a female FBI agent, while Remy and Michael silently listened. Then Smith had sent her off to her room with the polite advice that she pack whatever she needed. That had been half an hour ago, and she was still waiting for one of them to come and get her.

She hadn't been exactly sure what to pack. What, after all, did you take to jail? So, by candlelight, she had packed everything. Whatever she didn't need or couldn't keep could be stored or delivered to her apartment or shipped to her father.

One thing was certain: she couldn't leave anything here. She would never be coming back here again.

Now she sat on her bed, knees drawn to her chest, listening to the low murmur of voices down the hall. The woman, Shawna something-or-other, had left a few minutes earlier. As far as Susannah could tell, that left only the three men. She supposed Smith would take Remy to his apartment in New Orleans, at least until the power and phone service could be restored here and until he had an opportunity to hire someone else to help out.

And she supposed Michael would take *her* to jail.

The thought of jail terrified her, although it was no less than she deserved. Still, she'd never had so much as a parking ticket, had never told anything more than a white lie. Now she faced charges of aiding and abetting a known felon, participation in a criminal enterprise and conspiracy to commit murder—those were just a few of the charges the female agent who was in authority had tossed around.

And all she'd been trying to do was protect her brother.

Now she didn't know if Skip was all right or if he was even alive.

But at least Remy was safe.

That was one prayer answered.

Outside a car door slammed, then an engine started. Susannah wondered whether it was Michael or Smith leaving and whether Remy had gone with him. Maybe he wanted to get away from her so much that he wouldn't even tell her he was going. She certainly couldn't blame him.

Even if the thought did make her hurt way down inside.

With a sigh she got to her feet. Whichever of the two men had remained behind to take her into custody would be coming for her any moment now, and there was one more thing she needed to do. Earlier, while everyone was still busy outside, she had reclaimed her embroidery from the sewing basket in the parlor. Now she took it and the note she'd written to accompany it from the desk and, finding her way by moonlight, she went across the hall to Remy's room. She positioned the linen on the dresser and the note on top of it; then, with one last touch of her quilt—of Remy's quilt, which he would probably no longer want—she returned to her own room to wait.

It was another ten minutes before footsteps finally approached. Getting to her feet, she pulled on her jacket and was waiting beside the bed, beside her bags, when Remy stopped in the doorway. "Are you about ready?"

He hadn't left without saying goodbye, she thought with a sudden surge of hope, but it faded as quickly as it had come. Did he want to accompany her to jail? Did he want to actually see her locked up for what she'd done to him? "Yes," she whispered.

He played the flashlight he carried across the room, bringing it to a stop on the bags beside her. "You packed an awful lot for one night."

"I—I didn't know what to take."

"I think just a toothbrush and a change of clothes will be plenty."

"Oh. I didn't know."

"Michael's going to board up the door where they broke in, and I'm going to get my stuff together. Then we'll go."

She listened to him leave, then lifted one bag to the bed and opened it, removing a set of clean clothes. From her tote bag she took out a plastic case containing both her toothbrush and toothpaste, then closed everything up again. She wrapped her clothes around the case and slid the entire bundle into her purse. Then, suddenly, his last words registered in her mind. *I'm going to get my stuff together.*

She bolted from the room, crossed the hall in one step and stopped abruptly beside his bed. His flashlight was sitting on the dresser, its beam pointed across the room, and he was holding her note in one hand, the linen in the other. Just holding them. Looking at them.

Tears stung her eyes. She had left them in plain sight to be sure he found them, but she hadn't wanted him to find them before she was gone. She hadn't wanted to be here to face his pain or anger or rejection. She had hoped she could at least be spared that.

He didn't turn, didn't look around, but he was aware of her. "Susannah, where do you think we're taking you tonight?" he asked, his voice oddly pitched.

"To jail."

"Do you think I would let them arrest you?"

"That woman—Shawna... She said..."

"Shawna's in charge of the investigation, and you're right. If she had her way, you *would* be going to jail. She can arrest you, but Smith is the one who would prosecute you. She'll defer to his recommendations."

"But...I broke the law. What I did was wrong."

"You had a good reason for it. And you tried to make it right before anyone got hurt."

"But I almost got you killed," she whispered sadly.

"My *job* almost got me killed. It happened once before I met you, and it might happen again. Susannah, you played the least significant role in Falcone's plan. They didn't do anything that they couldn't have managed without your information. What happened tonight wasn't your fault."

At last he turned to face her. "So…that takes care of this." He held up her note, a simple and very brief apology—*I'm sorry*—then laid it on the dresser. "Now let's talk about this."

Her gaze dropped to the linen. She couldn't see the stitches from this distance in the dim light, but she could picture them: the fat heart embroidered in gold, decorated with a few simple pink flowers and one flowing ribbon, and the message in script across its center. The words were as blue as his eyes, as blue as her own heart.

"Do you mean this?"

"Remy—"

He silenced her with a gesture. "Do you mean this?"

"Yes," she whispered. "I do."

"'I do.' Now there's an answer I've been looking forward to getting out of you. But somehow I thought we'd have an audience of at least a few hundred when you said it."

She recognized his tone—that sweet, teasing, charming tone he had used so often with her—and slowly sank onto the bed. "Why aren't you angry with me?"

"I *was* angry. I got mad, I lost my temper and I yelled at you in the kitchen." He shrugged. "I'm not angry anymore."

"But I—"

"You made a mistake, Susannah, but you did what you could to correct it. Why would I hold that against you?"

"Remy, a mistake is when you add up the numbers wrong in your checking account and write checks for more money than you have, or you forget to put oil in your car and burn the engine up. My 'mistake' almost got you killed!"

He sat down in front of her, still holding the linen. "You put your life on the line for me tonight. You could have easily escaped into the woods, but you didn't go because I surely would have gotten caught without you. You could have stayed hidden in the barn, but you didn't. You came out and stalled them so I could have a little more time. For God's sake, Susannah, you knew they intended to kill you, but you put yourself out there anyway, just to give me a chance. That more than makes up for what you did." He glanced at the embroidery. "*This* more than makes up for it."

She stared at him for a long time, wanting desperately to believe him but afraid. "Can it be that easy?" she whispered. "Can you forgive me just like that?"

With his free hand he claimed both of her hands. "Remember that Sunday afternoon when we sat out in the yard reading, the first time I kissed you?"

She nodded. It was that day that the woman, Greta, and her partner had shown up.

"I announced to you that I intended to get married."

"Just as casually as if you had decided to have bacon and eggs for breakfast the next morning."

"And you said that marriage was too important to be taken so lightly. You said I should get married because I'd fallen in love, because I couldn't imagine living without this woman, because she completed who I was, because there was an emptiness to my life that no one could fill but her." He smiled faintly. "That's how I feel about you, Susannah. You're the one I want to spend the next sixty or seventy years with. I could be angry with you for not confiding in me about your brother. I could send you away and nurse a grudge for the next few weeks or months or even years. I could refuse to forgive what you've done, could refuse to understand why you did it. But none of that would change the fact that I love you."

"But—"

With a chuckle, he drew her close. "Sweetheart, you have more arguments than anyone I've ever known. Answer one question for me: do you love me? And don't forget that I already have it in writing."

"Yes, but—"

"No more *buts*. Just a simple yes or no. Do you love me?"

"Yes."

"Enough to live with me? To marry me? To spend the rest of your life with me?"

She was preparing to offer a more complicated answer when he stopped her with a warning shake of his head. "Yes."

"And I love you, enough to live with you, to marry you, to spend the rest of my life with you." His grin was sweetly confident. "So what more could you possibly want?"

It *could* be that easy, she thought with growing delight. With love you could do anything—could resolve any difference, right any wrong, forgive any hurt. If you loved someone, and he loved you, too, what more *could* you possibly want?

"Susannah?"

She wrapped her arms around his neck and hugged him tightly. "I love you, Remy."

"I know. I love you, too." He kissed her, then solemnly added, "And I always will."

It was a lovely March afternoon, springtime warm and sunny. Susannah sat in the dining room of the apartment she shared with Remy, music playing softly in the background, her attention focused on the quilt frame in front of her. She had bought a few how-to books, had visited a quilt shop in the Quarter and had picked up a few tips from Michael's grandmother last weekend when they'd all gone to Arkansas for his and Valery's wedding. Her first project wasn't turning out badly at all.

Remy had chosen the pattern—Oh, Susannah, of course—and she had chosen the colors: ivory, gold and blue. They both had a romantic streak—and a sentimental one, she thought—that was darn near embarrassing. Take, for example, the ivory squares that formed the corners of each block. Most of them were plain ivory-shaded cotton, but two of them, the upper left and bottom right squares of the very central block, were fine linen. Each was embroidered with a gold heart, and a message was inscribed across each heart. The first was in her handwriting. *Susannah loves Remy.* And the second, in his writing—

"The mail's here." Remy bent to press a kiss to the top of her head as he came in. "You got a letter from your dad *and* one from Skip."

She laid her needle and thimble aside and took the envelopes he offered. The FBI had picked Skip up at Falcone's house and arrested both Jimmy Falcone and Nicholas Carlucci the day after the attempt on their lives. After he had cooperated fully with them and Smith's office, he had been allowed to return home to Nebraska. He would be brought back to testify—if they ever made it to court—but in the meantime, he was living at the farm, working hard and keeping his promise to stay out of trouble.

She hoped he managed to keep it for a long, long time.

She skimmed his letter, then her father's, before returning them to their envelopes. Instead of returning to work on the quilt, though, she settled back in her chair and studied Remy for so long that he began to squirm. "What?" he asked at last.

"You look good." His cast was off, and the physical therapists had worked wonders at rebuilding the muscles in his right leg. Of course, she liked to think that the love they made on a fairly regular basis had something to do with his recovery, too. He still needed the cane on occasion, when he was tired or his days at the office were impossibly long, but for the most part he was as fit and healthy as anyone she'd ever seen.

"I feel good." Remy grinned lecherously. "Want me to show you?"

"I'd like that," she replied with a smile that made him slowly turn serious. It was a soft, gentle smile, he thought, full of the serenity that had first drawn him to her. For much of their time together at Belle Ste. Claire, it had been missing but he lived with it now. He saw it in her smile every night, saw it in the sleepy, drowsy lines of her face every morning.

She gathered her supplies together, then bent over the quilt top to secure her needle in its layers. He wrapped his arms around her from behind, holding her close while he examined her handiwork over her shoulder. He had never taken much interest in any kind of craft, but this quilt interested him. He could sit and watch her work on it for hours. He could imagine all the nights of warmth it would give them.

He was already anticipating all the intimacies they would share underneath it.

"You do good work," he remarked.

"I come from a family of quilters," she reminded him.

He reached past her to trace across the fine stitches, to stroke over the hearts and their sentiments; then he pulled her around and kissed her. "Come upstairs with me, sweetheart," he invited hoarsely. "There's something I want to show you."

Such as how much he loved her.

Or maybe the two embroidered pieces in the center of the quilt said it best.

Susannah loves Remy.

But Remy loves her more.

* * * * *

*Brittany Grayson survived a horrible ordeal at the hands
of a serial killer known as The Professional...
who's after her now?*

*Harlequin® Romantic Suspense presents a new installment
in Carla Cassidy's reader-favorite miniseries,*
LAWMEN OF BLACK ROCK.

*Enjoy a sneak peek of
TOOL BELT DEFENDER.*

*Available January 2012
from Harlequin® Romantic Suspense.*

"**B**rittany?" His voice was deep and pleasant and made
her realize she'd been staring at him openmouthed through
the screen door.

"Yes, I'm Brittany and you must be..." Her mind suddenly went blank.

"Alex. Alex Crawford, Chad's friend. You called him
about a deck?"

As she unlocked the screen, she realized she wasn't
quite ready yet to allow a stranger inside, especially a male
stranger.

"Yes, I did. It's nice to meet you, Alex. Let's walk around
back and I'll show you what I have in mind," she said. She
frowned as she realized there was no car in her driveway.
"Did you walk here?" she asked.

His eyes were a warm blue that stood out against his
tanned face and was complemented by his slightly shaggy
dark hair. "I live three doors up." He pointed up the street to
the Walker home that had been on the market for a while.

"How long have you lived there?"

"I moved in about six weeks ago," he replied as the

walked around the side of the house.

That explained why she didn't know the Walkers had moved out and Mr. Hard Body had moved in. Six weeks ago she'd still been living at her brother Benjamin's house trying to heal from the trauma she'd lived through.

As they reached the backyard she motioned toward the broken brick patio just outside the back door. "What I'd like is a wooden deck big enough to hold a barbecue pit and an umbrella table and, of course, lots of people."

He nodded and pulled a tape measure from his tool belt. "An outdoor entertainment area," he said.

"Exactly," she replied and watched as he began to walk the site. The last thing Brittany had wanted to think about over the past eight months of her life was men. But looking at Alex Crawford definitely gave her a slight flutter of pure feminine pleasure.

*Will Brittany be able to heal in the arms of Alex,
her hotter-than-sin handyman...or will a second
psychopath silence her forever? Find out in*
TOOL BELT DEFENDER
*Available January 2012
from Harlequin® Romantic Suspense
wherever books are sold.*

Harlequin® A *Romance* FOR EVERY MOOD™

CLASSICS

Quintessential, modern love stories
that are romance at its finest.

Harlequin Presents®
Glamorous international settings…
unforgettable men…passionate
romances—Harlequin Presents
promises you the world!

Harlequin Presents® Extra
Meet more of your favorite Presents
heroes and travel to glamorous
international locations in our regular
monthly themed collections.

Harlequin® Romance
The anticipation, the thrill of the chase
and the sheer rush of falling in love!

Harlequin® A *Romance* FOR EVERY MOOD™

PASSION

For a spicier, decidedly hotter read—
these are your destinations for romance!

Silhouette Desire®

Passionate and provocative stories featuring rich, powerful heroes and scandalous family sagas.

Harlequin® Blaze™

Fun, flirtatious and steamy books that tell it like it is, inside and outside the bedroom.

Kimani™ Romance

Sexy and entertaining love stories with true-to-life African-American characters who heat up the pages with romance and passion.

Look for these and many other Harlequin and Silhouette romance books wherever books are sold, including most bookstores, supermarkets, drugstores and discount stores.

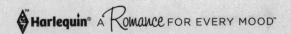

Harlequin® A *Romance* FOR EVERY MOOD™

SUSPENSE & PARANORMAL

Heartstopping stories of intrigue and mystery—
where true love always triumphs.

Harlequin Intrigue®
Breathtaking romantic suspense. Crime stories that will keep you on the edge of your seat.

Silhouette® Romantic Suspense
Heart-racing sensuality and the promise of a sweeping romance set against the backdrop of suspense.

Harlequin® Nocturne™
Dark and sensual paranormal romance reads that stretch the boundaries of conflict and desire, life and death.

Look for these and many other Harlequin and Silhouette romance books wherever books are sold, including most bookstores, supermarkets, drugstores and discount stores.

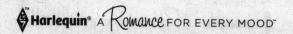

Harlequin® A *Romance* FOR EVERY MOOD™

HEART & HOME

Heartwarming romances where love can
happen right when you least expect it.

Harlequin® American Romance®

Lively stories about homes, families
and communities like the ones you know.
This is romance the all-American way!

Silhouette® Special Edition

A woman in her world—living and loving.
Celebrating the magic of creating a family
and developing romantic relationships.

Harlequin® Superromance®

Unexpected, exciting and emotional
stories about life and falling in love.

ook for these and many other Harlequin and Silhouette
mance books wherever books are sold, including most
okstores, supermarkets, drugstores and discount stores.

HHCATR

Harlequin® A *Romance* FOR EVERY MOOD™

INSPIRATIONAL

Wholesome romances that touch the heart and soul.

Love Inspired®
Contemporary inspirational romances with Christian characters facing the challenges of life and love in today's world.

Love Inspired® Suspense
Heart-pounding tales of suspense, romance, hope and faith.

Love Inspired® Historical
Travel back in time and experience powerful and engaging stories of romance, adventure and faith.